OTHER BOOKS BY LINCOLN JAMES
VINTAGE THRILLERS • MODERN NIGHTMARES

<u>Coming Spring 2026</u>

All We Wanted
A Supernatural Thriller

They make your dreams come true. Then you disappear.

It was supposed to be our college formal—one weekend of open bars,
rented tuxedos, and bad decisions at a luxury resort in Las Vegas.
But the casino has unveiled something new.
Buried behind the lobby stands a glass display case housing three
mummified figures adorned in gold—a ring, a tooth, an eyepatch.
By day, they're on display.
By night, they hunt.
They slip into borrowed skin.
They feed on desire, envy, regret.
All they need is one phrase.
I wish.
Because in this hotel, dreams don't come true.
They come for you.

<u>**Now Available in Print and eBook**</u>

The Ninth Layer
A Claustrophobic Survival Thriller

This wasn't a field trip... It was a burial.

It was supposed to be extra credit.
A simple research descent into the caves beneath Pendleton
University.
But the deeper Alex and his classmates go, the stranger things become.
The air hums.
The walls glow.
And the silence feels like it's listening.
Then the lights go out.
And something starts screaming in the dark.
By the time they realize there's no way back up, the ground itself is
shifting.
Breathing.
Hungering.
In the dark, they know they're not alone.
And the cave has no intention of letting them escape.

We Are Human
A Gripping Sci-Fi Thriller

They said it was evolution... He knew it was murder.

In 2040, Tyler Alcaster disappears.
When he wakes, his reflection isn't his own.
His skin is flawless. His pulse is wrong.
His memories—fractured.
They tell him he's special. Reborn. Immortal.
But Ty knows something still hurts. Still remembers. Still dreams.
Now he's trapped in a facility where nothing dies.

The people around him aren't people anymore—
a girl with glass eyes who never blinks,
a woman sewn together like a secret.
They all whisper the same question in the dark:
What are we becoming?
Because immortality isn't a gift.
It's the end of everything human.

Written Just For You
A Romantic Psychological Thriller

Some love stories are written in the stars. This one was written in blood.

Will wasn't supposed to stay in town. Jean wasn't supposed to meet
him. And the book she gave him? It wasn't meant to be read.
Depoe Bay is a place of whispers—where the fog clings too close and
stories go unfinished. The town says Jean is a ghost, a siren, a memory
that never made it out of the water.
But Will knows she's real. He's seen her. Heard her laugh.
Felt something shift.
And now that he's read her words...He can't let her go.
As the town turns colder, the secrets grow louder—about
the past, the dead, and what love refuses to bury.
Some girls don't make it out of their stories...
But Will's about to make sure this one does.

Devils Like Us
A Tense, Gritty, Chase Thriller

Some devils hide in the shadows... Others build a maze beneath your feet.

In 1997 Los Angeles, the sewer system stretches 40,000 miles beneath
the city—endless, rotting, and designed to be forgotten.
For two killers, it's the perfect hunting ground.
When college student Jason Murich is carjacked outside a North

Hollywood diner, he's thrown into the dark alongside two runaway
teens. But this isn't a kidnapping. It's a game.
They've been set loose in the tunnels.
The rules? Run.
The prize? Survive.
As the trio navigates collapsing passageways and echoing screams,
Jason realizes this isn't just a chase. It's a blueprint—built by those
who kill for sport and designed to trap you until you break.
Because down here, there's no help.
No light.
And no way out—unless you take it.

The Vanishing Eight
A Pulse-Pounding Survival Thriller

Disappearing was only the beginning.

Eight friends. One missing.
The town of Piedmont had always whispered about them—
too close, too wild, too perfect.
Then Roy disappeared.
Now, Jonathan is racing to hold what's left of their group together.
But the deeper he digs, the more he realizes: Roy's not the first to go
missing. And if Jon's not careful…
He won't be the last.
In a town built on secrets, nothing stays hidden forever.
And some friendships don't survive the truth.

Also available in audiobook.

FOREWORD

Content Warning

This story contains themes and depictions that may be distressing to some readers, including parental illness (Alzheimer's), grief, loss, and emotional trauma. There are also moments of intense emotional vulnerability, discussions of mental health struggles, and themes of identity and belonging. Please take care of yourself as you read and know that it is okay to pause or step away if you need to.

A Note on Themes

All the Time is, at its core, a story about the fleeting nature of time and the lengths we go to for the people we love. Through Carter's journey across decades, this book explores themes of memory, identity, and human connection—both the beauty and the pain that come with it. It's about learning to reconcile with the past, finding strength in the present, and holding on to hope for the future.

This novel also reflects the complexities of relationships, from family to friends to romantic connections, and how they shape us into who we are. At its heart, this is a story for anyone who has ever felt lost and sought a way back to themselves, even if the journey required navigating through pieces of a broken past.

Thank You

To my readers—thank you for taking the time to join Carter on this journey. Writing this book has been an emotional process, and it means the world to me that you're here, willing to step into his world. I hope this story resonates with you and offers something meaningful, whether it's comfort, catharsis, or just the feeling of being understood.

To my friends, family, and loved ones—your support has been the anchor that kept me grounded while I wrote this book. You were there during late nights and long edits, and for that, I'm forever grateful.

Finally, to anyone who has felt the weight of time and wondered if they could rewrite their story—this book is for you. Thank you for trusting Carter with your heart, and thank you for trusting me with your time.

Respectfully Yours,
Lincoln James

ALL THE TIME

LINCOLN JAMES

ISBN-13: 979-8-9904966-6-8 (Hardback edition)

ISBN-13: 979-8-9904966-7-5 (Paperback edition)

ISBN-13: 979-8-9904966-8-2 (Ebook edition)

Library of Congress Control Number: 2025901171

This is a work of fiction. Names, characters, places, and incidents either are the product of the author's imagination or are used fictitiously. Any resemblance to actual persons, living or dead, events, or locales is purely coincidental.

Published by: Lincoln James

P.O. Box 10660 Page Ave # PO 4034

Fairfax, VA 22038-4034

Edited by: E. Lee Caleca

Printed in the United States of America

First Edition: February 2025

CHAPTER 1

THE SUN BORE DOWN, relentless, like a prison guard with a grudge, watching every move, its heat a punishment that clung to my skin and settled into my lungs like a punching bag filled with wet cement, daring me to keep pushing, challenging every breath. It crawled into me, sticky and slow, dragging sweat down my back in jagged lines. Even the ground pushed against my steps, solid but mean, like it was trying to trip me up. Shadows flickered on the sidewalk—too fast, too sharp—like something was moving just out of sight, hunting, searching, dangerous. It all felt wrong, like the world was holding its breath, waiting for me to slip.

California. The place where dreams were supposed to bloom wild like weeds in the sidewalk cracks. But for me, it was a mirage, glittering and empty, its gold tarnishing the moment I touched it. My dream wasn't California. My dream was staying in Virginia, where life made sense, where everything wasn't already falling apart. But dreams don't count for much when someone else is holding the map.

A year ago, James—Dad—decided we needed a fresh start, as if packing up and heading west could erase the mess we were leaving behind. New job. New life. Just flip the switch, and everything's fine. Except it wasn't fine for me. I wasn't the one flipping switches. I was just another piece of luggage he dragged along for the ride, dumped into his version of paradise and told to figure it out.

It didn't feel like paradise to me. It felt like standing on the edge of something, watching the ground crumble away beneath my feet. I didn't know if I could make it work. Honestly, I wasn't sure I even wanted to try. But I never had a choice.

I slid into my Highlander, my escape pod that had been my lifeline since this whole mess began. Though today… it felt more like a cage on wheels. The cracked leather seats groaned under me, protesting as I settled in, the faint smell of dust and failed attempts at using leather restorer hanging in the air. The rearview mirror held a stranger's gaze —dark hair clinging to sweat, messy and growing out on the sides. My eyes were sunken and rimmed from sleepless nights, deep shadows etched onto my canvas like a face carved out of wax and left too close to the fire. A loose white T-shirt clung damply against me, along with wrinkled joggers and my Jordans—too clean, too bright, like they belonged to someone else. I looked like I'd given up trying. Maybe I had.

I viewed the Highlander as my little slice of "home." It was the only thing tying me back to the life I'd left. But every time I climbed inside, it only reminded me of how far away I was from that life—and how tempting it would be to just say screw it all and run away.

The freeway stretched toward the coast, where the ocean festered with the tides like a volcano that refused to erupt until it caught just the right victim in its path.

Its jagged waves gnashed against the shoreline, ready to swallow me whole.

I stared at it too long, wishing it could be somewhere else— Virginia Beach. With Mom.

She lived for the ocean. The coarse grit of sand still clings to my memory, burning underfoot as her hand gripped mine, pulling me toward the icy Atlantic waves. Her laugh echoed, bright and full, drowning out time itself—but even then, I could feel the tide stealing her away. "Come on, Carter. You're never too old for this," she'd say, her grin wide enough to challenge the warmth and intensity of the sun. Then the water would hit, cold and unforgiving, leaving us soaked and gasping. And still she laughed joyously and screamed at the cold, as though it was nothing but fun.

That grin feels impossible now, like trying to remember sunlight in the middle of a month-long storm. Her laugh came back to me in pieces, too loud and full, like she thought joy could keep time at bay. But even then, I could feel the tide pulling us apart—sand slipping through my fingers, faster and faster until there was nothing left. For a moment, I was back there with her, just us and the waves. Time had stopped just to give us that.

We'd spend hours at the sun-bright sea, ducking under the waves, daring each other to stay under just a little longer. And whenever we found shells washed up on shore, she'd pick them up like she'd found treasure. "This one's magic, Carter," she'd say, examining each one carefully. "Keeps the nightmares away if you put it under your pillow." I'd laugh, but I'd kept them, these little "magic" pieces of who we were scattered around my old room, mostly buried under other stuff now. Or maybe just lost in the mess that used to be my child-hood, my life.

But even then, those hours with her… they felt like some kind of shield. And now? It was all slipping away, like sandcastles just melting back into the ocean.

I didn't know then how quickly time could pull things out from under you. Or that someday I'd be fighting just to see her again, just one more time. Before there was nothing left to come back to.

THE VIBRATING hum of the old engine under me jolted me out of my thoughts, the freeway stretching on. Sunlight flashed like the bare bulb of an interrogation room swinging over the dust-caked wind-shield, sharing bits of the logjam that was the LA freeway, daring me to look at it with my eyes open and blinding me to my private thoughts. And no matter how far I drove, sitting on the Highlander's cracked seats with their thousands of stories, I was still here, sitting in traffic, stranded in Los Angeles, where everything was too bright and everyone was too happy. Like they'd never heard of broken families, unpaid bills or people who got left behind.

I muttered to myself, "Well, Carter, welcome to your life now. Two hours into your drive, and you're still stuck in Los Angeles. Just me and this beat-up SUV, held together by bad decisions and duct tape, going nowhere fast."

Not like the car cared. It just chugged along, oblivious. I let out a laugh, dry and hollow. "Yeah, sure, laugh it up, Highlander. You're just as stuck as I am."

The silence in the car swallowed my words, but I kept muttering to myself anyway. I guess it was easier to act tough with no one else around. Easier to pretend I wasn't totally lost... in my memories, my misery, my soul.

And then, before I knew it, I was back at that memory again. Mom's smile, wide and sure, telling me I was "never too old" for a little fun. I felt like she was right there, saying it to me now, encouraging me, like she knew this whole mess of a life could somehow turn around.

I sighed, staring out at the road. "Yeah, well... I feel too *young* for this now, Mom," I said to the empty car, half-wishing she'd answer back. "I just hope... I'm not too late." The words echoed around me, settling in that uncomfortable silence that always knows more than you're ready to admit.

When I finally made it out of the city, the road stretched out ahead, endless and flat. I stayed quiet for a while, letting the empty road fill up the silence, like maybe if I drove far enough, the questions would stop chasing me. But deep down, I knew there was no outrunning this. Not here, not anywhere. Just me, an empty highway, and a blur of dry fields and crooked fences on the verge of collapse. Like my old room, my car seats, my memories... Miles of nothing all going nowhere, and none of us in any hurry to get there.

I glanced at my iPhone 5S sitting in the cup holder, half-expecting some miracle—a text, maybe even a rogue call from an old friend that would make me feel like I wasn't totally forgotten. But nope. Just the usual, soul-crushing "No Service." Go figure.

Then it buzzed once. Then again.

"What? You suddenly have things to say?" I muttered, picking it up.

My screen lit up with a new voicemail, of all things. From Mom. I didn't even remember seeing her name pop up. Weird. I stared at the "play" button like it was some kind of trap, then tapped it, feeling a lump in my throat before I'd even heard a word.

"...don't forget your lunch, Carter... late for school... you need to visit soon."

Her voice crackled, fragmented through the static, like a ghost clawing its way out of some distant memory. Each word carried a sharpness that cut through me, but it was wrong—too young, too alive, like a piece of her had escaped time just to haunt me. My grip tightened around the wheel, knuckles blanching as her voice faded into the silence, leaving behind the weight of something I couldn't name. "Late for school"? I'd been out of school for months now. And "visit soon"? I was already halfway across the country. This didn't make any sense.

I hit "play" again, half-hoping I'd misheard. But it was the same message, all fragmented and strange, like someone had spliced together old recordings and sent them straight to me. It made the hairs on my neck stand up. Was I was missing some obvious detail, some hidden message buried in all the noise? I tossed the phone back into the cup holder, my grip tightening on the steering wheel. The car felt even smaller now, like the walls were closing in, and all I had was that memory of her voice, hanging in the air.

Once upon a time, her voice could fix anything. Bad grade? She'd laugh and tell me about the time she skipped an entire week of high school just to go to the beach with her friends. Bad day? She'd pull out the cheesiest joke you could imagine and practically dare me not to laugh.

But Alzheimer's didn't just take her—it hollowed her out, piece by piece, like watching a statue crumble into dust. One minute, she'd be right there, smiling at me like everything was fine. The next, she'd stare through me, her eyes searching for something I couldn't see, somewhere I couldn't follow. And now I was out here, hundreds of miles away, trying to make sense of memories that were slipping through my fingers faster than I could grab them.

James said the move would be "good for us," like putting a thousand miles between us and the truth would somehow erase it. Clean slate, fresh start—empty words, dripping with the kind of hope only he could believe in. But you can't outrun something like this. It clings to you, heavy and relentless, no matter where you go. He didn't have to feel the way her absence dug in, like a barbed weight, gripping, pressing down until I couldn't breathe. He didn't have to sit around, trying to pretend everything was fine when he knew it wasn't.

I already had my mind made up for the upcoming school year: keep my head down, survive my last year of high school without breaking, maybe even fool a few people into thinking I was holding it together. But then James had to go and drop the real bomb. "If you want to see her, Carter, really see her, you'll need to go back to Virginia. Before…" And he didn't have to finish. The hourglass was already flipped, and there I was, watching the sand drain faster than I could take it in.

So, I packed the car. Stuffed some clothes into a bag, grabbed my phone charger, plugged in the aux cord and hit the road. No plan, no goodbyes—just the hum of the engine and the caffeine pounding through my veins. The highway stretched ahead, jagged and endless, like an old wound that refused to heal, each mile a ribbon of remorse. The car smelled like stale coffee and exhaustion, wrappers piling up like gravestones for every hour I'd lost on this trip. Outside, the world blurred into something shapeless, a ghost of the life I had to leave behind.

Thirty-eight hours later, Fairfax rose up around me, blurry and off-kilter, like a dream I'd half-forgotten. The streets felt too small, too quiet, the kind of place that had learned how to disappear when no one was looking. It greeted me like a stranger wearing my old friend's face—familiar but all wrong. My first stop? The Starbucks on Main. Because nothing says "welcome home" like fluorescent lights and the bitter taste of regret.

THE STARBUCKS WAS DIM, the air thick with the smell of burnt coffee and something too sweet, like syrup left to rot. Everything about the place felt stuck, its edges worn down by years of footsteps and conversations long forgotten . The tiles clung to the past, sticky with memories no one wanted to clean up. It had the same old floors, same stale smell, same dim lighting casting shadows over customers hunched over laptops, probably Googling *"How to Escape Your Hometown"* or whatever people did when they were looking for an exit.

Or maybe I was just projecting.

And there she was—MaryAnn. She hadn't changed. Not even a little. She looked like she'd been cut out of the wallpaper, part of the scenery, her messy bun and tired eyes blending into the dim light. Seeing her here was like stepping into a room where time hadn't bothered to move on, a room that never knew I left. But I did. And I've changed. Standing across from her was like looking into an old photograph, except I wasn't in the frame anymore.

She looked up at me, eyes narrowing, and I could see it—the way she was piecing together some distant memory, like trying to remember the lyrics to a song you haven't heard in years.

"Well, well," she said, her voice slow and warm, like a spoon stirring something heavy. "Look who decided to show up." There was a tired kind of sweetness in her tone, a faint edge that said she'd seen too much and didn't expect much more. "Carter Sullivan, back from the dead. How's life in California?"

I forced a laugh, though I felt like I might come unglued. "As good as it could, I guess… but I could use something to clear my head. Just drove halfway across the country, so… you know."

MaryAnn tilted her head. "Gimme just a minute sweetie," holding up a finger, a smirk tugging at her lips. She returned and handed me an iced chai latte—my old usual. One sip, and I was hit with a wave of too much—too sweet, too weak, too familiar. It tasted like a memory that had been left out too long, the edges warped with over-analyzation, the details smudged like a fever dream. The kind of thing that makes you want to hold on but leaves you wishing you hadn't. But I couldn't tell her that, not after all this time.

"Careful with that, sweetheart," she teased, her eyes softening. "Too much of that stuff, and you'll be jittering off the walls. That's not the ride you want."

"Guess I'll take my chances." I tried to play it cool. But it was weird being back. Nothing seemed to have changed but it felt like everything had. I was suffering; thoughts moved faster than I could keep up and I tried to keep my outer composure, for the sake of appearances.

I glanced around. Her granddaughter, grown up now and working the register, moved with a focus I barely recognized. Last time I'd seen her, she was just a middle schooler, avoiding this place like the plague. Now? She moved around like she'd been doing it forever. Like time had just… moved forward without me, leaving me behind.

"Must be looking forward to graduation," MaryAnn said, her tone a little forced, filling the silence before it got too heavy. "2015's just around the corner! I remember when you were just a kid, hiding out in here to dodge your homework. Now look at you, about to take on the world."

"Yeah," I said with a half-smile. "I'm… as excited as I can be. Feels like the world's racing past, and I'm just stuck watching."

She looked at me for a moment, her gaze softening, like she was gearing up to give me one of those life lessons she kept tucked away for moments like this. "Look at you, already dreaming up plans," she said, her voice dropping to that low, serious tone. "But don't forget—life doesn't wait. Sometimes it throws you in the deep end. Speaking of which," she said, her voice gentle, careful. "Your mom—I—I've heard… well, you know how word gets around." Her eyes searched mine, hesitant, like she wasn't sure she wanted the answer, wasn't sure it was okay to pose the topic at all.

The question hit me harder than I expected, and a knot began tightening in my chest. *Guess my family is the town's favorite topic.* "She's… fading," I said, the word catching in my throat. "Like one minute she's right there, smiling at me, and the next… it's like she's already gone." I paused, the heaviness settling over me. "That's why I came back. Just for a little while. Before…" I trailed off, letting the silence fill in the rest.

"Oh, sweetheart," she said, her voice dropping into something softer, sadder. "I know that road. It's like trying to hold onto sand in a storm, isn't it? Watching them slip away, piece by piece, even when they're standing right in front of you. It's… cruel."

I nodded, the ache in my chest growing heavier. I held in a gasp of defeat that threatened to choke me. "Yeah, but... it's–uh... nice to be back. I guess." I offered a sad smile and blinked back a weak tear.

She reached across the counter, giving my shoulder a warm squeeze. "You're not fooling me, Carter. That tough act of yours? It doesn't work on me. I've seen enough kids trying to play it cool to know when someone's barely holding it together. And trust me—it's okay to not have it all figured out. None of us do. Life doesn't come with a map."

I nodded, feeling the ache lessen, just slightly. "Yeah. I just don't know if I'm ready for what's coming."

She chuckled softly, like she'd heard it all before. "If I had a dollar for every time someone told me that, I'd own this place by now." She paused and leaned closer, lifting my chin with her finger. "We can never be ready for this kind of thing, Carter. It'll just happen and you'll deal with it. Don't forget—you're tougher than you think. If you ever need someone to listen, you know where to find me. I've got coffee and an ear. That's all I can offer."

"Thanks, MaryAnn," I murmured, feeling the warmth break through my defenses. "I mean it."

She waved me off, her smirk sharp but kind. "Don't go getting all sentimental on me now. Place is dead without you coming around to stir things up. It's you or the caffeine addicts— and I'll take you any day."

We let the small talk linger, each line holding off the silence like a lifeline. After a bit, I took my iced chai to a seat by the window. The taste hit hard—nostalgia too sweet to be real. And regret. But I sipped anyway, holding on to whatever pieces of the past I could.

I pulled out my phone, the smudged screen catching the light in muted, blurry blots. Mom's message sat there, glowing faintly, like it was waiting for me. My thumb hovered over the "play," button again, trembling just enough to make me pause. When her voice spilled into the silence, it was like hearing a ghost, distant and fractured, pulling me somewhere I wasn't ready to go.

"Don't forget your lunch, Carter... late for school... you need to visit soon."

Maybe it was nothing. Just her mind pulling old memories out of the dark, tossing them like breadcrumbs for me to follow. Or maybe it was her, somewhere in there, trying to tell me something. Trying to reach out before it was too late.

I sat there, the coffee cooling my hand, surrounded by strangers who didn't look at me twice. I set the phone down on the table with a hollow click, the darkened screen facing up, daring me to keep looking. My hand lingered for a second, reluctant to let go, before I leaned back and stared out the window.

The street outside was alive with the usual buzz—cars crawling through intersections, a kid sprinting after a ball, the faint hum of cicadas cutting through the heat. It felt normal. Ordinary. Like the rest of the world was still spinning, even if mine had ground to a halt.

I let out a slow breath, turning back to the phone. And that's when I saw it.

A new voicemail.

The notification sat there, just above the one I'd already listened to, the timestamp fresh, impossible. My heart kicked against my ribs as I picked it up again. My thumb hovered over 'play,' trembling as if tapping it might crack something fragile inside me. I wanted to throw the phone, to silence whatever answer it was about to give—but I couldn't.

When her voice came through—clearer this time, sharper—it cut through me like glass, fragile and deliberate, as if time itself were daring me to listen.

"Carter..." She paused, like she was searching for the words. "You have to come soon. Please. Before it's too late."

Her voice lingered, echoing in my head even after the message ended. I stared at the phone, my pulse pounding in my ears, my world narrowing to that tiny screen.

I tried to call her back, but the dial tone wouldn't even ring. Voice-mail. *Something's not right.*

Outside, everything stilled—the cars, the kid chasing the ball, even the cicadas went quiet. The air felt heavy, the kind that presses down before a storm.

Then, the rain started.

A single drop streaked down the glass, blurring the sidewalk. Another followed. And another, until the world outside dissolved into a smear of gray, mirroring the fog that was distorting my senses, choking my chest like a torrent.

CHAPTER 2

THE RAIN CAME DOWN in jagged sheets, sharp enough to leave marks on the skin, heavy enough to crush the air from my lungs. This wasn't just a storm—it was a judgment, the sky was close, thick, dark, relentless, like it had decided I didn't belong here, like the volcano that had finally found its victim. By the time I reached the Highlander, my clothes clung to me like second skin, heavy and useless, my shoes squelching with every step, water dripping down my face and stinging my eyes.

Thunder tore through the heavens, a jagged sound of domination that made the ground shiver, like the earth itself wanted to crawl away. Each crack felt closer, louder, the storm closing in on me, alive and angry. I yanked the door open and flung myself inside just as a burst of lightning turned the parking lot into a blinding flash of white.

You missed, I thought sarcastically, feeling like it was a sign for me to look to the future with some kind of hope, whatever that was. The audacity of hope. What a concept.

I slumped into the seat. The rain was hammering against the windshield so hard it felt like the glass might give. My phone lay unconscious in my hand, the black screen swallowing what little light crept into the car. All it gave me was a warped reflection of myself, stretched and distorted, unrecognizable. I shoved it under my thigh, like hiding it would make the storm outside—and the one in my chest —ease up.

I sighed and reached for the ignition, ready to pull out of this strip mall wasteland, when, through the rain's relentless curtain, a figure emerged—flickering in and out like a bad signal. Her arms jerked against the storm, jagged and uneven, as if she were trying to fight off something invisible. Her figure shifted and blurred with the rain, like a holographic image trying to reach me from another space or time, her soaked dress clinging to her like the storm was trying to swallow her whole. For a second, she was just part of the storm, something pulled from it, until her voice cut through the pounding rain.

She looked stranded—not just here, but in time, like she didn't quite belong in this world. Her hair hung in dark, dripping tendrils, twisting and writhing like something alive, caught in the storm's violent discord. Her eyes burned through the rain, wide and unblinking—too steady, too sharp, like a predator caught in a night-vision camera, waiting for the right moment to pounce.

Against every ounce of good sense I had, I rolled down the window, bracing myself against the elements. "Uh… you okay?" The words felt weird coming out, like I'd just invited the universe to hand me more weirdness.

"Oh, you're a savior," she gasped, her voice floating over the storm, soft and trembling, dripping with practiced sweetness. It felt too smooth, like a melody hummed for an audience that had long since stopped listening. Her Southern drawl clung to every word, sweet and sticky, but there was something in it—something just a little off, out of time, out of frame, like it didn't quite belong here, didn't quite belong now.

Her smile stretched too wide, like she'd been rehearsing it for an audience that never came. "I thought you'd drive right by! I'm Colleen, Colleen Prescott. My car died on me and I've been walking for ages," she said, her tone too light for someone stranded in a storm. "I don't live far, just past the diner. It's funny—it isn't even my car. Borrowed it. But it looks like it didn't want me to make it home."

Every instinct screamed "no," but there she was, drenched and shivering, her dress clinging to her like she was barely holding herself together. Maybe it was the way her voice trembled, or maybe I just couldn't stomach the idea of leaving someone out here in this mess. The storm felt angry enough to swallow her whole. So I shrugged. "Alright, hop in." *Fuck it, I guess.* I should've told her to use the phone at Starbucks, send her back to MaryAnn, but my mind was already miles away. And frankly, I was fresh out of small talk.

Colleen slid into the seat, her movements sharp and jerky, like fitting herself into the space of a car seat was a new concept for her. *This is how people behave when they're nervous, hiding something, uncomfortable.*

Her presence was suffocating. Her energy—dynamic but disquieting, disturbing, discordant, off-putting—spilled over the edges of the seat and filled every corner of the car. My hands tightened on the wheel, knuckles pale against the dark leather, as the wipers screeched across the glass, their struggle to gain purchase against the rain no match for the storm's fury.

The road blurred into a smear of shadows and sharp flashes, each puddle glowing black and bottomless under the Highlander's jittery headlights. Colleen sat beside me, water dripping from her hair and pooling on the seat. She smiled, wide and unnerving, her teeth catching the light like the glint of a blade. "You're a lifesaver," she said, her voice soft and sticky, almost swallowed by the roar of the rain. I could feel her watching me, like she was studying me from the corner of her eye.

"Truly, you're a godsend," she murmured, her voice dipping lower, curling into the spaces between the storm's noise, like she was whispering a secret she wasn't supposed to share. "Funny, isn't it? How some people can vanish without a trace. And no one ever notices."

I raised an eyebrow. "Uh, yeah… sure," I replied, not really knowing what to say but finding it quite eerie that she'd said it. Was it just a profound coincidence or was she offering a message in there… for me? Honestly, I didn't need a delusional woman's existential crisis on top of my own. But there was something in her tone that made it hard to brush off. "Where am I turning?"

"Oh, just past the diner," she said, waving a hand like it was some grand destination. "Used to work there. Best apple pie in town. Not that I've had a slice in ages."

"Right… cool." I still wondered why she didn't use the Starbucks for refuge. I mean, it was right there. Shelter, a phone, food, people she probably knew… I kept my eyes on the road, trying not to get sucked in. She was like the storm, this energy that filled up the car, leaving no room for me to breathe or think. "Guess you've been on quite the adventure, huh?"

She laughed, this short, breathy sound that sounded as exhausted as it did amused. "Oh, sweetheart, my life's been a series of missteps, one after another. You lose track of the road, and soon enough, you're wandering in circles, wondering if the way out even exists anymore. That's when you learn the truth about yourself—what you're made of, or what's left of you."

I shrugged, trying to brush her words off, but they rang heavy considering what I was going through. For the second time that day, my chest felt like a weight was forcing air out of my lungs and not allowing any back in. "I don't know about all that," I muttered. "Mostly feels like we're all just muddling through. Some of us just happen to get luckier than others."

Colleen sighed, leaning back like that answer didn't satisfy her. "You know, it's easy to feel like you're invisible. Just a ghost in the background of everyone else's life. But I think we're meant for something greater. Something *grand*. Don't you?"

I felt her words sink in, like they were talking to some part of me I tried not to look at too closely. "I guess…" I cleared my throat, trying to steer the conversation back to something less… heavy. "So, what were you doing out here, anyway?"

"I just came from a revival," she said, her voice trembling with something between awe and fear. "The kind where the air becomes so tense and burdensome that it feels like the whole world's holding its breath waiting for you to be humbled. Deferential. Like if you didn't get down on one knee you would be struck down on the spot. People were screaming, crying, speaking in tongues—like they could feel the end coming, a foreboding, just out of reach but near enough to be menacing. Frankly, it was frightening."

I nodded along, fighting a smile. "Wow. That's… that's a lot. Sounds like things got pretty intense."

She kept going, not noticing the faint grin creeping onto my face. "Then I heard about this evolutionist convention in DC." She wrinkled her nose, her tone dipping into a sneer. "Can you believe it? All those people, trying to plot the downfall of everything good and decent."

I nearly choked, pressing my lips together to hold back a laugh. "People have all kinds of… interests, I guess."

She sighed, like she'd just realized she'd have to do this whole thing alone. "That's the problem. No one sees the bigger picture anymore. Everyone's too wrapped up in their own little worlds."

I nodded, glancing over. "Yeah, that sounds about right," I muttered, my mind drifting back to the mess waiting for me. I didn't know which was scarier—Colleen's world, or mine.

We finally pulled up to her place, a house that looked like it was being held together by sheer willpower. It just sat there, hunched and peeling, secrets holding up its walls. And Colleen, with her constant chatter and little sighs, just added to the feeling that I was stepping into something strange. I wasn't sure what, but I felt like I'd wandered into some story I wasn't supposed to hear. And she wouldn't stop talking.

Before I realized it, the words slipped out: "Mind if I use your bathroom?" It wasn't a choice, not really. The storm had drained every ounce of patience I had, and I just needed a second to breathe, to shake off the surreal cloud that seemed to follow her. She was talking, endlessly talking, and the idea of sitting in the car with her energy still spilling over every edge was worse than taking a risk inside her house. Besides, I could tell she wasn't going to let me go without dragging this moment out. A quick stop, and I'd be out the door.

Her face lit up, her nod too quick, too eager, like she'd been waiting for me to ask or looking for some reason to get me to stay. "Of course, darling," she chirped, her voice syrupy-smooth. Her reaction made it harder to back out. The words were already carved into the moment. My stomach twisted, but I forced a smile and slid out of the car. *Just a quick stop*, I told myself. *In and out.*

The rain continued to drumbeat steadily and, together with the shimmer of heat from the wet asphalt, they hit like a cartoon slap machine—no chance to recover, to catch my breath between onslaughts. I barely had time to react before—*crack*. A sharp, jagged sound tore through the quiet. I looked down, pulse spiking.

There it was, lying face-down on the pavement like it had been discarded, abandoned. My stomach dropped, cold and hollow, as I picked it up. The screen shattered into a web of jagged cracks, each one catching the flash of lightning like veins set alight with fire. My breath hitched, cold and sharp, as though the break in the glass had torn through me, exposing something raw and fragile I hadn't realized was there. It buzzed weakly in my hand, flickering orange and electric, like it was alive and struggling to hold on. *Perfect. Another broken piece of a day falling apart.*

I ran my thumb over the screen to unlock it, wincing as a splintery shard slid under my skin. "Ah—dammit!" I exclaimed quietly, taking in the crimson bead trailing down my thumb.

The words that bled through the broken screen were faint and trembling: "*Don't forget your red jacket, Carter. You'll need it.*" Mom's voice wasn't there, but it lingered in the air anyway, soft and steady, like she was standing just behind me. The jacket had been gone for years, but I could still feel its rough fabric, its weight bearing down on my skin.

My stomach twisted, an uneasy memory bubbling up like something dredged from a dream, vacant yet real. She used to make me wear that old jacket everywhere—school, the grocery store, even to bed when the nights got too cold. "It'll keep you safe," she'd say, tugging the zipper up to my chin, her hands lingering just long enough to make sure it stuck. I hated it—the way it scratched, the way it smelled faintly of her perfume—but now, I'd give anything to feel its weight. To hear her voice again, soft and certain, telling me it would all be okay.

I stared at the message, watching it blink once before it vanished just as quickly as it had appeared, like it hadn't been there at all. My stomach knotted tighter. *Was my phone broken and glitching out, or was something else going on? And... why now?*

I was standing on the edge of something… something I wasn't sure I wanted to see. I shoved the shattered phone into my pocket, as if I could bury everything it had stirred up.

THE STORM'S roar vanished the moment I stepped inside, overtaken by a heavy, unnatural silence, thick and unmoving, like the air hadn't shifted in years. Everything felt staged, too precise, like a museum exhibit left to rot. The walls leaned inward, heavy and expectant, like they were waiting for me to make a wrong move so they could swallow me whole.

The faint smell of vanilla candles and mildew hung in the air, sharp and sour against the wet, electric tang of rain clinging to my skin. It was the kind of place that feels more like a memory than something real, a ghost-like set from a movie. Trinkets and knick-knacks cluttered every inch of the shelves and tables, tiny, frozen bits of a life that was miles from my own.

I drifted into the living room, eyes catching on a cluster of framed photos all staring back like they were waiting for me to call them back to this plane, to life. There was one that grabbed me—a kid, maybe ten, smiling like he thought the world was some great adventure waiting to happen. It was that kind of smile that makes you wonder if he knew how fast life could turn on you. Maybe he didn't. Maybe he hadn't figured out yet that there are wolves in the world and some-times life just… throws you to them.

"That's Ryan," Colleen's voice cut through the stillness, snapping me back. She'd appeared beside me, quiet and unsettling, with that smile stretched across her face like it was painted on. "My darling son. I've given him the best of everything—homeschooled him, hired only the finest tutors, spared no expense. Only the best for my boy. You might even see him soon. Which reminds me—"

She paused, her eyes gleaming with a pride that felt too sharp, like it had claws. I watched as she reached for an old rotary phone mounted on the wall, fingers brushing it gently before stopping. The thing looked ancient, like it had been bolted to the wall since the dawn of time. There was this heavy feel to it, like it was strapped to some past that wouldn't let go.

"Sweetie, would you mind if I used your phone to call him?" she asked, her voice soft and too sweet, like sugar hiding something sour. "My landline's disconnected, and I left my cell in the car. I should let him know I made it home safe."

"Uh, sure," I muttered, handing over the phone. "Just, uh… the screen's kind of busted." I tried to shrug it off, but I felt her eyes on me as she clicked numbers, slow and deliberate, like she was handling some kind of ancient artifact.

Straight to voicemail. Not that I was surprised. People don't pick up for unknown numbers anymore; everyone knows that. She didn't seem fazed, though. Instead, she left this syrupy-smooth message: "Hello, Ryan, darling. It's Mother. Just checking in to say everything's fine. I'm using my new friend Carter's phone. Call me back when you get the chance, sweetheart. I miss you."

As she hung up, her face softened for a moment, and I caught this flicker of something in her eyes, like she knew he wasn't going to call back. Her fingers lingered on my phone a beat too long, tracing the cracks like she was trying to read them. I felt my chest tighten, my breath catching as she finally looked up, her smile faint and bitter-sweet, like she knew something I didn't—and wasn't planning to tell me.

"Isn't it strange?" she said, her voice soft and slow, like she was savoring each word. "Sometimes, you meet someone and it's like the universe planned it. Like you were always meant to cross paths, whether you wanted to or not." Something about her voice sent a chill crawling up my spine. "Doesn't that make you wonder?"

"Yeah… I guess it does." The words slipped out, hollow and unsure, and I felt that same chill settle into my chest, colder, deeper.

She handed the phone back to me, her smile still perfect but just… a little too polished. Like something in her had been rehearsing that look for years. A Stepford wife without the movie. I stammered an apology about the shattered screen, but she waved it off, brushing it aside with an airy shrug.

"Don't fret, darling," she said, her fingers brushing the splintered glass. "Life's nothing but cracks, isn't it?" she murmured, her fingers trailing across the screen like she could feel the fault lines. "They start so small—barely noticeable—but they spread before you even realize. And then it's too late. You're left trying to piece together something that'll never be whole again." A pause punctuated the room and she looked at me with an expectant expression. When I didn't reply, she pointed down the hall. "If you still need the bathroom, it's just down there. Sorry to keep you waiting."

"Thanks," I said, trying to sound casual, but every instinct was screaming. Something about her house, her voice—it all felt like it was closing in on me. "But, actually… I should probably get going. It's been… a day."

"Of course, darling," she replied, that eerie, perfect smile never slipping. "Take care. And don't be a stranger."

"Right," I muttered, my voice barely steady as I backed toward the door. "I'll, uh, keep that in mind."

I opened the door and the storm still roared outside, more beast than weather, its claws scraping at the windows, testing the glass with every relentless gust. It wasn't just a storm—it was a presence, watching, waiting, daring me to enter. Lightning split the room open, filling it with a searing, unnatural light. Colleen's shadow twisted against the walls, taller than it should've been, sharper, like it didn't quite belong to her. And then the thunder followed, crawling through the house like it was searching for someone to challenge it.

With a deep breath, I stepped out into the onslaught, the rain slashing at my skin, sharp and punishing. The air felt heavier now, thick with something unnamed, and the storm didn't just wash over me—it pushed, pulling at my clothes, urging me to run before it was too late.

The wall of precipitation punched at me like a heavyweight boxer, making it hard to breathe. *See, Carter? This is why you don't pick up hitchhikers.* But somehow, I knew this day was far from over. There was this feeling, gnawing at the back of my mind, like a thread that wouldn't stop unraveling, and all I could do was follow it, no matter where it led.

And as I ran to the Highlander, I could've sworn I saw Colleen watching me from the window, her eyes following me like I was just another piece in her perfect little world... and how it would be too late until I finally figured out why.

CHAPTER 3

THE RAIN CAME DOWN in slanted, brutal waves, battering the windshield like fists, like the heavy waves of my childhood when the sea rolled so hard it pushed me to the sand. Thunder grumbled low in the distance and prowled, circling closer, like a predator that had picked up my scent, snarling behind some unseen bush, with me in the open savanna.

The air inside the car was cloyingly thick and too still. I wanted the road to open up, to stretch out endlessly under the storm, but instead, the rain pounded harder, the wipers struggling to keep up like a thimble trying to empty an ocean. The world outside blurred into a smear of water and shadow, hemming me in, forcing me forward at a snail's pace, each roll of the tires moving with trepidation against the forces of nature.

I shoved the aux cord into my phone and cranked the volume up, but the storm swallowed the static whole. The bass rattled weakly beneath the rain's roar, losing a fight it hadn't asked for. Lightning slashed across the sky, in front of me, around me, the flashes catching the cracks in my phone's screen like a fire demon had possessed it.

Instantly, ABBA poured out of the speakers, syrupy and saccharine, trying too hard to be cheerful. Each note clashed against the storm, a cracked smile on a corpse that wouldn't stay buried. I turned the volume down, but the music clung to the air, stubborn and wrong, like it didn't want to leave. I glanced at the screen—nothing. Just a cracked display blinking back at me. Frantically, I punched in Mom's address before chucking the phone back in the cup holder. Taking a deep breath, I muttered, "It's alright Carter. You're almost home. You're good. You can make it."

The phone buzzed in the cup holder, a low, needling hum that sliced through the storm, electric and alive, like the device knew something I didn't. Its screen flickered weakly, splitting the light into jagged, frantic patterns, the fire demon trying to claw its way out. "Probably just junk," I tried to convince myself. "Someone asking about my 'car's extended warranty.'" But when I glanced down, there it was. *James.* His name burned on the screen like a match held too close to my skin. The notification glowed faintly, pale and cold against the flickering light of the storm. Thunder cracked overhead and jolted me, a sharp reminder of everything I didn't want to think about.

I stared at the screen, my thumb frozen above "play." Rain lashed against the glass, the sound like nails scratching at the edges of my thoughts. *'Hey, it's Dad'*—His voice already felt like a punchline to a bad joke, one I didn't have the strength to laugh at. Still, I tapped it, letting his voice fill the cabin, awkward as ever.

"Hey, it's Dad." His voice crackled through the speakers, familiar and useless, like the ghost of someone I didn't ask to haunt me. "Just checking in. Hope everything's, you know, going alright. We haven't talked in a while. Anyway, call me when you can... or whenever."

I almost laughed. Deleting it crossed my mind. What did he expect? That I'd call him back and pretend like we were just... fine? That he hadn't bailed on our lives the second things got real? That voicemail was just another half-hearted attempt to patch things up without actually doing the work. I swiped it away. Another empty message from a guy who never really got it.

The road twisted like a snake, its edges smudged by water and melting into the shadows that marked my journey. The trees lurched out of the gloom, their branches thrashing in the wind, twisted and desperate, like they wanted to pull me under. All I could see was James walking out the door, dragging me with him, leaving Mom to crumble one forgotten memory at a time. How he'd sent me back here to deal with this alone. He could apologize all he wanted, send these flimsy "hope you're doing well" messages till the sun burned out, but none of it mattered. Not really.

This drive home was supposed to be easy. A straight shot, routine. But just as I veered toward Lee Highway, the universe decided now was the perfect time to mess with me. You know that feeling? When you walk into a room and something's off… wrong. Only this wasn't a room. This was the whole damn road.

Siri went silent, GPS cut out, but I tried to follow roads I thought I knew by heart. The trees lining the road seemed different somehow, leaning in closer, their bony fingers watching me in silent judgment. Even the road betrayed me, the yellow lines dissolving under the relentless downpour. Water pooled and shimmered, turning the asphalt into a fractured mirror. The horizon blurred, folding in on itself, as if the world was caving under its own weight.

My heart slammed against my ribs, my breath hitching in uneven bursts and I didn't know why. Landmarks twisted into shadows, slipping past before I could name them. The world shifted under me, fragile and somehow incorrect, a dishonest replay of what I thought I knew. I couldn't keep hold of anything real. I felt like I was in a wicked fun house with distorting mirrors, where everything was contorted and warped, not as it seemed. The trees swelled into a solid wall of limbs, shutting the sky out completely.

My fingers dug into the steering wheel, the rough leather biting into my palms. My knuckles turned white; every muscle locked like letting go would send me spiraling into the void. Like maybe, if I held on tight enough, I could bring everything back into focus. But it didn't work.

The world outside melted, warping like wax under a flame. Trees stretched impossibly tall, their trunks curling like smoke, and the road split apart beneath me. The car tilted, the wheel pulling at my grip, and for a second, it felt like gravity had come unhinged, the whole world slipping sideways. Panic clawed at my chest. Before I knew it, I was speeding—gunning it—to Mom's house.

My stomach twisted, the kind of sensation that hits when an

elevator drops too fast. The roaring storm was suffocating, like I was underwater with no way out.

The trees loomed closer, their branches jerking and splintering like marionettes in a violent wind. Lightning continued to tear through the sky in jagged white scars that burned into my eyes. The thunder followed—deafening, apocalyptic—shaking the car, threatening to tear it apart at the seams. The rain hit harder, a deafening roar, my SUV skidding violently onto Mom's street. Then suddenly—.

The storm vanished like a curtain yanked from a stage. No rain. No thunder. The wipers screeched uselessly against dry glass, the sound grating like teeth on metal. Outside, the silence sprawled wide, hitting me like a punch. No clouds, no wind—just a pale, too-bright sky stretching out above an empty field. Even the engine's hum felt wrong—thin and distant, like it was coming from somewhere underwater.

I slammed the brakes, my hands gripping the wheel tight enough to hurt, and rolled down the window. The air was sharp, metallic. Each breath scraped against my lungs like I'd been running for miles. I glanced at my hands—they were shaking. The world outside was just too still, as if time itself had stopped, holding its breath and waiting for me to enter from the wings so it could continue on.

And where Mom's house should have been, there were only rows of trees standing tall and silent.

"Okay, no. No way," I muttered, my voice loud in the unnatural quiet. The storm couldn't just vanish—not like that. But I couldn't deny what I saw. It was a dry road stretching endlessly ahead, the trees still and holding their breath along with the rest of the world. No sway, no leaves drifting to the ground, no life living in its branches. Just the eerie quiet the precedes the murder in a horror flick.

"Perfect. Just perfect!" I shoved the SUV into reverse, peeling down the road. Wrong turn? No. This was Elm Street. The same street that used to hold my life—where I'd gotten grounded for sneaking out with that girl from tenth grade, where I'd suffered through my fifteenth birthday party in that "charming" sweater Mom swore looked great. But now it felt gutted. Like someone had peeled it off and pasted a ghost of it back in its place, too clean, too empty to be real.

I circled the neighborhood, taking turn after turn, but each one led me right back to where I started. No house. No Mom. Just shadows and empty spaces, like the whole town had shrugged and decided to erase itself. The old courthouse loomed in the distance like a monument to something forgotten, its bricks stained and darkened with time.

And then I saw it, a faded, hand-painted sign that read *Fairfax High School, Home of the Rebels.* It peeked out against a backdrop of trees, like some creature watching me from the forest.

What I thought should be reality was a frayed wire, sparking, jumping in and out of focus like an episode of the Twilight Zone, being controlled by something somewhere just out of reach. If this was a joke, the universe was playing it slow, letting me feel every twist.

I let out a breath, a sigh really. Fine. If everything was falling apart, might as well take a closer look.

Fairfax High rose from the trees, its silhouette jagged and sagging, like a tombstone no one had bothered to visit in decades. The windows glared back at me, dark and unblinking, like a face that had been watching for me long before I showed up. The bricks were faded to the color of spoiled milk, their edges crumbling where time had chewed them away. My pulse thrummed in my ears, the lingering echo of thunder that wasn't there anymore still fresh on my mind. The storm had swallowed me whole then spit me out into a hollow world. Too bright, too still, like it had discharged me somewhere I didn't belong. A stranger in a stranger world.

I parallel parked into my old spot, the only thing that felt even remotely real.

Only… it wasn't.

I stared out the window for a few moments. The school looked like it'd been pulled from another universe. Apparently, it was no longer in use and it seemed the town had forgotten it existed. The windows were clouded over, dull and lifeless, as if the building itself had stopped trying. *But I haven't been gone that long.*

I turned off the SUV, heart pounding in the unnatural silence. Everything about the school felt familiar but completely wrong, like it was pretending to be something it wasn't. And as I sat there, staring at it, I couldn't shake the feeling that I was right on the edge of something massive, something that would flip my world inside out. *What the hell is going on...?*

"Alright, Universe, you win." I muttered. "If you're trying to freak me out... mission accomplished."

Fairfax High sat there like an abandoned film set, its edges softened in the afternoon haze. The parking lot was cracked and faded, tire tracks ghosting over the pavement like the echoes of kids who had been here before me, their laughter worn down to static, just a hissing electrical interference from the atmosphere.

Faded pastel cars sat scattered around like relics, each dent and scratch etched in like a timeline of forgotten stories. Everything looked sun-bleached and dulled, like this place had long ago accepted it was nothing special and had just settled for being halfway decent. Every crack in the pavement felt staged, like some artist had gone out of their way to make it look "authentic." But I wasn't buying it. I could see right through the carefully orchestrated emptiness.

Beside me, my phone lay in the cupholder, fractured and dark. I reached for it without thinking, hoping it'd somehow light up and give me a clue, a message, even just a weather update to tell me I was still part of something normal. But nothing. Just that broken screen staring back at me, a reminder that things had slipped out of my hands a while ago. The longer I sat there, the more I felt it—the heavy, gnawing sense that I was way out of my depth, caught in a loop that wasn't about to end anytime soon.

This wasn't some bad dream or a Matrix glitch waiting to snap back to normal if I blinked hard enough. Nope, this was real. My life now—stuck in the last place I should ever belong.

The cars sat scattered like fossils, antennas bent like broken limbs, their cracked windshields clouded with dust. A cassette player glinted through one window, its eject button halfway jammed, like it had been abandoned mid-song and never touched again. Everything here felt preserved and forgotten, like a snapshot of a time I wasn't supposed to see.

I felt this strange, cold weight settle in my stomach. I'd punched a one-way ticket out of everything I knew, and no one had bothered to tell me how to get back.

For a minute, I just sat there, breathing in the thick, heavy silence that clung to the air like an old coat that had seen better days. My heartbeat felt loud, pounding against my ribs, each beat reminding me that, somehow, I was still here. Alive, or something close to it. Maybe I was losing it a little, but there was this stubborn part of me that knew better. I wasn't crazy—I was just… lost. And sitting around wasn't gonna fix that.

CHAPTER 4

THE PARKING LOT stretched out in cracked silence, and the school glared at me, hollow and watchful, waiting—like it knew I'd return. Then something moved—just at the edge of my vision—too sharp, too sudden, like a knife slipping through fabric. I turned, and for a second, I thought they were shadows, the kind that don't go away when you blink. Two figures, silhouettes against the pale light, moved through the bushes like they didn't belong here either. I froze, my pulse hammering. For a second, they seemed like they might disappear altogether. They looked about my age, eighteen, with this worn-down, rough-around-the-edges look that said they'd seen more than they should've.

Curiosity tugged at me, settling in before I could think better of it. What was I hoping for? No clue. But sitting around wasn't getting me anywhere, so I got out of the SUV. The heat hit me, heavy and brutal, clinging to the air, nowhere else to go. I could feel the warmth of the burning asphalt underfoot. The cicadas droned on, loud and careless.

When I finally caught up to them, I nearly tripped over myself, skidding to a stop just before I face-planted into the gravel. My heart pounded, half from the sprint and half from the nerves that were already twisted tight inside me. "Uh… yo," I said, trying to sound like I had even an ounce of chill, though it came out rough and kind of pathetic.

They turned at the same time, too precise, like actors hitting their mark. Their eyes locked on me—sharp, quiet, and far too knowing for two strangers. The girl tilted her head, taking me in like some abandoned thing who'd wandered out of the woods and didn't belong here.

"Who's the stray, Nat?" the blond kid asked, his voice casual, clean and sharp, like a blade sliding out of its sheath. His eyes flicked over me, curiosity glinting in them like a question he already knew the answer to.

"Never seen him," the girl—Nat—said, her voice low and steady, as if she'd already decided I didn't matter. She looked me over, slow and deliberate, her expression unreadable but pointed, like she was waiting for me to say something worth hearing.

I cleared my throat, trying to sound like I had even a little control. "I know this is weird," I started, my voice coming out rough. The words tumbled before I could catch them. "But I'm lost. Totally turned around. Like… none of this makes sense."

Nat raised an eyebrow, barely looking at me. She had this casual, lived-in look—jeans and a white tee that somehow managed to look like armor. A small silver necklace around her neck caught the sun, flashing like a tiny warning. Her gaze was more amused than dismissive, like she was deciding if I was worth the effort.

"Where exactly are you trying to go?" she asked, her voice smooth and calm, as if she had the time.

I took a breath, realizing how absurd this was going to sound. "Drove in from California," I started, feeling ridiculous. "Trying to find my mom's place on Elm. Phone's busted, lost service back there, and… figured I'd take a shot in the dark."

Nat raised an eyebrow, her mouth curving with a hint of a smirk that didn't quite reach her eyes. "California, huh?" she responded, her voice edged with a dry amusement. "That's cute." She said it like she didn't believe a word out of my mouth. "New in town?"

"Sort of," I muttered, feeling my situation settle in. "I'm Carter. Used to live here, but I've been kind of moved around. So… yeah. This place? Feels like another planet."

Nat's smirk twitched at the corners, something dark glinting in her eyes. Amusement? Pity? I couldn't tell, and the not knowing made my stomach twist tighter. "Nice. I'm Nat. And this is Ethan."

Ethan smiled wider, his expression full of mischief. He had this restless energy, the kind that made you feel like he'd be the first to walk straight into a haunted house just to see what would happen. His cargo shorts looked like they'd been through a hundred adventures, and his tank top was frayed at the edges like it was barely holding on.

"So, Cali boy, what's it like out there? Visit any haunted beaches? Seen any ghosts hitchhiking through Malibu?" His grin was too wide, like he was testing how far he could push.

I blinked, caught off guard. "Uh… no?" I said, my voice catching slightly. For a moment, there was silence—so sharp it made the cicadas' drone feel louder, closer, like they were out there waiting to pounce on me like Gulliver.

Ethan let out a disappointed sigh, shaking his head. "Damn… That's half the reason people travel, you know? Sightseeing, trying new food, coming face-to-face with the supernatural. If you haven't done all three, are you even living?"

I chuckled awkwardly, unsure if he was kidding or dead serious. "Guess I missed that part?"

"Don't worry, my guy. Stick with us, and maybe you'll get lucky." He leaned closer, eyes glinting with something between a dare and a promise. "Fairfax has its fair share of mysteries. Just gotta know where to look."

Nat rolled her eyes. "Dammit, Ethan. We were *this close* to having someone think we were cool. You're such dork, you know that?" she said, smirking, but there was no warmth in it—just sharp edges.

Ethan beamed, totally unfazed. "Thank you." He turned back to me, still looking like he was about to drag me into some whirlwind adventure. "So, you a senior? You, like, shred? Surf? You're from California, so you must be able to do something cool."

"Uh, yeah… sure," I said, not really sure where he was going with this.

He clapped his hands together. "Hell yeah, new kid! We'll figure out your thing. Everybody's got one. And if you don't… hang with us.

Adventures, questionable decisions, maybe even a ghost sighting. You'll be a Fairfax legend by Halloween."

I laughed, feeling like I'd just wandered into some bizarre parallel universe where every moment was half-dare, half-trick, and everyone had their own hidden agenda.

Nat gave me a skeptical look. "Alright, thrill-seeker, so you're trying to get to Elm?"

"Yeah," I replied. "Crazy I haven't met you guys before, I knew the school was big but... Any chance you have a phone? Mine's totally busted."

Nat snorted, glancing at me like I'd asked if she had a spaceship. "Phone? What are you, royalty?"

Ethan joined in, casual and unfazed. "Dude, I had a pager once. Lost it on a Ferris wheel. Rest in peace, little guy. Gone but not forgotten."

I forced a laugh, something dry and humorless. "A pager, huh? Retro. What's next, dial up?"

Ethan just blinked, completely unbothered, while Nat rolled her eyes, clearly already over it.

"You said Elm?" she asked again, flicking her cigarette, the ash scattering like tiny stars in a fairytale landscape. "Those houses haven't even gone up yet." Her voice was smooth, too casual, like giving me directions to a place that didn't exist was the most normal thing in the world.

I blinked hard, my chest tightening. "What do you mean? They've been there forever." My voice came out weaker than I'd meant, like I was trying to steady myself on ground that wasn't there.

She gave me a deadpan look. "Nope. Construction's on hold. Heatwave. Guess you missed the memo?"

Ethan leaned closer, like he was letting me in on a joke I wasn't ready to hear. "You're way off, man. Try again in... I dunno... '96?" He said it like he didn't care, but the words crawled under my skin, heavy and wrong.

96. The number punched the air from my lungs, leaving me cold despite the heat pressing down. My stomach twisted, a vertigo I couldn't shake. *They had to be fucking with me—right?* But the thought clung to me, heavy and wrong. The cicadas shrieked from the trees, their sound clawing at my temples, an inexorable static that made my pulse stutter. They were relentless, a chorus of something desperate trying to break free, to grab my attention; a warning perhaps.

Nat shot Ethan a look that shut him up fast. When she turned back to me, her voice softened, but her eyes stayed sharp, searching mine for something I didn't understand. It wasn't pity—it was something colder, harder, like she was trying to decide if I was going to fit into her malicious intent. "Ignore him," she said, her words careful, measured. "But yeah… this town? It doesn't like to play by the rules. Runs on its own weird timeline. But if you're done chasing ghosts, we're heading up to the bleachers. Not much to do in this place—but it's better than being alone."

"Right…" I forced a laugh, but it came out thin. "Well, you're the first people I've seen who aren't old enough to remember Woodstock. What's there to lose?" The words felt hollow in my mouth, like they didn't quite belong to me anymore.

"That's the spirit, *Cali*," Nat said, her voice laced with something I couldn't place—like she'd known all along I'd agree to go with them. Her smirk twitched again, her cigarette burning low, smoke curling up, trying to escape a death of its own making.

"Welcome to the Twilight Zone, man," Ethan said, throwing his arms wide with a smile too big for the moment. "Population: you." He laughed, the sound sharp against the empty air, but it didn't feel funny. "Stick with us, and you might just survive this place. Or not. Who knows? Either way, it'll be a trip."

He turned, gesturing dramatically like he was leading me into some grand adventure. "So, how do you feel about haunted bridges? Headless ghosts? Time travel? C'mon, I know you've gotta be into something out of the ordinary."

I raised an eyebrow, playing along. "Guess I've never put much thought into it before."

Nat turned without a word, moving like she was part of the landscape, her figure slicing through the still air. She didn't glance back, didn't hesitate, as if she'd always been here and I was the one out of place. I stood there for a second, my feet rooted to the cracked pavement. Every instinct told me to stay put. But the idea of being left alone in the bitter silence—no answers, no noise, just me—felt worse than whatever they had waiting for me. I had to move, even if it was a mistake. I took a step forward, then another, each one landing like a question I didn't want to answer.

But what choice did I have? I followed. Each step landed like a warning—sharp, brittle, like glass that could shatter and drop me into something worse. I glanced back at the SUV, expecting it to vanish, swallowed by the strange emptiness of this place. But it sat there, still and hollow, like it was watching me, daring me to go and hoping I wouldn't come back. A tether to somewhere familiar. Still, I kept moving. I didn't know where this would lead, only that staying put felt worse. And in the end, I had nowhere else to go.

CHAPTER 5

WE MOVED toward the stadium like shadows slipping through a place that didn't want us anymore. Not heroes, not rebels—just ghosts, leaving footprints in dust that didn't care that we were there. The stadium slumped into itself, its joints groaning under the weight of a thousand forgotten Friday nights. The wind scraped through the bleachers, hollow and restless, searching for conversations from a bygone era. Somewhere in the rafters, a bird cawed—sharp and sudden—before the quiet swallowed it, heavier than before.

The benches were cracked, bleached to the color of old bones, warped where rain had pooled and rotted through. My fingers brushed the railing, rust flaking away like dead skin, the smell of damp metal sharp and sour. The field before us was mostly dirt, with scraggly patches of grass and weeds clinging on like they had something to prove. The whole place felt like it was holding onto something heavy, like it was exhausted but didn't know how to stop, fighting to be heard where there were no ears.

The quiet here wasn't calm—it throbbed, slow and bitter, like something alive and waiting, a curtain that obscured the life behind the lack of life. It seeped into the spaces between our words, curling tighter, until it felt like I couldn't breathe without breaking it. My shoulders tensed, a cold ache pooling at the base of my neck, the hollow silence penetrating me, pushing me down, pulling me back, trying, in need of showing me something it was holding onto, something it wanted to let go of but could not allow itself to be seen—not out in the open where living eyes knew things. It wormed into my ears, crawled under my skin, like it wanted to pry me open and see what was inside. My pulse quickened, too loud in the quiet stillness. It felt like that soundless world could hear it, that it would figure something out about me. I swallowed hard, my ears ringing. It wasn't waiting for us to break it; it was watching to see if we'd disappear. I could almost hear the cheers that had been swallowed by time, chatter from some universal feedback, echoes that no one bothered to listen to anymore.

We climbed up the bleachers, boards creaking beneath us in a chorus of groans that echoed my uneasy thoughts. By the time we got to the top row, I flopped down, letting the wooden planks jab into my back. Around us, the cicadas were loud and unfiltered, an edgy buzz that spoke of endless encounters with the likes of us. They didn't care whether we were here or not. Somehow, it felt more real up here than anywhere else in town. Too real. Like I'd wandered into a dream that begged for me to be here, wanted me to believe in it. That I was really back in Fairfax.

"So, California," Nat said, her voice slicing through the drone of cicadas like the sudden response of an astronaut who's been lost in space. "What's it like living somewhere people actually give a shit? Somewhere that doesn't feel like it's falling apart under your feet while you're still standing on it?"

I shrugged, playing it cool. "Well, LA's a little different from Fairfax." The words felt thin, like they didn't belong to me. "It's another planet, really. People care way too much about what kind of coffee you order. It's practically a personality test."

Nat's laughter was light but layered, like she still wasn't sure if she believed me. "Right, of course. Mr. *Hollywood* over here." She tilted her head, giving me a look that felt like she could see right through me. "Do people just float around in designer sunglasses, sipping on lattes, acting like nobody else exists?"

Ethan scooted closer, his grin stretching wide, eyes practically glowing with curiosity. "Yeah, like, are there a ton of famous people?

And you just bump into them at random?" He leaned forward, his voice dropping into a stage whisper, like we were swapping secrets in a dark alley. "Have you ever run into someone huge? Like, you're getting gas, and boom—there's Arnold Schwarzenegger or someone!"

They were both staring, wide-eyed, like I was the only connection they had to the mythical land derogatorily referred to as Hollyweird. So I leaned in, pulling out every shiny, exaggerated detail I could think of about LA. I talked about the beaches that went on forever, crowded streets where you could barely see your own feet, people who never looked back, and traffic jams that went on for miles day in and day out. I threw out a couple names, mostly people I'd seen at a distance once or twice, and I hoped they'd eat it up, hang on every word like I was handing them pieces of another world.

But Nat's gaze dropped to the field, her lips parting like she'd thought of something worth saying but decided it wasn't safe to share. Slowly, she chose to anyway. "Can you... skip over the postcard descriptions? What's it all *really* like? It can't be all that great."

"You want the truth?" I sighed, surprised. "The city swallows you in pieces. First, the stars disappear, swallowed by smog and neon signs flickering like they're about to give up. Then the quiet goes. All that's left is the hum of headlights—circling, scanning for something they'll never find. And in the end, no one's even looking at you, but you can feel their eyes, heavy as heat against your skin, like you might burn if you stood still too long."

"Man," Ethan muttered, quieter this time. "That sounds like the loneliest place on earth." He picked at the edge of the bleacher, the sound of splintering wood too loud. "Packed with people... and you're still invisible. What'd you do to stay sane? You must've had a ton of friends, right?"

The question hit me, a little too real, and I felt my answer stick in my throat. "Yeah, sure," I said, shrugging it off. "I had friends. But... you know... LA's big. People come and go all the time. Everyone's got places to be." I turned away, hoping they'd buy it.

Nat tilted her head, her expression softening, like she could see past what I was trying to sell. "Must be weird, being out here without them," she said, her voice dropping just a bit. "I don't know if I could do it. Leaving all my friends behind, everything I've known..." She trailed off, her eyes slipping away to the field below us.

I just nodded, swallowing back the truth. "Yeah," I mumbled. "It's... strange."

Nat gave a small smirk, hugging her knees to her chest, staring out over the field with a look I hadn't seen before. "Sometimes I dream about leaving—just driving until the road disappears behind me. But being nowhere, being no one? That feels worse than staying. Like the road would stretch out forever, and I'd just... disappear. Vanish, like I'd been erased—a blip no one even knew was missing."

I nodded, feeling like I'd glimpsed some hidden part of her. "I get that... Sometimes you don't realize how much a place shapes you until you're not in it anymore."

Ethan, sensing things were getting too real, threw an arm around Nat, pulling her in tight. "C'mon, Nat," Ethan said, his laugh cracking a little too loud, a little too bright—like he was trying to chase something away. "It's too hot for existential crises, alright? We'll plan our getaway after graduation. Don't kill the vibe now."

She smirked, breaking the tension. But under the smile, I felt something shift, like I was seeing the two of them differently. And I wondered if maybe they could see parts of *me* I didn't want them to find.

"So," she said, dragging the word out like it might unravel me. "What was it? Why'd you leave Cali?"

My chest tightened. The truth clung to the back of my throat, but no way was I coughing that up—not now, not to them. Instead, I leaned into the absurd. "Oh, you know. Trouble at my last school. Nothing major—just a vampire infestation. Had to burn down the gym to save the cheer squad. Real hero stuff."

Ethan froze, his jaw dropping like I'd just told him I was an alien. "Vampires? Like, real vampires?"

"Obviously," I deadpanned. "What else was I supposed to do? Let them turn the entire class into their undead minions? That would've ruined prom."

They just stared at me. Not laughing. Not blinking. Just... staring.

"Oh, come on!" I threw up my hands. "You've never seen Buffy? Total classic."

Nat squinted at me like I'd started speaking a foreign language. "Wait—Buffy? Like, the movie?"

I blinked. "The movie?"

"Yeah, with Kristy Swanson," Nat said, her brow furrowing. "You're acting like it has some kind of cult following."

"Oh my god," I muttered, dragging my hands down my face. "The show! Buffy the Vampire Slayer! Sarah Michelle Gellar? Stakes? Leather jackets? Jesus Christ, are you guys messing with me, or am I losing my mind?"

Nat exchanged a baffled look with Ethan, who shook his head like I'd just handed him a Rubik's cube made of algebra. "Dude, what are you even talking about?" Ethan asked. "Trust me, there's no show—I'd know. The macabre is kind of my thing."

For a second, I just stared at them. My brain spun in place, hitting a wall every time it tried to make sense of this. "You're totally screwing with me," I said finally, pointing a finger between them. "You're still on this whole '90s' thing, right? What're you trying to do, gaslight me?"

Nat looked confused, her arms still crossed. "Gaslight? What are you talking about?"

"Oh, please," I muttered, shaking my head. "You're committed, I'll give you that. But let's be real. Buffy exists. And you not knowing it? Super sus."

Ethan opened his mouth, probably to ask what "sus" meant, but I cut him off.

"Let's just say I played along with this whole thing for a second… what's the *actual* year?"

They looked at each other, brows raised. Then they lost it, laughing like I'd said the funniest thing they'd ever heard, but my features didn't move. I just watched them.

Nat's expression dropped. "Fuck, you're serious." Her gaze bore into mine. "What are you, high? It's… 1994, genius. You're not in the future, alright?"

"Yeah," Ethan leaned in, taken aback before a confused smile painted his face. "What'd you think? You landed in 2099? Robot butlers, cyborg baristas... maybe a world where people actually know what to do with themselves?" He let out a small laugh, but there was something brittle about it, like a joke he didn't want the answer to.

I forced out a chuckle, praying it sounded believable, pretending my heart wasn't trying to break out of my chest. "Haaaa! Got you! I totally knew that!" I said, my voice barely steady.

But inside, everything was spinning, unraveling, like I'd just stepped off a cliff and had no idea how to land. It hit me like a punch to the chest—sharp, hollow, leaving me frozen as the air rushed out in a soundless gasp. The world tilted, colors smearing together like paint running down a wall, draining until there was nothing left. My ears rang—a sharp, high-pitched whine, splitting the air, splitting me. It felt like time itself was cracking open. I gripped the bench, but it felt like I wasn't holding onto anything at all—like I was falling through. *1994.* The number echoed, heavy and real, like it didn't belong in my head but couldn't get out. My vision swam. My hands went clammy. My throat tightened. This wasn't a dream. It was real.

Nat playfully shoved me, her smirk returning, pulling me back to reality. "Damn, you really had me going!" She laughed, those brown eyes bearing into me. "You're scary good at that, you know?"

I shrugged, forcing another smile that probably looked insane. "Hey, just trying to... keep life interesting."

She rolled her eyes, her smile turning playful again. "Right on. Well, around here, that's a plus. Welcome back to Fairfax."

"Rust, splinters, and all," Ethan added, gesturing around the stadium with a flourish. "Get ready to embrace small-town life, *Mr. Hollywood.*" He winked. "By next week, you'll be missing California, wishing you never left."

"Yeah, I'm sure I will," I said, chuckling despite the ache in my chest.

Nat spoke again, her tone softening. "Okay, now if you're done dodging the question, what's the real reason you left? None of the vampire bullshit."

Her eyes pinned me in place, and for a second, I thought about telling her the truth. About Mom. About why I'd really left. But instead, I shrugged. They didn't need to know it all. Maybe I could just pretend. "Nothing special. Parents needed a fresh start. Figured dragging me along for the ride would fix things, like a change of scenery could stop everything from falling apart."

Nat tilted her head, her gaze sharpening again, but she didn't push. "Uh-huh. So, what's your home life like now? Got any siblings?"

"Nope, only child," I said quickly, then added, "My parents are still together, totally in love."

It sounded fake even to me, but Nat just nodded slowly, like she was filing the information away. "Must be nice," she said quietly.

"Yeah," I replied, my voice sticking in my throat. "It is. They must've told me the wrong address or something, but they're on their way with the U-Haul now. They figured I should go on ahead and 're-learn' the town with my car, now that I can drive and all."

Ethan broke the moment with his usual energy, his face lighting up as he asked, "Wait, wait, wait. So... if you didn't burn down the gym, does that mean you've never *actually* been in trouble? Or are you secretly, like, a rebel undercover?"

I snorted. "Oh yeah. I'm a total rebel. Watch out. Might jaywalk later."

Ethan beamed. "Well, if you do, let me know. I make an *excellent* accomplice."

"Accomplice?" Nat rolled her eyes, finally smiling again. "More like a liability. You always fold under pressure."

"That's so not true!" Ethan said, puffing out his chest. "I just can't say no to a good deal."

Nat just shook her head, laughing quietly. "See, Carter? He's a sellout. But hey, either of you want to grab a burger or something? I'm starving."

"Nah, I've got dinner waiting at home. Speaking of which—" Ethan checked his digital watch with a loud sigh, then stood as he shook his head. "Shit. I better bounce before my mom totally freaks. You guys go ahead though—I'll catch you later in the land of the living!"

He gave us both a lazy salute, then hopped down the bleachers with a series of exaggerated, bouncing steps, like he couldn't leave without one last dramatic exit. "Awesome meeting ya, Carter! Don't let Nat corrupt you too much," he called over his shoulder, his laughter lingering in the air as he disappeared into the twilight.

"What about you, Carter? You down?" Nat asked, her gaze lingering.

I gave a sorry smirk, knowing I couldn't. My thoughts were spiraling, and a part of me didn't want to overstep. "Wish I could, but I should probably try and figure some stuff out— with the folks," I fibbed.

She crossed her arms, giving me a knowing look. "Understood," she said with a half-smile. "Guess it's just me, myself, and a Big Mac. Not exactly glamorous, but—"

Nat watched Ethan's silhouette go in the distance, her gaze lingering, thoughtful. Then she looked back at me, her expression softening, as if she wanted to say something else, something that might break through this invisible wall between us. But then she just shrugged, giving me a small, tired smile. "Guess I'll see you around, Carter," she said, her voice soft, almost hollow and lifeless, like she was trying to believe it for both of us. Her shadow stretched thin across the bleachers, like it didn't want to let her go. Then the dark swallowed her whole, and the field felt emptier for it. The hum of cicadas filled the space where her voice had been. I almost called her back—almost— but the words stuck in my throat.

She was gone.

"Yeah," I nodded, my voice barely a whisper. "See you around."

I leaned back, staring at the sky as it bled into black, the last hints of light sinking like stones. The quiet crushed down on me like dirt, shovelful by shovelful, until it felt like I might disappear under it.

I let my feet drag as I made my way back to the parking lot, not quite sure of my next move. My car sat there, its chipped paint catching the last bits of sunlight, a confounding display that somehow actually seemed beautiful, like a piece of modern sculpture made from trash and little fairy lights. I slid into the driver's seat and closed the door, unaware that I was unaware, just moving like a ghost with no direction. I sat there for a moment, the air thick as the inside of a vampire's coffin. My breath fogged the windshield, smearing the dark into an endless abyss. It felt like if I didn't move, the night would seal itself around me like a tomb. The seat creaked under me as I shifted, the engine ticking faintly, like a clock running out of time. *Tick, tick, tick*—each sound scraped at the inside of my skull. I stared at my hands, empty and shaking, like they didn't know what they were supposed to hold onto. *Maybe being swallowed by the void wouldn't be so bad*, I thought. *At least it would stop the spinning.*

The shadows curled in tight, swallowing the empty field and the sickly yellow streetlights slid in from the perimeter. Somewhere outside, something snapped—soft and distant, like this secret world was shifting, warning me to get out before its tentacles pulled me into a deep sleep from which I could not return. I gripped the wheel, holding on like it might stop me from slipping under.

The dream had ended, and I was alone in a world that didn't know what to do with me. I rested my head on the steering wheel, closing my eyes, and let out a slow, shaky breath. I'd made it all the way to Fairfax—38 hours under my belt. But where was I? I couldn't shake the feeling that I'd ended up somewhere I wasn't supposed to be—that I'd somehow slipped through cracks in time, in space, to a parallel universe no one else could see, and the world had already closed up behind me.

CHAPTER 6

For those first few weeks, I wasn't even a ghost—more like a stain, spreading thin at the edges of this sun-bleached town. The streets felt brittle under my shoes, cracked and tired, like they'd given up long before I showed up. Everything here tasted like old dust, bitter and metallic, sticking to my tongue like the scraps of a life that didn't want me. Nat and Ethan dragged me through their world like smug tour guides, pointing out empty lots and crumbling walls like they were landmarks worth remembering. It felt like someone had handed me a map scrawled in pencil, no compass, no destination—just endless arrows leading nowhere.

There was the gas station that smelled like it'd been frozen in time since the 70s, a lake whose sign was spray-painted with words no one could read anymore, and an arcade hanging on by the last bits of wire. The place was a graveyard—machines frozen mid-die, their screens dark and quiet. All except one: a pinball game in the corner, blinking and chiming like it still believed someone might save it. *OUT OF ORDER,* the paper read, its edges curling, left to rot. It chimed weakly anyway, its lights sputtering like an old man's spittle, flickering on a loop. The air around it smelled faintly of hot metal, like something trying too hard to stay alive. I stared too long. The hum in my chest echoed back: *same. Still running. Still broken.*

Half the town was like that—buzzing with a sound you could feel in your bones—like the faint hum of old power lines, still alive but too tired to spark. Nobody here knew how to stop. Or maybe they were just waiting for permission.

In Nat and Ethan's world, mysteries were everywhere. To them, everything had some kind of legend hiding just under the surface, like maybe if you looked hard enough, you'd figure out the town's big secret. Except the biggest news here was who kissed who at last weekend's party, and even *that* was old news by Monday morning. Everyone around here had a role—a place. And me? I was just orbiting, a background character who'd missed rehearsal.

Sometimes I'd let myself think, *Maybe this could be my life*—some old movie shot in washed-out colors where no one pretends to be anywhere but here. No missed calls. No hospital visits. Just cheap flannels, burned CDs, and parents who didn't walk out when things got hard. But that wasn't my reality. My reality was more like that pinball machine in the arcade: a big, blinking OUT OF ORDER sign taped to my chest, still trying to light up and get the ball down the alley anyway.

Nat and Ethan spoke a language built from laughter and broken promises, words that felt like they'd been carved into the walls of this town. I tried to listen, to decode the rhythm of their lives, but all I got were static bursts and fragments that slipped through my hands. I watched them the way you'd watch a movie through a dirty window— half the picture obscured, but still close enough to know what I was missing. I was just the extra weight in the backseat, tagging along because it was easier to let me than to tell me to get lost. They were my guides, dragging me through this place like they had all the time in the world, but I was the one without a second to waste. Worst of all, I kept waiting for them to pull the rug out from under me. To tell me to beat it. Scram. That I was just some out of touch kid, some 'lost cause' they wanted to cut loose before school started. And if that happened, I wasn't sure if I could handle it.

ONE SATURDAY, Nat leaned against her faded '85 Beetle, her arms crossed and her head tilted, giving me this long, hard look like I was some hopeless thrift shop find she couldn't decide to keep or toss. Her dark, shoulder-length hair fell in soft waves—effortlessly cool, like she'd woken up that way, even though it probably took work to look so careless. A silver butterfly clip pinned one side back, subtle but enough to make her look like she belonged on the cover of some moody alternative magazine.

She wore this pale, baby blue tee under an oversized cream cardigan that made her look like she'd walked straight out of a *Clueless* wardrobe raid. Her high-waisted jeans hugged her hips and flared out just slightly at the ankles, where her black platform Mary Janes peeked out. That same simple silver pendant rested against her collarbone, catching the light when she shifted, and her makeup—if she was wearing any—was undetectable, letting her sharp, knowing eyes do all the talking.

With a sigh, Nat shook her head in mock disappointment, her lips quirking into a half-smirk. "Carter, Carter, Carter," she said, drawing out my name. "What am I gonna do with you?"

Her tone was teasing, but her gaze was piercing, like she wasn't just joking. Like she was actually calculating whether I was salvageable or a lost cause.

"You cannot keep looking like this. Honestly, you might as well be wearing a sign that says, 'Lost Tourist from the Land of Bad Fashion.' I mean, do you even own anything that's *not* a t-shirt and sweatpants?"

The sad truth was, I didn't. All I had packed were joggers, some shirts, a tooth brush, and deodorant. Easy stuff for a long car ride and short stay, but how could I explain that to them? For all they knew, my parents were already here— my new house somewhere on a street I couldn't remember the name of.

Nat's eyes hit my sneakers, and she flinched like they'd bitten her. "And those? They belong in the Smithsonian for tragic footwear. Or on fire. I can't decide."

I shifted, tugging at my shirt. "They're Jordans. From California," I said, quieter than I meant to, like the word itself could wrap me up in a different life. Like it meant I still belonged somewhere.

Her brow shot up, disbelief etched all over her face. "Wait—excuse me, what? Are they knock-offs or something? I've seen Jordans—I *own* Jordans. They *don't* look like that."

I stiffened a little. "Maybe here, they don't," I said, forcing a bit of conviction into my voice. "Listen, I waited in line for hours to get these. They're definitely not knock-offs."

She let out a small, amused huff, giving me a sideways look. "Hours? Honey, if only you could go back in time and save yourself the effort."

Ethan, who'd been watching this whole exchange with an amused grin, leaned casually against a lamppost. His floppy sun-bleached hair fell into his eyes, and he pushed it back absentmindedly. He wore a loose green flannel over a white graphic tee with some abstract swirl. His dark cargo pants were cuffed over scuffed Doc Martens, and all I could think to myself was, *Really? Was I about to take fashion advice from these kids?*

Unable to hold back, Ethan burst out laughing, nudging me with his elbow. "She's right, man. I mean, it's like those shoes don't even know where they are." His tone was mock-serious. "But hey, no worries! With me and Nat on your side, you'll be blending in like a pro in no time!"

Nat rolled her eyes, but Ethan's enthusiasm was too contagious to ignore, his easy energy turning even my wardrobe disaster into a joke worth laughing at.

BEFORE I KNEW IT, I was being dragged through the mall like I was on some kind of strange, 90s crash course. The malls I knew were mausoleums—airless and hollow, footsteps lost to their own echoes. But here? Here, it heaved like a living thing, kids swarming like ants around dead food courts and neon-soaked walls. The place was alive, but in the way something might still twitch before dying.

We were bombarded by the thick smell of fried food, cheap cologne, and old leather, all stuck together in an awful mix that seemed to come right out of the walls. And the sound—voices and music all mashed together in this chaotic, pulsing beat. I had to shout just to be heard, but somehow, in here, none of it felt strange. Here, you could disappear in the noise. I could disappear, and maybe that's what Nat and Ethan wanted for me.

Nat led us into a store where the lights burned too bright, turning every corner razor-sharp and every shadow a little too dark, like they were hiding something waiting to jump out at me. She went straight to the racks, tossing clothes around like she was looking for something she'd lost. Finally, she pulled out a baggy flannel and tossed it at me.

"Here," she said, looking me dead in the eye, her tone serious. "Put. It. On."

I pulled it over my T-shirt, checking my reflection in the dressing room mirror. I stared at the reflection, and for a second, the kid looking back didn't budge. The flannel swallowed me whole, jeans puddling at my ankles like they were trying to bury me. My reflection looked pale, unfinished—flickering in the harsh light, like someone had sketched me into the wrong decade and forgot to erase the mistakes. I blinked, but he was still there. Still me. Almost. My dark hair was even messier than I remembered, curling slightly at the ends from the static in the dry mall air. It was impossible to tell the sides were ever shaved, and the oversized flannel made my shoulders look smaller, my whole frame a little shrunken, like I was trying to hide in plain sight.

I opened the door and Nat leaned against the doorframe, giving me a satisfied nod, her arms crossed like she was examining her work.

"Better," she said with a smirk.

"Much better," Ethan chimed in, his smile stretching from ear to ear as he leaned against a pile of neon shoelaces. "It's like... the East Coast version of you, man! You can't look like everything you own is from California forever! Now, all you need is a portable CD player, and boom! You'll be Fairfax's hottest new kid." He snickered, throwing in an exaggerated wink.

Nat picked out three more shirts and another pair of jeans, layering each one into my arms. Then, just when I thought we were done, Nat turned her attention back to my shoes, her expression shifting from approval to absolute scandal.

"Oh, no. No, no, no." She shook her head, as if physically pained.

"You *cannot* walk around in those. We're getting you real shoes, Carter." She yanked me over to a wall of high-tops, pointing to a pair of black Converse with white laces.

"These," she said, her voice dropping to a serious, almost grave tone. "You need these."

I held up a pair, skeptical. "Converse? Really?"

She gave me a look, like I'd just asked if the sky was blue. "Yes, Converse. They're, like, a rite of passage around here. You can't even be seen without a pair of Chucks. Trust me, I'm saving you from social suicide."

Ethan nodded, giving me this over-the-top sympathetic look. "She's not kidding, dude. It's, like, a local mandate. If you don't get those, they'll probably revoke your 'cool' privileges. Seriously, kids here don't mess around."

I sighed, tried them on, and stared at myself in the mirror again. The Converse pinched at my feet, stiff and new, testing my will to fit in. Like they knew I didn't belong here and wanted me to prove I deserved them. My Jordans had been mine. These? They felt borrowed, but they made sense here—like a second skin I wasn't sure I wanted. *I knew I should've bought the retros.*

Nat tilted her head, her smile hovering between smug and soft. "See?" she said, quieter now, like maybe she meant it. "Now you don't look like you wandered in from a different planet."

I paid for the clothes with the little cash my dad had slipped me before the trip, my heart sinking as I watched it disappear from my wallet. The cashier handed over the bag, and I walked out wearing an oversized flannel in muted blues and greens, its soft fabric drowning my frame in a way that felt simultaneously comforting and foreign. The loose jeans hung awkwardly around my hips, just a little too long, bunching over my Chucks. It was a look that screamed *trying to fit in but not quite there yet*, which was painfully accurate. The rest of the haul hung beside me in a plastic bag, feeling like a dead weight in my grasp.

When Nat, Ethan, and I wandered into the food court, the smell of stale popcorn and greasy pizza hit us like a wall. The food court hummed under buzzing neon lights, casting everyone in electric blues and greens that made their faces look surreal. Kids sprawled across tables like abandoned mannequins, limbs draped carelessly, voices ricocheting off plastic trays and metal chairs—a noise so loud it drowned itself out. Some sat slumped in chairs, others perched on the backs of benches, their whole demeanor screaming *we've got nowhere else to be and all the time in the world to waste.*

"You act like you've never seen a mall before—" Nat caught me staring. "I know it's probably nothing compared to LA, but this place… It's like its own universe. The mall has a gravity, and it's the only place that sucks us all in. Where our parents won't kill us for spending time in."

She was right. The mall was like this planet, circling itself, and everyone here was caught in its orbit. Maybe if I kept coming back, I'd feel that pull too, feel like I was actually part of something. But for now, I was still on the outside, watching them from my lonely little satellite.

Ethan nudged me, smirking. "Congrats, Carter. You're practically a local now." He nodded at the flannel and Converse, shaking his head in mock admiration. "You've got the look and everything. Just don't, like, freak out and start wearing socks with sandals or something. Trust me, it's… a slippery slope."

We drifted through the mall in silence after that, a comfortable silence, just the three of us moving through the crowd, slipping in and out of shops like we belonged there. I caught kids glancing at me with these curious looks, like I was some kind of exhibit they hadn't seen before. But for once, it didn't bother me.

Maybe now, I looked like I belonged. But looking like something isn't the same as being it. The flannel clung to my shoulders like borrowed skin, too soft, too new. Like it was waiting to wrap itself around me, tighter and tighter—until I couldn't tell where it ended and I began.

CHAPTER 7

After a while, we fell into this routine that almost felt natural. Like we were on the same wavelength, but mine kept drifting, like I was tuned just a little off. Nat and Ethan? They still had that unspoken language, the kind that makes you feel like you're missing half the conversation. Sometimes, I'd manage to make Nat laugh, but I'd catch Ethan looking at me, his smile slipping for just a second, like he wasn't sure if I was just another speck in his life, something to get used to, or something he would eventually want to get rid of. And there were these little things—like when his hand brushed hers, and she'd pull away just a little too quick, leaving him staring like he was losing something he couldn't name.

Then there'd be moments when I'd catch Nat's eye across the room, just a spark, just a second. Long enough for my pulse to jump. But the second I looked back, Ethan was there, his easy grin gone, something harder in its place. It made me wonder if he saw me as some kind of trespasser in his world, a stranger who didn't quite fit the mold he was preparing.

Still, each day felt like a different kind of adventure, though not the kind you brag about. More like the kind where you're not sure if you're the hero or just the extra who's gonna trip over something and mess up the shot. The whole *town* had this feeling. It was like it was clinging to some memory that nobody wanted to let go of. But there was no endless scroll, no notifications. Everyone was just killing time in a place where the biggest news was the possibility of a new song on the jukebox at the diner. Here, time had hit pause, and we were all just floating, trying not to crack the surface. But for me, everything always seemed to be moving in slow motion. There was always this itch, this nagging sense that maybe this wasn't the dream it pretended to be. Like everyone was just playing along, hoping they'd make it out before the train finally went off the rails. Or maybe that was just me.

Even with all the reckless laughter, the long nights that bled into mornings, I couldn't shake the feeling that something was missing. Like I was the only one who could see the cracks spreading while everyone else danced on top. Being stuck in this pastel-colored past made me miss the glitchy, complicated present even more—especially my mom. For all I knew, time was marching on without me, leaving a gap in the future where I should be. Maybe by now I was just another face on a milk carton, a name that showed up in whispers on the news. It was almost like living in a snow globe someone kept shaking, and with every shake, I was getting pulled further away from wherever I was supposed to be.

MOST NIGHTS, I'd end up at Ethan's place. His house felt like it was straight out of some bizarre adventure comic, with layers of half-organized chaos stacked in every corner. The walls of his bedroom were covered in faded posters, some of them fraying at the edges, relics of past interests Ethan had never quite outgrown. His parents barely blinked when they saw me hanging around, like I was just another piece of the furniture, just another casualty of an ill-equipped high school that prepares students for a world that doesn't exist. They'd either breeze by, juggling coffee mugs, tend to half-finished paperwork scattered across the kitchen table, or debate conspiracy theories from late-night documentaries like it was family tradition. And there was always something buzzing in the background—the old TV in the living room, the hum of a heater that sounded like it was gearing up for a fight, or the faint beat of whatever burned CD Ethan had going upstairs. Chaotic was definitely a word for the place, but hey, at least it had a shower, and a place for me to lay horizontal. And it was a family.

The couch in the living room was this saggy, overstuffed thing, the kind of couch that had borne too much weight over the years, too many children bouncing on it, too many dogs or cats tearing at it, until it finally swallowed itself and just surrendered. It was covered in weird stains Ethan swore were from "science experiments," though, of course, he'd never say which ones. The TV in the corner, one of those old boxy ones that sat above a VCR, had a crack on the screen, and Ethan *loved* to tell people it was the result of an "epic showdown" with his older brother. In reality, though, I had a feeling it was more of a stray basketball situation. Either way, it fit the house's vibe—patched up, a little beat-up, but hanging on like it had a personality of its own.

Ethan's "nest," as he called it, was his dad's ancient armchair, a hulking thing with the stuffing coming out at the seams. He'd sprawl out like he was on a throne, feet kicked over the side, one hand in a bag of chips and the other picking at the frayed fabric like it was some clue to a mystery he was solving right there in the armchair. He'd stare at the TV with that wide-eyed curiosity he had, his expression bouncing between half-asleep and completely wired, as if he was waiting for aliens to drop out of the screen or for some cartoon character to give him a message from the beyond.

Truthfully, we didn't really talk about big things. We just existed in the same space, letting the cartoon voices of *The Simpsons* fill the room, each of us drifting in and out of our own thoughts. I'd stretch out on the couch, sinking into it, watching the flickering screen and letting the weird comfort of Ethan's world settle over me. It was like his house had a pulse of its own—this quirky, tired rhythm that didn't need to impress anyone. Just hanging on like it always had, ready for whatever disaster Ethan decided to drag into it next.

And on the nights I couldn't stay there, it was just me and my car. I had to keep up the lie that my parents finally made it to town, that our house was beautiful, filled with home-cooked meals and people who didn't have a worry in the world. But in reality, I was just... here in some lot. I'd plug in my phone, watching the bars flash "SOS" like some cruel message. I guess it was the universe's way of showing it had a sense of humor. I'd lean back, let some old song fill the quiet, telling myself this was all normal. Just another episode in the Chronicles of Carter Sullivan. But even then, sometimes that gnawing silence crept in, whispering, reminding me of all the things I didn't want to hear.

Sometimes, it'd be Dad's words, his voice sticking like gum to the back of my brain. That warning, that if I wanted to see Mom again—really see her, while she still knew me—I needed to get back to her. And it was there, under a sky that couldn't care less, I'd feel so small, like I was folding in on myself. It was then I'd find myself doing something I hadn't done in years, but seemed to do all the time now: I'd hope, even pray, for something I couldn't even name. Just...a way back. And for her to still be waiting.

AFTER A FEW OF those not-so-fun nights, I finally caved. I burned through what little cash I had left on a room at this washed-up, beaten-down motel just past the edge of town. I used to drive by it all the time as a kid—this odd, lighthouse-inspired spot, but in reality, it looked closer to some poor, misshapen cigarette. Even in this time, its white paint was chipped and peeling under layers of grime and sun exposure. Best of all, it rested nowhere near the ocean, *but* I guess you didn't need to be close to anything real to pretend you had purpose.

The bed creaked when I sat down, the whole place smelling like it'd been sealed up since the Stone Age. I wondered how many people had passed through here, laying down their troubles on the same lumpy mattress before disappearing back into their lives. This place wasn't fancy. It wasn't anything. Just four walls and a bed that sagged in the middle, as tired as the people who had lain wearily on it year after year: the exhausted businessman, the homeless spending their last dollar for the chance at one hot shower, the man on the run, sleepy children, maybe even a dog or two... It was just tired of holding people up. But hey, a roof over my head. That's something, right? At least, that's what I told myself.

I sank into the scratchy comforter, the faint odor of unwashed bodies, lovers clinging to each other, and shattered dreams assaulting my senses. I clutched my phone out of habit like a safety blanket, a pacifier. The no-signal icon blinked back at me like it was laughing, the grand wizard in the carnival machine where, if you put a coin into its mouth, it would tell your fortune; even *it* was against me in all this. The whole world was moving on without me, and all I had was that stupid SOS symbol. I tossed the phone aside, letting the silence settle, and for the first time in hours, I tried to let myself relax.

But then, against every shred of logic, my phone buzzed.

Bzz-bzz-bzzz!

My heart shot up to my throat as I grabbed it, clinging to that little sliver of hope. It was a voicemail— from Mom.

I just stared at it. Couldn't move, couldn't breathe. *How was this even possible?* With a shaky hand, I tapped play.

"...Come home, Carter, I need... you." Her voice crackled through the static, faint, like she was barely hanging on. But it was her. It hit me like a punch I hadn't seen coming. My mom's voice—calling out to me. There was something in it, too, something raw, desperate.

I played it again, tried to hold onto every word, but it cut off half-way, swallowed by static. Like the universe was swallowing her words, like it didn't want me to hear. My chest tightened, walls closing in around me. *Come home.* That's all I'd been trying to do, but how was I supposed to do that when I didn't even know how I ended up here? Was time just leaving me behind, like I didn't matter? Like I was just another person passing through?

Where are you, Mom.

I tried everything to reach her—to send a message back, to get any sign she could hear me. But the phone just sat there, mocking me with that SOS symbol. After a while, I let it slip from my hand. It hit the floor with a dull thud, as lifeless as I felt.

Then the screen lit up again, blinking in little bursts like a broken beacon. *Missed call.* My heart lurched, but then I saw who it was.

James.

I groaned, swiped it away, but something kept my thumb hovering over the list. Three voicemails. Unopened. *He never called this much.* Against my better judgment, I tapped the latest one.

"Hey, Carter. Look, I know things have been… strained between us. I just… I want to talk. About the move. The job. I don't know, maybe I should have explained things better before. Anyway, I'm here if you want to talk. Let's… I don't know, try again? Call me when you get the chance."

His voice faded out, just static now, like the phone itself couldn't even handle him. Maybe that was his guilt, maybe mine—I didn't know. Didn't care. I tossed the phone onto the nightstand and pressed my fingers into my eyes. *He could wait.* What could I even say? "Oh, hey, Dad, I'm having an existential crisis in a motel on the outskirts of nowhere because you decided to blow up our lives? Oh. And by the way. I'm stuck in the 90s."

I grabbed the remote, flipped on the TV, hoping for something— anything—to drown out the quiet in my head. *Friends* crackled across the screen, its canned laughter bouncing around the empty room. I stared, not even watching. I didn't need to. My mind was somewhere else. Thinking of her.

Mom had this joke. Every time we'd sit down to watch a movie, she'd lean over and whisper, "I bet the dog did it." Didn't matter if it was a horror movie, a serious crime drama, a period piece with knights and betrayal and doom—she'd say it. Every. Single. Time. Like it was the funniest thing in the world. And somehow, it always was.

I could almost hear her beside me, leaning in with that little smile, nudging me. "I bet the dog did it." And I'd roll my eyes, pretend it was the lamest thing I'd ever heard. But I couldn't hide my grin. Not from her.

I'd give anything to hear her say it again, just like that. To feel her nudge me, waiting for the dog to show up. But that felt like it was slipping away, too. *How long until she forgot that joke?* Until I was just a stranger she had to work to remember, another face in the crowd of her mind?

The colors on the TV blurred as I blinked back the ache creeping up. I turned the volume down until it was just a faint hum. Even with the sound nearly gone, the memories were louder. So loud they drowned out everything else.

I knew that if I closed my eyes, I'd see her face, right there next to mine, and I didn't know if that would make me feel better or... if it would tear me apart.

CHAPTER 8

WHEN SCHOOL FINALLY STARTED, it was like stepping into some warped dream version of my old life. Same halls, same lockers, but everything felt… wrong. Like somebody tried to paint over reality but messed up all the details. Fairfax High was still here, still standing, but it felt like a skeleton of itself—its walls hollow, its air damp with the ghosts of long-forgotten mornings. The place reeked of old cafeteria grease and wet chalk, the kind of smell that sank into your clothes and made you wonder if it would ever wash out. I used to wish with everything in me that I'd be back here, that maybe being forced to transfer to Reagan High back in LA was the start of all my problems. But, hey, "be careful what you wish for," right? Who actually listens to that? Definitely not me.

Blending in wasn't hard. I walked into the front office on day one, told 'em I was the new kid, threw out some vague story about my "parents being on vacation in California," chasing some kind of dream or sun-drenched fantasy or whatever people think California's about. I promised they'd be back soon, and… Nobody questioned it. I was just another shadow sliding through the halls, melting into the peeling paint, grimy linoleum floors, and the lingering smell of cafeteria pizza, which seemed to be soaked into the air permanently. Places like this? They chew you up, spit you out, and forget you ever walked their

halls. If you're not loud, strange, or wearing spikes, you're wallpaper—
just another stain blending into the grime. I wasn't here to be seen. I
was here to disappear.

I dragged myself through homeroom, then history class, with my
next stop being Dr. Mercer's physics class. First day was as expected—
roll call, "here's your syllabus," try not to doze off. But I knew Nat and
Ethan would be in this class with me, which meant a small island of
familiar faces in the sea of monotony. As I walked in, Nat sat with her
chin propped on her hand, her dark, shoulder-length waves framing
her face, while her oversized denim jacket hung loose over a cropped
black tank top and plaid skirt. She looked effortlessly cool, the kind of
person who could make boredom seem intentional.

Ethan, by contrast, was dressed like he'd just stepped out of a skate
park. His black hoodie had a faded logo plastered across the chest, and
his loose khaki pants were frayed at the cuffs, giving him a scrappy,
lived-in look. Scuffed Vans peeked out from under the desk as he
tapped his foot to some internal rhythm, his floppy hair falling into
his eyes every time he moved.

Maybe this could be my new hideout. Somewhere to disappear,
where no one cared who I was or why I was here. I slipped into the
back row behind Nat and Ethan, and settled into the desk, letting the
local indifference wash over me.

Then the door creaked open.

It was slow enough to make the sound crawl under my skin. A
shadow spilled into the room first, long and jagged against the floor.
Then he stepped in, his movements unnervingly deliberate. The air
thickened, like it had sucked all the sound out of the room. Heads
turned one by one, pulled as if by invisible strings, their movements
slow and synchronized, like an audience waiting for the first strike of
lightning.

I squinted, trying to place him. He looked like he'd stepped out of
some vintage noir, all clean lines and controlled elegance. His blond
hair gleamed too bright under the flickering fluorescents, the kind of
perfection that felt designed, not lived-in. His face was a polished
sketch of sharp lines and smooth edges, like someone had taken a

scalpel to marble and decided to carve out ambition. He moved with a kind of studied grace, like he'd already mapped out every step, his expression cool and unbothered, as though the rest of us were just background noise to his performance. He wore clothes that were pressed and casual but tailored to perfection, an easy style that felt just a little too practiced. And those eyes—dark, keen, cutting—swept over the room, seeming to take stock of everyone's secrets, daring anyone to question his. He moved like he was the only one who knew where this story was headed, and something about him... didn't sit right. His aura hovered somewhere between "hardened outsider" and "potential cult leader," and neither made me feel any better.

I leaned forward, catching Nat and Ethan's attention. "Hey, who's the mysterious stranger?" I muttered, nodding toward him.

Nat glanced over her shoulder with a raised eyebrow, giving a faint, dismissive smirk. "Oh, that's Ryan Prescott," she said, her voice dripping with bored indifference. "Apparently, he's the smartest kid in school. Practically a local celebrity. Or, you know, legend—in his own mind." She rolled her eyes. "He's honestly just a walking ego trip with a perfect GPA."

Ryan. My heart froze. *Could this be Colleen's kid?* Her words echoed in my mind, sending a chill up my spine: *"You might even see him soon."* Was he the reason I was here?

Ethan snorted, leaning in with this gleam in his eye. "Oh yeah, *Ryan*," he said in a hushed, overly dramatic voice, like he was narrating *Dateline*. "Our school's resident boy wonder. He's got the charm, the A's, the whole 'prodigy' package. Basically, he's every parent's dream and every kid's worst nightmare. Watch out, man—he's supposed to be some kind of genius or something." He rolled his eyes. "Get ready for teachers drooling over him like he's the next big thing. And trust me, it gets old. Fast."

Nat smirked, leaning back like she couldn't care less. "Honestly, he's more Frankenstein than Einstein. Either everyone'll be too busy obsessing over him to notice us, or we'll be stuck dealing with the 'gold standard' he sets." She gave a dramatic sigh. "Obviously, I'm rooting for option one."

I glanced back at Ryan, trying to understand why every instinct in me was on high alert. He was standing at the front, talking to Dr. Mercer with the kind of confidence that seemed custom-made to draw attention. Something about him was just... too sharp, too perfectly placed, like he wasn't even trying to fit in, like he knew he didn't belong and didn't care. He had a purpose, and whatever that was, he was confident in his ability to get there.

"Must be nice," Ethan muttered, squinting at Ryan like he was inspecting a suspicious artifact, "to have everyone think you're some kind of legend. Bet he doesn't even realize us mere mortals exist." He gave an exaggerated sigh. "Ah, the life of a teenage genius."

Ryan's gaze swept across the room, sharp and cutting, before locking on me. My chest tightened, my breath hitching like my lungs had forgotten how to work. He didn't just glance—he held, as though he was waiting for something to crack open. I froze, hoping he'd move on, but he didn't. His steps were unhurried, deliberate, the kind of pace that stretched time thin, turning every second into something unbearable. I couldn't help counting them, each one dragging heavier than the last. By the time he stopped beside me, my pulse felt like a drumbeat in my ears.

In front of me, Nat and Ethan both went tense, staring straight ahead like they were hoping to melt into their seats. Nat mumbled under her breath, "Oh god. Here we go."

"Maybe he'll just... go away?" Ethan whispered, sounding anything but convinced.

But Ryan didn't change course. He slid into the vacant seat beside me like it was his throne. The chair creaked as he leaned back, watching me with a look that said he'd already figured me out and was waiting to see if I'd catch up.

I tried to keep it casual. "Hey, you're Ryan, right? I'm Carter." The words felt weird, but I forced them out. "Met your mom the other day —Colleen?" I said, trying not to trip over my sentence. "She mentioned you'd been homeschooled. You new here too?"

Ryan's smirk spread slowly, like he'd been waiting for this exact moment, savoring it. He looked me over, a glint of something dark and amused in his eyes, sizing me up with the lazy confidence of someone who knew exactly how to get under your skin. "Homeschooled?" he echoed, voice dripping with mock surprise, like he was humoring me. "Guess, you've had the pleasure of hearing one of my mother's fairytales. Let me guess, you two talked over apple pie at the diner?" His tone oozed with sarcasm, and that grin stayed in place, like he'd already won some game I didn't even know we were playing.

I blinked, caught off guard, my brain scrambling for something to latch onto. "But... she said—"

He cut me off with a low chuckle, the kind that crawls under your skin and settles there, making you feel like you'd missed a beat. "Yeah, well, Colleen says a lot," he said, dragging out each word as if he were tasting it. "Has quite the imagination. Helps her sleep at night. But if I were you..." He leaned in just a fraction, his gaze locking onto mine, cold and unblinking, "I wouldn't take everything she says at face value. She has a tendency to... *exaggerate.*"

Heat prickled the back of my neck under his stare, and he seemed to enjoy every second, watching like he was savoring my discomfort. Nat and Ethan stayed frozen, pretending they weren't listening but catching every word. Ryan leaned in, voice dropping to a near-whisper, his eyes shining with something that felt like a warning. "People in places like this? They love a good rumor. And you..." He paused, letting his eyes drag over me in a way that felt invasive, almost like he was peeling back layers I hadn't even known were there. "You look like the kind who'd make a great story."

A chill crawled up my spine, cold and deliberate, like the brush of an unseen hand. This wasn't just a game—it was a trap, and Ryan was already holding all the strings. He wasn't just another kid. He was the kind who wore his strangeness like armor, who'd pick you apart just to see what was inside, and somehow, I knew I'd just stepped into something I wasn't ready for.

I forced a laugh, hoping it sounded casual, though it felt hollow. "Right. Well, thanks for the... heads-up." I muttered, trying to act like I wasn't totally rattled. The words sounded thin, and he knew it.

Ryan tilted his head, his gaze lingering on me, sharper now, calculating every reaction. "Just be careful," he said. "The quieter you are, the more people notice when you finally speak up."

I held his gaze, refusing to look away, but it felt like staring into something endless and dark, like I was reaching for something just out of view. And then he turned, that smirk still curving at the edge of his mouth, like he'd just peeled back a corner of me and liked what he'd found. It was then I realized I'd never been great at staying quiet. Maybe that's what he was counting on.

Ryan leaned back in his seat, stretching out like he owned the space already, like he'd decided he had me exactly where he wanted. "So, Carter" he drawled, letting my name hang in the air as though it was his to play with. "Are you just here to fill a seat, or is there a real story under all that mystery?"

Frustration flared up in me, that instinct to pull my defenses tighter, like I was already losing ground. "Oh, I'm *definitely* here to fill a seat," I shot back, dry as dust. "Big plans to take up space, make people look at me. You know, for the aesthetic."

He raised an eyebrow, like he was both amused and unimpressed. "Is that what you tell yourself? That you're just… *here?*"

"Yup," I replied, letting the sarcasm drip, letting it cover the fact that he was under my skin. "Just here to wander the halls, stare at lockers, maybe unravel the mysteries of… this place." I gestured, lazily. "What do they call it? Limbo? Purgatory?"

He smirked, the gleam in his eyes turning darker, more pointed. "Sounds deep. Almost interesting." His gaze roamed over me one last moment, like he was deciding whether I was worth some serious time or just another pawn to toy with. "Guess I'll just have to see for myself."

Just as his words hung in the air, the bell rang, cutting through the quiet like a cold splash of water. *Thank. God.* Students shifted in their seats, rustling papers and books as Dr. Mercer clapped his hands, signaling the start of class. But even as Dr. Mercer launched into his introduction, Ryan's gaze stayed locked on me, lingering, like he'd left something unsaid.

Nat and Ethan gave each other uneasy glances, both of them straightening up as Dr. Mercer's voice filled the room. But Ryan's stare lingered, unsettling and thick with energy, like static in the air after lightning.

As Dr. Mercer started writing on the board, I chanced a look back at him. Ryan hadn't turned away, that smirk still there, like he knew something the rest of us didn't. And in that moment, with the hum of the class around me, I had this creeping feeling that whatever secrets he was holding? They weren't meant to stay hidden for long.

And me? I wasn't sure if I was ready to find out what they were.

CHAPTER 9

THE REST of the semester dragged on, drifting past in a blur of half-finished assignments and tired routines. My hair had grown longer than I typically liked, but Nat insisted it suited me. That it "gave me an edge." But no matter how much I tried to blend in, stay cool, and just let time pass, my mind kept getting yanked back to Ryan. Every time I sat down next to him in Physics, it was like he already knew every single thought bouncing around in my head, just waiting for me to crack. He had this way of staring at people that made you feel like he was reading a book you'd never be allowed to see. Like he'd been clued into some deep, dark secret about life that the rest of us were too scared—or too dumb—to understand.

After a few units that went in one ear and out the other, Dr. Mercer shifted us to the upcoming science fair. Everyone went into panic mode, scrambling for any project idea that might save them from embarrassment. Me, Nat, and Ethan? We just wanted to get through without accidentally creating some toxic spill in the lab. Sure, I could've come up with something wild, some... *future-tech* invention that'd leave them speechless in the '90s, but somehow, I didn't think "secret government experiment" was a good look on me.

Ryan, though? Different story. He was all in. While the rest of us were trying to figure out if baking soda volcanoes still counted as science, Ryan was off talking about "the linear passage of time and its path to immortality." Casual, right? Just another Tuesday for him.

The thing is, I couldn't get the idea out of my head. I knew I should stay out of it, but something about time itself was clawing at me. So one day, while we were packing up, I leaned over, lowering my voice like we were exchanging state secrets. "So, Ryan… got any thoughts on time travel?"

He paused, glancing over at me with this glint in his eye that was half-curious, half-amused, like he'd finally stumbled across something worth his time. "Time travel?" he echoed, letting the words drag out, lazy and sharp at the same time. "What, you planning on stealing a Tardis? Planning on rewriting history?"

I let out a laugh, but it sounded hollow, even to me. "Nah, just curious," I said, trying to shrug it off like I wasn't hanging on his every word. "You're basically the school's brainiac. Figured you'd have some kind of theory."

Ryan slung his backpack over one shoulder, giving me this look— half smirk, half I'm-way-smarter-than-you, the kind of look that made you want to roll your eyes and punch him in the same breath. "Everyone's so obsessed with rewinding the clock, aren't they?" he said, like he was sharing some dark truth meant only for me. "People think they can just go back, fix their mistakes, live in some romanticized *good old days.'* But time doesn't grant favors, Carter. It's forward or nowhere at all. You move forward, or you're left behind. Simple as that."

There was a weight to his words, something that lodged itself deep in my chest and refused to budge. *If he was right, then what was I doing here?* His words stuck like thorns. *'You're left behind.' Was that what happened? I moved backward while the rest of the world kept marching forward?* Regardless, I was done going back—it was about finding a way forward, even if everything in me wanted to look over my shoulder.

"So… you're saying going back is impossible?" I asked, barely a whisper, like I was afraid he'd laugh.

He leaned in just a little, his gaze unreadable, his voice dropping lower, and suddenly it was like there was no one else in the room.

"Impossible? Sure, we'll go with that. *Improbable?* Definitely. If it *were* possible, it'd take something none of us have ever seen. Some element that doesn't exist, some method we haven't dreamed up." He tilted his head, watching me in this way that was both curious and… something sharper. "If it *were* possible, you'd be messing with things no one fully understands. Time isn't like flipping through TV channels. You start toying with it, and it toys right back. And trust me, that's a game you don't win."

He paused, studying me for a long moment, like he was deciding whether to keep going. "But honestly? I don't think you're the type to settle for just getting by. Something tells me you'd take that risk if it was handed to you, am I right?"

There was something in his voice that made my pulse quicken, like a taunt wrapped in a dare. I felt my cheeks heat up, my mind scrambling for a comeback that didn't make me sound like an idiot. But he just watched me, that smirk flickering back, as if he enjoyed watching me stumble, like I was some puzzle he couldn't quite crack.

"Still," he murmured, his gaze lingering a second too long, "some things are best left buried. Digging up the past isn't all it's cracked up to be. Sometimes, it's better to let the ghosts rest."

And there it was—that look, that edge in his voice, like he'd just handed me a loaded gun and dared me to pull the trigger. And maybe that's exactly what he wanted. The pull in his voice was magnetic, unsettling. It left me wondering if I was supposed to trust him or keep my distance. The thrill of both was enough to make my head spin.

Then he gave me one last, crooked smile and turned to leave, just like that, like he hadn't left something burning inside me. I watched him go, feeling a mix of anger, intrigue, and… something else, something like… shit. *Admiration?*

"Time travel catch your interest, Carter?"

I nearly jumped out of my skin, snapping back to reality. Dr. Mercer was standing a few feet away, watching me with that too-intense stare of his, like he'd been listening to every word.

I cleared my throat, suddenly feeling exposed. "Um… no," I said a little too fast. "Just… thought it was cool."

Dr. Mercer's gaze didn't waver. He kept watching me, looking through me, searching for something beneath the surface. Finally, he raised an eyebrow, a faint, almost amused smile tugging at his lips. "Curiosity's a dangerous thing," Dr. Mercer murmured, almost too soft to hear. The words hung in the air, brittle and sharp. My stomach turned, but I forced a shrug, trying to act like his comment didn't stick like barbs under my skin. *Dangerous?* What did he mean by that? I didn't want to ask. I didn't want to know. But the way he looked at me, like he was measuring something, made it impossible to ignore. Then his voice dropped, low enough that it almost felt like he wasn't talking to me anymore. "It leads people down paths they might not be ready for. And some paths... they don't let you come back.'" he added before turning away, like he hadn't just planted that thought in my head to fester.

I forced a shrug, trying to look casual. "Yeah, well... I'll try not to wander?"

He left me there with a strange feeling settling over me, like he knew more than he was saying. Like maybe this was all leading somewhere I wasn't prepared for.

I watched him go, my thoughts still spinning around Ryan's words, the challenge in his smirk, and the unspoken dare in every word.

I HATED TO ADMIT IT, but I couldn't shake Ryan's voice from my head. He was the kind of person you couldn't forget even if you wanted to—a walking reminder of everything that made me feel like I didn't belong here. Untouchable. Smug. Smart enough to make sure the rest of us knew it. *Can't travel backward in time?* He couldn't be right. I mean, I was here, wasn't I?

But avoiding him was just wishful thinking, and Dr. Mercer seemed intent on making sure of that. And in the one class I hoped would be my escape, the universe had pulled me even closer into Ryan's orbit.

Dr. Mercer strolled in like he always did, looking like some dinosaur pulled from a museum exhibit. His graying hair was combed back and his shirt was meticulously ironed within an inch of its life, complete with knife-edge creases down the sleeves. The guy carried himself like he'd built this whole school brick by brick, like he knew every secret that had passed through it. His gaze slid over the room, barely stopping on anyone until it landed on me. This time, there was something different in his eyes, something colder, sharper—like he was trying to uncover something fragile, something that would crumble the moment it was exposed.

A slow smile crept onto Dr. Mercer's face, that twisted kind of smile he got when he was about to make an example out of some poor soul. "All right, everyone," he began, his voice practically dripping with condescension. "You'll be working in pairs for the upcoming science fair. Look to who you are sitting beside." His gaze settled on me again, lingering like he'd already decided I'd be the one to mess it up. "That, will be your partner. So Nat, you'll be paired with Ethan." He said it as if he were handing out punishment, not partners.

Ethan's eyes lit up, and he immediately threw his hand in the air, shouting, "All right!" He turned to Nat, hand out for a high five, grinning like he'd just won something. Nat let out a little sigh, her shoulder-length hair twirling as she glanced sideways at him with an amused smirk.

"Sure, Ethan. Living the dream here," she said, raising her hand half-heartedly to meet his, her tone dripping with playful sarcasm. But there was a glint of familiarity in her eyes, like she'd expected nothing less from him.

I felt my stomach twist, that sickening sense of inevitability settling in before Dr. Mercer even opened his mouth again. I knew what was coming, like the universe had already decided I'd be the punchline to this never-ending joke.

"And Ryan," he continued, his smirk widening just a fraction, "*you'll* be working with Carter." My stomach dropped. *Of course. Of course, this would happen.* I could feel Ryan's gaze before I even turned my head, the heat of it crawling up the back of my neck. I chanced a glance, and there it was—that smirk, like he'd been waiting for this, like he'd orchestrated it himself. My hands curled into fists under the desk, my nails digging into my palms as I tried to ignore the dread coiling in my chest.

"I trust your shared… *interest* in the mysteries of time will make for an *enlightening* partnership." Dr. Mercer finished before continuing through his assignments. A wave of muted groans passed through the class with each one, but all I could feel was this slow dread creeping up my spine.

Ryan leaned in, his voice low and deliberate, each word landing with the precision of a scalpel. "Think you can handle the pressure?" he asked, his tone dripping with fake politeness, as if he were already laughing at the thought of me even trying.

I wanted to say yes, to throw it back in his face, but my mouth stayed dry. "I'll... do my best?"

Ryan tilted his head, studying me like a problem he was already halfway to solving. "Let's hope your best is enough," he said, and for a second, something flickered in his eyes—curiosity, maybe? Whatever it was, it held me there, frozen, like he'd caught me in some strange gravitational pull I couldn't shake off.

He turned back to the front, but not before I caught the hint of a smirk tugging at the corner of his mouth, like he knew exactly what he was doing. And maybe he did. Maybe he knew I couldn't figure him out, couldn't decide if I wanted to prove him wrong or get as far away from him as possible. But I knew one thing: *whatever this project was, it wasn't going to be simple.*

Dr. Mercer's gaze lingered on me a moment longer, as if he, too, was waiting to see what I'd do, what kind of disaster I'd be pulled into next. And then he turned away, leaving me with the unsettling feeling that he'd set me up to fail.

As class dragged on, I couldn't shake that look Ryan had given me. There was something beneath it, something I couldn't pin down. Like he was enjoying every second of watching me squirm. Like he was circling, watching, waiting—seeing how far he could push me before I broke.

When the bell rang, he didn't rush to leave. He gathered his things slowly, taking his time, like he was waiting for something to happen. I caught his eye again as I walked past, and he leaned in, close enough that I could feel the warmth of his breath, close enough to unsettle me all over again.

"See you soon, partner," he murmured, his voice curling around the word like smoke, soft but suffocating. He let them hang in the air, watching me for a reaction I refused to give. But inside, my pulse was thrumming, my mind racing through every meaning he might have hidden in that single word—*partner*. He smiled as he turned away, and it wasn't until he'd disappeared out the door that I realized I hadn't breathed since he spoke.

As I walked out, his voice still echoed in my head, a thread I couldn't untangle. He wasn't someone you ran from—or toward. He was the kind of storm you stood still for, hoping it would pass before it tore you apart and left you scattered—just another name swallowed by time, forgotten before it ever mattered.

CHAPTER 10

THANKSGIVING BREAK crept in like a ghost whose heavy footsteps were here to recap my life: I had no one and nowhere to go. It strangled my chest and rattled every corner of my thoughts. A chill settled in my bones reminding me I had nothing to be thankful for. This was it. This—whatever this was— was here to stay. It wasn't just a feeling of dread; it was the quiet, insidious kind of hesitation that made you second-guess every breath. *I was <u>still</u> stuck here.*

Somehow, I'd wandered into Nat's world—a stray cat slinking into a warm house it had no right being in. Her parents were polite enough, but there was this edge, this carefully managed kindness, like they were merely hosting a guest and trying not to let anything personal spill.

The table was set perfectly, the kind of meal that looked like a Martha Stewart magazine page came to life: candles flickering, dishes steaming, silverware clinking softly against ceramic plates, white with a thin line of gold around the rim. There was this faint static beneath it all, like a radio station just out of tune, the kind of noise that burrowed under your skin and made you want to claw it out. It hummed in my ears, an echo of everything I didn't belong to. It wasn't loud, wasn't something you could point to—just small things. A pause before her dad passed the mashed potatoes. The way her mom's smile didn't quite stick or show up in the eyes. Nothing you'd notice unless you've already seen it all fall apart.

Nat sat cross-legged in her chair, totally at ease in the chaos. The glow of the Christmas lights tangled in her cranberry sweater, softening her edges in a way that felt almost too deliberate, like someone had painted her into the scene to make everything feel less hollow. And when she reached across the table for the stuffing, her hand brushed against mine.

It was barely a touch—over in a heartbeat— but it left this ember smoldering in my chest. It was warm, dangerous, something I didn't trust myself to touch. I glanced at her, and she didn't seem to notice, too busy piling her plate with rolls. But my hand tingled like it had just happened, a faint, pleasant electric jolt, and I couldn't decide if I wanted to pull away or reach out again.

If the whole table hadn't been groaning under the weight of more food than I'd seen in months, I might've spiraled into that feeling. But the turkey was too tempting, the sweet potatoes so sweet, the rolls so fluffy I couldn't stop grabbing for more. I wasn't just eating—I was *inhaling*. Every bite felt like it was filling some pit I hadn't even realized was carved into me—weeks of cold sandwiches and gas station snacks erased in seconds. It was almost too much, like I didn't know how to hold it all.

Nat's dark waves framed her face as she continued to tease her dad, little jabs thrown with a grin that made it impossible to tell if she was joking or serious.

He laughed it off, but his laugh came a beat late, like he'd only just caught the punchline. "Well, next time you want to chop down a tree, maybe don't pick the one with a hornet's nest," he said, pointing his fork at her with mock indignation. "That one's on you, kiddo."

"Oh, please," Nat fired back, rolling her eyes. "You're the one who thought hornets 'don't bother people this time of year.'"

Her mom's chuckle was thin, a hollow note that landed somewhere between polite and resigned, like she was laughing for someone else's benefit or heard it so many times already that it wasn't all that funny anymore. Her eyes flicked to Nat's dad, catching on him for just a second before skimming away. "It wasn't exactly the best plan, was it, Michael?" she added lightly, passing the sweet potatoes without looking at him.

Michael's smile faltered just slightly, but he recovered quickly, taking a bite of turkey like it was nothing. "Live and learn," he muttered, brushing it off. The tension barely flickered, just long enough for me to notice, before Nat's attention jumped to me.

She smirked at me between bites, her fork poised in mid-air. "Hungry much?" she teased, waving her fork at my overfilled plate, her voice light but carrying this edge of curiosity.

I mumbled something around a mouthful of stuffing, the words garbled but vaguely resembling, "It's good."

Her dad laughed, shaking his head. "Glad someone's enjoying it. You've got quite the appetite, Carter. Haven't eaten like this in a while, huh?"

My fork froze for half a second before I forced another bite. "Yeah… guess not," I mumbled. "I mean, no sir," I conceded, my words sticking to my tongue like something stale. The truth sat heavy in my chest, an ache I couldn't name: *I hadn't tasted a meal like this in a couple months, maybe longer.* Living out of my car left more gaps in me than I realized.

Her mom smiled, kind but quiet, before glancing toward Nat. "You should send him home with leftovers," she said softly, her voice carrying that same managed politeness as the rest of the night.

Nat waved her off, scoffing. "As if! He'll have to fight me for them."

The room filled with light laughter, and I let myself relax, just a little. But that ember in my chest flared again. Her laugh, the way it danced over the clinking silverware, the way she leaned into the table like the moment couldn't hold her in—it all stuck in my head, warm and unshakable.

But at some point, the warmth of it all—the lights, the food, the easy laughter—started to feel like quicksand. I wasn't sinking into it; I was sinking *through* it. Because all I could think about was another kitchen, another table, another Thanksgiving that felt both too far away and too close all at once.

· · ·

THE SMELL of turkey and cranberry sauce swirled in the kitchen. My mom was at the counter, her hands coated in flour as she worked dough into something magical. Her laugh filled the room, warm and whole, stitching the world back together like it had never been broken. It was the kind of sound I hadn't heard in so long, I almost couldn't believe it had once been real.

"Carter, you ready with the oven mitts?" she asked, her voice warm with just a touch of impatience. "The rolls are ready."

"On it!" I called, fumbling with the mitts and nearly dropping one in the process. The oven creaked open, heat pouring out in waves that wrapped around me like a hug, pulling me closer to the kind of safety I didn't know I'd been missing. "Ta-da."

She glanced back, her smile tugging at the corners of her mouth. "You didn't burn them. I'm impressed."

I rolled my eyes but couldn't help smirk. "You're welcome."

Her laugh came again, lighter this time, and for a moment, everything else disappeared. The world narrowed down to the sound of her voice, the smell of home, the way she turned to me with that look like I was her whole world.

A SPOON CLATTERED AGAINST A PLATE, and I blinked, yanked back to the present. Nat was telling some story about a disastrous camping trip, her dad chiming in with corrections and side comments that made her roll her eyes dramatically. Her mom laughed along, but there was something in her gaze—focused, almost too calm—that lingered before she glanced away.

"Carter," Nat's dad said suddenly, shifting the focus onto me. His voice was friendly but had this testing edge, like he wanted to see what I was made of. "It was nice of your folks to let you spend the holiday with us. You got family in town?"

The words hit like a sharp knock on a hollow door, echoing in all the places I didn't want anyone to look. My fork froze halfway to my mouth, but I forced myself to nod like the lie wasn't already unraveling. "Uh… yeah," I said, forcing a nod. "They're, uh, here from California. Long drive." The lie slipped out with an ease that surprised even me. *Guess I was getting used to this.*

Nat's mom gave me this small, understanding smile, but again, it didn't quite reach her eyes. She didn't push, though, just took another sip of wine and eyed me the way mom's do when they know something about you you're trying to hide. Nat's dad nodded, like that was enough of an answer for him. "Well, good. Glad to hear it," he said, spearing a piece of stuffing like he was trying to prove something. "You'll have to introduce us soon. Would love to welcome your mom and dad to the neighborhood."

Nat glanced at me from across the table, her brow furrowed just slightly like she could see through my cracks. "Don't worry, my dad's just *starved* for friends," she said, nudging the bowl of rolls toward me with a soft smile. "But hey. Eat up, *Mr. Hollywood*. We can save the introductions for another day."

I grabbed one, muttering a quick thanks, and stuffed it into my mouth so I wouldn't have to say anything else. The warmth of the food, the low hum of conversation—it all felt too normal. Like I was a little kid peeking through a window, watching an adult life I didn't belong to but couldn't stop staring at.

But, of course, real life isn't a warm, friendly dinner table. Real life was getting back to school and grinding through the last weeks before Winter Break—a looming deadline for freedom that felt impossible to reach.

As if school wasn't enough of a prison, working with Ryan was the barbed wire around it. He was the worst thing that'd happened to me in a long time, and I'd had plenty of "worst things" by now.

Every time we sat down, his whole vibe just... leaked out, like some kind of arrogant gas seeping into the room. I'd catch him glancing at me sideways, like he was looking for something, like I was some equation he couldn't quite solve. And that seemed to bother him —a lot.

"I'll handle the calculations," he told me, eyes already fixed on his notebook, like he was tossing me a bone. "You can, uh, glue the poster together or something."

My jaw clenched. "Right. Because that's the hard part."

He didn't even bother looking up. "Just trying to play to your strengths."

I threw him my best "seriously, dude?" glare, but it bounced right off his wall of smug. "Must be nice thinking you're always the smartest guy in the room," I muttered, half to myself, half to him.

His smirk widened, but this time, there was something else in it. "I don't think, Carter. I know."

And here's the worst part: he wasn't wrong. Ryan was good—too good. He just moved through the work like it was a game he'd already mastered, while I was out here just trying to keep my head above water. And he knew it. He loved it. The way he acted, it was like he needed everyone to know he was the best, like he was keeping score on some invisible board and couldn't stand the idea of ever losing a point. But he kept glancing at me, like he was watching to see what I'd do next.

ONE NIGHT IN THE LIBRARY, I caught a crack in the armor. We'd been working late, long after everyone else had called it a night. Ryan sat across from me, his pen gliding over his notebook with precise, almost surgical strokes. His blond hair was perfectly tousled, like he'd spent five seconds making it look like he hadn't tried at all. The collar of his crisp white shirt peeked out from under a charcoal sweater, the sleeves casually pushed up to his elbows, revealing a sleek silver watch that looked more expensive than my entire wardrobe.

He didn't look up, his sharp jawline set in concentration, but there was something about his posture—his shoulders slightly hunched, his eyes flickering over the page like he was searching for something he couldn't quite find. The usual smirk he wore, the one that screamed *I'm untouchable*, was gone, replaced by something quieter, almost vulnerable.

I glanced at him, trying to see past the wall he always seemed to carry around with him like a shield. Now, there was a crack, just enough to glimpse the person underneath.

"So… you really think about this stuff all the time?" I asked, breaking the silence because, well, the silence was getting heavy.

He blinked, like he'd forgotten I was there. "What? Time? Of course," he said, leaning back with a sigh that felt more intentional than casual. "It's like a Rubik's cube you can't solve but can't put down, no matter how long you stare at it."

I studied him for a moment, squinting, trying to see through the facade. "Why's it matter so much to you?"

He turned, looking me over with something unreadable in his eyes. "Time doesn't care about you, Carter," Ryan said, his voice sharp but brittle, like it might shatter if he pushed too hard. "It doesn't care if you're a genius or a ghost. It just keeps moving, leaving everything behind." He leaned back, his gaze wandering to the window. "You try to beat it, twist it, make it mean something… but you only end up a failure."

Something about the way he said it caught me off-guard—like he was talking about something way bigger than just numbers or theories. "Sounds kinda lonely, dude," I said, aiming for a lighthearted quip but missing the mark a little.

A smirk twisted his lips, the kind that looked more like a challenge than a smile. "Loneliness builds character, doesn't it? That's what people tell you, anyway. But if that's true, I should have more character than anyone by now." he added, his gaze flicking over me, lingering just a beat too long, "Besides, someone has to win the game. May as well be me."

The moment passed, but the weird feeling didn't. It just sat there, hanging in the air, like dust that refuses to settle. And suddenly, I didn't know if Ryan was invincible or just some guy pretending to be because he was terrified of something he couldn't even name. But the way he kept looking at me, sizing me up like I was something new, something different—that was fresh.

We were both quiet for a while, letting the words fade. I thought he was done talking, but after a beat, he went on, his voice lower now, almost distant.

"My dad's been gone since I was a kid," Ryan said, his voice flat and controlled, like he'd practiced saying it without flinching. "One second he was here, the next… gone. Just another thing time decided to erase."

I blinked, caught off guard. "Oh. Wow. Uh… sorry."

He shrugged, but it wasn't the kind of shrug that said he didn't care. "It lingers, you know? Like this shadow just hovering around. Like… yeah, time's in control, and one day it's just going to decide 'game over,' and there's nothing you can do."

It felt strange to see Ryan look… human. And a little haunted. I shifted, not quite sure what to say, so I just nodded. "Yeah… I mean, that sucks."

A smirk flickered back onto his face, almost like he was trying to shrug it off too. "My mom works all the time now. The diner on Main. Early morning, late night. She hardly even sees me… not unless I bring something impressive home."

"Like… awards? Grades? That kind of thing?"

"Exactly," he said, giving me this look that was both annoyed and amused. "The only way to stand out, right?"

"That's… really messed up," I muttered, feeling a little embarrassed. "Sorry. I mean, you do know she probably just, you know, wants the best for you, right?"

He let out a small, cold laugh. "Optimistic of you. But I'll let you keep thinking that." He looked at me with a flicker of curiosity. "You're a bit of an enigma, Carter. Just when I think I have you figured out, you say something… unexpected. It's rare."

I felt a weird warmth spread in my chest—like that look across the table with Nat but different, sharper. I brushed it off, leaning back in my chair. "Thanks, I guess."

We sat there in silence, his words hanging heavy in the air. I hadn't expected it, but somehow, Ryan didn't look like the arrogant, untouchable guy who had all the answers. He looked… just like anyone else.

The silence between us stretched, thick with all the things we hadn't said. Ryan's eyes drifted to mine, and I could feel the tension buzzing between us, as if I'd moved an inch closer without realizing it.

I wanted to ask him what he thought he'd figured out, or what made him so sure he even wanted to. But something held me back.

Ryan finally turned back to his notebook, the pen tapping softly against the table, though he seemed lost in thought, as if our conversation was just something to file away for later. But I caught him glancing at me, and his expression was that same mix of curiosity and something else, something half-hidden. Like he'd decided to put me on hold but not hang up, leaving our conversation suspended, a question with no answer yet.

I thought that was the end of it, and maybe it would've been. But then I felt it again—that prickling feeling, like eyes on the back of my neck. I glanced up, and there he was. Dr. Mercer was drifting down the row toward our table, moving almost too quietly for someone with shoes as old and creaky as his.

"Carter, Ryan," he said, coming to a stop in front of us. His voice was smooth and cool, like water sliding over stone. And his gaze? Like he could see right into my brain and pick out whatever stray thought he wanted.

"Good evening, sir," Ryan said, barely looking up from his notebook, as if Dr. Mercer was just some vaguely annoying background noise.

"Busy, are we?" Dr. Mercer's gaze latched onto me, unblinking and too steady, like he was peeling back my skin one layer at a time. It wasn't just a look—it was a surgical blade, searching for whatever I was trying to hide.

I forced myself to look casual, even though my heartbeat had picked up. "Just… the project," I said, sounding almost convincing.

"The project," he repeated, as if the words themselves amused him. He looked between us, his eyes finally settling on Ryan. "I hope you're not taking over the entire workload, Ryan. Collaboration is key, wouldn't you say?"

Ryan's mouth twitched. "I'm sure Carter's contributing what he can."

A tiny flicker crossed Dr. Mercer's face—gone before I could even be sure I'd seen it. Then he looked at me again, those eyes heavy with something unreadable. "Time doesn't wait, Carter," Dr. Mercer said, his gaze lingering like he was trying to pin me in place. "And it doesn't forgive."

I felt a weird, cold trickle down my spine, like his words had dropped an anchor somewhere in my stomach. "Got it, sir," I managed, nodding a little too fast.

He gave me one last, lingering look before he turned and slipped back into the shadows between the stacks, leaving a silence so thick you could almost feel it settling over the table.

Ryan picked up his pen again, tapping it against the surface, his eyes distant, like he was already slipping back into that impenetrable world of numbers and formulas. I watched him, wondering if he'd just pretend this whole night never happened—like his walls hadn't slipped, like I hadn't seen something behind them that didn't quite fit with the image he tried so hard to present.

Then, without looking up, he spoke, his voice low. "You know... maybe this isn't a total waste of time after all."

"What do you mean?" I said, raising an eyebrow, though I couldn't help the smirk tugging at my lips.

He glanced over at me, his gaze flickering with a strange intensity. "Maybe you're not as hopeless as I thought." There was that little smirk again, but softer, almost teasing. "It's rare, you know. Not many people surprise me."

I felt a weird, unfamiliar heat in my face, and I shifted in my seat, brushing it off. "Guess that makes one of us."

Ryan's smirk lingered as he turned back to his notes, but there was something in his eyes, a flicker that hadn't been there before. It was like he was starting to look at me less like an annoyance and more like... well, something else. And as much as I hated to admit it, there was a part of me that didn't entirely mind the attention. *Maybe he could actually help me. Maybe he's how I get home.*

Maybe this was all we'd ever be—a tightrope stretched between rivalry and something heavier, darker. Something I couldn't name but didn't want to walk away from. And maybe that was enough—for now. It wasn't safe, but safety wasn't what I was looking for anymore.

As he went back to scribbling down equations and I glanced back at my own half-finished work, I could feel that pull, that weird tension between us, hanging in the air like a question with no easy answer.

But for now, it gave me hope— and that's all I could ask for.

CHAPTER 11

THE WEEK before the science fair, I made a fatal discovery—one I knew would give me hell. The formulas sprawled across the page like a map to nowhere. My car felt smaller with every passing second, the air inside thick and stifling as my iPhone calculator blinked its refusal to cooperate. *Error. Error.* Like it was mocking me, reminding me that I didn't belong here—not in this project, not in this time. And after an eternity of trying, I was positive it couldn't have just been me—it must've been the numbers. They were off. Not just *off*, but wrong in a way that could tank the entire project and fail us right out of Physics. And I knew I had to do something.

The next morning, I found Ryan sitting in the farthest corner of the library, exactly where someone plotting world domination or hiding from their feelings would go. The place felt unnaturally quiet, the kind of silence that makes you hear your own breathing. Light filtered through the blinds, harsh and sterile, cutting across the table like it was dissecting us. His plaid button-up was tucked neatly into black jeans, the sleeves rolled just enough to say he was cool without trying too hard. His polished boots tapped lightly against the floor, the sound too even to be accidental.

The papers hit the table harder than I meant, the slap echoing through the quiet room. "Ryan, these numbers are wrong," I said, my voice sharper than I intended, anger curling at the edges.

He didn't even blink. Just sat there, like he'd been waiting for me to say those exact words. It made me want to take them back, but the damage was already done. Ryan's smirk spread slowly, savoring the moment the way a cat watches a bird just before pouncing. "Good morning to you too, Carter. And what exactly do you think is wrong?"

"I triple-checked," I said, jabbing a finger at the highlighted sections. "If we run with this at the science fair, the judges are going to eat us alive. And not in the fun way."

He tilted his head, like I was a mildly amusing bug on his windshield. "You triple-checked. Impressive. Tell me, did you also triple-check your credentials while you were at it?"

My jaw tightened. "It's not quantum mechanics. It's basic math. The energy inputs don't match the outputs. See for yourself."

Ryan picked up the papers, flipping through them with the lazy air of someone who already knew how the conversation would end. "And here I thought you were just riding my coattails for the glory."

"Coattails? Are you kidding me?" I leaned in, my palms flat on the table. "Ryan, I'm not doing this to show you up. I'm doing this because if we don't fix it, we'll look like idiots."

"Correction," he said, smirking. "*You'll* look like an idiot. I don't make mistakes, and I definitely don't see an error."

"Seriously?" I said, throwing my hands up. "You're that sure of yourself? You can't even entertain the possibility that maybe, just maybe, you're human like the rest of us?"

He leaned back in his chair, his smirk faltering for just a second. "People like me," he said quietly, "don't get second chances. A mistake isn't just a mistake—it's proof. Proof I don't belong, proof they were right about me all along."

"But why?" I shot back, louder than I meant to. A librarian shot me a glare, and I lowered my voice. "Why don't you get to make mistakes? What, does the universe have some special rule for Ryan Prescott? 'He must be perfect at all times or suffer the wrath of God'?"

Ryan's eyes darkened, his jaw tightening. "You wouldn't get it."

"Try me," I said, crossing my arms. "Because from where I'm standing, you're just being stubborn for no reason."

Ryan exhaled sharply, dropping the papers onto the table. "Because when I mess up, it's not just about me. It's about expectations. Reputation. Everything. People like me are judged on every little thing we do, and if I screw up? It's proof I don't belong. That I'm not good enough."

His words hit harder than I expected, like he'd reached into the part of my brain I tried to keep locked away. I thought of Mom, the stress of everything now, and the hollow ache of wanting to be there for her while knowing I was falling short.

"I get it," I said, my voice soft but firm. "That pressure—like the whole world is just waiting for you to fail. Like every step you take is on a wire, and one slip means the fall. But here's the thing—making mistakes doesn't mean you don't belong. It just means you're human. And if you can't accept that, you're going to drive yourself insane."

Ryan looked at me, his smirk completely gone now. "Why do you care so much? Seriously, what's in it for you?"

I blinked, caught off guard. This was it. My *in*. For a second, I thought about spilling everything—the truth about his mom, about me, about how none of this was supposed to happen. But the words clung to my throat, too heavy to push out. What was I supposed to say? That I was here by accident? That I didn't belong, either?

"What? Nothing's in it for me."

"Sure, Carter." His voice was sharp, cutting. "Because you're just that selfless."

The words stung, more than I wanted to admit. "I'm trying to help you, Ryan. Not because I want something, but because this project matters to me. And… yeah, okay, maybe I see a little of myself in you."

He seemed taken aback. His expression softened, averting his gaze from mine just for a moment, before his defenses snapped back into place. "You don't know me at all," he shot back, his voice tight, like he was daring me to dig deeper but terrified of what I'd find.

"No," I said, my voice low but steady. "But I know what it feels like to carry the weight of the world on your shoulders. And I know what happens when it gets too heavy."

Ryan stared at me for a long moment, like he was trying to figure out if I was serious. Then he sighed, running a hand through his perfectly styled hair. "Fine." he muttered, his gaze flicking to the floor for a second before meeting mine again, sharp as ever. "I'll look at the numbers again. But if I find out you're wrong—"

"You won't," I said, cutting him off. "But thanks for the vote of confidence."

As I turned to leave, Ryan called after me. "Hey, Carter?"

I glanced back, raising an eyebrow. "Yeah?"

"You really think I'm like you?" His tone was light, almost teasing, but there was an edge of vulnerability beneath it.

"Nah. You're way prettier," I said with a smirk, masking the tension with humor, even as something about his question lingered too long in the air.

His laugh followed me out of the library, sharp and unexpected. For a moment, it almost felt like a win.

AFTER HOMEROOM AND HISTORY CLASS, I dragged my feet into the Physics lab. I scanned the room, project materials tucked under my arm like they were my shield. The air in the lab was stale, heavy with the faint tang of dry-erase markers and dust. It clung to my skin like something alive, watching, waiting. Comforting wasn't the word—it was more like a truce between me and the space around me. Ryan was already at our table, lounging back in his chair with his usual nonchalance. He didn't even bother to look up when I dumped my backpack onto the table, the thud loud enough to startle half the room but apparently not him.

The sound *did* draw the attention of Nat and Ethan, who had just strolled in, sliding into their seats in front of us as the bell rang. Ethan twisted around, beaming, and shot me an enthusiastic thumbs-up. "Looking alive, Carter!" he said, cheerfully oblivious to the tension brewing. Nat smirked faintly, tucking a strand of dark hair behind her ear as she turned her attention to her notebook.

Before I could return Ethan's wave or reply, Dr. Mercer's voice cut through the air like a blade, sharp and deliberate, pulling every gaze toward him as if he thrived on attention. "Carter, a word at my desk."

I froze, the churning of my gut doubling. *Great.* Behind me, I felt

Ryan's gaze flick up briefly, probably grinning to himself like he'd already won whatever game he thought we were playing.

With a sigh, I trudged to Dr. Mercer's desk. Every step reminded me of why I hated situations like this—confrontations where I already knew the odds weren't in my favor. Dr. Mercer didn't look up immediately, shuffling some papers with deliberate care before he spoke.

"I had a conversation with Ryan this morning," he began, his voice carrying that flat, clinical tone teachers use when they've already made up their minds. "He's informed me that things haven't been working out between the two of you."

I opened my mouth to argue, but he raised a hand, silencing me before I could get a word in. "And, after seeing the two of you in the library the other evening, let's just say that conversation left *quite* an impression."

I frowned, my brain scrambling for context. "Wait, wait, wait," I stammered, trying to cut in. "What are you—"

Dr. Mercer's stern expression hardened further. "I don't want excuses, Carter," he said sharply. "It's clear you haven't been contributing as you should. You seem far more interested in *distractions* than in the actual work."

"That's not—" I started, then stopped, clenching my fists at my sides. "Look, Ryan and I just… we work differently, okay? But I'm not —*slacking!* I might not live and breathe *math equations*, but I'm trying!"

Dr. Mercer studied me for a moment before shaking his head. "Trying isn't enough, Carter," he said, each word landing like a stone in my gut. "I've reassigned you to a group more… suitable to your abilities. Consider it a *better fit*." He handed me a slip of paper, his tone almost condescending. "You'll be joining Ethan and Nat. I'm sure a papier-mâché volcano will suit you just fine."

"A volcano?" I muttered under my breath, staring at the slip. "Seriously? That's just insulting."

Behind me, Ethan whooped, his chair creaking as he leaned back. "Hey, volcanoes can be awesome! Welcome to the cool kids' table!" he yelled, loud enough for Nat to elbow him lightly. She glanced up at me with a bemused smile, her expression somewhere between sympathy and amusement.

"This is your chance, Carter," Dr. Mercer said, his thin smile curling like smoke as he ignored Ethan entirely. "Let's see if you're capable of more than just excuses—or if Ryan's instincts about you were right."

From behind me, I caught the faint sound of Ryan chuckling under his breath. My shoulders stiffened as I turned back to the table, feeling the sting of frustration clawing at me. Ryan's smirk was waiting for me as I dropped into my chair.

"Sorry, buddy," Ryan murmured, "there *wasn't* a mistake." His voice was low and cutting, the smirk on his lips sharp enough to draw blood. "The only person going down for your error is you—and I'll be watching."

I forced a laugh, the sound bitter in my throat. "Glad you're getting a kick out of this, *buddy,*" I said, shooting him a glare. "Screw what I said earlier. You're not that pretty."

The smirk didn't falter; if anything, it deepened. "Maybe not," he replied with maddening calm, leaning closer. "But I'm clearly entertaining enough to keep you interested."

"Don't flatter yourself," I snapped, crossing my arms and trying to look unimpressed. "I'd rather glue papier-mâché for a week than go down with your sinking ship."

Ryan chuckled, leaning back like he had all the time in the world. "Trust me, not even *God* could sink this ship," he said, his tone light, teasing. "You'll miss me, Carter, you'll see," he said, the smirk curving like a question mark. "People always miss the things they hate most."

I rolled my eyes, letting out an exasperated sigh just as Dr. Mercer called for attention at the front of the room.

Ethan twisted around in his seat again, giving me an encouraging grin. "Cheer up, Carter. We're about to make the coolest volcano this school's ever seen," he said, managing to look genuinely excited.

Nat leaned slightly in my direction. "Ignore him. But hey, at least you're stuck with us now, right?"

I nodded, forcing a small smile, though my mind was still racing. As class began, I tried to focus on Dr. Mercer's voice, but Ryan's last words hung over me, the unspoken tension sticking like glue. Across the table, Ryan leaned back, giving me one last knowing glance, the faint smirk still tugging at the corners of his mouth.

CHAPTER 12

THE LIBRARY SMELLED of glue and paint, the air sticky with chaos. Nat and Ethan were lost somewhere in the wreckage, buried under strips of newspaper and splattered colors like they were part of the mess itself. It wasn't just a volcano—they'd made a war zone out of art supplies. Glue bottles and paint tubes were scattered like shrapnel, wires sticking to everything within reach. And thank God for it. I needed this—anything to break up the weird fog that'd been sitting in my brain for weeks. Ethan's face lit up when he saw me.

"Welcome to the coolest team in school!" he said, throwing his hands up in this exaggerated cheer, like he was inducting me into some secret society.

Nat rolled her eyes, smirking as she wiped her hands on her already paint-stained flannel. "Carter, you sure you can handle the *intense* pressure of the volcano project? It's not for the faint of heart."

I tried to smile back, but it felt... strange, like my face had forgotten how. My skin felt stretched too thin, like paper about to tear, every nerve buzzing with an unease I couldn't name. Was it the stress clawing at me, or just time itself pulling me apart? Either way, I didn't feel like I belonged in my own body anymore.

I dropped my bag onto the table and sank into the chair, feeling a weight ease off my shoulders now that I wasn't stuck with Ryan.

"Honestly? This is exactly what I need right now. A big, ridiculous volcano."

Ethan tossed me a roll of tape, his mouth twisting into a smirk. "Welcome to the dark side, my friend. We've got paper-mâché and *zero* expectations."

A laugh slipped out before I could even stop it, like it'd been sitting in my chest just waiting to escape. And just like that, some of the tension from the last few weeks started to melt away, piece by piece, like ice cracking in warm water. I grabbed the tape and started working, wrapping it around the base of the volcano while Nat and Ethan debated if the lava should be bright red for drama or orange because, as Nat put it, "accuracy matters."

"You sure about that?" I asked with a smirk.

She raised an eyebrow, grinning. "Science is *important*, Carter," Nat said, deadpan, her paint-streaked hand waving like she was delivering a solemn vow. "This is *serious* business."

"Oh yeah, for sure. Super serious." I was trying to sound sarcastic, but it just… felt good. The glue dried on my fingers, the paint streaked across my hands—messy and imperfect, but it felt real. It grounded me here, to this moment, to Nat and Ethan, keeping me from floating too far into the haze that had been pulling me under for weeks. I wasn't trying to solve a cosmic riddle or navigate the weird maze that was Ryan's brain—I was just here, shooting the shit with the only people who made life in the 90s feel… not like hell. It was simple. Safe.

Ethan poked his head up from his paintbrush, studying me for a second. "You look weirdly happy, man. You good?"

"Good as glue and no expectations can get me," I said, shrugging. I couldn't tell him what was actually on my mind—that sometimes I didn't feel like myself, like I was aging while everyone else stayed the same, or I was confined to some time-warped version of reality without a way out. Sitting here, with glue drying on my hands and laughter filling the air, the anxiety in my chest lifted—just a little. It wasn't gone, not really. But for now, the mess anchored me, kept me from slipping under.

Nat glanced at me, her face softening. "Screw Ryan, man. You know with us you can just be… you, right? You don't have to carry the world on your shoulders or whatever. Just be Carter for a bit."

"Right, Carter," I said, chuckling. "Whoever *that* is." I wasn't even sure I knew anymore, but with them, it felt okay. I picked up a brush and dunked it in the paint, letting myself sink into the mess of it. Sticky hands, streaks of paint everywhere, a volcano that looked a little more like a lopsided hill.

And for the first time in… way longer than I wanted to admit, I felt like maybe, just maybe, I could survive this twisted version of reality without completely losing my mind. Guess we'll see.

THE NIGHT of the science fair was chaos—kids rushing around like their projects were on fire, teachers squinting at displays with these suspicious, "Are you for real?" expressions, and parents pretending to care deeply about whether their kid's lemon battery could power a tiny flashlight for a whole ten seconds. All around, tables were covered in poster-boards, paper rockets, and jars full of who-knows-what fizzing over like some mad scientist's dream.

And there it was, smack in the middle of everything—Mt. Cartethanat stood proud and ridiculous, streaked with lava that looked more like spilled condiments, surrounded by plastic dinosaurs frozen mid-scream. It was a monument to chaos, and somehow, it felt perfect. Ethan, being Ethan, had dumped in enough baking soda to make it look like the whole thing might erupt if you even looked at it funny. It was ridiculous. It was over-the-top. And somehow? It was kind of amazing.

Then there was Ryan.

I spotted him hovering over his setup at the edge of the room, giving us this look every now and then, like he was waiting for Mt. Cartethanat to topple over or set itself ablaze. His setup, meanwhile, looked like it had beamed in from some dated sci-fi fantasy, complete with sleek monitors and neatly arranged wires. He was totally in his element, glancing over his setup like a king surveying his realm.

After a while, he drifted over like a shadow slipping into place, hands in his pockets, his smirk sharp enough to cut. "So," he said, voice low and drawling, leaning in a little too close, like he was sharing some big secret with me. "Miss me yet?" Ryan asked, his voice low and taunting, each word deliberate. "You could've been on the winning team instead of… whatever you're calling this." He gestured at Mt. Cartethanat like it was a personal insult.

I rolled my eyes, folding my arms. "Well, you can't beat the classics." I jabbed a thumb at our volcano. "Some people actually like to have fun, Ryan."

He leaned in, close enough that the faint scent of his cologne—something sharp and dark, like pine and ash—wrapped around me. It was calculated, like everything about him, designed to keep people guessing if they wanted to get closer or run the other way. "Oh, I'm sure the judges are going to *love* it," he said, dripping with sarcasm. "Let me guess—you're planning to wow them with a little vinegar and baking soda? That's… adorable."

I could feel my face getting hot, but I forced myself to stay cool, raising an eyebrow. "Oh yeah? At least ours doesn't have errors in the data. Some of us know how to make stuff that just works." I leaned in too, not backing down an inch. "But hey, good luck impressing them with your fancy graphs and time warp stuff. I'm sure they'll be… captivated." I added a slight smile, as if daring him to argue.

He paused, his eyes narrowing just a bit, like he was really seeing me, beneath it all. His smirk didn't falter, but there was something else there now, something unreadable. "Good luck, Carter," he said softly, his tone a mix of challenge and arrogance. He didn't look away, didn't even blink. I could feel my heart start to pound harder, and I knew he could probably hear it too.

"Thanks, uh—" I replied, my voice steady even though my insides were doing a weird little flip. "Good luck to you, too."

Ryan's smirk deepened, and he shook his head, giving me one last look before sauntering back to his setup, flashing a little wave over his shoulder like he was the star of his own show.

Shortly after, the judges came into view, working their way from project to project. They glanced at Ryan's display, then moved toward Mt. Cartethanat, with matching expressions somewhere between amusement and pure skepticism. Nat held the vinegar bottle with the intensity of someone who had a bomb in her hands, eyes gleaming with barely contained excitement. Ethan and I shared a quick, conspiratorial look, like we were about to initiate a serious operation.

"Ready?" I whispered.

Nat didn't answer, just poured the vinegar in.

And bam—The volcano roared to life, a tidal wave of red and orange foam spilling out like it couldn't wait to destroy everything in its path. It splattered the ceiling, the walls, and half the judges, leaving streaks of chaos in its wake. Around us, kids cheered like we'd just launched a rocket to Mars.

One of the judges was Dr. Mercer, and with an unimpressed look on his face—dabbed at the foam splattered across his glasses, his mouth twitching like he wasn't sure if he should be amused or annoyed. The other judge, a woman with a perfect poker face, actually cracked a smile as she swiped foam off her jacket.

"Well," she said, her voice warm with a barely suppressed laugh, "I think you've earned a solid B for... enthusiasm."

Nat looked like she was holding in a giggle, while Ethan beamed proudly, totally unbothered by the mess we'd created. Mt. Cartethanat was definitely low on science, but it was high on pure chaos. I couldn't have been prouder.

Then, the judges moved on to Ryan's display.

His setup was spotless, almost sterile, like he'd spent hours making sure everything was exactly where it should be. He cleared his throat, that usual confidence radiating from him like he was about to reveal some great discovery. "Good evening," he began, sounding like he'd practiced this in the mirror a thousand times. "My project explores The Linear Passage of Time and Its Path to Immortality." He paused, savoring the words. "I've developed a program that, using data points and predictive modeling, can show us how certain variables affect time's movement, even hinting at possibilities for achieving immortality through precise manipulation."

The judges leaned in, intrigued, as Ryan gestured to his monitor. The screen showed a simple, looping curved line, going up and down in this hypnotic little wave. Honestly, it didn't look like much, but the way he spoke, you'd think he was curing cancer.

"This," he continued, tapping a key with dramatic flair, "is the initial display. But when I input my findings..." He tapped a few more keys, "...you'll see the model expand, with calculations predicting patterns far beyond human lifespan."

But instead of his display expanding, the entire screen froze.

For a second, Ryan just stared at it, his smirk hanging there like it didn't realize it was no longer needed. Then he forced a chuckle, a little too loud, a little too awkward. "Uh... minor hiccup," he said, flashing the judges an uneasy smile. His fingers moved over the keys like he was just coaxing it back to life, his face carefully calm. "Just... refreshing the data," he muttered, still tapping keys. "These calculations take time, you know. Complex stuff." His laugh this time was tight, like he was holding his breath.

The screen stayed frozen.

The judges exchanged wary glances, and by now, the other kids had started to notice, craning their necks to watch the great Ryan Prescott stumble. The looping curve froze mid-wave, mocking him with its stillness. The calm Ryan wore like armor began to splinter—his fingers trembling over the keys, his jaw clenching tight enough to crack. And then, the final blow: a flicker, a flash of blue, and the words *Fatal Error* glowing like a neon sign, loud and merciless.

Beside me, Ethan leaned in and whispered, "You think we should help him?"

I didn't take my eyes off Ryan. "Not a chance."

The blue light of the screen reflected across Ryan's face, washing him out. His fingers flew over the keyboard, his movements growing more erratic, his jaw tightening like he was biting back a scream. He pulled the keyboard closer, practically cradling it like he could somehow fix the problem by holding it tighter. In his desperation, he forgot that he wrapped the keyboard cord around the monitor and tower for aesthetics. He gave the cord another frantic yank, and in one horrifying moment, the entire setup slid off the table.

Ryan reached out in panic, but it was too late. The monitor crashed to the floor, the tower followed with a heavy thud, and all that was left standing was the poster-board—the one I'd spent hours gluing together, because apparently that was my strong suit. For me, it was a strange, twisted little victory.

The cafeteria went dead silent as everyone stared at Ryan's mess. A few kids stifled laughter, some whispered, and the judges backed up, eyes wide with barely concealed horror. Ryan's fists clenched at his sides, his breathing shallow, his face blazing red. He looked down at his ruined display, his expression shifting from panic to something almost blank, like he was bracing himself for impact.

"And that'll—uh. Conclude my presentation. Thank you," he muttered, his voice tight and shaky, each word landing awkwardly in the tense quiet.

Ryan didn't wait. He turned and walked out, his steps sharp and deliberate, his shoulders stiff like he was bracing for an impact that hadn't come yet. The cafeteria doors slammed shut behind him, and the sound echoed in the silence he left behind, like a ghost lingering in the air.

Next to Mt. Cartethanat, I felt a weird, grim satisfaction bubbling up inside me, like this was the universe balancing things out. For all the times he'd made everyone around him feel small, talked down to them, shoved them aside—this felt like justice. The project he'd lorded over me for weeks was crumbling, right in front of him. It felt like the universe had tilted, giving Ryan a taste of the chaos he usually controlled. But the thing about chaos? It doesn't stop when you want it to.

His exit felt like a thread hanging loose, unraveling in the back of my mind. I couldn't stop myself—I had to see where it led, even if it meant stepping into the storm with him. Maybe it was curiosity, or maybe it was the pull of something I didn't fully understand but couldn't ignore.

Nat caught my arm. "Don't, Carter. Let him go," she said, her voice low but sharp.

"I can't, Nat." I shook her off, already stepping into the hall. "I need to see where he went," I finished, the words feeling flimsy even as they left my mouth. Something pulled at me, a thread I couldn't leave hanging, even if following it meant unraveling everything.

"You're gonna regret it!" she called, her voice echoing behind me as

I walked away, leaving her words hanging in the empty space between us.

The hallway stretched ahead of me, dim and endless. Every step felt heavier, like I was moving toward something I couldn't see but already knew would break me. Maybe I was chasing answers. Or maybe I was stepping into a storm I couldn't outrun, one that had been waiting for me all along.

CHAPTER 13

THE HALLWAY STRETCHED like a vein through the school's hollow body, its dim light smothered by shadows that clung to the lockers in uneven streaks of blue and gray. It felt like I was standing inside a bruise. And there was Ryan, his back to me, fists clenched so tight his knuckles were white. The whole place was quiet, but somehow the silence buzzed, like the school itself was holding its breath.

"Ryan!" I called after him. My voice felt strange, like it didn't belong to me. I tried to keep it steady, ignoring the weird knot twisting in my chest. "You alright? Look, that error, I—"

Ryan's laugh scraped the air, jagged and hollow, the sound of something breaking just beneath the surface. It wasn't humor—it was a wound left open too long. "Error? You think this is about the project?" He looked at me like I was a puzzle missing half its pieces, like he couldn't quite figure out how I was supposed to fit in his world.

"Uh… yeah?" I replied, crossing my arms. "Kind of? You're the one upset over this whole thing."

He shook his head, his expression twisting like he was barely holding something back. "You don't get it, do you? You come in here, out of nowhere, acting like you know everything. Like you can see right through my work, through *me*." He paused, jaw tight, and I could see it—him clamping down on all that anger, on whatever he didn't want to say. "You don't know what it's like," he said, his voice trembling. "To have everyone looking at you like you're already perfect. Like you don't get to make mistakes. Like you're not even allowed to break."

I swallowed, words catching in my throat. "Maybe I get it more than you think," I said, my voice splintering under the silence that followed. The air between us felt sharp, like stepping too close would draw blood. "You're under all this pressure. You're trying to *be* perfect, to know everything, but that's too much, dude. No one should have to deal with that."

For a second, he almost softened, something flickering in his eyes. But just as quickly, his gaze hardened, and he looked away. "This fucking project. It actually meant something to me, dammit! I was so close to a breakthrough, to understanding… everything. And now—" His voice cracked, and I saw his shoulders shake, just barely. "Without this… what am I? I've spent my whole life chasing answers, but now it's like they don't even matter." His chest heaved. "It's all just… gone. I'll be nothing. I *am* nothing."

The knot in my chest tightened. "Your project mattered to me too. And so do you." The words slipped out before I could stop them. "Look, I don't know how or why, but you and I are tangled up in something. I don't know what it is, but you're… you're the only person who can help me make sense of it."

Ryan stared at me, his gaze intense and searching. I could practically hear the gears turning in his head, like he was trying to figure out what I wasn't saying. "Help you? Is that what you think I'm here for?" He shook his head, his voice barely a whisper. "You're just like the rest of them. You don't see me—you see a shortcut. Someone to use. And when I'm not enough, you'll throw me away, just like everyone else has."

"No, that's not—" I reached out, desperate, but he was already turning away, shoulders hunched, the fight draining out of him.

Without thinking, I grabbed his arm. "Ryan, wait, I—"

Ryan spun, his palm colliding with my chest so hard it felt like my ribs might cave in. The force sent me flying into the lockers, my head snapping back into one of the metal grates with a sharp, splintering pain. The jagged edge bit into my scalp, and for a second, the world tilted as a hot, wet sting bloomed at the back of my head. Blood. His fist crashed into the locker beside my head, the metal screaming under the blow. The sound ricocheted down the hallway, sharp and jarring, but not as loud as his voice.

"What do you want from me?!" he choked out, his voice thick, almost breaking. His chest heaved, his breath coming in jagged bursts like it hurt to inhale. Weak tears welled in his eyes, then began streaking down his face even as his jaw tightened. His body trembled, and I realized with a jolt that he wasn't just angry—he was falling apart. Completely unraveling right in front of me.

I tried to speak, but the words caught in my throat. I was scared—scared he might snap completely—but I stayed rooted, my back pinned to the cold metal. His fist hovered beside my head, the knuckles scraped raw, shaking like he couldn't decide whether to hit the locker again or me. The tears came faster now, cutting streaks through the fury etched into his face. "Tell me, Carter! What do you want?"

My voice came out hoarse, shaking but steady enough. "I don't want anything from you, Ryan. I'm just trying to figure it out. Just like you."

He froze, but the tears didn't stop. For a moment, I thought he might collapse right there.

The cafeteria doors slammed open, the principal's sharp footsteps slicing through the charged silence. "What the hell is going on here?!" he barked, his voice cold and cutting. Ryan's fist remained frozen in midair, inches from the dented locker, but his tears didn't stop. Slowly, he turned to face the principal, then back to me, his chest still heaving, his face a raw, broken mask. Blood dripped down my neck, hot and sticky, pooling at the collar of my shirt. The principal's gaze locked on it, his eyes narrowing as he noticed the jagged metal slit behind me, faintly streaked with red. He darted a sharp glance between me and Ryan, the calculation in his expression as cold and clinical as the air in the hallway.

"Ryan. My office. *Now.*"

Ryan didn't move at first, just stood there, his eyes locked on mine.

His breath hitched as the tears spilled, falling fast and hot onto his cheeks. His chest shuddered with every exhale, like each breath was a battle he was losing. No smirk, no cocky grin—just exhaustion. Defeat. And something else, something that felt like it could've been everything or nothing at all. Ryan's gaze lingered, heavy and unreadable, like he was memorizing the cracks in my armor—or showing me his own. When he turned to leave, his shoulders slumped as if the stress of it all had finally broken him.

He trailed the principal down the hall, and I just stayed there, feeling this weird weight lifting off my chest. It was over. The rivalry, the games—he'd lost. He'd lost whatever he'd been clinging to like a lifeline. My stomach twisted violently, a cold wave of nausea rising in my throat. I doubled over slightly, squeezing my eyes shut as the hallway spun, the metallic taste of fear and blood coating my tongue.

From behind me, someone called my name. I turned, and there was Nat, stepping out of the cafeteria, brow furrowed as she walked toward me.

"Carter," Nat's voice cut through the haze, sharp and urgent, pulling me back from the edge. Her eyes darted to the streak of blood trailing down my neck, widening in alarm. "Oh my God, Carter— you're bleeding."

I swayed slightly, the hallway tilting again. "I'm fine," I muttered, but the words felt hollow, like I wasn't sure they were true. My knees threatened to buckle, and Nat reached out, grabbing my arm to steady me.

"Fine? Are you kidding me?" Nat's voice rose, sharp and insistent as she moved closer, her hand brushing lightly against my head. She pulled it back, her fingers streaked with blood. "Carter. You need to sit down—now." Her voice softened as she guided me to the floor, her grip firm but careful, like she was afraid any wrong move might send me crashing down.

I leaned back against the lockers, wincing as the cold surface bit into the knot forming at the back of my skull. The nausea lingered, coiling tight in my gut. Nat crouched beside me, her expression a mix of worry and barely contained anger. "What the hell happened? What did I miss?" she asked, her voice low but trembling with emotion.

"I think I…" I said, my voice barely above a whisper. "I think I just fucked everything up."

She hesitated, her hand brushing against mine. "Fucked what up? Carter, Ryan could've—" She stopped, swallowing hard, her eyes scanning my face like she was looking for something she couldn't find. "You should've listened to me—you shouldn't have followed him."

I let out a weak, humorless laugh that hurt more than it should. "Yeah. Probably."

Nat's expression softened as she inched closer, not asking questions, not pushing for details. "We need to get you looked at," she said, her voice low but insistent. She slid beside me, her shoulder leaning into mine, grounding me, but the heaviness in my chest didn't budge.

After a moment, she gave my arm a nudge. "Look, whatever happened, it'll work itself out. Just another day in paradise, right?" she cracked, but my expression didn't break. The feeling in my chest didn't lift. Her gaze took me in, before resting her head on my shoulder. "I know you don't like to talk a lot, but you don't have to carry all of this alone," she said, her voice soft but firm. "Whatever you think you've screwed up… it's not all on you. It never is."

I nodded, though the ache lingered. Ryan was gone, his future messed up because of me, because I'd barreled into his life without a second thought. I'd been clinging to this idea that he'd be the one to help me find my way back, that he'd have the answers. But seeing him now, he was just… another kid. And I just screwed up his life.

Nat shifted, glancing at the principal's office door. "Come on," she said, voice soft. "Let's just go. Get out of here. I'm taking you to the ER."

I shook my head, eyes fixed on the closed door. "I can't… not yet."

She looked at me, waiting. "Why? You really want to hear what Ryan Prescott has to say after—" she gestured. "All this?" Her voice softened, but I could see the tension in her jaw, the way her fingers trembled slightly as she clutched my arm. She wasn't just angry at Ryan—she was scared for me.

I swallowed, the words stuck in my throat. I couldn't go to the doctor. Couldn't afford it, didn't have insurance. I didn't even *exist* yet. Not here. But she couldn't know that.

Nat leaned on the locker beside me, her shoulder brushing mine again. "You and Ryan," she said softly, shaking her head. "You're like two storms colliding—tearing each other apart, and neither of you even knows why."

I let out a shaky breath, but my chest felt tight, the nausea still curling in my stomach. "Maybe we're both just trying not to drown," I muttered, not sure if I meant it for her or myself.

She gave me a long look, her eyes softer now, full of something like understanding. "Well, maybe it's time one of you learned to swim."

I let out a small puff of air, but my eyes stayed glued on the front office door. I didn't know why I needed to stay, just that something felt unfinished, like the whole thing had cracked open, spilling out parts of me I didn't even know I'd been carrying. I stayed quiet, and so did she, just watching with me.

A few minutes later, a younger Colleen walked through the doors at the end of the hallway, diner uniform and all, her eyes sharp and worried. Her wired red hair was fuller, but still had that frantic energy I remember. She powered past us, her steps quick and clipped, and slipped into the principal's office. The door clicked shut behind her, and I could only imagine what was happening inside.

Soon, the door swung open again, and I heard Colleen's voice, distinct and insistent, her Southern charm spilling through. "So you're telling me my son—the smartest kid in this whole school—can't just finish up his diploma here?"

"It's school policy, Mrs. Prescott," the principal replied. "Given the recent incident, regardless of Ryan's academic history... We have no other option but expulsion."

"Unbelievable," she muttered. Then she turned to Ryan, the two shuffling back into the hallway. "Ryan, sweetheart, this isn't fair. None of this is fair," she said, her voice breaking as she reached for him. Her hands trembled, fluttering uselessly before gripping his arm like it was the only thing keeping her steady. "We'll make homeschooling work, I promise. You'll earn the highest honors. You always do. You... have to."

The word hung there, heavy and rough. *Homeschooling.*

Ryan's gaze snapped up, his expression shifting as he looked directly at me. In that instant, his eyes sparked, a sudden clarity dawning on his face. I watched his expression change, watched him connect the dots, recalling the time I'd asked him—out of nowhere—if he'd been homeschooled.

The moment his eyes locked with mine, I saw it—the flicker of recognition, sharp and electric, like he'd pieced together a puzzle I hadn't even realized I'd handed him. His gaze was a question and an accusation, one I couldn't answer.

Nat squinted at me, glancing between me and Ryan, picking up on the silent exchange. Her brow furrowed, and she whispered, "Wait... Carter, how'd you know about that? Are you, like, psychic or something?"

I looked down, swallowing hard before meeting her eyes, managing a weak smile. "Something like that."

Ryan's gaze lingered a moment longer, intense and unblinking. I could see it in his eyes—the realization that I'd been keeping secrets, that I didn't belong here in any sense he understood. The last little mystery about me was solved, and for once, it didn't make him look victorious. It just made him look... sad.

Watching him walk away, his shoulders hunched and his fists still trembling, I felt something twist deep in my chest. As much as he'd pissed me off, as much as I wished I could hate him, I couldn't. Because I saw it—the crack in him, the part that was breaking under the load of everything he couldn't say. It wasn't anger, not really. It was pain. And I just made it worse.

I took a shaky breath, trying to keep my face steady, but Nat could see right through me. She gave my arm another gentle squeeze, her voice soft. "Carter... come on. Time to go."

I nodded, letting her lead me, though everything inside me felt like it was unraveling. As we left the school, I couldn't shake the feeling that I'd lost my only hope to finding my way back. I'd thought Ryan was my answer. But now, all I could see were the pieces of his life I'd scattered, like I'd been playing with something fragile I didn't know how to hold. And the idea that I had somehow impacted the future, before I had even gotten stuck in the past, terrified me.

. . .

EVERY SECOND I spent in this 1994 limbo felt like a gift wrapped in razor wire, reminding me that time wasn't on my side. Sooner or later, the clock was going to run out. Ryan's whole crash and burn felt like a neon sign flashing just for me. Like, "Hey, you're one wrong move from losing it too." I couldn't stop thinking about my own mess, looming bigger and closer with every second. And my mom, somewhere out there in the future, waiting for me—waiting in a way that was eating away at her memory, minute by minute. It all hit like a weight in my chest.

In the days after Ryan got booted, everything felt... weird. Off. His seat sat empty next to mine, just staring at me like a reminder I didn't need. Every time I looked over, it was like the universe was whispering, *Congrats, you blew it.*

I kept trying to catch him somewhere, maybe explain, or... I don't know. Spill the truth? But every time I got close, he was like smoke. One day, I drove by his house, working up the guts to knock and just... tell him everything. But no one was home, just an empty driveway and the faint smell of burned leaves from someone's yard down the street. The next day, I stopped by his mom's diner—that dingy little spot off Main where you could taste the grease in the air before you even walked in. But apparently, she'd quit her job. Left to "spend more time with her son." Probably meant I was officially erased from Ryan's life, a footnote that never mattered.

And with that? My last shot at getting home went up in flames, one "Now Hiring" sign on the diner window away from being stuck for good.

But, despite the cosmic slap in the face, I was starting to feel weirdly... at home in this retro limbo. Christmas slid by in its quiet, lonely way. A one-man show, starring me, in the sad, silent movie that was my life. New Year's Eve? Now that was a different beast. I debuted at the local hotspot otherwise known as Ethan's basement, rocking a pair of '1995' glasses like a bad punchline. I don't know— just for a second, in the glow of that cheap string of lights, things felt almost normal.

Then, of course, there was my Toyota Highlander—a rust bucket in the future but a sci-fi superstar here. The whole town practically drooled over it, like Spielberg himself had dropped it off. Some kids even asked if I was "from the future." I just shrugged and played along, but inside, it was… I don't know, kind of sad. They thought it was a big deal; I just saw a busted reminder of where I was supposed to be.

And then, there was my prize possession, the cracked iPhone. A whole future trapped in one shattered screen. It sat in my pocket like a bad omen, whispering, *You don't belong here.* Every time I pulled it out, those jagged fractures glinting in the sunlight, it was like the universe was spelling it out for me in broken glass: *You're stuck.* Sure, maybe I was here physically, but mentally? I was everywhere but.

And by the time I'd run out of cash—surprisingly easy to stretch in a 90s economy—I had to turn in my motel key and head back to the only thing that still felt familiar. Most nights, I'd just sit in my car, staring at the cracked screen, letting the leather seats cradle me like some last shred of sanity. The last bits of daylight would filter through those fractured lines, reminding me of all the places I wasn't.

My backpack, full of clothes that didn't belong to this world, was my silent passenger. It slouched in the seat beside me, like it was waiting for the day I'd finally wake up and get out of this simulation. Sometimes, when the night got too quiet and everything pressed in around me, I'd turn my gaze to that busted screen and let myself hope. Just for a second.

And then, like clockwork, I'd hear Mom's voice, faint and foggy, like a distant memory tugging me back. I could picture her on our old porch, the humid air thick with crickets and her gentle advice.

"Life's not a straight line," she'd say, that knowing smile flickering on her face. "It zigzags, loops back, sometimes even slams into a wall. But no matter what, you keep moving. Even if you're just guessing where 'forward' is."

At the time, I'd nodded, maybe rolled my eyes, thinking it was just one of those things moms say to make you feel better about failing a class. But now? Stuck in this 90s snow globe, losing people left and right? Yeah, I got it. Moving forward was all I had left.

"Just keep moving," I muttered to myself, gripping the wheel like it was the only thing keeping me anchored. "Just… keep moving."

But every day was like wandering through a museum of ghosts.

Living in this world was like taking a tour of memories that weren't even mine. And sure, the 90s had its charm, its neon lights and chunky tech, but it was all just a shiny trick to distract me from the truth. My real life, the one that mattered, was slipping through my fingers, second by second. No amount of retro nostalgia could replace the cold, hard fact that my future was ticking away. And if I didn't get back, if I didn't find a way out of this? I'd be nothing more than another ghost haunting this place.

So I pushed the memories away and gripped the wheel a little tighter, the cracked phone charging silently in the cupholder like it was on life support. The thought of Mom, somewhere in the future, waiting for me, kept me from losing it. I had to get back—to her, to the life waiting for me on the other side of this mess.

"Keep moving, Carter. Forward. Even when it feels like you're running out of road." The words stayed with me, a faint ember in the cold expanse of everything I'd lost.

I stared at the phone, its fractured screen still reflecting the last streaks of daylight. It felt like a mirror, one that showed me all the places I was breaking, all the pieces I hadn't figured out how to hold. And yet, it hummed faintly in my hand, a reminder that maybe, just maybe, I could still find my way back.

CHAPTER 14

DAYS BLED TOGETHER IN A GRAY, sluggish blur, like I was stuck behind the static of a broken TV screen. Everything felt slowed down but too loud at the same time—a world off-key, sharp edges dulled by repetition. Nat, Ethan, and I—we weren't some neat little trio. We were stray dogs circling the same rusted-out junkyard, picking through scraps and hoping to find something worth holding on to.

But lately, it was like the script had changed. The easy rhythm we'd found started snagging, fraying around the edges. Especially when it was just Nat and me. There was this… charge. A weird electricity crackling between us whenever our hands brushed or our eyes met for just a beat too long. It was like standing on the edge of a cliff and feeling the pull of something I couldn't name. Or maybe didn't want to.

And Ethan? He felt it too. I caught it in the way his grin turned brittle, his laugh clipping off too fast, like it didn't belong to him anymore. His eyes darkened, flickering to me and Nat like he was seeing something he couldn't unsee. When he looked at us, the air between us turned heavier, like the room was closing in just for him. The jokes he threw at Nat started sounding hollow, forced, like he was trying to hang on to something slipping right through his fingers.

We weren't some fairytale friendship, but there was a time when it felt like we could've been something solid, something worth keeping.

Now it was more like a half-erased memory, the kind you try to hold onto even as it slips further out of reach. But Nat was the anchor in all this, the one thing that kept me from spiraling completely off course. Yet, of course, nothing stays that simple for long. And what happened next? It could've been straight out of some tragic sitcom heading for cancellation.

It was Ethan who broke. He'd been stewing for weeks, and today, it finally boiled over. I barely set my tray down when he appeared, his floppy hair falling into his face as he stopped right in front of me. He brushed it back with a quick, agitated motion, but the rest of him didn't match the sharpness in his movements. His posture sagged, and his hands twitched at his sides before diving into his pockets, like he didn't trust them to stay still. His foot tapped once, then stopped, like the motion betrayed him.

"Carter." His voice came out forced, light enough to be brittle. His jaw twitched, the tension there threatening to crack through his words. "Got a sec?"

"Uh… yeah?" I replied cautiously, my eyes narrowing as I tried to figure out where this was going.

Ethan shifted his weight, the chain on his pocket jingling faintly. "Look, don't take this the wrong way, man, but… things have been a little weird. With Nat. With you. I mean, you're cool and all, don't get me wrong. But it's just… different now, you know?" His voice softened, dipping into something almost apologetic. "Like, you're my friend, but…"

I blinked, thrown by how much he wasn't saying. "But… what?" I asked, my voice tentative.

He sighed, glancing around like he was checking to make sure no one else was listening. "It's just… Nat and I, we've always had this thing. Like, not a *thing* thing, but… you know what I mean. And now it's like you just…" He trailed off, his hands coming out of his pockets to gesture vaguely. "I don't know. Like you just strolled in and—."

"Strolled in and what, Ethan?"

We both froze, his head snapping toward the source. Nat was standing a few feet away, her arms crossed over her leather jacket, her expression ice cold. Her hair was perfectly tousled, the faint light catching the butterfly clip on one side. She looked like she'd been waiting for this moment.

"Nat," Ethan started, his voice faltering. "It's not—"

"What do you think is happening here, Ethan?" Her voice cut clean through the cafeteria noise, sharp as glass under bare feet. She didn't raise it—she didn't have to. She stepped forward, her leather jacket catching the light, and for a moment, it didn't matter that she was half his size. She could've leveled him with a glance. "You really think Carter just strolled in here and ruined everything? Like I don't have a say in my own life? God, Ethan, do you even hear yourself?"

Ethan's bravado faltered, his hands falling to his sides as he scrambled for words. "It's just… it's different now, Nat. *You're* different." He paused, his voice softening. "I mean, we used to be a team. Just us. We had a thing going, you know? It was like—"

"Like what? Like we were best friends?" She tilted her head, her expression a careful blend of clarity and challenge. "Yeah, Ethan, we were. But that doesn't give you the right to act like I owe you something." Her voice was level, but there was an undercurrent of hurt, just enough to make him flinch. "I've been there for you. For everything. And now you're throwing this at me like… what, I'm supposed to date you?"

Ethan opened his mouth, but nothing came out. He looked wrecked, like she'd just torn him open in a way he didn't know how to put back together. "Nat, that's not—"

"No, it is," she said, her voice quieter but unbreakable. "You don't get to be mad that I'm getting close to someone else. That's not how this works, Ethan."

I stood there, rooted to the spot, like I'd wandered into a room where I wasn't supposed to be. Their words lashed out, sharp and jagged, and I could feel every one of them carving into me, a reminder that I wasn't just a bystander—I was the crack in their foundation. And all I could do was stand in the middle of it, a ghost trying not to be seen.

Ethan's fists clenched at his sides, his jaw tight as he tried to keep it together. "I just—" He stopped, swallowing hard. His fists opened, closed. "I don't want to lose you, Nat! That's all." He paused, swallowing hard, his voice cracking. "I thought you'd always be there. Solid. Something I could count on. Like we mattered. But now... now it's all slipping."

Her face softened, just for a second, and I thought maybe she'd reach out, say something to pull him back. But then it was gone, and her expression hardened again, like a door closing. "You didn't lose me. But after this? You might."

The silence that followed was thick, heavy. Ethan looked at her, his face pale, his shoulders slumping. For a second, I thought he might argue, try to claw his way back. But he just nodded, his shoulders sagging as if it all had finally crushed him. His footsteps dragged across the floor, each one a faint echo of something he'd broken, something he couldn't put back together.

As he disappeared through the doorway, I turned back to Nat, my mind still reeling from everything that had just happened. "Uh... you okay?"

She sighed, running a hand through her hair, the coolness of her earlier words slipping just a little. "I don't know, Carter. I think... I think I just ripped something open that I can't put back."

I nodded, feeling her words sink in. "Yeah. But maybe it's better this way? Like, no more pretending?"

She looked at me, her eyes softening. "Maybe. But it doesn't make it hurt any less."

The cafeteria around us buzzed with voices and laughter, but all I could hear was the sound of broken hearts.

I glanced at Nat, the mess around us feeling way too loud, way too public. "Hey, uh... you wanna get out of here?"

She nodded, her eyes meeting mine, and I could feel it—that pull, that charge, like the edge of a cliff I wasn't quite brave enough to jump off yet. But maybe she was right there with me, ready to jump too.

In the aftermath of that showdown with Ethan, it was like something in Nat had shattered, and everything she'd been holding back came rushing out in a flood she couldn't stop. She practically dragged me out of the cafeteria, her grip tight on my wrist, like I might disappear if she let go.

We ended up in her Beetle in the parking lot, surrounded by rows of cars buried under a thin, fresh layer of snow. The car smelled like her—stale smoke clinging to the upholstery, softened by the faint floral perfume she always spritzed on before heading home. Both the cigarettes and the bottle were stashed in the center console, like a little survival kit she never bothered to hide from me or Ethan. It wasn't unpleasant, just... Nat. Complicated and unapologetic.

The snow fell heavy and slow in big, soft, dry flakes, smothering the windshield until the outside world dissolved into pale, shapeless nothing. The cold seeped in through the windows, brittle and sharp, pressing against us like something alive. It muffled everything—the parking lot, the rows of empty cars, the words we couldn't find for each other. The silence between us stretched, thick and suffocating, like the snow wasn't just outside—it was inside too, filling the space between us, making it impossible to speak.

Sometimes, silence was the best I had to offer.

Nat gripped the steering wheel, her knuckles white as her fingers dug in, so tight they could've left marks on the plastic. She stared straight ahead, her breath fogging the window as her chest rose and fell unevenly.

"I don't get it." Her voice broke, so soft I almost missed it. "How could he just... say that? Like it's nothing. Like... I don't even know who he is anymore."

I didn't have an answer for her. Truth was, I wasn't sure there was one. I kept quiet, just letting her fill the silence.

"We've been through everything together," she continued, her voice sharper now, teetering between anger and something that sounded a lot like heartbreak. "I've known the guy since kindergarten, for God's sake. And now? Now it feels like he's just some stranger I thought I knew."

I shifted in my seat, the scratchy upholstery doing nothing to make the moment easier. "He's... scared, I think," I said slowly, each word feeling like a risk. "Feels like he's losing you. Maybe he's been feeling that way for a while."

She let out a bitter laugh, shaking her head. "Losing me? Carter, I was never his to lose. He's like… family, you know? But he doesn't see it that way, does he?"

Her jaw was clenched, and her words came out sharper, colder. "He thinks because we're close, I'm supposed to feel something more."

I shrugged, looking down at my hands. "Maybe. But he doesn't get it. He's so wrapped up in his own feelings, he can't even see how he's hurting you. It's like… he's trying to hold onto you so tight he's forgetting to let you breathe."

The words just hung there, heavy and sharp. Nat looked down at her hands, her face softening in a way I wasn't used to seeing. "I feel like I'm drifting," she said, her voice cracking. "Like everything that held me together is coming undone, and I can't stop it. I'm falling apart, piece by piece, and it feels like no one even cares enough to try to catch me." Her lower lip quivered. "Everything that used to feel solid—Ethan, my family—it's coming undone, like a thread pulling loose from a sweater until there's nothing left but a pile of useless yarn. And I can't grab hold of it fast enough to stop it." She paused, tears brimming at the edges of her eyes. "I thought Ethan would always be there, like some kind of anchor. But now? Now I don't know who he is. Or who I am, half the time."

She looked so small, folded into herself. Vulnerable. I wanted to reach over, maybe tell her it'd all be okay, that things would eventually work themselves out. But that would be a lie, and I wasn't feeling like adding another one to the pile.

She sighed, her voice breaking through the stillness. "I'm sorry," she said, words barely audible. She brushed her fingers under her eyes, like she was wiping away invisible tears. "I'm dumping all of this on you when you've got your own mess to deal with. I just… didn't know who else to turn to."

I shifted, feeling her words settle on my shoulders. "Don't apologize. I'm here, Nat. You don't have to… carry all this alone."

She looked at me, her eyes searching mine, like she thought maybe I had some kind of answer that'd make sense of all this. We sat there, both tangled in our own messes, both of us too stubborn to say what was really on our minds. The stuff we couldn't put words to—our confusion, her falling out with Ethan, the weight of it all—just sat there between us, unspoken but understood.

Then, after a few long seconds, she took a shaky breath, her voice barely more than a whisper. "My parents… they're finally doing it. They're splitting up." Her voice cracked, eyes glued to the dashboard. "I haven't told anyone. I don't even know how to deal with it."

A pang shot through me, like a hit to the chest. "Nat… I'm sorry. That's… heavy."

She nodded, her voice flat, empty. "Yeah. It's been coming for a while. They tried to hide it, I guess, but I'm not blind. I'd hear them fighting, even when they thought I was asleep. And now… it's official. My dad's moving out, and my mom wants us to move halfway across the country."

She turned to me, eyes sharp, filled with this mix of anger and something deeper. "It's not just them. It's… everything. They've got this perfect little life planned for me, this perfect little future, but it's not mine. It's like they don't even care what I want."

I nodded slowly, feeling the ache in her words, the way it suffocated the air. I'd always thought of her as unbreakable, like steel forged in fire, but now I could see the cracks spidering across the surface, everything too heavy to bear. Life was closing in on her from every angle.

"Trust me," I said quietly. "I get it. More than you'd think."

She let out a soft, humorless laugh, her breath fogging the air. "Do you, though? I mean, you've got your family, your new house—"

"My parents are separated too," I said, surprising myself. The words were out before I could even think. "They split a while back. My dad's out in California, doing his own thing, living this other life. And my mom… she's the reason I came back here."

Her expression softened, her eyes widening a little. "Why didn't you ever tell me? Is… is everything okay?"

I hesitated, feeling the words get stuck in my throat. I hadn't meant to bring this up, but it was out there now. "No," I admitted, my voice barely a whisper. "She's got Alzheimer's."

Nat blinked, taking it in. "Is… is that why she got your house's address wrong? I'm sorry, Carter… That's… really tough," she murmured, her voice quiet.

I nodded, managing a faint smirk, but the words were harder to find. "Yeah. Something like that. But the disease? It's not what people think it is. It's not just forgetting addresses, or names, or faces. It's forgetting your life. I'll call her, and some days she's there, you know? But other days… it's like talking to a stranger."

Nat's face softened even more, her gaze full of something close to understanding. "I can't imagine what that's like."

I ran a hand through my hair, a heaviness I couldn't shake dragging at me. "I don't know how to handle it. It's like there's this clock somewhere, ticking louder every day. I can't see it, but I feel it—this constant burden in my chest, like the hands are carving seconds into my ribs, counting down to the day she won't know me anymore. Not my name. Not my face. Nothing. I'll disappear."

Nat didn't say anything, just sat there, staring out at the parking lot like she was seeing it all for the first time. "I'm sorry," she broke, her voice barely a whisper. "I didn't know."

I shrugged, leaning back against the seat. "I don't really talk about it. But yeah. Every time I think about her, I know it's all going to come to an end soon. Faster than I can handle."

Nat looked over at me, and I could see something change in her expression, like she was finally letting her guard down. "That's got to be horrifying," she said softly. "It's like… how do you even deal with something like that? How do you keep going, knowing what's coming?"

I let out a breath, looking down. "I don't, really. I just keep moving because… what else can I do? But the thought of her forgetting me? It's terrifying, Nat. Really, truly terrifying."

She reached over, her hand brushing against mine. It was brief, just this quick touch, but it was enough. Enough to remind me I wasn't alone, even if sometimes it felt like I was.

"I'm sorry about your mom." She paused, her voice quieter now, like she was testing the words. "I don't even know what to say. That's… it's too much, Carter."

I looked at her, feeling her sympathy and the strange comfort of her presence. "Yeah. It is what it is."

She met my gaze, and for a second, it was like every wall she'd built came down. "I guess we're both pretty messed up, huh?"

I managed a weak smile. "Guess we are."

The silence that followed felt different, almost lighter. Like something had shifted between us. We weren't just two people going through the motions—we were two people trying to make sense of a world that felt like it was slipping through our fingers, a game whose rules changed before we'd had a chance to learn them.

Nat shifted beside me, pulling her knees up to her chest, and I wanted to hold onto her like she was holding onto me, but the truth was... I didn't know if I could be there for her. I wasn't even sure how to be there for myself.

The bell rang in the distance, breaking through the moment. "Feel like going back inside?" I asked, trying to gauge her reaction, like I didn't really know what I wanted her to say.

"Why bother?" she said, a faint smile tugging at the corner of her mouth. "They're lucky if I ever bother going back. Let's just pray they cancel school early."

I grinned. "Well if we're already late, what's the point in showing up? Wanna skip the rest of the day and head to the bleachers? I've got something I want to show you." I didn't even wait for her response. I threw open the door and climbed out. "Come on!"

She blinked, but then her face softened, her confusion replaced with something close to relief.

We ran, the pavement slick under our shoes. Our breath came in ragged bursts, clouds dissolving into the air. The cold hit us hard, cutting through our jackets like shards of ice. My breath came fast, sharp in my chest, and I could hear Nat's boots clapping the frozen earth behind me. We weren't running toward anything—we were running away, the burden of it all snapping at our heels like hungry dogs. The mess we'd made. The things we couldn't fix. For a moment, with the snow whipping around us and our laughter cutting through the cold, it almost felt like we could outrun it. Like we could leave it all behind. But we were wrong.

CHAPTER 15

THE SNOW CONTINUED to fall in thick, heavy flakes, smothering the field and bleachers in silence. Each flake hung in the air like it didn't want to land, drifting, taunting, dragging the world into a strange, suspended stillness. It was the kind of quiet that made you feel like the last person alive. But I wasn't. Not with Nat.

She and I trudged up the steps, her boots crunching against the fresh layer while I stumbled a little, my sneakers slipping on the ice hiding beneath the layers of fluffy white. Nat moved ahead without a word, carving a path only she could see. Her scarf trailed behind her, whipping in the wind like some kind of banner. There was something unrelenting about the way she walked, like she was chasing a truth only she could find. And somehow, I felt like I was slipping further back with every step, like trying to run in a dream where the ground keeps falling away beneath you. Not old, exactly. Just… out of sync. Out of place.

The bleachers loomed above us, the darkened wood shimmering faintly under the gray, heavy sky. They had this ancient, almost regal quality about them, like they'd been there forever and would still be there long after we were gone. Like the ruins of the Coliseum that had seen great gladiators fall under the rule of men who had no feelings, men whose thumbs turned up or down at their whim. The many lives who had passed over these bleachers whispered to me, urging me to keep moving or be locked into a thumbs down.

I followed her to the top row, dragging my feet while she practically floated, and we plopped down, the cold biting through the layers of fabric between us and the wood.

Nat stretched her legs out, her boots tapping lightly against the sodden rung below, and tilted her face up to catch the snowflakes. They caught in her dark hair, clinging for a moment before melting away, like the world was trying to crown her before it lost its nerve.

"So," Nat started, propping herself up with that sharp look she gives when she's already got you figured out. "What's the big deal? Come on, spill. New CD? Tickets to a show?"

I smiled. This was it. I was finally going to do it.

Slowly, reluctantly, I pulled my phone from my pocket, the cracked screen catching the pale light. "Not quite," I said, the breath puffing out of my mouth in a cloud. "Prepare to have your mind blown."

This thing felt like a mockery of the world around us, all slick and high-tech in a place where dial-up was still, you know, the *thing*. "Check it out," I said, keeping my voice low, like I was letting her in on some giant, cosmic secret. In a way, I guess I was.

Nat's face twisted, skeptical, like I'd just shown her a magic trick she wasn't buying. "What is this, some Frankenstein pager from RadioShack?" she asked, her tone dripping with mockery, though her eyes stayed locked on the screen.

"No, no. Just… watch." I held down the power button, the apple logo flaring up against the broken glass, and Nat's mouth dropped open, just slightly.

"That's… actually kind of insane," she said, her voice soft with shock. "Is it… what, like a makeup mirror?" She leaned in, unable to look away.

I smirked, tapping the home button as it flickered to life. "It's called an iPhone."

"An eye-what?" she shot back, her voice dripping with skepticism. "Look, if you're gonna show me something, at least make it something that's, you know, *real*."

"It's real, alright," I replied, tapping my passcode in, the screen unlocking. Texts, photos, music—all the pieces of my life, right there. "This is me," I said quietly, holding it up like some fragile artifact. "Everything I was, everything I left behind—it's all crammed in here. Like a time capsule I didn't mean to bury."

Her words came out slower, like she was piecing together her reaction as she spoke. "And where'd you find this 'time capsule'?"

I shrugged, putting on a bit of a show. "Bought it a few months ago… or, y'know, a couple of decades in the future. Whichever way you want to look at it."

Nat blinked, her expression twisting between confusion and a smirk. "Are you serious? What, are you… like, some kind of alien or something?" Her tone was playful, but I could tell she wasn't entirely joking.

I laughed, a real one, even if it was edged with disbelief. "The fuck? No! Definitely not an alien," I said, cracking a grin. "Just a guy from the future. Guess what year."

Her eyes narrowed, her hand brushing against mine like she didn't even realize it, and I felt the shock of it straight to my core. "You're serious?" Her tone was half-amused, half-disbelieving, like she didn't want to be played. "Alright, I'll bite. When are you from, *Mr. Future Man?*"

"Not gonna guess?" I teased, a smirk creeping up.

"Just tell me," she said, her voice flat. But I could see it—a flicker of excitement, like she was looking for a way to make it all make sense.

"2014," I said, watching her face shift, seeing the impact of that number land. I swiped through the images on my phone—my friends, the places I missed so much, all here but impossible to touch.

Nat's mouth opened, a half-formed laugh caught there, like she didn't know whether to believe me or not. "Wait… 2014? That's… that's insane." Her voice dropped, as if saying it too loud might break the moment. "You're serious?"

I nodded, watching the disbelief and excitement flash in her eyes as she leaned in, staring at the screen like it was some ancient artifact with the answers to the universe.

"So… this is real?" she whispered, her fingers brushing the cracked screen like it might shatter under her touch. "Like... this is really you?"

"Yeah. That's me, Sophomore year. Fairfax High, before everything got flipped upside down." I felt all of it pressing in, the familiar faces staring back from the photos, impossibly far away but so close I could feel them.

She was quiet for a moment, studying the photos like they were from some foreign world. "That's *Fairfax?*" she asked, her voice barely above a whisper. "God, it actually looks... different. Cleaner or something."

I laughed, shaking my head. "Not exactly. It's like, the same—but not. They probably remodeled."

She looked at me, her face softening. "So... the future." She said it like she was testing the word, turning it over in her mouth. "2014. You seriously came all this way?" Her voice softened, like she didn't know if she was supposed to believe me or laugh it off.

"I seriously did," I replied, voice dropping. "Not that I planned it or anything. One minute, I was in the car... next, I'm here. Stuck. It doesn't make any sense, Nat. But I have to get back... My mom's sick, and I don't know if I'll make it in time. Sometimes it's all I can think about."

Her expression softened, something shifting in her gaze. "Carter, I... I'm sorry. That's... I can't even imagine." She hesitated, the edges of her usual bravado slipping. "If there's anything I can do..."

I tried to laugh, but it sounded hollow even to me. "If only it were that easy— and I'm not exactly holding out hope. Figured maybe Ryan could help—guess you can see how that went."

She snorted, shaking her head. "What did you expect? All Ryan Prescott cares about is being the smartest person in the room. If you want real help, you look at people who actually care about you."

The cold bit through the bleachers, the snow soaking into the back of my jeans, but I barely noticed. Nat shifted beside me, her boots tapping softly against the wood as she reached into her coat pocket. She pulled out a crumpled pack of cigarettes, tapping one loose with practiced ease. The flick of her lighter broke the silence, a sharp burst of orange against the muted gray sky. She took a slow drag, the smoke curling upward in thin, pale wisps before disappearing into the cold.

"You're really set on going back, aren't you?" she asked, her voice soft as she stared out at the empty field. She didn't look at me, just flicked the ash onto the snow, where it disappeared like it had never existed.

I nodded, swallowing the lump in my throat. "I don't have a choice."

She turned then, her eyes sharper than I expected, like she was trying to memorize every detail of my face. "You always have a choice," she said, her voice softer now. She stubbed out the cigarette on the snow-covered bench. "I'm just saying, you don't have to make it alone."

I didn't know what to say to that. The words caught somewhere between my chest and my throat, refusing to budge. She leaned closer, her breath a mix of smoke and spearmint gum, her fingers brushing against mine, and for a moment, I thought that might be it. Just a small, fleeting moment of connection.

But then she kissed me.

It wasn't tentative. Nat didn't do tentative. It was full of something sharp and desperate, like she needed to say everything she couldn't with words. Her lips were warm, the kind of warm that cuts through the cold and lingers, leaving a trace like the faint burn of sneaked whiskey. Her hand slid up to my jaw, steady but not hesitant, her fingers cold against my skin, making me shiver in a way that had nothing to do with the weather.

For a second, I froze. I'd always been terrible at this—at letting people in, at knowing what to do when they got too close. But I leaned into it anyway, because it was her, and because I didn't know when—or if—I'd ever feel this again.

When she pulled back, her face hovered close to mine, her breath curling in faint clouds between us. Her eyes searched mine, and for the first time since I'd met her, she looked almost afraid.

"Don't forget me," she said, her voice breaking just enough to make my chest ache. "Even if you end up somewhere else, even if I'm just a memory you try not to think about—don't let me disappear. Promise me you'll remember this."

I nodded, my heart thudding in my chest. "I promise," I said, and I meant it. Even if I wasn't sure I could.

She gave me a small smile, the kind that almost looked real. "Good. I just… hope you're not stuck here forever. The '90s suck. Don't let anyone tell you otherwise."

I laughed. "Yeah, sure. Says the girl who's living in it. If you only knew what's coming next. I'll say one thing, though—the world doesn't end in 1999. Or maybe it did, and I'm just a ghost from the future."

She rolled her eyes, crossing her arms. "Really? That's all you're giving me? No 'heads up, here's what's coming'? Nothing to bet on?"

I looked down, trying to keep the smirk from falling. "Honestly, even being here… it could be messing things up. I could be… I don't know, erasing stuff, changing lives without even trying."

She looked at me, and for a moment, something softened in her expression. Then, without warning, she slung her arm around me. Her head rested on my shoulder, and the world stopped spinning. Her warmth steadied me, grounding me in a way I didn't know I needed. And just as quickly, it was gone. She lifted her head, her eyes locking onto mine with a mix of defiance and something softer, something unspoken.

"You've already changed my life, Carter," she said, her voice breaking just enough for me to hear it. "So don't think for a second this doesn't matter. *You* matter. Just tell me what you need, and I'm there. Always."

My eyes caught on the battery icon—*56%*. Every percent felt like a countdown, every second slipping away, not just on my phone but on whatever thread still tied me to my world.

Before I could respond, my phone buzzed in my hand. Nat jumped, and I glanced down, feeling my stomach twist. A voicemail. From Mom.

"Sorry, it uh— does that." I played it off. But internally, my mind was already sprinting. I tapped 'play', holding the phone to my ear, my pulse hammering as the static-filled message played.

Mom's voice crackled through the speaker, faint and disjointed, like it was fighting its way through some distant, crumbling connection. "Carter... it's fading. You need to—" The static swallowed her words, then her voice came back, weaker, fraught with urgency. "Don't let the reflection fool you... He's not—" Another burst of static cut her off, leaving only the hum of dead air. "The man in the window —He isn't James!"

And then it was gone, the line cutting out, leaving me with nothing but the ghost of her words and the stillness of the moment.

I sat there, the screen dark in my hand, her words circling in my mind. None of it made sense—the reflection, the man in the window —but it was her voice. It cut through me like a shard of glass, jagged and cold and painful. I gripped the phone tighter, like holding onto it might keep her closer, and for a second, I thought I might break.

Nat's hand slid back over mine, pulling me to reality for just a moment. "Everything okay?" Her voice was soft, but I could feel the worry in it, like she'd seen something break in me.

"I don't know," I whispered, eyes glued to the broken screen. "I really don't know anymore," the words barely scraped past the lump in my throat. My mind was screaming, trying to make sense of it all, but the more I tried, the more it felt like I was falling into some endless void. "Let's just... hope for the best," I managed, though the words felt weak, even to me. Deep down, I felt that ticking, pulling me toward something big, something I didn't know if I was ready to face.

CHAPTER 16

THE COLD HAD SEEPED into every fiber of the wood beneath us, making it hard and unforgiving. Clouds lingered in the sky, pale and indifferent, while the sun barely broke through, casting a weak, washed-out light that struggled against the waning day and did nothing to warm us. The whole world had gone quiet, hushed by the blanket of secrets that fell around us, anticipating, waiting for something to happen.

Nat hugged her arms across her chest, her breath curling in faint clouds in front of her. Her eyes were distant, flicking over nothing, like she was trying to work out an equation she didn't have the numbers for. She hadn't said much since the phone call, but her silence spoke volumes.

Me? I was a mess. My brain wouldn't shut up. For every question I had, fifty more were lined up waiting to be asked. I was flipping between a rush of satisfaction and a sinking sense of dread. Showing Nat the future was something big. I crossed a line. And the thing about crossing lines? You don't get to walk back over them.

Then I saw him.

Dr. Mercer stepped out of the gym's shadow, his coat snapping in the wind like some phantom made of sharp edges and bad intentions. A film noir character in slow motion, his squinted eyes wary, moving from side to side as if looking for some lurking criminal. He pulled up his collar and swiftly crunched across the frost-covered grass, zeroing in on us like a heat-guided missile, a hunter who'd been tracking his prey. My stomach dropped, heavy and sharp, and every instinct screamed for me to run. But I couldn't move. Not yet.

His eyes flicked up to us, my phone's cracked screen reflecting a sliver of dull winter light. Then his expression shifted—part triumph, part something darker. Like he'd finally gotten his hands on the key to Pandora's box, and he was all too eager to open it.

"Carter," he called from the bottom of the bleachers, his voice cutting through the cold like a knife. "You're in trouble."

There it was. Three words, and they hit me like a truck. I blinked, trying to play it cool, but my hands were already clenching into fists in my lap. "Hey… Dr. Mercer. How's it going?"

His eyes narrowed. No humor. No hesitation. He closed the distance between us and snatched the phone out of my hand before I could react.

"Hey!" I shouted, my voice cracking. "What's your deal?"

"My deal?" he mocked, his tone as frosty as the air around us. He held the phone up, turning it over in his hands like he was handling some ancient artifact. "You really thought I wouldn't notice? You've been careless, Carter. Flashing this around like it's nothing. But it's not nothing, is it?"

My mouth went dry. My brain scrambled for an excuse, something —anything—to get him to back off. "It's just a phone," I said, forcing a shrug even as my heart pounded in my chest. "From California. Nothing illegal about that."

His lip curled into a smirk, cold and cruel. "You really think I'm that stupid?"

My gut twisted. "It's uh— new," I muttered. "Scout's honor. You can catch it at your local Target. I got it on sale."

He didn't laugh. Instead, he leaned closer, his breath coming out in white puffs. "You don't think I know," he said, his voice low and almost... excited. "But I do. And if you're hoping I'm going to keep letting you play with it, you're wrong."

I swallowed hard, my pulse hammering in my ears. "If that's the case, what's your plan, then? Call the FBI? Have me locked up for having cool tech?"

His smirk deepened, and that's when I knew I was in real trouble. "I don't *need* anyone. I have all I want."

My fingers twitched at my sides, itching to grab the phone back, but I couldn't see an opening. Not yet. Nat shifted beside me, her breath quickening, but she stayed quiet. She didn't trust herself to speak. I didn't blame her.

"Seriously, Dr. Mercer," I said, trying to keep my voice steady. "I really need that back—"

"You don't know what happens yet, do you?" He turned the phone in his hand, inspecting it like it was a precious gem. A laugh erupted from him, but there was no warmth in it. "The way you've been keeping this thing hidden like it's some kind of secret weapon." His eyes flicked back to mine, sharp and cold. "You never fooled me, Carter. I knew from the second I saw your name on my roster. I've been waiting for this moment."

My chest tightened. My hands were already moving before my brain could catch up. I lunged forward, snatching the phone in one desperate motion. "Run!" I hissed, yanking Nat's arm so hard she stumbled and almost fell. My legs burned as I shot to my feet, the cold air slicing into my lungs with every step.

Behind us, Dr. Mercer's shout cracked through the atmosphere like a whip. "Carter! Stop right there!"

"Hell no!" I shouted over my shoulder, my grip on the phone so tight my knuckles ached.

Nat kept pace beside me, her breath ragged. "This is bad," she gasped. "Like, really bad."

"Understatement of the year!" I shot back, dodging around a stack of snow-dusted chairs. My brain screamed at me to come up with a plan, but all I could focus on was running.

We ducked around the back of the gym, our footsteps crunching against the frozen ground. Dr. Mercer's heavy tread followed, slower but unrelenting. "You think you can outrun me?" he shouted, his voice threatening and winded at the same time. "You're just making this worse for yourself!"

Nat's face was pale, her breath coming in quick, visible bursts. "What's the plan?" she asked, her voice sharp despite the panic slipping through. "Keep running and hope he has a stroke before he catches us?"

"Plan?" I said, glancing over my shoulder. "There is no plan! There's just not-getting-caught. That's the plan."

"Great plan," she muttered, her voice dripping with sarcasm. "Really inspired."

We slid behind the old equipment shed, collapsing against the cold metal as we tried to catch our breath. My heart was racing so fast I thought it might explode. Nat peeked around the corner, her expression darkening. "He's still coming."

"Of course he is," I said, rubbing a hand over my face. "Because why wouldn't he? Today's clearly my day."

Nat glared at me, but her fear softened it. "You're impossible."

"And you love it," I said, though my grin was shaky.

Before she could respond, Dr. Mercer's voice rang out, closer this time. "You can't hide forever, Carter! This only ends one way."

Nat's eyes darted to the other side of the shed. "We need to move."

I swallowed hard, gripping the phone so tight it hurt. "Yeah. Or we need a miracle."

We weren't getting one. Not today.

"Maybe we can reach my car," I muttered, scanning the distant lot. But it was farther than I'd thought, and Dr. Mercer was closing in, one determined step at a time.

"You really thought you could avoid this?" he huffed, his face red from effort. "Hand it over, Carter." His twisted smile spread wider, like this was all going exactly the way he wanted. "It was only a matter of time," he said, his voice low and brittle, like he'd been rehearsing this moment for years. "You were trouble the second you walked into my world. And now you're going to fix it."

"Jesus, Carter! What'd you do to the guy?" Nat asked, exasperated.

"How the hell am I supposed to know! I barely talked to him!"

"Fuck, we're so screwed," Nat whispered beside me. Her eyes darted to the open space ahead, then back to me. I could tell she was trying to calculate how far we could get if we ran.

I swallowed, my throat dry and tight. My chest felt like it was being squeezed by something I couldn't see. "It's either we take a shot now... or I end up on an episode of *Unsolved Mysteries.*"

Too late.

"There you are!" Dr. Mercer said, lurching around the corner with a finality that made my stomach flip. He loomed over us, his breath visible in the cold air, and his eyes locked onto the phone in my hand like it was a prize he'd just won. His voice was sharper now, colder. "End of the line, Carter." he cracked, puffing up like he'd just delivered some heroic one-liner. "Hand it over," he demanded, his tone cool and sharp. "We both know its power."

I tightened my grip, the cracked edges digging into my palm. "It's just a phone," I muttered, stalling. "What's the big deal?"

His lips curled into that same twisted smirk, the kind that made my skin crawl. "The big deal," he said, his voice dropping like he was sharing some sinister secret, "is that you're lying."

"What are you even talking about?" I shot back, trying to keep my voice steady even though my brain felt like it was scrambling to keep up. His expression wasn't just angry—it was something else. Something that made me want to bolt again.

He stepped closer, his shadow stretching over us. "I tracked you from the start," he said, almost conversationally, like we were just discussing the weather. "I watched the way you hid it. The way you acted. You took *everything* from me."

I stared at him, my chest tight. "You're insane."

"Am I?" he said, leaning down slightly, his eyes glinting in the dim light. "You don't even realize what you've done, do you? It almost hurts to see you like this—so naïve, so blind to what's coming. But I've seen it. I know what's waiting for you, Carter. And it's going to tear you apart."

My throat felt like it was closing up, but I couldn't let him see that. "You've lost it," I choked out, my voice trembling as my chest tightened. My hands twitched at my sides, itching to bolt but frozen under Mercer's stare. "It's just a phone. I don't know what you're expecting, it's not a weapon!"

"You don't get it," he snapped, his voice low and sharp. "I've seen the signs. Tracked the ripples. I can help you get back. To your time. To your *mother.*"

The words hit me like a punch to the gut. My mouth went dry, and my pulse roared in my ears. "How do you—"

"I know enough," he said, cutting me off. His hand remained outstretched, his gaze locked onto mine. "You're out of your depth, Carter. If you want to fix this, you'll give it to me. Now."

The air felt colder, heavier, like the whole world was closing in around me. My grip tightened on the phone. Beside me, Nat shifted, her face pale and tense, her breath quick and shallow. I glanced at her, then back at Dr. Mercer.

I wasn't sure what terrified me more—handing over the phone, or what would happen if I didn't.

Something wasn't right. The way he loomed over us, the way his voice slithered under my skin. He had the kind of authority you didn't just shake off, like an avalanche bearing down on you. I looked at Nat again, her eyes wide but fierce, and felt everything pressing in on me. *It couldn't end like this—not after everything I'd been through.*

But my hand moved on its own, trembling as I held the phone out to him. The fight drained out of me, replaced by this sinking feeling, like I was giving away the last piece of myself.

"Good boy," he sneered, snatching the phone with greedy hands. He held it like it was a trophy, his fingers curling possessively around the edges. He pushed the home button, the screen flickering to life, and then he punched in the passcode—my passcode.

I froze, the chill running down my spine as if I'd just locked myself in a freezer and no one knew I was in there. *How does he know that?* My stomach twisted as he tapped at the screen, his grin growing wider like he'd just won some twisted lottery.

As he pounded his fingers on the screen, Nat's hand found mine, her grip grounding me for just a second. Then she did something I didn't see coming—she shoved me forward, hard.

"Go!" she shouted.

I didn't think, didn't hesitate. My body moved before my brain could catch up. I lunged for the phone, ripping it from Dr. Mercer's hands before bolting toward the trees on the edge of the school parking lot. The screen glowed an eerie orange in my palm, the light flickering like it had a mind of its own.

Behind me, I heard Dr. Mercer's furious roar. "You're not going anywhere!" His voice cracked like ice, followed by a scuffle of movement.

I glanced back just in time to see him grab Nat, his grip like a steel trap around her arm. She twisted, her face a mix of rage and panic.

"Get your hands off me!" Nat spat, her voice slicing through the cold. She twisted violently, her breath coming in sharp bursts as she fought against his grip.

I stopped just past the tree line, my chest heaving, heart hammering so loud I could barely think. My head spun as I watched her fight, every second dragging out like it might snap under the tension. My feet were frozen, my brain screaming at me to move, to do something. But every option ran headfirst into the same dead end. I couldn't leave her. I couldn't stay. *What the hell was I supposed to do?*

"The fuck is wrong with you?!" Nat's voice rang out, sharp and furious. Her free hand clawed at his grip, her eyes blazing with a mix of rage and panic. She looked at me, just for a second, and it hit me like a punch to the chest—the trust in her gaze, the unspoken plea to leave her behind. But I couldn't.

"This isn't about you, Ms. Thompson," Dr. Mercer snapped, his gaze cutting toward the trees. "You can run all you want, Carter, but this is your only chance! It's this—or oblivion. I've seen what happens to you. I've witnessed the void. And soon, you will too!"

His voice carried, echoing off the parked cars like a bad omen. I ducked behind my Highlander, barely breathing as I crouched low. The glow from the phone intensified, spilling out between my fingers, bright enough to make me squint.

I looked down at it, the screen flickering wildly, the orange light pulsating like a heartbeat. My fingers brushed over the glass, a chill creeping up my arm. And then it happened.

Everything stopped.

The air thickened around me, squeezing in from all sides like I'd been dropped underwater. Time itself seemed to twist, stretching out and pulling tight all at once, like a rubber band about to snap.

And then, the world shifted.

It didn't feel like moving. It felt like breaking.

The world fractured around me, colors bleeding and stretching like spilled paint on glass. The ground sank beneath my feet, crumbling into something that wasn't quite air or solid, and the silence roared louder than anything I'd ever heard. My breath hitched, my hand clutching the phone like it was the only thing keeping me tethered to anything real. My breath caught in my throat, my legs trembling as everything around me twisted into something unrecognizable.

It wasn't just breaking—it was pulling me apart, every nerve in my body screaming, trying to hold onto something that wasn't there anymore. And then, it was gone. I blinked hard, my eyes stinging, and when I opened them, everything was blank.

Nat. Dr. Mercer. The school. All of it—gone.

One second, I was hiding, my heart pounding like a drum. The next, I was standing… somewhere else. The shift hit me like a punch to the gut, and I stumbled, trying to get my bearings.

The air here was different—warmer, drier, and eerily still. My breath came out in shallow gasps as I took in my surroundings. The schoolyard had vanished, replaced by an empty parking lot stretching out under a sun that felt too bright, too foreign. The cracked asphalt beneath my feet radiated heat, the kind that made the air above it shimmer in waves.

But it wasn't the heat that unsettled me. It was the silence. No voices. No movement. Just this crushing, unnatural stillness that settled over everything like a heavy blanket.

I looked up, and my stomach twisted. In the distance, the skyline of Los Angeles loomed, but it looked… wrong. The buildings were familiar, but not. Like someone had taken my memories of the city and stretched them just enough to feel off.

I looked down at the phone, still glowing faintly in my hand. My knuckles were white as I gripped it, the cracked screen reflecting the warped skyline back at me. It felt cold, foreign, like it wasn't even mine anymore. But it was all I had.

The realization hit me like a collapsing building, heavy and suffocating. I was alone—no Nat, no snow, no lifelines. Just this vast, empty parking lot stretching endlessly under a cruel sun. The world I knew felt impossibly far away, its warmth and familiarity reduced to a ghost I couldn't touch. And the worst part? I wasn't sure if I'd ever feel like I belonged anywhere again.

I couldn't move. Couldn't think. My mind screamed at me to do something, but what was left to do?

Time had moved forward.

And it left me behind.

CHAPTER 17

ONE MOMENT, I was gripping my phone like it could anchor me to something solid; the next, I was free-falling into a world that felt wrong in its bones. Everything around me twisted and warped, like reality had been melted and reshaped in a furnace, its edges hissing and crackling in the air. The smell of scorched oil and something chemical clung to my throat, making each breath thick and heavy.

I staggered forward, trying to make sense of the scene. A diner's sign buzzed faintly, its letters flickering in and out of focus like they were struggling to stay alive. The sound burrowed under my skin, a relentless mosquito hum that made my teeth itch and my head throb. Beneath it, a rusted-out payphone swung in the breeze, its cord twisting like a noose waiting for a neck.

The whole place felt... wrong. Like someone had tried to rebuild a memory from spare parts but didn't have all the pieces. The streets were too empty, the silence too loud, and the space too big; a deserted Hollywood movie set waiting for a new script, new actors, new life. And I guess I was it.

The pavement crackled and splintered beneath my Chucks, stretching out into an endless horizon. Above it, billboards loomed like decaying giants, their faded messages half-lost to time. One advertised a brand of cigarettes with a smiling couple that looked too perfect to be real, their joy leaching into something eerie the longer I stared. Another, a soda brand I didn't recognize. Both of them felt less like ads and more like warnings: *stay here long enough, and you'll rot, too.*

My eyes caught on a final one perched high above the chaos. It was sleek, shiny, and way too polished for the grime that clung to the city around it. "Michelle Lopez: The Face of the Future!" the words shouted down at me, stamped across a smile too polished to believe. Her eyes gleamed with confidence, her pose sharp against a glittering skyline that belied the one I saw across the horizon. It wasn't hope—it was a reminder. A future that felt out of reach, mocking me from a distance I couldn't close.

I stared at it for a second longer than I meant to, something about the words digging into my chest. *The face of the future.* "Fuck you, Michelle," I muttered. But the ad stood there, towering over everything like a promise I didn't believe in. It only made the world around it feel smaller, dimmer.

A car rolled by in the distance, chrome bumper gleaming like it belonged to a spaceship from another timeline. Its engine growled low as it passed, the sound fading faster than it should've, like it was in a hurry to escape. I turned back, my stomach dropping as I realized my car was gone—poof, vanished, along with any shred of logic I had left. All that remained was my phone, the only thing that felt remotely real, even with its shattered screen glowing faintly in my hand like a broken portal to nowhere.

The air was heavy, oppressive, like every sound, every movement, had to fight to exist. Faint notes drifted through the haze, carried on a breeze that barely moved. I knew the song—Hall and Oates—but it sounded wrong. Warped. Like it had been stretched too thin and played through a speaker buried under miles of dirt. Familiar, but broken, the way memories get when you try too hard to hold onto them. *Was this... the 80s?*

Then came the laughter—low and hollow, threading through the silence, another character off-script. It curled around my thoughts, echoing in a way that made my skin crawl, like it was trying to burrow under my skull. It didn't belong here. It didn't belong anywhere. It faded as quickly as it came, leaving behind a silence so sharp it felt like a knife pressed to my throat. I spun around, trying to find the source, but the street behind me was empty. The diner, the payphone, the stretch of pavement—it all felt like a stage set, and I was the only one in the scene. The laughter faded, leaving behind a silence so sharp it felt personal. My heart kicked up a notch, and that's when it hit me: this wasn't just some weird dream. I was lost. Really, actually lost.

The panic came slow, a cold knot in my stomach that unfurled with jagged edges. It clawed its way up my spine, a thousand icy fingers digging into my ribs, until my breath hitched and the world tilted under my feet. My chest tightened as my mom's face flashed in my mind, vivid and too clear, like a punch to the gut. I could see her, sitting at the kitchen table, her hands wrapped around her coffee mug, her laugh spilling out with warmth I'd taken for granted. The thought of her—of being stuck here, so far from her—slammed into me hard, knocking the air out of my lungs.

I clenched the phone tighter, my fingers brushing over the jagged cracks on the screen. It was all I had. The one thing fastening me to anything familiar. But it wasn't enough. Not by a long shot.

I spun in a slow, desperate circle, my sneakers scraping against the asphalt. "Okay," I muttered under my breath, my voice shaking. "Okay, this is fine. Totally fine. Just stranded in some kind of alternate-reality nightmare where everything smells like car exhaust. Great. Love that for me."

The words didn't help. If anything, they made the crushing silence feel even heavier.

Somewhere in the distance, another car passed, its engine cutting through the hazy afternoon. I thought about flagging it down, but my feet stayed planted, frozen by the overwhelming wrongness of the whole place. The city skyline rose in the distance, hazy and warped, like I was seeing it through dirty glass. It looked familiar—close enough to trick me into thinking I knew it—but the longer I stared, the more it felt like something I'd seen in a dream. Familiar, but wrong; obvious but difficult to understand.

The phone in my hand flickered, the glow shifting slightly before fading, and I felt a pang of hope that dissolved as quickly as it came. I glanced down at it, the cracks in the screen looking as broken as I felt.

"This can't be happening again," I whispered, my voice barely audible. "This can't be happening." My legs felt weak, like they might buckle if I stayed still too long. But where was I supposed to go? There was nothing here!

The silence wrapped around me, I felt it deep in my chest: the weight of being alone.

I clutched the phone tighter, like holding onto it might somehow fix everything. But deep down, I knew the truth. This wasn't something I could fix. Time had shifted again, leaving me in the cracks, and there was no one here to pull me out.

And the worst part? I didn't even know *when* I was anymore.

I shuddered involuntarily. My feet dragged me to the edge of the sidewalk, every step feeling heavier, like the pavement was laughing at me for thinking I had a plan. This city—Dad's city—felt stretched, twisted, like someone had taken the blueprint of my life and dumped it into a funhouse mirror. The buildings loomed overhead, all sharp angles and glass windows jutting against a grayish-brown sky, neon lights flickering like they knew their time was limited before burning out. The buzzing sound wormed into my brain, just loud enough to be annoying. The city itself was daring me to stare too long, to wonder too loud, and to care too much.

Then I saw it.

Victory Blvd. The name hit me like a half-formed memory, tugging at something just out of reach. It should've felt solid, familiar, but instead, it twisted in my chest, a reminder of everything I couldn't hold onto. *I... lived off this street. Or I would. Or I did.* The timeline didn't make sense anymore, and neither did I.

I tore my eyes away, focusing on the street again, trying to get my bearings. But the more I looked, the tighter the knot in my stomach twisted. It wasn't just unfamiliar—everything was wrong and I couldn't put my finger on it. My phone had thrown me straight here, like it expected me to find something solid, something real. A breadcrumb trail leading back home. Except there was nothing waiting for me.

I already knew it. Our apartment—my apartment—wasn't here. There was no point in looking. What would I even say to the current tenants if it was? No. No, it was just me. Me, a greasy diner, and a sad, empty parking lot that looked like it hadn't seen life in years. It hit me hard and fast, like running full speed into a brick wall. Like the universe was leaning over my shoulder, whispering, *this is what you get for getting comfortable.*

The realization left me dizzy. And then it sank deeper, heavier, like an ice pick driving straight into my gut: *What if this was it?* What if I was stuck here for good, while Mom was back in the future, slipping away piece by piece? I could miss it all—her laugh, the way her eyes crinkled when she smiled, the last time she said my name and meant it. The thought hit me like a sledgehammer, and my breath caught in my throat, coming out in shallow gasps as the cold realization clawed at my chest.

My eyes drifted back to the parking lot, hollow and useless, like a cruel joke with no punchline. I replayed every moment in my head, every choice, every twist of fate that had led me here, looking for some crack in reality I could use to crawl back out—or back in. But all I found was this sinking certainty: I was slipping, falling, and there was no ground left to catch me.

I turned toward the diner window, desperate for something steady. My reflection stared back at me, shadowed and strange, like I'd been pulled out of my own body and shoved into someone else's. My hair was in full shag, the circles under my brown eyes darker than I'd ever seen them, and—*was that a wrinkle?* No. Couldn't be. But the question lodged itself in my head and refused to leave: *Was this what the past was doing to me?* Stealing pieces of me with every second I didn't belong here, wearing me down until I wasn't even myself anymore. Just a shadow, stretched thin and unraveling.

"Hey, you look lost, man," a voice called from the shadows near the diner.

I froze, my heart jumping into my throat as I turned toward the sound. A guy leaned casually against the wall, his cigarette glowing faintly in the dim light. Smoke curled around him, soft and lazy, but it wasn't the cigarette that stopped me in my tracks. It was him.

The hair hit first—thick, dark waves that fell into place with the kind of effortlessness that felt unfair. Then the jacket: a faded Dodgers bomber that carried years of stories stitched into its worn seams. But it was his face that stopped me. *James.* Younger, sharper, alive in a way I'd never seen. My dad, but not. A stranger wearing the bones of someone I thought I knew.

For a second, my brain stuttered, struggling to catch up with reality. My tongue felt too heavy, my voice caught somewhere deep in my throat. "Uh… yeah," I managed finally, my words stumbling out like I'd forgotten how sentences worked. "I'm… looking for something."

James cocked an eyebrow, his lips twitching into a faint smirk as he took a slow drag from his cigarette. He exhaled the smoke in an easy swirl, his other hand resting loosely in his jacket pocket. "Yeah, aren't we all?" he said, his voice smooth and warm, like the notes of a half-forgotten song, but there was a flicker in his eyes—something restless and searching, like he was looking for answers even he couldn't name. "This city's funny," he said, his voice low. "Feels like every time you think you've found what you're looking for, it slips through your fingers. Like you're always chasing something you can't catch."

The words hit like they were meant for me, like he knew—somehow—that I didn't belong here, either. My chest tightened as I tried to swallow the lump in my throat. "Yeah," I said, barely above a whisper. "I know exactly what you mean."

His gaze lingered on me for a second longer, his eyes narrowing slightly, like he was trying to figure out my deal. Then he shifted, flicking the ash off his cigarette with a practiced ease. "Well, good luck, kid," he said, his tone easy but not unkind. He straightened, adjusting the collar of his jacket with a smooth, almost theatrical James Dean kind of shrug. "Hope you find whatever it is you're looking for."

His words were casual, tossed out like they didn't mean anything, like he didn't know he was talking to *me.* He turned, stepping out of the shadows and into the sunlight. His walk was loose, confident, the kind that said he wasn't in a hurry to get anywhere but also wouldn't stick around long.

I stood there, rooted in place, my chest tight enough to crack. Every instinct screamed at me to call after him, to say something—

anything. But what could I say? This wasn't my dad. Not yet. And maybe that was the cruelest part: knowing he'd walk away without ever realizing what he'd left behind.

A part of me wanted to ask the questions I'd carried the past year: *Why did you leave? How could you abandon her? Abandon our lives?* But this wasn't the man who'd made those choices yet. He was just a guy, standing on the edge of everything, trying to figure out where he fit.

Just like me.

I watched him disappear down the street, his silhouette fading into the haze of city. And for a moment, I let myself believe that maybe I could still find the answers I was looking for—if I could figure out the right questions to ask.

I forced myself to look away, back at the empty parking lot, but my thoughts wouldn't settle. Everything about this moment felt tangled, frayed, like I was holding pieces of a story I couldn't put together. My parents' story. The one I'd always been too afraid to ask about.

I turned toward the road, my breath hitching as Mom's voice echoed faintly in my head, distant and distorted: *Be careful of reflections. The man in the window isn't James.* The warning gnawed at me, even as I forced myself to take a step, then another. Her message from the future had to wait. The only place that made sense now was Reagan High—the one spot that might still be here. The school where everything had started. Or maybe ended. Hell if I knew anymore.

All I knew was that I couldn't stay here, standing still. Because if I did, the memories of everything I'd lost might finally take me down. I gripped the phone tighter, the cracks digging into my palm like the past refusing to let go. Every step felt heavier, like the world was dragging me down, pulling me deeper into a place I didn't understand. But I couldn't stop. Not when she was still out there. Somewhere, waiting for me to find my way back to her.

CHAPTER 18

REAGAN HIGH ROSE out of the ground like a jagged scar, its gray stone walls streaked with rain and years of neglect. The ivy crawling up its sides seemed less like decoration and more like nature's attempt to choke the life out of it. The windows, tall and narrow, glinted in the pale light like empty, watching eyes.

A row of wide stairs led up to the main doors, their edges worn and rounded having survived generations of stomping feet and bad decisions. The doors themselves were these heavy, dark slabs of wood with iron handles that belonged on a dungeon, not a high school. It didn't feel like a place you'd go to learn geometry—it felt like you'd walk inside and end up in a trial by combat or cursed into a ghost story.

I sank onto the bench at the base of the stairs, my legs folding like they'd finally given up the fight. Sitting there, I felt it all closing in— this place, this time, this endless sense of being caught in a story that didn't belong to me. I tugged off my coat and threw it down beside me. The California sun warmed my scalp. The whole scene buzzed with this uncomfortable quiet under a sky that stretched out in this sickly shade of gray that made the building's stone walls look even heavier, like they might just cave in if the clouds pressed too hard.

The courtyard stretched out like an abandoned battlefield, the pavement cracked and scarred in deliberate patterns, warning me to stay away. The air felt charged, thick and waiting, holding its breath, waiting for me to make my next move. To where? A stray bird hopped along the edge of the walkway, pecking at nothing, and I watched it like it might have the answer I didn't.

Through open windows, the muffled hum of the school carried on like everything was normal, like I wasn't caught in some surreal nightmare. Laughter leaked out in bursts, followed by the occasional distant thud of a slammed locker. But the courtyard? Dead quiet. *Too* quiet. The kind of quiet that leaves you alone with your thoughts, whether you liked it or not.

And I didn't. Not even a little.

I sat there, staring at the cracked pavement and hoping for the bell to ring. Hoping the flood of students would knock something loose in my brain, like maybe one of them had the answer for what to do next. How to fit in, how to exist... *here*. But my mind didn't stay on the school. Mom's face pushed its way to the front of my mind again, uninvited but impossible to ignore. The way her smile had started to falter the last time I saw her, the moments where she paused mid-sentence, searching for words that had slipped away. It all came rushing back, sharp and unrelenting. I could practically hear the clock ticking, counting down the time I had left to figure all of this out. Every second here felt like a step further away from her, and every second closer to...

The school door slammed open, the sound echoing off the stone walls like a warning shot. I flinched, my heart leaping to my throat as my head snapped up.

There he was—a teacher, storming out with this kind look in his eye, like I was just another lost kid. His approached me, his steps practiced and swift, and my stomach dropped.

"What are you doing out here?" he asked, confused, his voice slicing through the eerie quiet like a razor.

My heart hammered harder as I stared at him, the pieces clicking together a second too late. *It... it was Dr. Mercer. Only... not the Dr. Mercer I knew.* This version moved with the confidence of someone who hadn't yet been worn down by life, his sharp features untouched by time. Seeing him like this was like stepping into a glitch, a crack in reality where time folded in on itself. My stomach turned, my pulse racing as I tried to piece together how he could exist like this—*why was he here?*

My brain froze, struggling to process what I was seeing. *Did he know who I was? What I was? Who I would be to him?* The questions swirled, tugging at the edges of reality, but I forced them down. Panicking wouldn't help. I had to keep it together. For now.

"I'm, uh…" My voice cracked, and I coughed, trying again. "Just waiting for a friend, sir." I got to my feet, grabbing my coat and shoving my hands into my pockets like that would somehow make me look less suspicious. "Heading in now."

Dr. Mercer's expression didn't budge. It pinned me in place, sharp and heavy, like he was trying to peel back my layers and find whatever secret he thought I was hiding. "Don't worry about it. Just get to lunch," he responded, gesturing at the doors like they were some portal to salvation. "Don't let me catch you out here again."

I nodded, swallowing hard as I forced my legs to move. The door creaked shut behind me, the sound echoing through the hallway like the closing of a tomb. Everything about the space felt familiar but, again, somehow wrong—lockers lined up with military precision, fluorescent lights buzzing faintly overhead, and that faint, greasy smell of cafeteria food. It was a snapshot of high school life, distorted and off-key.

"Welcome back," I muttered under my breath to no one, the words bitter and sour as they left my mouth.

But back to *what?* That was the question. A past that didn't belong to me, a present that didn't make sense, and a future I wasn't sure I'd ever get to see again. The thought sat heavy on my mind as I walked, each step dragging like I was moving through quicksand. I didn't belong here—not in this hallway, not in this year, not in this life. Every step felt like walking through a stranger's dream, the edges blurry and wrong, the air too thick to breathe.

But there wasn't anywhere else to go. So I kept walking.

. . .

As I DRIFTED down the hall toward the cafeteria, the run-in with Dr. Mercer stuck to me like the smell of something burnt—stubborn and impossible to ignore. Seeing him there, in that polyester suit, left this gnawing feeling in the back of my head, like finding a crack in a windshield. You know it's there. You know it's going to get worse. But you can't stop looking at it.

Stepping into the cafeteria was like walking into another world. The noise hit first—voices tumbling over each other, trays clattering, bursts of laughter cutting through the chaos. High school kids doing their thing, carefree in a way I could barely remember how to mimic. They tossed fries and cracked jokes like nothing in the world could touch them. For them, maybe nothing could. For me? I was watching through a one-way mirror, close enough to see the cracks in their world but too far to feel the warmth of it. Normalcy was a mirage, shimmering just out of reach.

Then I saw him.

He stood by the vending machines, perfectly at ease, like the whole cafeteria existed just to frame him. His blonde hair caught the light in a way that seemed accidental, and his grin was the kind that pulled you in whether you wanted it to or not. Everything about him screamed untouchable, the kind of guy who didn't just own the room —he owned the world.

His green eyes sparkled like they had some kind of secret they weren't sharing, and he wore a light-washed denim jacket over a graphic tee, the sleeves casually pushed up to his elbows. His jeans were cuffed just enough to show off his white sneakers, so clean they could've been part of the cafeteria floor.

When he turned and caught me staring, his smile practically knocked the air out of my lungs. It was wide, easy, and confident, like he already knew I'd been looking and didn't mind one bit.

"Hey!" he called out, strolling over like he owned the place. "You new 'round here? Did I miss the memo?"

It took me a second to remember how to use words. "Yeah," I said, my voice a little too quiet. "Just moved here from... DC."

He raised his eyebrows, his smirk widening. "DC? Fancy. What, they run out of monuments for you to hang around?"

That pulled a chuckle out of me, small but real. "Something like that."

"Well, welcome to LA, the land of smog, celebrities, and overpriced tacos," he said, gesturing around like he was giving me a personal tour of his kingdom. "I'm Max, your official guide to surviving Reagan High."

"Carter," I said automatically. Just saying my name out loud felt strange, like it belonged to someone else. But Max's whole vibe had this weird magnetism, like he could pull you into his orbit whether you were willing or otherwise.

"Carter from DC," he repeated, nodding like he was filing it away for later. "Nice. So, what's the verdict? LA too weird for you yet, or are we growing on you?"

I shrugged, glancing at the organized chaos around us. "It's different."

Max laughed, clapping a hand on my shoulder like we were already best friends. "Oh, man, different doesn't even cover it. I moved here last year from this tiny town in Washington. Piedmont. And when I say tiny, I mean blink-and-you'll-miss-it kind of tiny. Doubt you ever heard of it."

"Piedmont," I repeated, rolling the name over in my head. "Nah. Doesn't ring a bell."

"Exactly," he said, grinning like it was the funniest thing. "We had one stoplight. One. You could see the whole town in about ten minutes, which is about five more minutes than it deserved."

I chuckled despite myself. "Sounds… cozy?"

"That's a generous word for it," he said, shaking his head. "Coming here? It was like landing on another planet. I mean, Piedmont didn't even have a decent mall, let alone traffic jams or enough kids to fill this cafeteria." He gestured around at the chaos. "But hey, I figured it out. And you will too. LA's weird, but it's a good weird. Trust me."

Good weird. I wasn't sure I believed that, but the way Max said it, so casual and sure, made me want to try.

"So," he said, nodding toward the crowd. "Meet anyone else worth talking to?"

I hesitated, shoving my hands into my pockets. "Just… Dr. Mercer."

Max stopped in his tracks, then let out a laugh so loud it turned a few heads. "Oh, man, you started with Dr. Mercer? Bold move."

"What's his deal?" I asked, trying to sound casual, though my pulse quickened at the thought of it.

Max leaned in, dropping his voice like he was about to tell me a secret. "Word on the street is he's into some serious science stuff. Like quantum physics, way past what they're teaching us in class. Rumor has it his PhD dissertation was on messing with time."

My heart skipped. "Messing with time?" I echoed, my voice steady, but my mind spinning like a top.

"Yeah," he said, shrugging like it was no big deal. "Apparently. He's some kind of genius. Always off in his own world, working on stuff nobody understands. Kind of a mad scientist vibe, you know? Not sure if he's actually cracked the code or just wants to fry his brain trying."

I forced a laugh, but inside, my thoughts were racing. *Time. Quantum physics.* This version of Dr. Mercer wasn't just some younger, less cranky version of the guy I knew. He was playing around with what I needed to understand. What could get me home. Maybe this was more than coincidence. Maybe he could help.

Max nudged me with his elbow, breaking me out of my thoughts. "Hey, don't overthink it. The guy's harmless. Quirky, but harmless."

"Right," I said, my voice distant, already chasing the possibility. "Quirky but harmless." My chest tightened as the idea latched onto me, refusing to let go. If Dr. Mercer knew something about time—if he really was messing with it—then maybe there was a way out of this. A way back to my life. Back to Mom.

"Anyway," Max said, flashing that easy smile again, "if you want the real tour, stick with me. I'll show you all the secret spots. You know, where the cool kids hang."

I couldn't help but laugh at that. "Cool kids like you?"

"Exactly," he said, giving me a mock-serious look. "Just try to keep up, Carter from DC."

For the first time in hours, the tension on my chest eased; just a little. Max's easy grin and effortless confidence felt like a lifeline, pulling me out of the quicksand of my own thoughts. He made it seem like maybe—just maybe—I wasn't as alone as I felt.

CHAPTER 19

We grabbed our food and sat down, Max sliding his tray across the table with this casual confidence. My mind, though, was a million miles away. Max started talking about the school's football team, who to avoid, and the usual survival guide for a new kid. I nodded along, but my brain kept drifting—back to Dr. Mercer. It still didn't make sense, but somehow, pieces of it almost did, and that was… a lot.

Max, mid-sandwich bite, glanced around the room like he was scoping out potential recruits for some secret club. "Alright," he said, pointing his sandwich at me like it was an accessory. "First impression —what's the vibe? Miss home yet, or are you too dazzled by the fine educational establishment before you?"

I blinked, trying to focus. "Uh, yeah. I mean… it's complicated," I said, my voice catching as the thought of Virginia—and Mom— yanked at my chest like a hook I couldn't pull out.

Max raised an eyebrow, setting his sandwich down. "Complicated, huh? That's the go-to move for when things suck but you don't want to say they suck."

"Okay, fine. They suck," I muttered, leaning back. "You happy?"

He smirked, leaning in like he'd cracked the code to the universe. "Only if you are, my man. But hey, new places are a lot to handle. Trust me, I get it. When I first moved here, I couldn't tell the cafeteria fries from the mystery meat. Don't ask me how or why they taste the same. Pro tip: you don't want to know."

I huffed a laugh despite myself. "Thanks for the heads-up. I was just about to dive in."

Max waved a hand, like he was granting me clemency. "You'll figure it out. And when you do, you'll be running this place in no time. If not, I can show you the ropes. I'm basically an expert at making people think I know what I'm doing."

His confidence was almost contagious, pulling me into his orbit, but the heaviness in my chest stayed put, stubborn and unmoving. For now, I could fake it.

"Good to know," I said, poking at the limp fries on my tray. "I could use an expert."

He grinned like I'd just validated his entire worldview. "Alright, lesson one: avoid the math club like your social life depends on it."

"What, like mathletes or something?" I asked, raising an eyebrow.

"No, like a black hole that sucks up any chance you have of being cool," Max said, deadly serious. "One meeting with those guys, and BOOM—you're wearing suspenders ironically and debating the Fibonacci sequence for fun. Trust me, I've seen it happen."

I stared at him for a beat, then snorted, unable to hold back the laugh. "Fibonacci sequence? Really?"

"Dude, they're into prime numbers." He leaned in like he was sharing classified intel. "Once they get their hooks in you, it's game over. But don't worry—I got your back. Stick with me, and you'll survive."

His laugh was the kind that made everything else fade out for a second, like static clearing on a radio. Comfortable. Familiar. I found myself leaning into it, the chaos of the cafeteria melting away just a little. For a moment, I wasn't entirely drowning.

"I've got a stupid question," I said, trying to sound casual, "but what's today?"

Max tilted his head, giving me a skeptical look. "You mean, like, today-today? Or are we talking existential 'what is time' stuff? Because if it's the second one, I'm gonna need more fries."

"The date," I said, smirking. "Let's keep it simple."

"October 14th," he said with a shrug. "Why?"

I hesitated, fiddling with a fry to keep my hands busy. "Just trying to remember if I had something to do. What's the full date?"

Max stared at me like I'd just asked for the secret to world peace. "Okay, you're being weird, but whatever. October 14th, 1985. That clear things up for you?"

1985. The number rang in my ears like a note played on an out-of-tune piano. My stomach churned, and the room tilted slightly, the intensity of it all pressing down until I thought my lungs might give out. *Keep it together, Carter. Just keep it together.* "Yeah. '85. Guess it just slipped my mind. You know how it is—sometimes the years just blur together." *Right. Because that's totally how kids in the 80s talked.*

Max squinted at me, amused but clearly not buying it. "Blur together? Dude, you're talking like you're a hundred years old. Don't tell me you're one of those 'wise beyond your years' types. Please say no."

I shrugged, leaning into the absurdity. "Maybe I'm from the future. It's all chrome and jetpacks. Big upgrade, let me tell you."

Max laughed, loud and easy, drawing a few more glances from nearby tables. "Jetpacks? Alright, Marty McFly, let me know when the DeLorean's parked outside."

I grinned. "You'll be the first to know."

"But for real," Max leaned back in his chair, his smile widening like he'd just landed the punchline to a joke only he knew. Everything about him was loose, easy—like life bent around him instead of the other way around. "If you're really from the future. That jacket? Total dead giveaway. You're lucky this isn't a fashion police zone. What, were you expecting it to snow or something?"

I glanced at my coat, still streaked with mud from my encounter with Nat and Dr. Mercer. "Guess I missed the memo on what's *in* this year."

"You missed more than that," he said, shaking his head. "But hey, I'll let it slide. You're new. You get a free pass. This time. That hair though? Total surfer vibe. I dig it."

He leaned in again, his tone softening. "But seriously, dude— what's going on with you? You seem kinda spacey."

I shrugged, deflecting. "Just some stuff with my folks. It's... nothing major."

Max's expression shifted, more serious now. "Yeah, I get that. Parents, man. Always a trip. What's the deal? They on your case already?"

I hesitated. Telling the truth wasn't an option. "They're not here yet. Things are... complicated, I guess. They're late getting to town."

Max nodded slowly, taking it in. "So you're just stuck waiting? That's rough, dude. Hate to see it."

"Pretty much," I said, keeping my tone vague.

He watched me for a beat, then shrugged, his smirk returning like a light switch. "Hey, if you're stuck waiting, my place has room. No strings, no judgment. Just a roof and some pizza. Sometimes you just need a place to breathe, you know? And my dad's cool. Long as you don't mind my little brother Justin nerding out about Batman for, like, hours."

I blinked, caught off guard. "Really? That'd be... incredible." The words felt heavy on my tongue, like I was taking something I didn't deserve. "Are you sure? I mean, I don't want to..." My words trailed off, but Max just grinned, steady and unshaken, like he already knew I needed this more than I could admit.

"Dude, I wouldn't say it if I didn't mean it," he said, waving me off. "Consider it your official welcome-to-town package. Plus, it's a good excuse to make you pay for dinner every now and then."

I let out a breath I didn't realize I was holding. "Hell yeah, that's totally fine. Seriously, thanks a lot, man."

"Anytime," he said, leaning back with his trademark smile. "Besides, now you owe me a hoverboard ride when you get that thing out of the shop."

I chuckled, the tension loosening just a little. "Yeah, I'll see what I can do."

But even as we laughed, the shadow in the back of my mind remained, heavy and sharp. Mom. Every second I spent here was another second I'd never get back with her. The universe felt like it was watching, amused, waiting to see if I'd crack under the stress.

At least there was Max—a friend, a place to land, proof that even in chaos, there are anchors strong enough to hold you steady. He was like a rope thrown into a storm, giving me something solid to cling to when everything else felt like it was slipping away. It wasn't enough to quiet the ticking clock in my chest, but for now, it was enough to keep me moving.

MAX HAD DRIVEN me home after school, his red Corvette rumbling low like it had a personality of its own. He parked haphazardly in the driveway, tossing me a smirk as he hopped out. "Alright, man. Welcome to Casa de Max. Don't judge the decor; we're working on it."

He bounded up the front steps, throwing the door open like he owned the place. Which, in a way, he probably did.

As I stepped inside, it felt like cracking open a novel halfway through—lived-in, chaotic, and full of stories I didn't know yet. The faint smell of motor oil mingled with the warmth of something freshly baked, and the clutter was less a mess and more a map of the lives lived here.

The first thing that hit me was how small it was—smaller than the houses I was used to. But there was a strength to it, a kind of resilience in the worn siding and cracked driveway, like it had been through too much to give up now. Max didn't pause to let me process.

"Dad!" he called out, his voice echoing through the narrow hallway. "You home?"

"In the kitchen!" came a voice, rough and steady.

Max turned to me, his grin still intact but softer now, like he was bracing for something. "Alright, just… follow my lead, okay?"

I nodded, trying not to look as nervous as I felt. Max led me down the hall to the kitchen, where his dad stood at the counter, wiping grease off his hands with a rag. He was taller than I expected, his frame solid and lined with the kind of wear that comes from working long days. His uniform shirt had a patch that read "Dave," and there was a quiet steadiness in his movements, like he didn't need to prove anything to anyone.

Max didn't waste time. "Hey, Dad. So, this is Carter. He's… staying with us for a bit."

Dave's eyes flicked to me, sharp but not unkind. He didn't say anything right away, just sized me up like he was trying to figure out if I was trouble. Eternity stretched before he spoke.

"Alright," he said finally, his tone more matter-of-fact than anything. "You got clothes? Stuff you need?"

I froze. I hadn't thought this far ahead. All I had were the clothes on my back—90s jeans, that flannel shirt Nat made me buy, and chucks that I guess were as "timeless" as I felt. The silence stretched, and my stomach twisted.

Max stepped in without missing a beat. "He's got everything he needs," he said, his voice firm. "Anything he doesn't have, I've got covered."

Dave's gaze shifted to Max, his expression unreadable for a moment. Then he nodded, his focus returning to me. "Great. You're on dish duty tonight," he said simply. "Dinner's at six."

And just like that, the conversation was over. No third degree, no lectures about rules. Dave had assessed the situation, and apparently, I passed whatever silent test he'd given me.

"Thanks," I managed to mumble.

"Don't thank me yet," Dave said, giving Max a pointed look. "You break it, you fix it. Got it?"

"Yeah, yeah," Max said, waving him off. "We'll keep it all in one piece. Come on, Carter. Let me show you the lair."

He led me upstairs, the hallway narrow and lined with pictures. Family photos, mostly—Max and his older brothers, a younger kid I assumed was Justin, a woman with a warm smile who had to be his mom. But there was one that caught me off guard: Max with a girl who looked just like him but with red hair, her arm slung around his shoulder like *she* owned the world.

"That's Becca," Max said, his voice dropping like the weight of her name was too much to hold. His fingers brushed the edge of the frame, barely touching it, as if the glass might shatter under the heaviness of his memories. "My sister. She, uh… passed a few years ago. You'd have liked her."

I stopped walking, unsure of what to say. "I'm sorry," I said finally, the words feeling too small.

Max shrugged, his grin flickering back into place like a shield. "It happens. Everyone had their reasons for leaving Piedmont. Ours just… happened to be a little more colorful."

I raised an eyebrow. "Colorful?"

"Yeah, well," Max said, scratching the back of his neck. "Mom passed away first. Lung cancer. She smoked like a chimney, and it caught up with her. Becca though? She was the glue. After Mom, she kept us… steady. But then she…" His voice caught, his gaze falling to the floor like he could still see the cracks she left behind. "It's a long story. Not exactly a *first day* conversation."

I nodded, letting the subject drop. He didn't owe me the details.

"Anyway," Max said, his voice picking up again. "My older brothers took off for college, and Dad decided it was time to downsize. Piedmont was just… too big, for how small it was, you know? Too many memories, too much space. So, here we are. Welcome to the glamorous life of *Max Carleton*."

He opened a door at the end of the hall, revealing his room. It was a kaleidoscope of chaos—band posters layered the walls like a collage of rebellion, their edges curling from the heat of summers past. Clothes hung off the back of a chair in mismatched layers, and the bed sat rumpled in the corner, its sheets tangled like a storm had passed through. The air smelled faintly of guitar strings and old fabric softener, and a stack of VHS tapes leaned precariously next to a boxy TV.

"You're welcome to crash in here," Max said, gesturing to the room. "I can set up the couch downstairs if you want, but honestly, Justin hogs the TV, so good luck with that."

"It's fine," I said, taking it all in. "This is… cool. Thanks."

"Don't mention it," Max said, flopping onto his bed. "Seriously. Don't mention it. If Justin hears you're impressed, he'll never let it go."

As if on cue, the door burst open, and Justin bounded in, his energy filling the room like a firework. "Who's this guy?" he demanded, pointing at me.

"This guy," Max said, gesturing dramatically, "is Carter. He's staying with us for a while, so try not to scare him off."

Justin beamed, his eyes narrowing like he'd just been given a challenge. "I'm not scary. Am I scary?"

I smirked. "Terrifying."

Justin puffed out his chest like he was some kind of superhero. "Good. I'll keep you on your toes."

Max rolled his eyes, shoving Justin lightly toward the door. "Alright, that's enough. Go back to whatever cartoon you're obsessing over."

Justin stuck his tongue out at Max before retreating, his laughter echoing down the hall.

Max glanced at me, his smile softening. "Sorry about him. He's, like, 90% energy and 10% chaos."

"It's fine," I said, leaning against the wall. "He seems… happy."

Max's expression flickered, something unspoken passing behind his eyes. "Yeah. He is. And that's what matters."

I didn't push. Whatever weight Max was carrying, he clearly wasn't ready to unload it. And that was fine. For now, it was enough that he'd opened his home to me, given me a place to land. And maybe, for the first time in a long time, I didn't feel completely alone.

CHAPTER 20

DAYS BLED INTO WEEKS, then a month, the kind of endless loop you only notice when you're trapped inside it. 1985 clung to me like a second skin—sticky with Aqua Net, the squeak of vinyl seats, and neon lights that felt too bright, too fake, humming a synth soundtrack I couldn't escape. The whole year smelled like someone trying too hard to forget something, and I was starting to understand why.

There was no grand plan, no map scrawled in some back corner of my mind. Sure, there was Dr. Mercer. But the way his eyes fixated on me in the future left me... worried. So it was just me, me and whatever patience I had left—which, if we're being honest, was already on life support. The mysterious voicemails from the future? Gone. The cryptic warnings that had been chasing me through time? Silent. For all I knew, Mom could already be gone.

And the worst part? I couldn't stop thinking about it. Telling myself not to dwell on it was like sticking a "Don't Touch" sign on a big, red button. My brain just pushed harder. *What if she didn't remember me anymore? What if she was waiting, alone, counting seconds I wasn't there for?* It was this gnawing ache, a quiet, endless scream I couldn't tune out, no matter how hard I tried. The colors here were too sharp, the sounds too loud, and every single person around me seemed fine. Like this was normal. Like *I* was normal. I wasn't.

The only thing keeping me even remotely grounded was Max.

Max was the kind of person who didn't knock before barging into your life, all careless grins and easy laughter. He had this way of filling a room, like a heater that didn't work right but still managed to keep the cold at bay. It wasn't just that he made things suck less—it was how he did it, effortlessly, like he didn't even notice the nightmare he was pulling me out of.

To him, I was just the weird new kid from D.C.—a walking question mark with a shadow always hanging over him. And somehow, Max didn't care. Actually, he might've even liked it. I mean, who looks at a guy like me and goes, "Yeah, let's be friends"? Apparently, Max.

He made 1985 tolerable, which wasn't nothing. He'd drag me through this neon wasteland, introducing me to his friends—a group of loud, chaotic misfits who seemed permanently on the verge of setting something on fire. They were fine, I guess. Fun, even. But Max? Max was different.

With him, things felt less fake. Like maybe I wasn't as lost as I thought. Like the ground beneath me might hold, even if everything else was falling apart. We'd spend hours just talking—or, well, he'd talk. I'd listen, throwing in the occasional sarcastic comment to keep up the illusion that I wasn't constantly on the edge of spiraling. Max made the ache in my chest feel lighter, but it never fully went away. Not really.

Because no matter how much I tried to let this place feel real, there was always that ache. That constant, crushing reminder that I didn't belong. Every day I spent here felt like another day stolen from her. From us. I wanted to be home.

At night, the quiet wrapped around me like a weighted blanket, heavy and suffocating. I'd lie there on my makeshift bed of pillows and scratchy blankets, staring at the ceiling as the dark turned up the volume on every fear, every regret, until it was deafening. The kind of quiet that didn't just fill a room—it climbed inside you and stayed there.

When I was alone, I'd stare at the cracked screen of my phone, trying to count the days I'd lost, how long I'd really been gone. If I'd had a birthday, or if being reset in October negated that fact all together. But still, I'd wonder how Mom was doing. Was she getting worse? Did she even remember me?

The thought of her slipping away—of her forgetting me before I could make it back—wasn't just a fear. It was a slow drowning, the kind where you're kicking for the surface, but the light you see at the top is already disappearing, leaving you clawing at nothing but dark water and panic. Every second I stayed here was a second I'd never get back. A second closer to her light going out.

And then there was Nat and Ethan.

In this version of 1985, they were just kids. Probably running around some playground, their biggest worries being scraped knees and whose turn it was on the swings. Not the 18-year-olds I'd known back in the future, not the people I'd grown close to. They were these distant, younger versions of themselves, versions I'd never meet. Thinking about them like that—so far out of reach—made the distance feel even bigger. Memories slipping through my fingers, one at a time.

If they saw me now, they wouldn't recognize me. I wasn't their Carter anymore. I was just some guy. A stranger haunting a timeline that didn't belong to me, chasing ghosts of people I didn't even exist to yet.

And I didn't know how to stop any of it.

Ms. Thode's math class was in full swing, the usual chatter filling the scene 'til the announcement crackled over the PA, sharp and staticky, stopping us in our tracks like a teacher flicking the lights to get our attention. "Carter Sullivan, please report to the front office. Carter Sullivan to the front office."

A knot twisted in my stomach, tight and immediate. Being called to the office was never good. Even if you hadn't done anything wrong, it was like being summoned to a firing squad.

Max leaned over from the desk next to me, whispering just loud enough to get a glare from Ms. Thode. "Ooooh. What'd you do? Steal the principal's lunch?"

"I wish," I muttered, grabbing my bag. "Probably just my turn to get sent to the gulag."

Max grinned, his voice lowering as I stood. "Hey, don't leave me out of the rebellion. I'm coming."

I rolled my eyes but didn't stop him. I figured Max tagging along wasn't exactly going to make things worse.

The walk to the office felt longer than it should have, the echo of our footsteps bouncing off the tiled floor in that weird way schools had—like they were built to make you feel small. Max kept pace beside me, hands in his pockets, humming some half-recognizable tune under his breath. Probably his way of filling the silence.

When we reached the front office, the woman behind the desk looked up from her notepad, adjusting her glasses. Her smile was polite but thin, like she was used to dealing with kids who didn't want to be there.

"You must be Carter," she said, her voice light but not particularly warm. She glanced at Max and raised an eyebrow. "And you?"

"I'm Max," he said, flashing his signature smirk. "Moral support. I'm basically his life coach."

The woman didn't seem impressed, but she didn't kick him out, either. Instead, she gestured for us to sit in the chairs across from her desk. I sank into one, feeling the hard plastic dig into my back. Max slouched beside me, his legs sprawled out like he was about to give a press conference.

"So," the woman began, folding her hands neatly on the desk. "I wanted to let you know we received a call from David Carleton this morning. He mentioned that your parents are currently unavailable and that he's stepping in as your guardian."

The word landed like a punch I hadn't braced for. *Guardian.* The word was heavy, final. Like a door slamming shut on something I hadn't realized was open. I sat there, frozen, my mind spinning.

Max, of course, jumped in. "Yeah, that's right," he said, his tone casual but firm, like this was no big deal. "Carter's with us now. My dad's got it covered."

The woman nodded, her expression softening slightly. "That's good to hear. I'll update our records, then. If you need anything—supplies, transportation, anything at all—just let us know, alright?"

I managed a small nod, my throat too tight to say anything. Max, however, had no such trouble.

"Cool. Thanks for letting us know," he said, standing up and tugging me to my feet. "Come on, Carter. We've got important lunch plans to discuss."

The woman opened her mouth to say something else, but Max didn't give her the chance. He pushed open the office door, guiding me out into the hallway with that easy confidence of his. Once we were clear, he shot me a sideways glance.

"You okay?" Max asked, his voice quieter now, his smirk slipping into something softer. He shifted his weight, one hand raking through his hair, like he was debating whether to say more or just let me fall apart in peace.

"Yeah," I said, though it came out flat. "That just… makes it real, I guess."

Max frowned slightly, like he wanted to say something but wasn't sure how. "Look, it's not a bad thing. My dad's solid. And, you know, you're not in this alone."

I stopped walking, leaning back against the wall and crossing my arms. "Yeah, I get that. It's just… weird. Like things are already being replaced."

Max didn't argue. He leaned against the wall next to me, his hands still shoved in his pockets. "Yeah. Change sucks," he said, his voice quieter now, like he was feeling it too. "But, you know, sometimes it doesn't have to suck forever. You just gotta wait it out. Let it shift into something… less shitty. And I guess this means you're stuck with me now, and I'm pretty decent to be around."

That pulled a weak laugh out of me, which seemed to satisfy him. He clapped me on the shoulder, steering me toward the cafeteria like nothing had happened.

But as we walked, the woman's words hung in the back of my mind. *Guardian.* It shouldn't have felt like a big deal, but it did. I mean, fuck. I'd practically been homeless in the 90s. But this felt like my life was being patched together with other people's pieces, and no one had asked me if that was what I wanted. It seems the universe wasn't going to give me a choice.

Lunch passed in a blur of noise and motion, but I couldn't shake the thought. And later that night, when the house had gone quiet and the world outside seemed to stretch on forever, I slipped out the back door, searching for air I could actually breathe.

IT WAS LATE, the kind of late that stretched too long, where the silence wasn't just quiet—it was alive, watching, waiting. I was sitting outside the house, staring at the rows of identical homes lined up like teeth, their dark windows watching me back. The lawns were too perfect, unnatural, as though they'd been painted on.

I didn't even know why I'd stepped out. But Max's house wasn't where I needed to be—not tonight. The streetlights cast long shadows on the pavement, and for a second, I thought about going back in. Maybe Max would still be awake, or maybe he noticed I wasn't in my usual spot on the floor. Maybe he'd say something dumb and comforting in that easy way he always did. But my eyes stayed on the street ahead, frozen, debating whether it was finally time to visit Dr. Mercer's office.

Then my phone buzzed.

I flinched like it had burned me, the sound cutting through the quiet like a slap. I grabbed it without thinking, my breath catching when I saw the notification. Finally, a voicemail.

From Mom.

I stared at the screen, my thumb hovering over the play button, every nerve in my body screaming at me to expect the worst. Not to play the message. But I did. Of course, I did.

Her voice crackled through the speaker, faint and warped, like it was clawing through static, desperate to reach me but falling short. Each word felt like a knife dragging across my ribs, sharp and hollow. My chest tightened, the ache blooming like a bruise I couldn't touch. The words were a jumbled mess, slipping in and out of coherence, each one cutting sharper than the last. She didn't say my name. She didn't even sound like her. Just this hollow echo of someone I used to know. Like she didn't know who she was reaching for—or why.

I didn't cry. I just sat there, staring at nothing, letting the words sink into my chest like stones dragging me under.

My fingers moved on their own, scrolling through my phone for an out, for anything to distract me from the heavy silence that followed. A screenshotted meme. An old text. Whatever. Anything. But then it buzzed again.

Another voicemail.

This one from James.

I didn't want to. I didn't. But before I could stop myself, I hit play.

His voice broke through the speakers, clear and familiar in a way that hit like a sucker punch. "Carter," he said, like he was testing out the name to see if it still fit. "I don't know if you hate me. Hell, I understand if you do. But I need you to know something. About why I left."

I froze, my heart hammering so loud it drowned out the next few words. My thumb hovered over the pause button, but I didn't tap it. I couldn't.

"Your mom…" He stopped, his voice cracking. "She isn't the same. She's slipping, and I didn't know if I could handle it. I *couldn't* handle it. I thought—" Another pause, longer this time. "I thought it'd be easier if we just... weren't there. Easier for me. For you."

The night air felt too heavy, like I was sinking into the porch and the world was closing in around me. My grip on the phone tightened, the edges digging into my palm.

"I know that doesn't make it right," James continued, his voice quieter now, almost like he didn't want me to hear. "I know I should've gone with you. But I didn't. And I'm sorry, Carter. I'm so sorry."

The message ended with a click, leaving me alone with the sound of my own breathing and the hum of the streetlights outside. *I couldn't handle it.* Well, neither could I. But at least I tried, and I still am. What was his excuse?

"Cool," I muttered, my voice cracking as I stared at the screen. "Thanks for nothing, Dad. Really clears it all up." My hand tightened around the phone, the metal edges biting into my palm, but I didn't let go. I wanted to throw it, smash it, scream at it—but I couldn't. I wouldn't. I just sat there, letting the words claw at the edges of my mind, sharp and relentless.

I tossed the phone onto the cement beside me, my chest tight and my head swimming. Outside, the rows of houses stayed dark, quiet, like they hadn't been listening. But I was. And now, I couldn't unhear it.

I knew I couldn't let any of it show. I had to keep a game face on. Keep moving forward, even as everything kept piling on. Survival mode was all I had left—just one foot in front of the other, stumbling through this twisted, time-warped circus where the days blurred together like bad reruns. Nothing felt real, but I couldn't stop moving. I didn't know how to do anything else.

CHAPTER 21

IT DIDN'T TAKE LONG for the whispers to start, for the looks to shift. Teachers didn't say anything outright—no cloying "I heard what happened, Sweetie," or thinly veiled "I'm so sorry you're going through this." But there was a softness to the way they spoke to me, like I was glass and they didn't want to be the ones to break me. I wasn't sure which was worse: the pity they were trying to hide or the fact that I felt like I needed it.

They didn't look at me differently—not exactly—but they had this way of pausing just a little longer when I answered questions in class, like they were waiting for something else, some sign that I wanted help. Like maybe I'd crack open and spill everything right there on their carefully color-coordinated desk. I wouldn't. I couldn't. But the way their eyes lingered made it clear they already knew something was missing.

That's how it was with everyone lately. Not outright sympathy, but this subtle rearranging of how they treated me, as if I'd quietly shifted into some other category of student: not quite orphan, but close enough that they didn't know how to handle me.

One afternoon during my free period, I wandered the halls, dragging my sneakers against the tile like I could scuff my way out of my own head. The world felt too quiet, too still. I should've been heading to Dr. Mercer's lab to deal with the science-fiction hellscape that had taken over my life. But that felt like staring into the sun—necessary, sure, but almost guaranteed to fry me. Instead, I wandered.

I turned a corner and ran smack into Ms. Amory, my English teacher, who was walking down the hall like she'd just stepped out of a Crayola box. Her hot pink sweater clashed spectacularly with lime green earrings, and her teal bangles jingled softly with every step, like she was some kind of walking fireworks display in a building full of shadows. She didn't belong here—too bright, too alive—and I couldn't decide if that made me like her more or less.

"Carter!" she said brightly, flashing me a grin that felt almost too genuine for this building. "Roaming the halls, are we? Dangerous territory for a free spirit like you."

I shrugged, leaning against the wall. "Just trying to figure out how much aimless wandering it takes to wear down the floor."

Her laugh came light and easy. "Well, I'd say you've got your work cut out for you. This tile's older than both of us combined."

I smirked. "That's comforting. Love to know I'm walking on ancient ruins."

Her laugh was light and unbothered, like she genuinely appreciated the banter. "You've got a quick wit, you know that? Makes you stand out." Her eyes narrowed slightly, in that not-unfriendly way teachers sometimes look at you when they're trying to crack your code. "So tell me, are you out here because you're deep in thought, or are you avoiding something?"

I hesitated, the truth sitting heavy on my chest. "Can it be both? Like, multitasking?"

She raised an eyebrow but didn't push. "Fair enough. But let me ask you something, Carter. Is avoiding it working?"

"I mean…" I trailed off, scratching the back of my neck. "It's not *not* working."

That earned a soft chuckle, and she folded her arms, her bangles jingling again. "Life has a funny way of not letting us off the hook, you know. Whatever you're carrying, it's going to follow you around until you face it."

Her words landed a little too close to home, and I shifted uncomfortably. "Yeah, well, maybe I just need a break from being followed."

Her expression softened, and she stepped closer, dropping her voice. "You know, Carter, a little birdie told me about the Carletons stepping in for you. That you're going through a lot right now. I just wanted you to know—it's okay not to have all the answers."

The words hit harder than I expected, like she'd cracked open a part of me I was trying to seal shut. I swallowed hard, forcing a small smile. "Thanks, Ms. Amory. I appreciate it. Actually, I'm… heading to see Dr. Mercer. Got some… stuff I need to talk to him about."

Her expression softened into something gentler, and she nodded, crossing her arms in a way that made her bangles jingle again. "Ah, Harry. Dr. Mercer. Brilliant mind. He's got quite the reputation, doesn't he? Even teaches at UCLA on the side. Always talking about time this, time that. He makes it sound so straightforward, like we're all just riding a neat little train track."

I blinked at her. "Huh. That's… not exactly how I'd describe him."

"Oh, don't get me wrong," she said quickly, her tone lighter again. "He's sharp as a tack. But sometimes I think he gets a little too caught up in the mechanics of things. The gears, the levers." She tilted her head, her expression thoughtful. "What about you, Carter? What do you think about time?"

The question caught me off guard, and I shrugged automatically. "I mean, I try not to think about it too much. It's, uh… stressful. Like, existential-crisis-level stressful."

She chuckled, giving me an understanding look. "That's fair. Time can feel a little overwhelming when you get too close to it. All those possibilities, all those could-haves and should-haves. But you know what I think?"

I leaned against the wall again, crossing my arms. "Hit me."

"Time's not a train track," she said, her voice soft but steady. "It's not some rigid, one-way line. It's more like a river—twisting, turning, carving its own path. Sometimes calm, sometimes wild, but always moving, no matter how much we try to hold it back."

I raised an eyebrow, intrigued despite myself. "Okay, so what's the trick, then? Not drowning?"

Her smile widened, and she leaned in slightly, like she was sharing a secret. "The trick is learning to float. Trust the current, Carter. You're exactly where you're meant to be right now. Even if it doesn't feel like it."

I snorted, shaking my head. "Yeah, I'm not so good at the whole 'letting go' thing. Floating sounds like a good way to get swept over a waterfall."

Her laugh was warm, and she reached out to pat my shoulder. "It's not about letting go entirely," she said, her voice quiet but steady. "It's about knowing when to hold on and when to drift. I've had to learn that myself, Carter—it's not easy. But you've got instincts. Trust them, even when the water feels too deep. The sharpest minds can try all they want, but no one can steer every twist and turn. *That's* the beauty of it."

Her words sank in deeper than I wanted them to, like she'd cracked open a door I didn't even realize I was guarding. *Letting go. Drifting. Trusting myself.* I wasn't sure I was built for that, but the way she said it, like it was simple, like it was possible—it stuck with me.

"That's... a lot," I admitted, trying to keep it light. "You sure you don't moonlight as a motivational speaker?"

Her smile returned, bright and teasing. "Only for students who look like they could use it. And Carter? You look like you could use it."

"Gee, thanks," I said, rolling my eyes but smiling despite myself.

She gave my shoulder a squeeze before stepping back. "Alright, then. Off to Dr. Mercer with you. Don't let him intimidate you too much. He's all gears and math, but you've got heart. Don't underestimate the difference that makes. See you next period?"

"Uh, yeah. See you next period, Ms. Amory."

I watched her walk off, her neon colors fading down the hall like some kind of reverse rainbow. Her words stayed, though, echoing in the quiet as I stood there. *Trust the current. Float.* The words didn't erase the knot in my stomach, but they lingered, a small, steady pulse against the chaos in my head. Maybe it was enough to get me through this. Or maybe it wasn't. Either way, I didn't have a choice.

Taking a deep breath, I pushed off the wall and headed for Dr. Mercer's door. My hand hovered over the wood for a second before I knocked, the sound sharp and deliberate under the fluorescent hum of the hallway.

"Come in," called a familiar voice from the other side, younger and smoother than the version I'd known.

Here goes nothing.

I PUSHED THE DOOR OPEN, stepping into the lab like I was walking into someone else's memory. The air hit me first—a sharp mix of chalk dust, cleaning solution, and that faint, metallic tang that always clings to places built on science experiments and teenage panic. It was familiar in a way that felt wrong, like hearing a song you don't remember learning the words to.

The room looked exactly like every 80s physics lab you've ever seen in a movie. Rows of wooden desks scarred by generations of doodles and bad ideas. A massive chalkboard at the front, crammed with equations that may as well have been hieroglyphics for all the sense they made. Shelves sagged with dusty beakers and textbooks that looked like they'd survived a nuclear apocalypse. On the desk at the front, papers were scattered like fallen leaves, covered in neat rows of numbers and diagrams I was probably too dumb to understand.

And then there was him.

Dr. Mercer was hunched over the desk, a pencil moving in precise, deliberate strokes. He didn't look up at me at first, which gave me too much time to look at *him*. He had this messy look, like he'd just rolled out of bed and decided to make it a fashion statement. Dark curls that refused to stay put, wire-rimmed glasses perched slightly askew, and a blazer that somehow managed to look both casual and important. His shirt was unbuttoned just enough to say, *I work hard, but I'm also fun at parties,* and there was a faint smirk tugging at the corner of his mouth, like he knew something I didn't and couldn't wait to rub it in.

When he finally acknowledged me, he straightened, tilting his head like he was trying to place me. His dark eyes sparkled with curiosity and just a hint of mischief, the kind of look that makes you feel both fascinating and deeply judged. I could practically hear his thoughts: *Who the hell is this kid, and why does he look like he wandered out of detention?*

"Well," he said, his voice low and smooth, like he was narrating a documentary about my bad decisions. "You're not one of my students. At least... I don't think you are. Unless I've been exceptionally distracted."

I blinked, thrown off by how much he sounded like he'd just walked off a stage. "Uh, nope," I said, shaking my head. "Not a student. Definitely not."

His smirk widened. *Great start. A+ for me.* "Then what brings you here? Lost? Curious? Or just looking for a friendly face in this cold, chaotic universe?"

I shifted on my feet, suddenly hyperaware of how out of place I felt. "Uh. Sorry, Dr. Mercer. My name's Carter. We met. Outside the school. I'm, uh... new." The words tumbled out awkwardly, and I hated how small they sounded in the space between us. "And I need your help."

There it was. Out in the open. And boy, did it feel stupid.

"You can call me Harry," he said, offering a hand. The name felt disarming, almost too casual for someone surrounded by equations scrawled across the walls like a mad scientist's playground. His smirk faded into something more thoughtful as he set his pencil down, leaning against the desk like he was getting ready to hear my confession. "Help, you say," he mused, tapping his fingers lightly on the desk. "Intriguing. And what, exactly, is it that you think I can help you with?"

I hesitated, glancing around the room like the answer might be hiding somewhere in the mess of papers and gadgets. *This was a mistake. I shouldn't have come here. Why did I think this guy could help me?* My eyes caught on the chalkboard, its surface crammed with loops and lines that looked less like math and more like someone's attempt to summon a demon. "You study time, right? Time travel?"

His expression didn't change, but there was a flicker of something in his eyes—curiosity, maybe. Or amusement. "Ah, time travel," he said, drawing out the words like he was savoring them. "The ultimate forbidden fruit. Dangerous. Ambitious. Entirely theoretical. Unless, of course, it isn't." He tilted his head slightly, his smirk creeping back. "Let's say I do. Why exactly do you need my help?"

"Because," I said, forcing myself to meet his gaze even though my chest felt like it was caving in, "I think I'm stuck here. In time. And I don't know how to get back."

CHAPTER 22

THE LAB'S silence pressed down on me, heavy and unrelenting, as if the room itself was daring me to keep going. The air felt thin, brittle, and ready to shatter. Dr. Mercer—Harry—leaned back, his gaze sharp and dissecting, like a scalpel peeling away my defenses until I felt raw, exposed.

"Go on," he said, his voice too smooth, too practiced. "You're stuck in time, you said. Enlighten me. Try to keep the dramatics to a minimum."

I opened my mouth, then closed it again, words clumping together in my throat like they'd all decided to give up on me at once. My chest felt tight, each second dragging like lead. The air in the lab was suffocating, thick with unspoken judgments. *If he didn't believe me, if this went sideways, what then? What was left for me?* But it wasn't like I had a better plan. I shifted on my feet, my pulse hammering so loud I was pretty sure he could hear it.

"I'm not from here," I said, the words dragging out of me like they'd been trapped for too long. "Not from now." My voice cracked, the syllables fragile, like they might break before they fully formed.

His eyebrows lifted just slightly, the corner of his mouth twitching in what might've been a smirk. "Oh, well, that clears things up. You're not from this time." He gestured with one hand, his tone dripping with that charming, condescending flair that made me want to both listen and throw something at him. "I suppose this is the part where you tell me you're a time traveler on some noble mission to save the world?"

I frowned, my jaw tightening. "Yeah, no. That'd be way cooler than this train wreck."

His smirk deepened, but there was curiosity flickering behind it now. "Alright. I'll bite. When, precisely, are you from?"

I hesitated, the truth catching in my throat like a splinter. Then I swallowed hard and let it out. "2014."

His head tilted slightly, his eyebrows rising as a slow, disbelieving smile spread across his face. "2014," he repeated, the word rolling off his tongue like he was testing its weight. "That's bold. I like it. A solid twenty-nine years from now. You've really committed to the bit."

"It's not a bit," I said, my voice cracking a little despite myself. "I'm not joking, okay? I'm… from the future."

For a moment, he didn't say anything, just stared at me with that maddening, unreadable smirk. Then he leaned forward off the desk, crossing his arms as he shook his head. "You really expect me to believe that?"

Panic curled sharp and unforgiving in my chest, every breath catching on its thorns. If I couldn't convince him, everything—every fragile thread holding me together—would snap.

"Look," I said quickly, my voice pitching higher, "I know how it sounds. But I can prove it. I… I brought something."

I reached into my pocket, my fingers shaky as they wrapped around my phone, the only piece of home I had left. I pulled it out, the phone cold as ice in my hand. The cracked screen splintered the fluorescent light into shards that danced across the ceiling. Our warped reflections stared back at me, broken and incomplete, as if the phone was mirroring the fractures running through my life.

Harry's eyes gleamed, the amusement bleeding out as something darker took its place. He moved closer, his voice soft, almost reverent. "And this is… what?"

"It's a phone," I said, gripping it tighter like it might slip away. "From the future. *My* phone."

He tilted his head, his lips quirking back into a skeptical grin. "A phone. Right. Because nothing says 'time traveler' quite like an upgraded mirror."

I turned it on, the screen lighting up with a clean, white glow. The Apple logo reflected in his glasses, and his expression finally cracked —just a little. His smirk faltered, replaced by something closer to intrigue.

I unlocked it, the apps and icons glowing back at us like tiny lifelines. "I'm telling the truth," I said, my voice shaking. "It's called a smartphone. In 2014, we use these for… everything. Talking. Pictures. Music. The internet."

He blinked, the word catching his attention like I'd dropped a bomb in the middle of the room. "Internet?" he repeated, leaning in closer, his tone equal parts curious and skeptical. "That sounds… ambitious."

"It's real," I said quickly, flipping to the camera and angling the phone so he could see the lab through the screen in real time. "Look. It works. This is real."

He stared at the screen, his skepticism dissolving into something quieter, more thoughtful. Slowly, he reached out, his fingers hovering just over the device like he wasn't sure if he was allowed to touch it. "This," he murmured, his voice soft, almost reverent. "This is… incredible."

My stomach churned as my eyes flicked to the battery icon—39%. My charger was still in the Highlander, stuck somewhere in the future. The number stared back at me, stark and unyielding, a countdown to losing everything. My grip tightened, knuckles aching, as if holding on harder could stop the inevitable. *Without this, I'll lose everything. My only proof. My last link home.*

Harry's eyes flicked to mine, his calm cracking into something sharper. "If this is real," he said, his voice quieter now, "if you're telling the truth—"

"I am," I interrupted, desperate. "But it's dying. The battery won't last, and if it dies…" My throat closed around the words, too heavy to finish.

The bell shattered the stillness, a sharp, jarring sound that ripped through the tension like glass breaking. I jumped, clutching the phone to my chest as the noise from the hallway seeped in, loud and chaotic.

Harry stood, his movements suddenly brisk, purposeful. "Alright," he said, his voice low but urgent. "We'll table the time crisis for now. Come back. At the end of the day. And bring that."

I nodded, backing toward the door, my thoughts spinning too fast to grab hold of any of them. "Yeah. I'll be back. I promise."

The hallway swallowed me whole, its fluorescent lights buzzing too loud, the retort of lockers slamming and the hum of voices echoing in my ears. My mind stayed tangled in the lab's sterile light, Harry's words looping like a broken record: *"This changes everything."* My chest felt tight, like I'd shown him more than just a phone. I'd just trusted Dr. Mercer—_the_ Dr. Mercer—to help me figure this out. But as I glanced down at the phone, watching the battery tick down to 38%, I realized one thing for sure: I didn't have much time left.

MY FEET MOVED on autopilot towards the library, the cold glow of the overhead lights cutting through the static in my head. The air smelled faintly of dust and floor polish, sharp and sterile, the kind of cleanliness that didn't feel clean at all. It wasn't a refuge—it was just another holding pattern, another place to wait while the clock kept ticking.

Ms. Amory had declared today an "independent study," which was teacher-speak for *'keep yourselves busy while I drown under a sea of essays.'* She'd handed out some vague prompt about symbolism in *The Wizard of Oz* before vanishing into the back room, leaving us to sink or swim.

I followed Max and his crew to a corner table, hoping to fade into the background.

A girl named Jessica claimed the head of the table like a general surveying her troops, her notebook open and her stack of books arranged with military precision. Her pen moved in deliberate, controlled strokes, each one carving order into the chaos around her. She was tall, with long braids tied back with a black scrunchie, and dressed the part of someone who wasn't here to mess around. She wore black leggings, an oversized black sweater with the sleeves pushed up, and a chunky silver bracelet that caught the light whenever she gestured. She had the kind of intensity that made you feel like she was silently judging you for not being as prepared as she was—probably because she was.

"Independent study," Jessica muttered under her breath, her pen flying across the page. "What a waste of time."

Beside her was Josh, sprawled across his chair like gravity barely applied to him, his long legs stretched under the table in a way that made everyone else shift to avoid them. His green windbreaker hung off his wiry frame, the faded Van Halen logo across his chest cracking like it had lived a hundred lives before landing on him. His straight, dark hair flopped forward in a way that constantly made him swipe it back with a flick of his hand, and he was one of those guys who never sat still, always fidgeting, always talking, like he was scared silence might kill him. Right now, he was trying to rope Tyler into a debate about the upcoming Winter Formal theme, *How Will I Snow*, but Tyler wasn't biting.

Tyler sat hunched over his *Spider-Man* comic, his freckles blending into the pale flush of his skin. His mop of red hair stuck up in stubborn directions, like it couldn't decide where it belonged, much like him. His sneakers looked brand new, their crisp white soles at odds with the worn edges of his striped button-up.

As for Max, he was perched on the table's edge. There was something about him—steady, magnetic—that pulled you in without asking if you wanted to be anchored. He made it look effortless, like he belonged wherever he decided to land. His Members Only jacket sat over a plain white T-shirt, his jeans cuffed just above his sneakers. His blond hair was slicked back just enough to look effortless, and he had that thing about him—like he could walk into any room and own it without breaking a sweat.

I dropped into a chair, slouched low, and opened my textbook. Not that I was reading it. The words swam on the page, my brain refusing to focus. The phone was pressing against my thigh like a stone in my shoe, irritating me, reminding me of its presence every second, as if I could forget it was there. It wasn't just a device—it was my anchor, the only thing keeping me from floating away completely.

But each percentage it lost felt like another cord snapping, leaving me adrift in a place that didn't want me.

The table's voices blurred together, a low hum that barely touched me. It wasn't that I didn't care—I wanted to—but the world felt distant. I was trapped behind a pane of glass looking out, with no door, no key, and no plan. On top of it all, I felt like I'd aged years in a matter of days.

Everyone's voices were muted, their laughter cutting through the haze like static, sharp and grating against the hollow quiet in my chest.

Across the library, a group of girls clustered near the windows, their laughter floating over the buzz of quiet voices. One of them, a girl with a perfect ponytail and a smile so polished it practically shined, glanced my way. She caught my eye and smiled wider, tilting her head like she was waiting for me to do something about it.

Jessica noticed immediately. She didn't miss much. "So, are you gonna do something about that," she asked, not looking up from her notebook, "or just sit there like you don't see it?"

I shrugged, keeping my voice flat. "Not my type."

Josh swiveled in his seat, his long legs tangling awkwardly under the table as he glanced at the girl. "Not your type? Dude, that's a *cheerleader*. That's, like, *everyone's* type."

"Yeah, who even are you?" Tyler said without looking up, his tone light but cutting. "Maybe *Max* is more your style."

The table froze for half a beat, then Josh burst into laughter. Jessica smirked and went back to her notebook. Tyler barely reacted, his nose still buried in his comic, but Max raised an eyebrow, his grin turning sharp and amused.

"Well, Carter," Max leaned closer, his fingers drumming lightly on the table's edge. "If I'm your type, just say so. I'll clear my schedule."

My throat tightened, the words catching for half a beat too long. "Oh, totally," I smirked. "This is it. The moment everything's been building toward."

Max's grin grew, and he leaned back on his hands, the picture of mock-seriousness. "I knew it. All that mystery, all that brooding—it was for me. I feel *so* special."

Jessica didn't bother looking up. "Unbelievable," she said, the smirk in her voice sharper than the one on her face as her pen scratched across the page.

"No, there's… someone else," I said, brushing the comment off. "At another school."

Jessica's head snapped up. "Wait. Are you serious?"

Josh's jaw dropped, and he leaned forward, the excitement radiating off him like static. "Whoa, hold up. You mean you've got a girl waiting for you back in DC?"

I hesitated, my stomach twisting. "Something like that."

Nat's crooked smile flickered in my mind, her voice loud and unapologetic, cutting through the quiet like sunlight through heavy clouds. Her laugh echoed in my head, bright and unfiltered, the kind of sound that carried summer in it no matter the season. But it faded too quickly, leaving only the sharp ache of something lost. *What if that was all she'd ever be now? A memory, unraveling thread by thread, slipping further from my grasp with every second I spent in this place?* My fingers brushed against the phone in my pocket.

Tyler snorted, finally glancing up from his comic. "That's what everyone says when they don't wanna admit they're single."

"It's true," I said, sharper than I meant to. I caught myself, taking a breath. "She's… different. Not like—" I gestured vaguely toward the cheerleader, who had gone back to laughing with her friends. "Not like that."

Max tilted his head, his smirk softening into something thoughtful. "Different, huh?" He nodded, like he was weighing the word. "Alright, I get it. A man of mystery. You're keeping your cards close to the chest. Classic move."

"It's not a move," I muttered, staring at the blank worksheet in front of me.

"Oh, it's a move," Max said, pointing at me like I'd just proved his theory. "And a good one, too. But let me tell you—being mysterious only works if you play it right. Too much, and you come off like you've got something to hide. The trick is *balance*."

"Balance," I echoed, raising an eyebrow. "Is that part of your foolproof method?"

"Exactly," Max said, his grin snapping back into full force. "*All* my methods are foolproof. It's not my fault fools keep screwing them up."

Jessica groaned, finally looking up from her work. "We're not doing this again. Max, just because you managed to flirt your way into free Slurpees *one time* doesn't make you a relationship expert."

"*That*, would be strategy," Max corrected, wagging a finger. "Totally different. But thank you for recognizing my genius."

"Please," Tyler muttered, flipping another page. "The only strategy you've got is showing up without a date for Formal. Again."

Josh's eyes lit up, and he snapped his fingers. "Oh, right! Jess, are you finally saying yes to Tyler this year, or are we going for the three-peat rejection?"

"Gag me." Jessica snorted, leaning back in her chair. "Sorry, Ty. Never happening."

"Oof," Tyler said, mock-cringing. "Thanks Josh. You were supposed to ask her when I *wasn't* around."

The laughter around the table blurred into white noise, each sharp burst grating against the heavy quiet in my chest. My fingers brushed the spine of my textbook, the worn cover rough under my thumb, grounding me in a moment I wasn't fully in. The conversation shifted, Josh and Tyler diving back into Formal logistics while Jessica returned to her notebook. Max stayed perched on the table, his foot tapping lightly against the edge, and every so often, I caught him glancing at me. It wasn't nosy or pushy—just... there. Like he was watching me without needing to say anything.

Max, his smile steady in a way that felt unfair, never asked for more than I could give, never pushed. But that steadiness only reminded me of how unstable everything else was. How fleeting it all felt. With him, I could just exist, no expectations, no judgment. But the comfort felt fragile, like I was letting myself drift too far from the reason I was here. Mom needed me, and every second I sat here was one less I might have with her.

The phone in my pocket felt heavier again, its battery ticking down in my mind like the countdown clock to something I couldn't escape. Time was slipping through my fingers, faster than I could hold it, but Max's easy smile and their chatter wrapped around me like a lifeline. For a moment, I let myself breathe, even though I knew better. Things like this didn't last. Not for people like me.

And no matter how much I wanted to hold on, I knew I couldn't let myself get attached.

THE REST of the school day dragged by, the hours smearing together like smudged ink. Every lecture felt like white noise, every assignment like some cosmic prank. None of it mattered—not the classes, not the bell schedule. My mind was stuck, circling the same relentless thought: *the phone's gonna die soon.* When the final bell rang, I had one destination: Harry's lab.

When I stepped inside, the room felt different. Quieter. Heavier. The fluorescent lights hummed faintly, their cold glow bleeding over the mess of papers and diagrams strewn across the desk, like relics from a mind unraveling. Harry was hunched over a sheet of paper, his pen scratching furiously as though solving a puzzle that might save the world—or just ruin it a little less.

He didn't look up at first, so I stood there, awkward and uncertain, the quiet stretching long enough for my nerves to start buzzing. Finally, I cleared my throat. "Uh... Harry?"

His head shot up, his glasses slipping slightly down his nose. He blinked at me, and for a second, it was like I'd pulled him out of some deep, theoretical void. "Ah, Carter," he said, his voice smooth and deliberate, like he was narrating his own life story. "Right on time." He straightened, adjusting his glasses and setting his pen aside with an elegant little flourish. "You have no idea how much I've been looking forward to this."

I raised an eyebrow, stepping further into the room. "Yeah? Well, lucky you. My schedule was wide open, so I thought I'd drop by for some light existential dread."

That earned me a soft chuckle, and he folded his arms, leaning casually against the edge of his desk. "Always with the sarcasm. I like that about you, Carter. Keeps things... interesting." He gestured toward the desk, where papers covered in equations spilled over onto the floor. "I've been theorizing about your predicament."

"Great," I said, sliding into the chair across from him. "Because I've been thinking about it too. And let me tell you—it's not getting any easier."

He nodded, his expression slipping into something more serious. "No, I imagine it isn't. Your story... well, it defies everything I know about the natural order. And believe me, Carter, I know quite a lot about the natural order." His gaze flicked to the phone in my pocket. "But that device of yours—that's the real wild card, isn't it?"

Reluctantly, I pulled the phone from my pocket, holding it up between us like it might bite him. "Yep. The future in my hand. Pretty great, huh?"

His eyes lit up as he reached for it, handling it like it was some ancient artifact instead of a cracked smartphone. "Remarkable," he murmured, turning it over in his hands. "This... this is extraordinary. A device this compact, with this level of sophistication... Carter, do you even realize what you've brought me?"

"Yeah," I said dryly. "A headache and probably some really weird questions."

He ignored me, his focus locked on the phone like it was whispering secrets. "The possibilities," he murmured, his fingers tracing the edges. "Imagine what we could achieve with technology like this. Communication, medicine, education—it's a revolution in your pocket." He tilted the phone, his grin widening as the cracked screen lit up. "And the interface... oh, it's so clean. So intuitive. And this... what did you call it? An app? What does this one do?"

"Yes, app for application. That's my music library," I said, leaning forward to grab it back. "Can we focus on—"

"Music!" he interrupted, holding the phone away from me like a kid who didn't want to give up a new toy. "A digital catalog, easily searchable and transportable. This would transform the way we store and share media." He laughed, his voice tinged with awe. "It's... well, it's brilliant. Groundbreaking, even."

I groaned, slumping back in the chair. I was losing my patience. "Look, I didn't come here to give a tech demo. I came because I need to figure out how to get back. My mom... she's sick, and I can't lose any more time."

His smirk faltered, the curiosity in his eyes dimming as his gaze flicked from the phone to me. "Your mother," he said softly, the words careful, almost hesitant, like he was testing their weight. The shift in his tone was jarring, a reminder that even he could find limits to his fascination.

"Yeah," I said, my throat tightening as the words spilled out. "Alzheimer's. I was on my way to see her when all this... whatever this is... happened. And now every second I'm stuck here is a second I can't get back. I... I might even already be too late."

The room went still, the hum of the fluorescent lights suddenly too loud. Harry exhaled slowly, setting the phone down on the desk between us. His fingers lingered on it for a moment before he pulled back. "I didn't realize," he said quietly, his voice losing some of its theatrical edge. "I'm... sorry, Carter."

"Yeah, well," I muttered, rubbing the back of my neck. "I appreciate it but sorry doesn't fix it. I just need to get home. That's all I care about."

He nodded, his expression serious as he straightened up. "Alright," he said, his voice measured. "Leave the phone with me tonight. Let me study it, test it. If there's any way to use it to get you back, I'll find it."

I hesitated. "And what if you can't?"

His lips quirked into a faint smile, one that didn't quite reach his eyes. "Carter," he said, his voice soft but charged with something electric. "I've built my life on solving the impossible. And this? This is the kind of problem that could rewrite everything."

My fingers tightened around the phone like a tether. Letting go felt impossible, like cutting the last thread that held me to everything I couldn't lose. But I couldn't do this alone. Slowly, I slid it across the desk. "Fine. Just... don't break it. It's all I have left."

"Come back tomorrow," Harry said, his gaze fixed on the phone like it held the answer to every question he'd never dared to ask. "We'll see what secrets this holds—together."

I nodded, standing up and shoving my hands back into my pockets. As I turned to leave, the tension in my chest loosened—just a little. For once, there might actually be a way out of this.

CHAPTER 23

THE ENGINE'S hum crawled under my skin, steady and unfeeling. Outside, the horizon blurred—a bleeding canvas of gold and pink streaks, too fragile to hold onto. The sky felt like a trick, soft and endless, but suffocating me all the same. Memories twisted there—Nat's laugh, Max's grin—scraping against each other until they blurred, too. *Was this survival?* Letting one ghost carve its name in my ribs, only to make room for another? Nat's laugh still felt raw, like a fresh cut, but Max's grin wasn't a bandage—it was a blade, too clean and sharp for me to hold onto.

I leaned back, my eyes following the shapes of trees and power lines flashing by, but my head was somewhere else. Harry's voice echoed in my ears—slick, calculated, full of big words about how my situation was "groundbreaking" and "revolutionary." But the reality of it all felt like a thread around my throat—tight, thin, impossible to break. If he was right, if he could help me... it sounded amazing. Dangerous, but amazing. His pitch though was something you'd expect from someone who wanted to be the star of their own sci-fi blockbuster, not a kind old scientist.

The truth was, I wasn't here for world-shaping or reality-bending. I just wanted to go back to my life, the life I'd left behind. Back to Mom, before everything crumbled away. Trusting Dr. Mercer felt like trying to hold onto a greased-up rope. But what choice did I have? My stomach twisted at the thought, that uneasy buzz humming in the background no matter how hard I tried to shake it.

The hum of the Corvette was steady, almost enough to drown out the noise in my head. Almost. I glanced around the car, my gaze landing on the fuzzy dice dangling from the rearview mirror. They swung gently with the movement of the car, catching the dim light. I hadn't noticed them before. Or maybe I just wasn't paying attention.

"Fuzzy dice?" I asked, brushing my fingers over their soft, worn surface. They swung lazily, unbothered by the cracks in the road or the tension in the air. For a second, I envied them—their weightlessness, their ability to just exist without care. "Really leaning into the retro aesthetic, huh? You think they're actually lucky, or are they just for the vibe?"

Max shot me a smile, all teeth and easy charm, keeping one hand on the wheel. "What can I say? I'm a sucker for tradition." He gave the dice a flick, watching them spin. "Besides, you've got to have a little faith in something, right? Even if it's two squishy cubes on a string."

"Faith in dice," I muttered, letting out a hollow chuckle. "That's... oddly inspiring."

"Right?" Max said, his smirk widening. "Honestly, I think they're just fun to look at. But hey, if they want to bring me some cosmic good fortune, I'm not about to complain."

"Maybe I could use some of that luck," I said, half-joking, though my voice cracked just enough to betray the tension coiling in my chest.

Max glanced over at me, then nudged the dice again so they swayed a little harder, back and forth. "Tell you what," Max said, his voice dipping lower, softer. "One day, when you're really up against it, they're yours. For emergencies. The kind you can't face alone."

I snorted, a real laugh breaking through the haze for half a second. "Because nothing says 'save the day' like fuzzy dice."

"Hey," Max said, wagging a finger, "don't underestimate the dice, man. They've seen some things."

I shook my head, the laugh fading as quickly as it came. Still, I let a small smile linger, watching the dice swing in the glow of the dashboard lights. Max didn't push. He never did. He had this way of just being there, this quiet kind of presence that didn't demand anything from me. And right now? That mattered more than I wanted to admit.

But even Max couldn't pull my mind away from Harry for long. The way he'd looked at my phone like it was the Holy Grail. The way his voice shifted when he talked about all the things he could do with it, all the people he could "help." That wasn't my problem. It wasn't supposed to be. I wasn't here to fix the world, or even tweak it. I just wanted to make it back to mine. And trusting him? It was like standing at the edge of a cliff, hoping the ground wouldn't give way.

The rumble of the Corvette softened as Max turned onto his street, the neat rows of houses coming into view. The neighborhood was too still, its perfection cutting like glass. Porch lights glowed faintly, casting halos over the bikes slumped in driveways like they'd been left mid-flight. It was the kind of quiet that screamed, *You don't belong here*, and the ache in my chest agreed.

Max pulled into his driveway, came to a smooth stop, and cut the engine, leaving a stillness that felt too loud. "Home sweet home," he said, throwing the car into park and flashing me a grin like this was just another Wednesday night.

I nodded, my hands resting in my lap. "Yep. Back to reality. Or... whatever version of it this is."

Max tilted his head, giving me a sidelong look. "You've got that face again," he said, leaning his elbow on the steering wheel. "You know, the *'I'm thinking about something way too hard and it's probably not good for me'* face."

I blinked at him, caught off guard. "I have a face for that?"

"Oh, definitely," Max said, nodding sagely. "I'd rate it a solid 8.5 on the existential crisis scale. Maybe a 9 if you're feeling extra broody."

"Wow," I said, deadpan. "Good to know I'm so predictable."

Max smiled, leaning back. "Hey, don't knock it. Brooding's a great look. You're cryptic. Thoughtful. Just, you know, don't overdo it. People start thinking you've got secrets. Then they start *asking* questions, and who has time for that?"

I smirked, shaking my head. "Thanks for the life advice, Dr. Cool."

"Anytime," Max said, tossing me a wink as he popped open his door. "I've got a whole bag of wisdom. Stick around, and I might just share more."

I rolled my eyes, but there was a warmth in my chest now, something solid to hold onto, even if it wouldn't last. Max climbed out of the car, and I followed, stepping into the brisk evening air. The neighborhood was quiet, the kind that felt too perfect, like the set of a horror waiting for someone to yell "action."

But my mind stayed on the phone I'd left with Harry. His words echoed in my ears. Trusting him felt wrong. But what other choice did I have?

Max glanced back at me as we headed toward the door. "You good?" he asked, his voice softer now, less playful.

I hesitated, then nodded. "Yeah. Just tired."

Max nodded, not pushing, not prying. Just there. The way he always seemed to be. And for now, that was enough.

INSIDE, the house felt worn in, like an old leather jacket that carried hundreds of stories. The scuffed floorboards and mismatched chairs weren't imperfections—they were proof of something solid, something that didn't fracture under pressure. It was so Max, effortless in its honesty, and I hated how much I wanted to claim it. Call it mine.

You could feel the echoes—laughter, quiet fights, meals that ran too long, and moments that didn't need words. It smelled like dinner: roasted something, buttery something, and just enough burnt edges to make it feel human. Max's little brother sprawled on the carpet, cartoons painting his face in flickering blue light. It was ordinary, painfully so, and that made it worse.

"Justin!" Dave called from the kitchen, his voice carrying that perfect blend of tired and kind. "Turn that off and come eat!"

"Just one more minute!" Justin yelled back, never taking his eyes off the TV.

"Now," Dave replied, his tone firm but not sharp, the kind of voice you didn't argue with twice.

Justin groaned like the weight of the world had just been dropped on his back. He dragged himself off the floor with all the drama of a kid who wanted everyone to know he was suffering, turned off the TV with one last, longing look, and stomped into the dining room. Not enough to start a fight—just enough to make sure everyone knew he *could* if he wanted to. For a second, I envied him—his small rebellions, his freedom to demand without consequence. He still believed the world would bend to his will, rather than take everything without a goodbye.

I followed Max to the table, the layout of the room coming into focus in little pieces: the worn edges of the dining table, the stack of mail leaning precariously on the counter, and the faint hum of the fridge, like it was working harder than it had to. The whole place was small, but it felt solid, rooted, like it wasn't going anywhere.

Dave came out of the kitchen carrying a steaming casserole dish, his hands wrapped in a towel. He had that grease-under-the-finger-nails look you only get from working hard, the lines on his face deep enough to say, *I've lived a lot, and I'm still standing.* He still had on his work shirt, and it matched the smell of engine grease that clung faintly to him. He set the dish on the table, glancing at Max like they shared some unspoken language.

"Alright, let's eat," he said, pulling out a chair and plopping down with the kind of tired sigh that made me think he'd been standing all day.

Dinner moved like clockwork—plates passing with quiet rhythm, laughter filling the spaces between bites. I sat at the edges of their world, watching like a ghost smashed against the glass. The smell of butter and salt curled in the air, too warm, too real. It made the ache sharper, carving out a hole I couldn't fill.

Dave told some story about a customer at the shop who insisted their car was haunted because it made a clanking noise when they turned left, and Justin giggled through a mouthful of mashed potatoes. Max, being Max, chimed in with just enough flair to turn the story into a ghost-hunting comedy special, but I mostly stayed quiet, picking at my plate.

Nobody seemed to mind. Dave asked me how school was going, in that casual, obligatory way that adults ask teenagers. I mumbled something vaguely positive, and he let it drop without pushing. For a moment, I let myself sink into their rhythm, listening to the jokes bounce around the table like ping-pong balls.

Then Justin suddenly perked up, looking at me with wide, curious eyes. "Hey, Carter, Max said you're from the future. Is that, like, for real? Do you have a time machine?"

Max grinned, leaning forward like he'd been waiting for this. "Nah, Justin. Carter's hoverboard broke down. That's why he's stuck here."

"Yup," I said, stabbing a piece of casserole with my fork. "It's in the shop. Real bummer. Can't get the parts in this decade, you know."

Justin's eyes narrowed, like he wasn't sure if I was serious or not. "Do they have robots in the future?"

"Oh yeah," I said, deadpan. The memory of Ethan made me crack a smirk. "I even had a robot butler once. His name was… Steve. Great guy. Couldn't cook to save his life, though."

Max snorted, shaking his head. "Carter's future sounds *way* cooler than life here. Dad, when are we gonna upgrade? Ya know, beef up the tech in this place."

Dave chuckled, shaking his head as he leaned back in his chair. "Max, I can barely afford your *car*. You want robots? You're gonna have to build 'em yourself."

"Challenge accepted," Max said, grinning as he leaned back like he'd just won the argument.

For a while, the conversation swirled around me, warm and effortless. Max's dad started telling a story about their old house in Piedmont, something about how Max's sister Rebecca used to boss everyone around when she was Justin's age. Max groaned dramatically, insisting he didn't need another lecture about "how things were." But there was a softness in his tone, a kind of familiarity that made it clear these stories weren't just stories—they were threads holding everything together.

I glanced around the table, taking it all in. Dave, tired but steady. Justin, still vibrating with kid energy even while eating. And Max, leaning back in his chair with that easy smile, joking around like he didn't have a care in the world. The way they moved around each other, the way their jokes overlapped like second nature—it wasn't just comfort. It was trust, something I hadn't realized I was starving for until now. The ache in my chest sharpened, tangled with a guilt I couldn't name. Wanting this felt like stealing.

This wasn't my family. It wasn't my home. But for a second, I wanted it to be. Like I'd stepped into a space where everything made sense, even if I didn't belong in it.

Max caught my eye, his face softening just slightly. "Hey," he said, his voice quieter than before. "The food alright?"

"Yeah," I muttered, the fork trembling faintly as I stabbed a piece of casserole. "Just… thinking."

"About your hoverboard?" Max grinned, leaning forward like he could pull me out of my head.

I forced a smirk. "Yeah. Thinking I might just leave it in the shop forever." The words came out flat, too heavy for the joke to land. Max's smile faltered, just for a second, but he didn't push.

"I mean, I'd be okay with that. But only if you promise to share the Delorean."

"Deal," I said, my chest tightening, though I wasn't sure why.

As dinner wound down, the ache settled deeper, but I pushed it aside. For now, it was enough to be here, in the warmth of this imperfect house, with these people who didn't seem to mind that I didn't quite fit. It was enough to laugh at Max's quips and pretend, just for a little while, that I wasn't running out of time.

AFTER DINNER, Max and I headed upstairs, the sound of his little brother still faintly yelling at cartoons from the living room below. Dave had ducked out not long after dinner, leaving the house quiet in that way that felt too big, like it was holding its breath. Max pushed the door open to his room, and we both fell into the usual routine, comfortable as slipping into an old hoodie.

My makeshift bed was waiting for me on the floor, a pile of pillows and blankets that had seen enough nights with me that they almost felt like mine. It wasn't much, but I didn't care. The spot was cozy, a little shielded from the rest of the world, and—most importantly—it felt safe. And that feeling was a rarity these days.

Max peeled off his shirt with the kind of lazy grace that made everything he did seem effortless, tossing it onto the chair without a second thought. He flopped onto the bed, arms behind his head, sprawling across it like gravity didn't apply to him.

It wasn't fair, the way he made the air between us hum with ease while my chest tightened, everything I couldn't say choking me harder with every breath. I looked at him and felt both anchored and adrift. Watching him was a reminder of what I wasn't—untouched, unburdened, whole. Life's struggles didn't seem to know his name, and part of me wanted to hate him for it. But I knew I couldn't. I never could.

"Ah, home sweet kingdom," he said, grinning at the ceiling. "You know, Carter, I really should charge rent. You're getting five-star floor service here."

I smirked, kneeling down to spread out my blanket. "Oh yeah, five stars for sure. The lumpy carpet really seals the deal. You should start an Air B&B."

"A what?"

"I mean a B&B," I quickly corrected.

He snorted. "I'd call it Max-imum Comfort. Book now, and we'll throw in a free breakfast of Pop-Tarts and judgmental stares from my dad."

I shook my head, biting back a laugh as I focused on arranging the pillows. Max always made it seem easy, being this relaxed. Like the world's burdens had forgotten to land on his shoulders.

He shifted on the bed, the mattress creaking softly under him. "Long day, huh?" His voice was low, casual, like he was genuinely asking, not just filling the silence.

I hesitated, my throat suddenly tight. "Yeah," I said, keeping my voice light. "A real rollercoaster. You know, if the rollercoaster was on fire and designed by someone who hates fun."

Max chuckled, his smile audible. "Sounds about right. Honestly, I don't know how you do it. If I had half your stress, I'd probably just explode. Like, full-on cartoon fireworks."

"Not a bad way to go," I muttered, settling onto my makeshift bed and wrapping the blanket around myself. "At least it's quick. And festive."

He laughed again, softer this time, and the sound lingered in the room like the warm glow of the bedside lamp. I stared at the ceiling, trying to focus on the shadows the light cast across the walls. But my thoughts were loud tonight, louder than I wanted them to be.

There was something about the way Max had said it, something unspoken. The way he didn't press, didn't push, but left the door open, like he was waiting for me to step through when I was ready. It was easy with him—too easy. And that made it hard. *Dammit, Carter. Don't get attached!*

The quiet stretched between us, comfortable but heavy. Max shifted again, rolling onto his side to face me. "Hey, you've got this," he said, his voice soft, almost hesitant, like he wasn't sure I'd believe him. "Whatever's out there waiting for you—you'll handle it. You always do." His eyes met mine for a second too long, and I looked away, afraid of what he might see. "You're, like, secretly the toughest person I know."

I turned my head, raising an eyebrow. "Secretly, huh?"

"Well, yeah," he said, smirking. "You've got that whole brooding, mysterious thing going on. Makes people think you're all fragile and deep. But me? I see through it. You're basically a badass."

I rolled my eyes, though I couldn't stop the corner of my mouth from twitching upward. "Wow, thanks. I'll be sure to add that to my résumé."

"You should," he said, his grin widening. "It'd look great under 'special skills.' Right next to 'expert at avoiding cheerleaders.'"

I groaned, pulling the blanket over my head. "Please, I beg you. Let me die in peace."

"Not a chance," he said, leaning back against his pillow. "What kind of friend would I be if I didn't stick around to watch you squirm?"

The blanket muffled my laugh, and for a second, the tension in my chest loosened. Max had a way of doing that, of breaking through the mess in my head without even trying. I let the blanket drop, staring up at the ceiling again. The shadows looked different now, softer somehow.

"Thanks," I said quietly, the word slipping out before I could stop it.

"For what?" he asked, his tone casual but curious.

"For… letting me crash here," I said, my voice hesitant. "For not asking a million questions. For just… being cool."

He didn't say anything for a moment, and when he did, his voice was lighter, teasing again. "Well, *obviously*. I'm Max. Cool is, like, my whole brand."

I rolled onto my side, facing away from him. "You're unbearable, you know that?"

"Yup," he said, popping the "p." The mattress creaked as he shifted, and then his voice softened again. "Anytime, Carter. You know that, right?" The words should've felt light, tossed off like the jokes that came before, but they didn't. They stuck, settling in the spaces I'd been trying to keep empty.

I didn't answer, but my chest felt tight in a way that wasn't entirely bad. The room was filled with a comfortable silence, but my thoughts weren't quiet. Being this close to Max every night was a quiet kind of torture—the way his laugh settled into the silence, the way he filled the room without trying. It made the space between us feel fragile, electric. I couldn't name the longing it stirred, only that it scared me, made me want to pull closer and run all at once.

The sound of his soft breathing filled the room, and I couldn't help but wonder what he was thinking. There was something between us, something I wasn't ready to put into words yet, but I couldn't deny that it was there. I squeezed my eyes shut, willing the thoughts to disappear, but they only seemed to settle deeper into my chest.

Tomorrow, Harry would be waiting, and the world would tilt again. But tonight, lying inches from Max, his breathing steady and real, I held onto this fragile, fleeting moment like it was the only thing holding me to myself. I knew it wouldn't last. It never could. But for now, I let the thought of losing him sink into the shadows, hoping they'd hold it for me just a little longer.

THE MORNING LIGHT fractured across the Corvette's windows, slicing through the air like a scalpel, clean and merciless. The cracked window let in bursts of cool air, sharp against my skin, but it wasn't enough to calm the roiling mess in my chest. Outside, the streets blurred in a palette of gold and gray—too perfect, too alive—like the world was mocking the emptiness curling tighter inside me.

Max's hand grazed mine as he shifted gears, the touch feather-light but burning through the silence between us. I jerked away, the heat lingering like an echo I couldn't shake. My chest tightened as I stared harder at the road, as if willing it to swallow the ache. Attachments weren't just risky—they could be lethal.

I sank deeper into the seat, trying to disappear into the hum of the engine, but my thoughts coiled tighter with every mile. The sunlight was harsh, relentless, carving last night's moments into jagged edges that wouldn't dull. Nat's eyes flickered in my mind like static, blending into Max's, and for a second, I couldn't tell where one memory ended and the other began.

He made it too easy to forget, to breathe. But every time I let myself sink into that ease, the memory of Mom's face pulled me under again. Then Nat's face would flicker in my mind—her crooked smile, her laugh, the way she made me feel like I wasn't completely lost. But I knew she was already gone. And now, there was Max. Max, who'd let me crash at his place without asking a million questions. Max, who always seemed to know when to find the humor in life and when to just sit in the silence with me.

It was all starting to blur together—Nat, Max, this strange, fragmented timeline I was stuck in. And maybe that pull I felt toward Max was real, or maybe it was just me looking for an anchor in a world that didn't make sense anymore. Either way, it scared me. Because getting attached wasn't an option. Not to him, not to anyone. The more people I let in, the harder it'd be to leave when—or if—I ever made it back home.

I glanced at Max as he shifted gears again, one hand on the wheel, the other resting lazily on the shifter. He looked so relaxed, like this was just another day, another drive to school. The sunlight caught in his hair, making it look almost gold, and he had that easy smirk on his face, like the world existed purely to entertain him. He caught me looking and raised an eyebrow, the corners of his mouth twitching upward.

"What?" Max's voice cut through the noise in my head, warm and unbothered. "You're staring like I just solved world peace or something."

I blinked, snapping out of it. "Just thinking about how this car's *way* too nice for you."

He laughed, shifting gears smoothly as we turned into the school parking lot. "Too nice for me? This car *is* me. Sleek, fast, and always on point."

"Sure," I said, smirking. "That's one way to spin it."

We pulled into the school parking lot, the Corvette rumbling to a stop as Max threw it into park. I shoved my bag onto my shoulder, already bracing myself for the day ahead. My time here wasn't infinite. Mom. Saying goodbye to her was the only thing that mattered. That thought pushed everything else—Nat, Max, this whole tangled mess—into the background.

"Alright," Max said, leaning back in his seat and flashing me a grin. "Try not to get lost in there. You're new, but not *that* new."

I rolled my eyes as I opened the door. "Thanks for the pep talk, Coach. I'll try not to embarrass you."

"Too late," he shot back, his grin widening. "You've been embarrassing me since the moment we met. Just don't do anything I wouldn't do—which, I'll admit, isn't much."

I snorted, shaking my head as I stepped out of the car. "Later, Max."

The school buzzed like a hive, laughter and footsteps bleeding into a cacophony that clawed at my skull. It was a maze I didn't belong in, the walls closing in with every step. I forced my legs to move, but it felt like I was dragging myself through quicksand. Every step toward Harry's lab made my chest feel heavier, tighter. Nat's laugh, Mom's fading voice, Max's easy smile—they all tangled in my mind, pulling me in different directions until I couldn't tell where I was supposed to go. I wasn't sure I even wanted to find out.

My pulse quickened, and I shoved my hands deeper into my pockets, trying to keep from unraveling. Voices rose and fell around me, too loud, too bright, as I pushed through the crowd. Each step felt like wading against a tide pulling me further from myself. But before I got far, Max's voice called out behind me.

"Hey, where's the fire, Carter?" he ran up from behind me, leaning against the wall with his arms crossed. His expression was casual, but there was something curious in his eyes. "You sure you're okay? You look like you're on a mission or something."

I hesitated, glancing back at him. "I gotta see Harry—uh—Dr. Mercer," I called, trying to keep my tone light. "There's... some stuff he's helping me with."

"*Harry*, huh?" Max tilted his head, his smirk faltering for a second. "You've been seeing a lot of him lately. Didn't know you were on a first name basis." His voice was casual, but there was something else there—something that made my chest tighten.

I shrugged, my fists clenching. "Yeah, well, I'm full of surprises."

Max studied me for a second, like he was trying to piece something together. "Just... watch your back, alright?" Max's tone stayed light, but his eyes lingered on mine a moment too long. "Those science types... They always seem normal, right up until you're their next experiment."

I managed a laugh, the tension in my chest loosening just a little. "I'll keep that in mind."

"Good," Max said, his smirk returning full force. "And hey, if you need any advice on dealing with eccentric geniuses, I'm your guy."

I rolled my eyes, starting towards the lab again. "You're my guy for everything. Catch you later, Max."

"Don't forget to keep 'em guessing!" Max called after me, his voice light but careful. "And Carter?" He paused, the teasing edge in his tone softening. "Just… make sure you're still here tomorrow, okay?"

I raised a hand in mock salute but didn't look back. As I walked away, I could feel his gaze lingering, and for a second, I thought about turning around. But I didn't. I couldn't let myself get caught up in that pull—not now.

MY THOUGHTS CHURNED as I headed toward Harry's lab. Nat. Max. Mom. The lines were blurring, all of it pressing heavier on my shoulders. I forced myself to focus. There was no time for distractions. Not when the clock was already ticking.

By the time I reached his classroom, my steps had slowed. The door was cracked open just enough for me to hear the faint murmur of his voice inside. My stomach twisted as I stopped just short of the threshold, straining to catch the words.

Harry hunched over the school landline, his voice a low murmur that barely carried over the hum of the fluorescent lights. The words I caught— "preparing everything," "not too soon"—curled in the air like smoke, acrid and clinging. The lab felt off, colder than the rest of the school, with shadows stretching unnaturally across the cluttered tables. The fluorescent lights buzzed faintly, their flicker stuttering just enough to make my skin crawl. As the door creaked open, Harry glanced over his shoulder, his eyes narrowing before his expression shifted into something too cheerful to be real. Instantly, he hung up the phone with a *click*.

"Ah, Carter," he said. "Perfect timing."

I leaned against the doorframe, crossing my arms. "Who was that?"

He waved his hand like he was swatting at a fly. "Oh, just a…

minor detail. Nothing to trouble yourself with." He gave a thin smile, the kind that didn't reach his eyes, and turned toward one of the cluttered tables. Papers and books were scattered everywhere, a tornado of half-finished ideas. "We'll circle back to that later."

My stomach churned. *Circle back?* It was the conversational equivalent of shoving something under the rug. "Right," I muttered, stepping fully into the room. "So... what have you uncovered?"

Harry turned back to face me, his eyes gleaming with excitement again. "Before we get into the juicy details, I need you to tell me something. What's the last thing you remember before your first... temporal detour?"

I frowned, the question hitting me like a kick to the gut. "I mean, honestly? It was storming. I was driving home. It was late, sunset. The rain was terrible, and then—bam—I was in 1994." My hands made an awkward explosion gesture. "Not exactly a thrilling origin story."

He tilted his head, studying me like he was analyzing a particularly interesting bug under a microscope. "Just driving? No strange occurrences? Flickering lights? Radio static? Perhaps a swirling vortex of time-y wime-y... stuff?"

"Uh, no," I said, crossing my arms tighter. "It was just me, my car, and *ABBA*. Pretty mundane."

He started pacing, tapping his chin in that distracted genius way that screamed, *I'm having ideas that no one else will understand.* "Intriguing," he murmured. "And you felt no disruptions? No... sense of displacement until the moment it happened?"

I shook my head. "Not until it was too late. One second, I'm on the road; the next, I'm trying not to scream in public."

His pacing slowed, and he turned, his eyes gleaming. "Have you considered what might've caused it? Any theories of your own?"

The memory flared, sudden and electric—the phone slipping from my hand, the glass splintering like a scream. That glow. It wasn't just light—it was alive, twisting and writhing like it wanted to tear itself free from the moment. It burned into my vision, a searing orange that refused to fade, no matter how tightly I shut my eyes. I could still feel it now, flickering at the edges of my mind, like it was waiting for me to notice it again. It was the same glow I'd seen with Nat, the same one pulling me through time, and now it pulsed like a warning I couldn't ignore. *Was that when everything went wrong?*

I swallowed the truth, locking it behind my teeth. The way he looked at me, sharp and dissecting, made my muscles tighten. Like he was waiting for me to split open, to spill every secret he could twist into something useful. "Nope," I said, shrugging a little too hard. "I was kind of hoping you'd be the guy with the answers."

Harry gave a slow, knowing smile, like he was enjoying the challenge. "Ah, but answers are just more questions in disguise, aren't they? And I do love a good question." He turned back to his desk, grabbing a notebook and flipping through it with quick, practiced movements. "Let's consider some possibilities. Black holes, for instance. Theoretically, they could create massive distortions in space-time, bending reality in ways we can't fully comprehend."

"Black holes?" I repeated, still trying to shake the image of the orange glow from my mind. "I don't think I drove into a black hole, Harry."

He ignored my sarcasm, continuing eagerly. "Or..." He paused dramatically, looking over his shoulder. "Parallel universes."

I raised an eyebrow. "So what, I slipped into the multiverse and ended up with the Brat Pack?"

"Not quite," he said, chuckling softly. "But close. Imagine a fabric stretched too thin, tearing at the seams. You could have... fallen through, so to speak." He leaned against the desk, his hands gesturing wildly now. "Or—and this is my personal favorite—a temporal glitch. A hiccup in the space-time continuum."

"A glitch in the Matrix, huh?" I repeated, trying not to laugh.

Harry's brows furrowed. "Matrix?"

I rolled my eyes. *Too early, you idiot.* "Never mind."

Harry shook his head, clearly filing the comment away for later. "Regardless, it's either due to you, yourself having some... *super power*... which I find unlikely, or it's all due to your phone," Harry said, his voice a knife, cutting through the air. "You see, this object," Harry's voice dropped to a near whisper, "isn't just a device. It's a fracture—a tear in the fabric of time. It's pulling the past, present, and future together, twisting them into something fragile, something volatile. Do you realize what this means? You're holding the most dangerous object in existence, and you don't even know it." he paused, taking a deep breath. *"This device,* Carter," his eyes gleamed, feverish, as if he'd stumbled upon the divine, "is connecting it all. Advanced, powerful, damaged in ways we can't even fathom. It's not just from the future—it's a temporal anomaly in its own right."

The image of the orange glow flickered in my mind, and I felt a cold chill creep up my spine. *He confirmed it.* "So you really think the phone's to blame? That it's what caused all of this?" I asked, trying to sound skeptical instead of terrified.

"Not intentionally, no," he said, pacing again. "But it's likely a conduit, triggering temporal disruptions when used inappropriately. It's possible that its existence in the wrong time could have created a temporal disturbance—a ripple effect in the space-time continuum that drew you into it. It's possible that if it were somehow connected to your car, it transported you, along with everything inside of it, to another place in time."

My pulse quickened. *Could this really have been as stupid as me breaking it?*

"But that doesn't make sense," I said, shaking my head. "Everyone has iPhones in 2014. Unless you were an Android person—"

"There's Androids in the future? Cyborgs?" Harry interrupted, his eyes wide.

"...Not like you'd expect. But look, this phone isn't anything special. It wouldn't have caused a time warp just by existing in its correct time."

Harry's expression darkened, his eyes narrowing slightly. "Carter, it's not just about the phone being in the wrong time," his voice dropped to a near whisper. "It's about what the phone is doing to time itself. If you've jumped from the 90s to 1985, then time isn't just bending—it's breaking. You can't just freely jump around time without consequences. The Butterfly Effect. The Grandfather Paradox. For time not to collapse in on itself, you would have had to always exist in these points in history– with this phone. But every moment you're away, the cracks are spreading."

I stared at him, feeling my chest tighten. "What do you mean I… always existed…?"

He nodded, his gaze piercing. "In a sense, you've always been here, in each of these times, even if you never knew it. In old photographs. Old newspapers. Yearbooks. Otherwise, the timeline would've torn itself apart. That's why the phone matters—it's not about when it was made, it's about what happened to it. The moment it was damaged, that must've fractured something. And that's why you're here."

I felt a chill run through me. The thought hit me like a punch to the chest: I'd always been here, woven into history without my consent, without my knowledge. A ghost haunting a time I couldn't escape. It made my head spin, my stomach twist. I wasn't just losing Mom—I was losing myself, scattered in fragments across timelines I barely understood.

Harry straightened up, his eyes gleaming with the intensity of someone about to deliver groundbreaking news. "You and it are tethered somehow. What that means, I don't entirely understand yet. But I have my theories."

My pulse quickened, memories suddenly aligning in my mind as I rubbed the shard of glass still imbedded in my thumb. *I can't tell him about the piece still in me. If I do, he'll want to slice me open.* "There's… actually something else," I began, hesitant but feeling the pieces falling into place. "The first time it happened, when I was driving, right before everything went wrong… There was this woman. Colleen. I gave her a ride, and she used my phone to call her son. And then… while I was in '95, uh…" I hesitated. *He can't know. Not about who he'd become, nor who I was to him in the future.* "This… man… took it from me. Manipulated it somehow. And after that, I ended up here, in the '80s."

Harry froze, his eyes lighting up with renewed excitement. "That's it!" he exclaimed, his hands flying to his temples like he'd just had the epiphany of the century. "The calls. The usage. The phone *is* causing the fractures! Every call is a ripple in the timeline, anchoring you to each era."

"So… it's the programming? Maybe the hardware? What does that mean for me?" I asked, my stomach twisting.

"It means," he said, his tone both thrilled and grave, "you're chained to these times somehow. And unless we stabilize the connection, you're stuck riding the ripples. Have you tried bridging the connection to the future? Have you made any calls yourself?"

I stared at him, the realization settling in, then felt a pang as another thought crossed my mind. "I– I tried calling my mom," I said, my voice lower now. "Hoping it might pull me back. But it never works. It's like... everyone else has influence over where I am, except me. And every time I hear her voice—"

Harry's gaze sharpened. "You've *received* calls?"

"Yeah," I replied, feeling a chill. "They're... strange. Distorted. My mom has called, and sometimes my father too. But they're eerie— crackling with static, like they're traveling through miles of interference. When I try to call back, I can't."

Harry's eyes widened, his voice sharpening. "Carter, don't you see? These aren't just calls—they're signals, echoes breaking through to the timeline you're fused to. Every call she makes is a thread pulling you back, but the damage... it's severing the connection piece by fragile piece. The phone's damage may only allow incoming signals to you— and that interference you hear? It's likely a side effect of your unique position—caught between times. This would create a temporal barrier, preventing your active participation in your original timeline."

I sighed, his words settling over me. "So... stabilizing the connection. Til I do, I'm just... stuck?"

He placed a reassuring hand on his desk. "Precisely. I believe we can create a controlled signal—a sort of rope to pull you back to your correct time."

A flicker of hope rose in me. "You think that's possible?"

"It's more than possible," he said, a glint of determination in his eyes. "With enough data and further studies, Carter, I can help you get back."

A group of students suddenly burst into the room, their chatter shattering the moment. My stomach dropped, and I quickly grabbed the phone, shoving it into my pocket. Harry straightened, his expression calm again as he glanced at me.

"Come back after school," he said in a low voice. "We'll continue then."

I nodded, already backing toward the door. Harry's words clung to me like static, jagged and inescapable. *You and it are tethered.* The hallway stretched impossibly long, the walls rippling like reflections in broken glass. Voices around me bled together, sharp and distant, as if the world was cracking apart in slow motion. My legs felt heavy, each step dragging me deeper into something I couldn't name. The phone in my pocket was the only thing solid, its cold edges biting into my palm, anchoring me to this fractured moment. I gripped it tighter, a silent reminder that I wasn't just stuck in time—I was part of the fracture spreading through it.

CHAPTER 25

HARRY'S WORDS wormed their way inside me, a splinter under the skin. Every step out of his lab felt weightless and wrong, like walking on air that might collapse at any moment. My legs dragged, my breath caught, and the ground beneath me blurred into something I couldn't trust. My thoughts broke apart, looping on the same unbearable note, echoing *You've always been here... even if you never knew it.*

I waded through the day, struggling to stay afloat 'til the lunch bell rang. The cafeteria pulsed with life—laughter spilling like static, trays clattering like distant thunder. Too bright. Too loud. Everything was too much, and yet it didn't feel real. Max's laugh cut through it all, a single thread in a tangle of noise, but it wasn't enough to anchor me. The table felt miles away, their voices muted, like I was watching them from the other side of a one-way mirror.

He spotted me instantly, flashing one of his easy grins—the kind that said, *hey, no pressure here, you're safe.* It was like someone threw me a life raft in a storm. I slid into the seat next to him, letting out a long breath as I felt some of the tension in my shoulders finally start to ease.

Jessica hovered over her notebook like she could will the words to save her. The chains on her wrist caught the light, glinting like sparks in the dim, fluorescent haze. She didn't look up, didn't need to. Her presence hummed, sharp and untouchable, like static before a storm.

She was dressed in black as usual—a loose, oversized sweater tucked into a studded belt cinched around a long black skirt. Her dark eyeliner and deep red lipstick completed her goth aesthetic, a striking contrast to the colorful cafeteria around her.

Josh sat across from her, his lanky frame folding awkwardly into his chair. He was always way too tall for the table—and his skinny jeans and oversized striped sweater only made him look more like a scarecrow. His floppy dark hair fell into his eyes every time he leaned forward, which he did a lot because he could never seem to sit still. He was cracking a joke about zombies to Tyler, waving his hands for emphasis like the drama was necessary.

Tyler, meanwhile, had his head buried in another comic, his coppery-red hair catching the cafeteria's fluorescent light every time he moved. He had his polo shirt tucked neatly into faded jeans and sneakers that were just a little scuffed but still clean. His freckles were scattered across his nose, and when he finally glanced up, he gave one of those sheepish smiles that made him look younger than he was. Tyler always seemed to be a step out of sync with everyone else, but he owned it in a way that made his dorkiness kind of charming.

Max leaned into me just enough to remind me he was there, his smile like the edge of a knife—sharp enough to cut, steady enough to lean on. I didn't know why he kept pulling me out of the dark, or why I kept letting him. "Whoa. You look like you've been through it," Max said, leaning closer, his expression softening just enough to make me think he cared more than he let on. His shoulder brushed mine, and for a second, I almost told him everything. Almost.

"You have no idea," I muttered, running a hand through my hair. "Feels like my brain's been tossed into a blender, and someone forgot to hit stop."

Max snorted, leaning back with his trademark ease. He had that perfect California-cool thing going on, with his light-washed jeans, a white Henley shirt, and a letterman jacket slung over the back of his chair. His blonde hair looked like he'd just rolled out of bed, but somehow in a way that worked. "So, business as usual with Dr. Mercer, huh? The man's like a walking episode of *The Twilight Zone*."

"More like an unhinged version of *Bill Nye*," I said, grabbing a fry from my tray and jabbing it in the air for emphasis. "Except way less fun and with way more headaches."

"Who's Bill Nye? Friend of yours from back home?" Max asked, breaking his sandwich in half and handing me a piece. "Look, you survived, and that deserves a reward. Here. Food therapy. On the house."

I took the sandwich, trying not to notice how exhausted I always seemed to feel now. "Generous. Is this the part where you tell me I owe you forever?"

"Nah," Max said, grinning. "I'm building goodwill. Gotta keep my investments happy."

Before I could respond, someone approached the table. I looked up to see her—the cheerleader from the library. Her ponytail swayed like it had its own choreography, and she had this bright, practiced smile that could probably sell ice to a polar bear.

"You're Carter, right?" she asked, her voice lilting with just the right amount of confidence. "I'm Tiffany. We have English together."

"Uh, yeah," I said, already bracing myself for whatever was coming next.

Her smile hit me like a camera flash, blinding and cold. I hated how easily she stepped into my space, how her perfect, calculated confidence made my skin crawl. "Winter Formal, the... dance tomorrow?" She said, like the answer was already hers to claim. The words hung in the air, bright and polished, cutting through the static in my head. Her confidence felt out of place, almost obscene, like neon in a funeral home. I wanted to laugh, or maybe disappear.

My mind flashed to Nat—her messy, unfiltered laugh, the way her smile never felt fake. And then to Max, sitting right here next to me, his steady presence grounding me without him even trying. *No. Attachments.*

I opened my mouth, but the words evaporated before they made it out.

Max stepped in without missing a beat. "Carter would *love* to go with you," he said smoothly, his smirk so effortless it could've been rehearsed. "Right, Carter?" He smacked my back.

I blinked, heat flooding my face. "Uh, yeah. Sure."

Tiffany beamed, her victory practically lighting up the room. "Great! I'll... see you there, then!" She gave me a wink before spinning on her heel and strutting back to her table, where her cheerleader friends erupted into giggles.

Tyler glanced up from his comic, his expression as dry as ever. "You ever notice how cheerleaders always go for the guy who looks like he'd rather be anywhere else?"

Jessica rolled her eyes, setting her pen down. "Says the guy who's never been within five feet of a cheerleader."

"By choice," Tyler muttered, turning the page in his comic. "Gotta protect the brand."

Josh scoffed, pointing at him. "Yeah, sure. Lone comic book geek. Very *in* right now. Totally works for you."

Jessica ignored them, leaning over the table to nudge me. "See? It's about time you moved on, Carter. Can't stay hung up on that DC girl forever." She shot a glance at Max, her smirk sharp. "And we all know *Max* isn't taking you to the dance."

Max let out a laugh, brushing it off with his usual charm. "Hey, don't rule me out just yet, Jess. I'm a man of many surprises."

"Shocking," she said, her tone dripping with sarcasm, but she was smiling as she went back to her notebook.

Max turned back to me, swiping a fry from my tray and popping it in his mouth. "Alright, Carter. Big date. Big expectations. You're gonna need prep work. Lucky for you, I'm offering my services."

"Prep work?" I asked, raising an eyebrow. "What are you, my mentor now?"

"Absolutely," Max said, grinning. "*Step one:* dress sharp. *Step two:* don't trip over your own feet. *Step three:* keep just enough mystery to keep 'em hooked. *Foolproof.*"

"Here we go again with Max's 'foolproof method'," Jessica muttered, not looking up. "Otherwise known as a disaster waiting to happen."

Max smirked, unfazed. "Disaster? Please. I don't do disasters. *I'm* a miracle worker."

Josh laughed, shaking his head, and Tyler snorted something about "miracles being overrated." The conversation shifted back to their zombie-versus-alien debate, but I wasn't paying attention anymore. My thoughts drifted, circling back to Max.

I thought about everything he'd done—letting me crash at his place, lightening the mood when he could tell I needed it, never asking questions I wasn't ready to answer. With Max, it was too easy. He didn't ask for anything, didn't pry, just let me exist in the space he created. But the more I leaned into that quiet, the more I felt it—the way it filled something I didn't want to name, the way it made me need him in ways I shouldn't. And maybe that's what scared me—the way I was starting to need it, to need him, more than I wanted to admit. It was something I was getting used to, and it was valuable in a way that made me want to hold onto it, even if I shouldn't.

Max nudged me again, breaking me out of my thoughts. "Still with us, Carter? Or is this the part where you go all broody and poetic?"

"Maybe both," I said, smirking. "I'm versatile like that."

"Good to know," Max said, his face softening. "Versatility'll come in handy tomorrow night. Trust me."

The lunch table buzzed with jokes and easy laughter, their voices blending into a rhythm I didn't belong to. It felt warm, almost too warm, like stepping into a room with the heat turned up too high. I smiled when I was supposed to, nodded when it felt right, but the ache in my chest didn't fade. It never did. Still, for the first time all day, the storm in my head quieted. For a moment, it was enough—the laughter, the warmth, the illusion of normalcy. But I could already feel it slipping through my fingers, the storm creeping back in, the shadows waiting just outside the light.

The final bell rang, releasing its shrill decree over the school, and the hallways erupted into their usual chaos—a symphony of sneakers squeaking, locker doors slamming, and kids laughing way too loud about things I'd never find funny. I slipped out of my last class, clutching my books like they were some kind of shield, and let myself get pulled into the tide of students. My head was buzzing—part from the blur of the day, part from lunch with Max, and mostly from the tornado that was Harry and everything he'd said earlier.

As I drifted toward his lab, my mind wandered, running through half-formed plans and spirals of "what if" scenarios. I was so lost in thought I didn't hear the footsteps behind me until two hands clamped down on my shoulders.

"Gotcha!"

I jumped like I'd been hit with a jolt of electricity, my heart doing its best impression of a drum solo as I whipped around. Max's face greeted me, cheesing ear to ear, his laugh spilling out as he leaned back against a row of lockers.

"Geez, Max!" I snapped, clutching my chest. "What's your deal, man? Trying to send me to an early grave?"

He shrugged, his smile only widening as he crossed his arms. "Hey, I like to keep you on your toes. Keeps life interesting. Besides, if I don't scare the shit outta you, who else will?"

"Literally anyone else," I shot back, but the corner of my mouth betrayed me, twitching into a reluctant smirk. "You're a menace, you know that?"

"Yeah, yeah," he said, waving it off like it was the highest compliment. "A lovable menace, though. Admit it, Carter—you'd miss me."

I rolled my eyes but didn't bother denying it. He adjusted his backpack, slinging it over one shoulder like he'd practiced the move in a mirror. "So," he said, nodding toward the exit, "you ready to split or what? Day's not gonna get any better from here, and I've got a standing date with the couch."

"Almost," I said, the word slipping out before I could stop it. My eyes darted down the hall, toward Harry's lab. "I just... need to go see Dr. Mercer again. Won't take long."

Max's grin faltered for a split second, replaced by something more cautious. Concern, maybe? Suspicion? He tilted his head, his eyes narrowing slightly, but his tone stayed light. "Again? Man, you've been seeing that guy a lot lately. Something I should know about?"

"It's nothing like that," I said quickly, forcing a laugh that sounded too hollow. "I just... He's helping me out with something. Extra credit. Totally normal, non-weird student-teacher stuff."

Max didn't say anything right away, just held my gaze like he was trying to crack a code. Finally, he shrugged, the tension sliding off him as easily as his usual smirk slid back into place. "Alright, if you say so. Just don't let him rope you into one of his weird experiments or something. Next thing I know, you're gonna show up to lunch with a second head."

I smirked, relaxing a fraction. "Yeah, sure. I'll save the freakshow routine for next Halloween."

"Good call," he said, stepping back and adjusting his backpack again. "You've got five minutes," Max said, his hand lingering on my shoulder just long enough to unravel me. His smile didn't quite reach his eyes this time, and for a second, I thought he might ask the question I wasn't ready to answer. But he didn't. And I didn't stop him as he walked away, guilt twisting sharp and sour in my chest.

THE HALLWAY STRETCHED LONG and empty, the walls closing in with each step. The hum of voices and footsteps faded into nothing, replaced by the steady echo of my own shoes. It felt like walking into a void, a place where the edges of reality blurred. By the time I reached Harry's door, my chest was tight, and my pulse was too loud in my ears. My thoughts swirled, too fast to catch, but one thing was clear: *whatever else he had waiting for me, I wasn't sure I was ready to hear it.*

The door creaked open, a sound that sliced through the stale air like a warning. Inside, the room was a wreck—papers scattered across the floor like they'd been flung in a fit of rage, equations scribbled on the chalkboard so frantically they barely made sense. Harry stood in the middle of it all, adjusting his glasses with the calm precision of someone who didn't see the chaos he'd created.

He shrugged into his coat like he was getting ready to make a dramatic exit. When he looked up and saw me, his face lit up—not the warm, reassuring kind of smile, but the sharp, slightly unhinged grin of a guy who'd just solved a puzzle and couldn't wait to show it off.

"Carter!" he said, striding toward me with a burst of energy that made my heart skip. "You're *exactly* who I was hoping to see."

My stomach twisted as he locked the door, the click too loud in the suffocating silence. His smirk didn't reach his eyes, and for a moment, the room felt smaller, the walls closer. I gripped the phone in my pocket.

"Uh," I started, shifting awkwardly, "were you about to head out?"

"Not anymore," he replied smoothly, brushing off the question like it didn't matter. He adjusted his glasses with a quick, practiced flick of his hand, his movements loose but precise, like he'd done this a thousand times before. "In fact, your timing is impeccable. Truly. I mean, I could've waited another five minutes, but where's the fun in that?"

I blinked, already struggling to keep up. "What's going on?"

His smile widened, and he took a step closer, practically buzzing with energy. "Your phone, Carter. I need it. Just for a moment. Trust me, this is going to be... spectacular."

"Why?" I asked, my voice sharper than I meant it to be.

"It's all arranged," Harry said, his gaze sharp enough to cut glass. "A symposium, tonight, 7:30. A few of the brightest minds in physics, theorists who think outside the lines, who will understand the gravity of what you've brought me." He leaned in closer, his voice dipping into a conspiratorial whisper. "I didn't tell them everything, of course. Just enough to pique their interest. But when they see it, Carter, they'll know. They'll know we've unlocked the future."

The word symposium hit me like a punch to the gut. My breath caught, my chest tightening as the room seemed to tilt. This wasn't some abstract theory anymore; this was real, too real. A room full of strangers gawking at my phone, dissecting its secrets, maybe even ripping apart everything I was trying to hold together. "You told them?" I said, my voice cracking despite myself. "Harry, you don't know what this could do—what *they'll* do."

He waved off my concern like it was a fly buzzing around his head. "Specifics? No, no specifics yet. But once they see what we have— what you have—they'll understand. They'll see the possibilities, the brilliance of it all!" His voice rose slightly, his hands moving as if he were conducting an invisible orchestra. "You don't see it yet," he said, his voice low and almost reverent. "This isn't about you, Carter. This is about rewriting the rules of existence itself. You're just... a key."

His eyes didn't meet mine when he spoke, darting instead to the pocket where he knew I kept the phone like it was the only thing in the room that mattered. For a moment, I saw through the charm, through the carefully crafted words. This wasn't about helping me. This was about him. About his name in the headlines, his face on the cover of magazines. And if it came at my expense, well... that was just collateral damage.

I took a step back, the edges of the room blurring as his words spun in my head. "You can't do this," I said, my voice trembling but firm. "You don't understand what you're messing with. Changing time? Showing the world this phone? What about all the paradoxes? It's... it's not a good idea. It's a terrible idea!"

He stopped pacing, turning to face me with an expression that was somewhere between amused and exasperated. "Oh, Carter," he said, his tone dripping with a mix of charm and condescension. "You're thinking too small. Too... linear. But trust me, once you see the scope of this—once you understand what's possible—you'll see."

"I'm already regretting it," I muttered under my breath, my grip tightening on the phone.

He softened his voice, leaning toward me like he was trying to draw me into some grand conspiracy. "Carter," he said, almost whispering now, "imagine a life where you could go anywhere. Back to your mother, before she got sick. Back to your friends in the 90s, reliving every golden moment. Forward, backward, sideways—time as a playground, not a prison. No more missed chances. No more goodbyes. Think about what that could mean. For everyone. For *you.*"

For a second, his words hit me like a wave, pulling me under. The idea of seeing Mom again, of seeing Nat, of fixing everything I'd lost, made my heart ache in ways I couldn't describe. But beneath that hope was something darker—something sharp and possessive in the way he looked at me, at the phone. This wasn't the same Harry I'd trusted, not completely.

"So..." I said slowly, my voice carefully neutral. "You think we could control it? Just... go anywhere, any *time* we want?"

"Yes," he said, his smile spreading, his tone like honey laced with ambition. "But only if we work together. With this phone, Carter, we could make time ours to control. The symposium—these brilliant minds—they're all coming to help *you*. They'll help us to unlock its full potential."

His words should've sounded like salvation. They didn't. Something about the way he said "ours" felt more like "mine."

My fingers tightened around the phone, my pulse pounding in my ears. "This... feels like a trap," I said, my voice low, more to myself than to him. "How do I know I can trust you? That I'm not going to be carted off to some government lab?"

"Carter, this isn't just a discovery," Harry said, his voice sweet with the kind of reverence that made my skin crawl. "This is revolution! You think I'm doing this for a grant? For some fleeting applause from academics too blind to see the future? No. This is bigger than that. Bigger than you. Bigger than me. Together—we'll rewrite everything they think they know. I'm talking Nobel Prizes. No, even larger. I'm talking *immortality*, Carter! They'll remember my name for centuries. All because I've helped *you!*" He stepped closer, his voice soft but insistent. "This is our chance. Don't let fear hold you back. Together, we can shape history. We can *be* history!"

For a moment, I hesitated, his words pulling at the frayed edges of my hope. But that little voice in the back of my head wouldn't shut up, whispering that if I handed him the phone, I wouldn't just be giving him a tool. I'd be giving him control.

Still, my hand moved. Slowly, reluctantly, I held out the phone, my stomach twisting into knots. His fingers closed around it, gripping it like it was already his. The phone was warm in my hand, the edges pressing into my palm like a warning. When I let it go, it felt like losing a piece of myself. Harry's grin widened, and for a second, the room seemed to tilt, like reality itself was shifting beneath his gaze.

Harry's glasses caught the cold, fluorescent light. "Don't look so worried, Carter," he said, his tone light, almost playful. "You'll thank me when this is over."

But the way his words hung in the air, heavy and sour, made my stomach churn. I didn't believe him. Not for a second.

CHAPTER 26

THE CAR RIDE WAS QUIET, the kind of quiet that wasn't awkward but wasn't exactly comfortable either. Max's red Corvette purred down the road, the late afternoon sun spilling warm, golden light across the dashboard. The trees loomed like ghosts, their shadows clawing at the fading daylight as if desperate to drag it back. The world outside felt distant, untouchable, a cruel reminder of everything I'd lost. I stared out the window, my reflection faint and blurred against the passing world, my thoughts a tangled, spiraling mess.

Harry—Dr. Mercer's—face clung to my mind like a stain I couldn't scrub out. His eyes, sharp and hungry, had devoured the phone, his fingers curling around it as if it were a weapon he couldn't wait to use. It wasn't just a device to him. It was power, and I'd handed it over like an idiot. I could finally see it—the shadow of the man he'd become in the 90s. The same man who'd tried to control everything, no matter the cost. And now, I'd given him exactly what he wanted.

The sun dipped lower as we drove, casting the world in shades of orange and purple. The light caught on Max's sunglasses, making him look like he belonged in some glossy car ad. But his usual laid-back smirk was nowhere to be found. His hands rested firmly on the steering wheel, his fingers tapping out a restless rhythm as the silence stretched on.

Finally, he glanced over at me, breaking the stillness. "Alright, Carter. What's the deal?"

I blinked, startled out of my thoughts. "What deal?"

Max shot me a knowing look, his sunglasses sliding down just enough to reveal a raised eyebrow. "The deal where you've been acting like you just got dumped by the universe. You've been weird ever since we left the school. And not your normal brand of weird—like, extra-weird. Top-shelf weird."

A weak laugh slipped out before I could stop it. "Cool. Love that I've hit *premo* weird status."

"Hey, I call it like I see it," Max said, his tone teasing but his eyes steady on the road. "You've got that look again."

"What look?"

Max smirked, the edge of his usual charm creeping back. "The *'I just tanked my entire day and now I'm spiraling'* look. Very you."

I slouched further in my seat, leaning my forehead against the cool glass of the window. "It's complicated."

"It's always complicated with you," Max said, shaking his head but still smiling. "Mysterious is great. Very broody. Very intriguing. But you might be overplaying it. Even *I'm* starting to wonder if you're hiding a secret identity or something."

I let out a small huff of air, staring at the long shadows racing by. "What if I am?"

"Then you're doing a terrible job keeping it secret," Max quipped, but his grin faltered as he glanced at me again. "Seriously, though. Something's eating at you, and it's not exactly subtle."

My chest tightened. I glanced at him, taking in the way his hands gripped the wheel, his jaw tight. Max didn't do serious very often, and this hit harder than I wanted to admit.

"And while we're at it," he continued, his tone gaining an edge, "I don't like how much time you've been spending with Dr. Mercer. The guy gives me bad vibes. Like, *super* bad vibes. And I know vibes—I practically invented them."

I stared at the horizon, the guilt building in my chest. "You're not wrong," I said quietly.

Max glanced over, his expression softening slightly. "That's... not exactly reassuring."

I hesitated, struggling to find the words. I wanted to tell him everything—about the phone, the time jumps, Nat, my mom—but the thought of saying it all out loud felt like stepping off a cliff. Without the phone in my pocket, my last connection to 2014, the truth felt even more fragile. *There was no way he would believe me.*

"Max," I started, my voice faltering. "I—I don't know how to explain it."

"You don't have to," he said quickly, cutting me off. His voice softened as he adjusted his grip on the wheel. "Look, you don't owe me a play-by-play of whatever's going on. But you don't have to keep it all bottled up either. I'm here. That's all I'm saying."

I swallowed hard, the knot in my chest loosening just enough to let me breathe. "Thanks."

The car fell quiet again, the hum of the engine filling the space between us. The sun dipped lower, brushing the tops of the trees with gold before starting its slow fade into dusk. Finally, Max spoke again, his voice breaking the quiet.

"So, what's the plan? You just gonna sit there looking tragic all night?"

A small smile tugged at my lips, his teasing pulling me back to the present. "Actually... would you mind driving me somewhere?"

He raised an eyebrow, his curiosity clearly piqued. "Depends. Are we talking somewhere fun or somewhere ominous? Because I'm cool with both."

"UCLA," I said, sitting up straighter.

Max blinked, surprised. "UCLA? Like, *now?*"

"Yeah," I said, nodding. "There's a symposium. Dr. Mercer's gonna be there. And I think... I think I know what I have to do."

Max tilted his head, studying me for a moment before letting out a low whistle. "Alright, Carter. This is officially the most dramatic thing you've ever said."

"You have no idea," I muttered.

Max sighed, shaking his head, but his grin was back. "Well, lucky for you, I'm a sucker for a road trip. Buckle up, buddy."

"Thanks," I said, meaning it more than I could put into words. "I…
appreciate you."

Max glanced at me, his expression softening. "Anytime. But if this
turns into some kind of sci-fi horror movie situation, I'm leaving you
behind. Just FYI."

I snorted, shaking my head. "Fair."

The Corvette sped on, the golden light fading into a dusky blue as
we headed toward UCLA. The stress of what lay ahead bore down on
me, but with Max beside me, cracking jokes and grounding me with
his steady presence, it didn't feel quite so impossible. It finally felt like
I could breathe—at least for now.

THE LIGHTS from the college auditorium spilled out onto the sidewalk,
pooling in uneven patches on the cracked pavement. The auditorium
rose out of the darkness like a monolith, its sharp edges cutting into
the night. The crowd moved like a single, relentless current, dragging
me toward something I didn't want to face.

Max's Corvette idled at the curb, its low rumble cutting through
the muffled chatter. He shifted into park, his hand lingering on the
gear shift as he glanced at me, brow creased like he was trying to read
my mind.

"You sure you want to do this alone?" Max asked, leaning back in
his seat like he was playing it casual. But his fingers drummed against
the steering wheel, his eyes flicking to the glowing entrance ahead. "I
mean, if this guy's as shady as you say, maybe we come back with, I
don't know… a tank? Or at least backup."

I smirked, but it felt hollow. "Yeah, I'll just pop by the Army
surplus store and see what they've got on clearance."

Max smiled, but it didn't reach his eyes. He tilted his head toward
the building. "I'm serious, Carter. What if this is, like, the worst idea
you've ever had?"

"I mean, it's definitely in the running," I admitted, twisting the
strap of my bag in my hands. The truth sat heavy in my chest—I didn't
know what I was walking into. Dr. Mercer was already weird enough

back at school, and now I was willingly stepping into his lair of time-travel scheming. Brilliant plan, really.

Max's grin faded as he watched me, his gaze steady and maybe just a little too knowing. "Well do you need me to stick around?" His voice was softer now, careful, like he was trying not to spook me. "I can wait out here. Be your getaway driver or something. No one's better at peeling out of a parking lot than me."

I wanted to say yes. I wanted to tell him to stay, to come inside, to keep me close to something that felt real. But instead, I shook my head, forcing a smile that felt like it might shatter under pressure. "Nah. I'll be fine. Probably. Maybe."

Max didn't buy it, obviously. His fingers tightened on the wheel as he let out a long sigh. "Carter, come on. This isn't just about being fine. That Dr. Mercer guy? He's sketchy. Like, *'don't trust the dude with a creepy van'* sketchy. What if you need me?"

I hesitated, gripping the door handle like it might anchor me. The words were on the tip of my tongue: *Stay. Please. I changed my mind. I don't want to do this alone.* But the thought of dragging him into this tangled mess made my stomach twist. He deserved better than my wreckage. "I'll be careful," I said, and it sounded about as convincing as a note scribbled in crayon. "If it gets weird, I'll hunt down a payphone and call you."

Max's brow furrowed, his fingers tapping faster. "Okay, but *'if it gets weird'* is a low bar, considering everything you've told me so far. We're already at weird. What's your plan for when it gets, like, *'alien autopsy in a government bunker'* weird?"

I laughed, short and shaky. "Wing it? Maybe get abducted. You know, the usual."

Max shook his head, but there was a flicker of a smirk as he turned to me fully. "Alright, fine. But don't go pulling some lone-wolf hero act in there. If things get dicey, you call me, got it? I'll be here faster than you can say *'horrible idea.'*"

"Don't worry, my plan's *foolproof*." I said, cracking a real smile this time. It was small, but it was there.

Max studied me for a moment longer, his usual grin replaced by something softer, quieter. "Good luck, Carter," he said, his voice uncharacteristically serious. "And, hey—don't go doing anything stupid."

"No promises," I said, already reaching for the door. The cold air slapped me as I pushed it open.

I stepped onto the sidewalk and the sound of the car faded behind me. I didn't look back—I couldn't. The lights from the auditorium glared brighter as I got closer, spilling across the pavement like a warning. My chest tightened as I reached the entrance, gripping the strap of my bag until my knuckles ached. I wasn't ready for whatever was waiting for me inside. I wasn't even sure what to expect, what I was looking for, and what I would do when I found it. But I knew one thing for sure—there was no running behind a car, no easy escape.

Not this time.

CHAPTER 27

THE AUDITORIUM BUZZED WITH ANTICIPATION, a low hum that crawled up the walls and clung to the ceiling, heavy and electric. I hovered in the doorway, anxiety burrowing a knot in my chest. *Fuck. What am I doing? What if this is my only chance? If these people were really here to help me, I could lose everything!* But deep down, I knew something wasn't right.

Dr. Mercer stood at the podium, the projector's glow carving him out of the shadows like some false idol. His smile curled at the edges, too sharp, too knowing, as if he could see the strings of fate and was already pulling them. He wasn't just enjoying the attention—he was *feeding* on it, his self-satisfied smirk practically dripping with validation.

The phone—*my* phone—was held aloft in his hand, its cracked screen catching the light like some ancient artifact. The crowd of scientists, professors, and eager minds leaned forward, all eyes on him, their collective hunger for discovery filling the air. I wanted to yell, to scream that they had no idea what they were applauding, but my voice was locked somewhere in my chest, buried under panic.

"With this device," Dr. Mercer began, his voice smooth and deliberate, like he was narrating a nature documentary, "we hold the key to the future. To untold possibilities. This is not speculation, ladies and gentlemen. This is proof that time travel—yes, time travel—is not just a theory. It is *reality.*"

The room erupted into murmurs and scattered applause, and every clap felt like a slap to the face. My pulse pounded in my ears, drowning out the noise, my stomach twisting tighter with every word. This wasn't just a lecture—it was a spectacle, a performance meant to cement his place in history. And I was the sacrificial lamb he'd built it on.

My legs felt like they'd turned to lead, each step dragging me deeper into the lion's den. The air was thick with judgment; I felt every gaze as I made the slow walk down the aisle to the stage, and each one sliced through me like glass. But I couldn't stop. Not now.

The projector's light caught me as I climbed onto the platform. Gasps rippled through the crowd as I stood there, every pair of eyes now fixed on me.

Dr. Mercer tilted his head, his smirk unfurling into something serpentine, coiling around his words like a noose. "Ah, Carter," he drawled, his voice dripping with this performative kind of charm. He spread his arms wide, like a magician about to pull a rabbit from his hat. "Ladies and gentlemen, the man of the hour himself! After all, what's a demonstration of future technology without the future in attendance?"

The applause in the crowd swelled, buzzing like static. I could feel their eyes on me, sharp and expectant. The spotlight cut through the room like a blade, landing right on me. My skin prickled under the heat, my chest tightening. He wasn't just smug—he was thriving on this, like he already thought he'd won.

My voice cut through the noise before I could second-guess myself. "You can't do this!" I yelled, my voice raw, trembling. "This isn't right."

Dr. Mercer tilted his head, his smirk deepening into something almost reptilian. "Carter..." he said my name again, slow and deliber-ate, like he was savoring every letter. "Ever the humble one." He turned back to the crowd, gesturing toward them like he was a conductor and they were the orchestra he was about to dazzle. "Don't be shy, now! These are the greatest minds of our time, gathered here tonight to witness a technological revolution—a glimpse into the future! And you, young man, are at the very center of it!"

I could feel my fists clench at my sides, my nails digging into my palms. His words hung oily in the air, but all I could focus on was the sea of faces staring at me—professors, journalists, researchers, all of them waiting for something extraordinary. My stomach twisted. He wanted me to be his trophy, his proof, his pawn. And it was working.

For now.

"I—" The words jammed in my throat like traffic on a one-lane road. I glanced at the phone on the podium, its cracked screen glowing faintly under the stage lights. My heartbeat thundered in my ears, but I forced the words out. "I can't go along with this." I stepped forward, my sneakers squeaking against the polished floor. "I need to tell you all the truth!"

The murmurs in the crowd grew loud, rippling like waves in a storm. Dr. Mercer's smirk flickered, his hand twitching toward the phone like he was about to grab it, like he knew what was coming and wanted to stop it.

"This isn't what you think!" I said, my voice cracking under the weight of a hundred eyes. The words felt like a free-fall, each one ripping another piece of my armor away. "He's lying. All of this—it's a lie! This isn't some revolutionary device, it's a flashlight! A fancy flashlight, sure—but just a light!"

Gasps rippled through the crowd, sharp and disbelieving. The tension in the room snapped like a rubber band stretched too far. Dr. Mercer froze, his confident façade cracking like thin ice. He laughed, but it was strained and shaky, his voice laced with desperation. "Please," he said, holding his hand up like I was a misbehaving child he could gently scold back into line. "Now is surely not the time for jokes."

"This isn't some joke!" I shot back, spinning toward him. "You gave me this 'phone' to stage your little show and make it seem like you'd 'unlocked the secrets of time travel.'" I reached out, grabbing the phone off the podium, holding it up for the crowd to see. The glow of the screen was faint, but I tapped the flashlight button and the LED shone into the darkened room like a searchlight.

"See? It's just a bulb and some film. Not a portal to another dimension. Not a time machine. Just a flashlight."

The crowd roared to life, their whispers sharpening into accusations that cut through the room like shrapnel. The metal of auditorium chairs scraped as audience members leapt to their feet, the air buzzing with outrage and betrayal.

"A hoax?" someone yelled from the back.

"Are you kidding me?" Another voice cut through the din, angrier, louder.

"We came all this way for a flashlight?"

Dr. Mercer's face twisted, his composure fracturing with every shout from the crowd. His voice rose, thin and frantic, as if he could stitch the unraveling chaos back together with sheer desperation. "This is absurd!" he bellowed, stepping forward with all the grace of someone trying to balance on a tightrope made of bad decisions. His voice boomed, but I could hear the wobble in it, the edges fraying. "Ladies and gentlemen, this young man is confused—misinformed! He doesn't understand the significance of what he holds!"

"I understand just fine!" I shouted, my voice rising above the crowd. I held the phone higher, its faint glow casting long shadows across the stage. "This isn't some revolutionary discovery! It's not a portal to another dimension. It's a hoax, all of it!"

Gasps rippled through the room, sharp and disbelieving. The tension snapped like a rubber band stretched too far. More people stood, shaking their heads, muttering under their breath as they shuffled toward the exits. Their footsteps echoed through the auditorium, a low, hollow sound that should've felt like victory. But it didn't.

Not everyone was leaving.

"Wait!" a man in the front row shouted, his voice edged with anger. His sharp blazer crinkled as he surged forward, pointing at the phone. "That can't be right. Let me see it!"

Another person leapt to their feet, their chair screeching. "Kid, what are you trying to pull?" They demanded, their eyes darting between me and the phone like I was holding a piece of their salvation. "Give it here!"

The murmurs swelled again, angrier this time. A woman in a lab coat elbowed her way toward the stage, her voice sharp and impatient. "Hand it over! If it's a hoax, we'll see for ourselves!"

I backed up instinctively, my chest tightening as the first man climbed the stairs onto the stage, his polished shoes squeaking against the wood. "Stay back!" I shouted, gripping the phone tighter, my voice trembling. "You don't understand what you're asking for!"

But they didn't care. The man advanced toward me, his hands reaching out, his face twisted with disbelief. Another person followed close behind, their movements jerky and determined, and then another, their voices blending into a chaotic roar that drowned out everything else.

"Let us see it!" someone yelled from the shadows of the crowd.

"What's the big deal, kid?" another snapped, their tone sharp and accusing.

My pulse thundered in my ears as I stumbled back, my sneakers scuffing against the edge of the stage. My chest heaved as I glanced left, then right—both staircases on either side of the stage were filling with people, their shadows stretching long and jagged under the flicker of the projector light. Behind me, waves of them were clamoring up to the stage. The wooden floor beneath me felt too small, the distance to the crowd shrinking with every second. They were closing in.

"Stop!" I shouted, gripping the phone tighter, my voice cracking. But the noise swallowed me whole, the demands of the crowd roaring louder, closer.

A hand shot out from my left, grabbing at my backpack and yanking hard. I staggered forward, panic clawing at my throat as I twisted away, slipping free. My breath came in short, jagged gasps as I backed up again, my eyes darting to the opposite staircase where more figures swarmed upward, their movements frantic and disjointed.

Then I felt it—a sharp tug at my ankle. My breath hitched, my body freezing for half a second as I looked down. A hand seized my leg, fingers clutching tightly at the denim of my jeans. Before I could react, the grip tightened, and I was yanked backward. My balance tipped, the stage's edge catching the small of my back as the world tilted.

The impact knocked the air out of my lungs. My back slammed into the polished floor in front of the stage with a sickening thud, pain exploding through my ribs and shoulder. The phone slipped from my grip, its cracked surface skittering across the cold wood with a faint, mocking glow.

I lay there for a moment, stunned, the breath ripped from my chest. The voices above blurred into a cacophony of jeers and demands, their words sharp and biting, like shards of glass slicing through the air.

"Someone get it!" One person barked, their footsteps thundering as they jumped down from the stage, landing with a heavy thud a few feet from me.

"Grab the phone!" Another voice screamed, shrill with desperation.

My body jerked into action, driven by sheer panic. I scrambled toward the phone, my palms slipping against the slick floor as my ribs screamed in protest. My hands shook as I reached for it, my fingers brushing against the cracked glass just as another hand grabbed the back of my shirt, yanking me upright. Pain shot through my shoulder—sharp, hot, relentless—as I jerked free, clutching the phone to my chest like it was the only thing tethering me to reality.

"Stop him!" Dr. Mercer's voice rang out above the chaos, jagged and desperate. "Don't let him go!"

The crowd surged again, their bodies colliding in a frantic scramble. Someone's side slammed into me, sending me stumbling. My chest heaved, every breath tasting like copper as I spun toward the exit. Hands clawed at my shirt, dragging me back, their nails digging into the fabric.

I swung blindly, my fist connecting with something solid—a jaw, maybe. Someone cried out in surprise, and the grip on my shirt loosened just enough for me to tear free. My legs burned as I bolted toward the double doors, the phone's faint glow pressing against my chest like a fragile heartbeat.

The auditorium doors slammed against the wall as I shoved through them, the cold night air hitting me like a slap.

"Carter, you don't know what you've done!" Dr. Mercer's words echoed after me.

My legs burned as I ran, the roar of the crowd spilling out into the dark behind me. My lungs ached, my pulse pounding in my ears as I rounded the corner of the building, the shadows swallowing me whole.

I collapsed against a rough brick wall, the surface scraping against my back as I sank to the ground. My hands trembled, the phone shaking in my grip as I clutched it to my chest. My shoulder throbbed, and my ribs ached with every breath, but I didn't let go. I couldn't.

This must've been it. Why he hated me in the future. It was always going to come to this... Just like with Ryan. Inevitable. Like nothing I do ever to matters.

The sound of tires crunching against the roadside broke through the haze. I looked up, my vision swimming as Max's Corvette came into view. He jumped out, his face pale under the streetlights as he ran toward me. "Carter!" he called, his voice sharp with panic. "What the hell happened?"

I tried to answer, but the words caught in my throat, thick and choking. My hands felt too heavy, my chest too tight, as if everything —the phone, the past, the future—was crushing me all at once. Quickly, I hid my phone from him.

Max crouched in front of me, his hands gripping my shoulders, his voice cutting through the fog. "Hey! Look at me! Are you okay? Are you hurt?"

"I'm fine," I lied, my voice hollow and cracked. I forced a shaky breath. "I just... I finished it, Max."

Max's eyes flicked to the entrance, then back to me, his jaw tightening. He didn't ask questions, didn't push for answers. He just nodded, his hands steadying me as he helped me to my feet. My knees buckled, and he caught me, his grip firm but careful, like I might shatter if he held on too tightly.

The Corvette's door creaked as he guided me inside, the leather seat cold against my back. The engine rumbled to life, a low, steady hum that filled the silence. As Max pulled out onto the road, a clutch of angry scientists emerged from the building, shaking their fists and yelling into the night. And Dr. Mercer was at the head of the pack.

THE CITY LIGHTS BLURRED PAST, smeared like watercolors against the dark. My shoulder throbbed and my knuckles were raw, but the pain felt distant, muffled by the fog that wrapped around my mind. Max didn't speak, his hands tight on the wheel, his jaw set. The tension in the car was thick, closing in on me like the ghosts of everything I'd left behind in that auditorium.

I stared down at my empty hands, remembering how the phone's faint glow cast jagged shadows across my skin. The cracks in the screen seemed deeper now, splintering out like veins, like roots, like the map of everything I'd broken tonight.

I didn't know what I'd done. I didn't know what came next. All I knew was that I was slipping further away from home, from the life I'd been fighting so hard to get back to. And for the first time, I wasn't sure I would ever find my way again.

CHAPTER 28

AFTER THE SYMPOSIUM, Max's room became my refuge—a flimsy shield against the world outside. It was the only place I felt remotely safe, though the word "safe" was doing a lot of heavy lifting. I hadn't stepped outside since we got back. That morning, I stayed curled up on my makeshift bed of blankets and pillows, listening to the familiar sounds of Max getting ready for school. The soft clink of a belt buckle, the zip of his backpack, the low hum of his radio as he pulled on a shirt—it all should have felt like a calm start to a normal day. But instead, it just made the air in the room heavier, choking the air like a weight I couldn't shake.

It wasn't just Dr. Mercer I was hiding from—it was everyone. The man I'd trusted, the one who claimed he wanted to "help," had nearly unraveled everything. Exposed me to a room full of strangers. It was like I had a target on my back, and I couldn't get his self-superior expression out of my head. Every word he said still echoed in my ears, like a taunt I couldn't outrun.

I had to tell Max and his dad I was too sick to go to school, and, thankfully, they didn't push too hard. Dave was already leaving for work, and Justin was on the bus, so it should've been easy enough to keep up the lie. But Max—I knew he wasn't buying it. He saw the bruises. He knew I was scared. And by the way his eyes lingered on me, I knew he was waiting for me to crack, to finally say something real. But he wanted answers I didn't know how to give.

When I finally heard the low rumble of Max's Corvette fading down the street, the tension in my chest loosened just a little. I waited until the sound disappeared completely before pulling my phone out from under the pillow. The phone's pale glow spilled into the dark room, a fragile cord to a life slipping further away. It was like holding onto a ghost—there, but untouchable, fading faster the harder I tried to cling to it. Each flicker of light was a heartbeat, faint and uneven, as if the phone itself was barely holding on. Just like me.

"Already at 10%," I muttered, staring down at the screen like it was taunting me. The little red sliver of the battery icon might as well have been laughing.

I swiped through photos, my thumb hovering over each one, the cracked glass making every image feel fragile, like they could splinter apart if I stared too hard. There was Mom, mid-laugh in the kitchen, her chestnut hair catching the light like it had decided to be the main character for a day. I could hear it—her laugh. Loud, unashamed, spilling into every corner of the room like it didn't know how to stop. I could almost smell her: vanilla, coffee, and that stupid candle she swore smelled like fall but really just smelled like cinnamon.

I swiped again. My friends, blurry and chaotic, arms tangled around each other like we'd never imagine being apart. Smiling into the camera like life wasn't hurtling forward, like nothing would ever change. Another swipe, another wave of ache. It felt too far away now, like trying to go back to sleep to recapture a great dream that had vanished the moment you woke up. The edges were slipping, and no matter how tight I held on, I couldn't stop it. Any of it.

My thumb hovered over Mom's picture again. My chest tightened, the memory blooming so sharply it almost knocked the air out of me. I could feel her ruffling my hair, smell her sweater, hear her voice saying something goofy or ridiculous just to see me roll my eyes. For a second, it was real. So real it hurt.

And then, the phone slipped.

"Shit—ow!" I yelped as it smacked me right on the bridge of my nose. The sting was sharp, stupid, but it split something open—a bitter laugh tearing out of my chest before I could stop it. For once, the pain felt like mine to control.

I rubbed at my nose, glaring at the phone like it had done it on purpose, but the laugh wouldn't stop bubbling up. "Nice," I muttered, shaking my head. "Perfect. Just perfect."

The screen glowed faintly in the dim light, Mom's face still staring back at me. The ache came rushing in again, but quieter this time, like it was sitting beside me instead of clawing at my chest.

"Well," I murmured, swallowing hard, "this is it, huh? I never managed to say goodbye." The words cracked as they left me, soft and broken, but I couldn't stop them. "And soon, I guess my memory's all I'll have left."

The silence after felt heavy, like the room was absorbing it all, giving me space to breathe for just a second. But even that wasn't enough to stop the crushing sense of it overwhelming me. I closed my eyes, gripping the phone tighter, like holding onto it might somehow hold onto her.

"Thought you were sick," a voice cut through the quiet, making me jump.

I scrambled to hide the phone, looking up to see Max leaning in the doorway, arms crossed. His gaze pinned me, steady and unyielding, but something flickered beneath it—concern stretched too thin to hide the frustration creeping in. His hair was still a little messy, and the way he tilted his head made it clear he wasn't here to joke around. At least, not entirely.

"Max..." I sniffed. "I thought you'd gone to school."

"Obviously," he said, his tone light but edged with something sharper. "And clearly, you're *very* sick. Hope you don't strain yourself by avoiding life all day."

I sat up, adjusting the blanket draped over me and forcing a half-smile. "It's called 'advanced bedrest,' okay? Very cutting-edge. You wouldn't get it."

Max raised an eyebrow, pushing off the doorframe to take a step closer. "Oh, I get it. Hiding out. Being mysterious. Classic Carter move."

"Yeah, well, it's worked so far," I muttered, looking away.

Max sighed, his teasing grin softening as he sat on the edge of his bed, his foot brushing against the edge of my makeshift setup. He leaned forward, resting his elbows on his knees, his voice quieter now. "Look, you don't have to tell me everything. But from what I saw last night? This doesn't look like someone who's just 'too sick' to get out of bed." His eyes flicked to the blanket, then back to me. "Something happened. And, surprise, you're terrible at hiding it."

I swallowed hard, my throat tightening like it was trying to choke the words out of me before I could even think them. The air felt dense, stale, clinging to my skin like a damp sheet. Even the faint hum of the radio seemed too loud, too sharp, slicing through the suffocating quiet. Max sat there, his expression hovering somewhere between concerned and *don't-make-me-pry-but-I'll-pry-if-I-have-to*. His presence filled the space in a way that was comforting and terrifying all at once.

I wanted to tell him everything—the lies I'd swallowed, the truths I couldn't face. About Dr. Mercer's betrayal, the future slipping through my fingers like sand. About how I'd tried to shield him from the mess, to protect him from all the insane, impossible truths. But the words tangled together in my head, wrapped tight in fear. Fear that he wouldn't understand. Fear that I wouldn't be heard. Fear that if I said it all out loud, it would make everything real in a way I couldn't undo.

"It's… complicated," I sighed, the words small and pathetic, like they were apologizing for existing. My hands gripped the blanket draped over my legs, fingers curling into the fabric like it might anchor me to this moment.

Max shifted closer, the morning light hitting his jaw just right— sharp angles softened by concern—and his eyes caught mine like they were trying to read a book I hadn't written yet.

"Complicated how?" he asked, his voice softer now, more curious than pushy. Like he was giving me an opening to step through. No stress. No demands. Just a door left ajar.

I dropped my gaze, but everything in my head was a knot—a horrible, tangled mess of fear and shame and that stupid, awful weight of not knowing how to start.

"Max, I..." The words caught again, trailing off into the air like smoke.

After a beat, he sighed, the sound soft but loaded, and his head dropped. He was close enough that his hand almost bumped my knee, close enough that the warmth of him radiated through the blanket. It was grounding in a way that made my chest ache.

"Look," he started, leaning in. "You don't have to, like, give me the whole plot of whatever's going on in your head. I'm not asking for spoilers. But you're... not exactly subtle when something's wrong." He glanced sideways at me, his lips quirking in a half-smile that didn't quite reach his eyes. "And something's been wrong for a long time. It's not exactly a blast watching you shut down like this."

I winced, guilt twisting in my gut like a knife. *He was right.* I'd been hiding things, shoving everything deeper, like that would fix it somehow. Like the less people knew, the less real this insanity would be. Like burying it would make it disappear. But all it had done was make the space between us grow wider, the silence heavier.

Max shifted, his voice softening even more. "I'm not trying to make you talk if you're not ready. But..." He hesitated, then added, "You don't have to do this alone anymore, you know?"

My chest tightened, and I stared at my hands, at the floor, at anything that wasn't his face. I took a breath, shaky and uneven, and let the words start to form. "Last night... at the symposium," I said, my voice barely above a whisper. "I thought I could end this whole thing. Wrap it up, fix it, whatever. And... I did. Sort of."

Max's brow furrowed, his attention sharpening like a laser. "Sort of?" he repeated, turning to me, his tone walking the line between teasing and genuinely worried. "Carter, you've gotta give me more than that. 'Sort of' is what people say when they've set something on fire but don't wanna admit it."

I let out this jagged, bitter laugh, sharp enough to cut myself on. "Yeah, well, setting a fire probably would've been the *nicer* thing to do. Quick. Painless. Poof, gone." My voice cracked, but I didn't stop. Couldn't stop. "What I did—" My throat tightened, and I had to look away, like maybe if I didn't see Max, I wouldn't completely fall apart. "I ended it, Max. I hope I did."

The words hung there, heavy and sour, choking the air between us. My chest felt like it was caving in, like I'd swallowed every bad decision I'd ever made and it was sitting there, making itself at home. "I thought... I thought I was doing the right thing," I said, my voice barely holding together. "Thought I was finally fixing everything. Like —like if I could just... put everything back in place, everything would be okay again."

Max stayed quiet, his focus on me steady and solid, but not in a way that pushed. It was like he was holding the silence open, waiting for me to walk into it. I took a breath.

"I almost let it all go," My voice shattered. "Everything left of the life I had, the person I was—it was slipping through my fingers, Max." My chest shook. "But in the end... I *still* lost it all. For good. No escape hatch, no reset button. Now I'm just... stuck." It all felt unbearable, like dragging a lead blanket I'd never asked for. My fingers dug into the borrowed pajama pants I was wearing, the fabric soft but unfamiliar—just like everything else. "It's like the harder I try to hold onto what's left, the faster everything's ripped away. I mean, Christ. It's like no matter how hard I try—I can never do anything right..." Tears swelled in my eyes, blurring the room into this hazy, soft mess. "Being here, everything with Nat, all the shit with my mom, I just—"

"No, Carter, don't." Max interrupted, his voice gentle but firm, cutting through the mess in my head like a lifeline. "The mess with your parents—whatever it is—it's not your fault. You're just a kid. And <u>fuck</u> them for abandoning you. But what does all this have to do with Dr. Mercer?"

His words pulled me back into the present, anchoring me when my thoughts threatened to spiral. Crossing my legs, I rubbed at my face with one hand, my other still gripping the fabric of my pants. I felt exposed. Maybe because I was shirtless in someone else's pajamas, or maybe it was because there was no more hiding. Not from him. Not now. He leaned forward slightly, like he knew this was the point where it could all come crashing down. And maybe he was ready to catch me. Or maybe he wasn't. But either way, I had to say it.

The words were a tangle in my throat, like trying to pull a thread from a knot that just tightened every time I tugged. "Max... there's something I haven't told you. About... me," I finally said.

He didn't flinch. He just nodded, his expression calm and his voice quiet when he said, "Alright. I'm here. Whatever it is."

I hesitated. My voice felt stuck, buried under layers of fear and shame, but Max didn't look away. He just sat there, his eyes steady and unyielding, the only solid thing in a world that felt like it was falling apart.

I swallowed hard, my throat dry, and finally found the courage to start. "My mom..." I paused, my voice barely above a whisper. Saying it felt like peeling back a layer of myself I'd kept hidden for so long it had practically fused to me. "She's dying," I said, the words cutting into the air like shards of glass. "Alzheimer's."

Max didn't move, didn't say anything right away, and that silence was almost unbearable. But it wasn't empty—it was full, charged with something I couldn't quite name. I pushed forward, needing to get it all out before the silence swallowed me whole.

"The thought of her forgetting me—" My voice cracked again, and I pressed my palms into my eyes. "I just wanted to see her. I wanted to get back before she forgot me completely. Before I was… nothing."

Max's hand tightened slightly where it rested on the bed, like he was physically trying to ground me, steadying me as I finally let it all out. His presence, so open and steady, made it easier to keep going. I hadn't expected that. I hadn't expected *him*.

"I was on my way to her," I said, my voice catching slightly. "My mom. And then... something happened. My phone broke, and I—" I hesitated, the words too big, too ridiculous. "I somehow ended up in 1994."

I glanced at Max, expecting some reaction—laughter, disbelief, *something*. But he just sat there, his expression open and calm, like he was waiting for me to fill in the blanks. So, I did. The words spilled out, messy and tangled, as I told him about the 90s, and about meeting Nat and Ethan.

I exhaled, a shaky, uneven breath that felt like trying to push a boulder up a hill. "And then I ended up in the 80s," I said, the words jagged in my throat. "In Burbank. And, uh... I ran into my dad."

Max blinked, but he didn't say anything, his expression softening, almost like he'd expected this from me. Maybe not something this *weird*, but close enough. I pushed on before I lost my nerve.

"It was a younger version of him," I added, my voice starting to crack again. "Back before... well, before everything. He was just some small-town guy who moved from out-of-state."

The room felt impossibly small now, like the walls were inching closer with every word. My gaze dropped to my lap, my fingers intertwining with each other like it was the only thing keeping me from unraveling completely. "I always knew my parents lived in Burbank back then—uh. *Now*. I just never even thought about the fact that I might run into him... just see him standing there. Like that."

Max brows knit together for just a second before smoothing out again. His hand ran through his hair in that casual, slightly dramatic way he always did, and his grin flickered back onto his face. "I'm not him, right? Just checking. We're good?"

I blinked at him, caught off guard. "What? No! You're not him, Max. He's from Oregon. You're... good."

He nodded, his smile widening a little. "Awesome. Just had to make sure, ya know? Would've made this whole thing super awkward. Like, *'guess I can't hang out with you anymore'* awkward."

I let out a startled laugh, half-hysterical but real. Max always did that—knew when to lighten things up, when to pull me out of my head just enough to breathe again.

He exhaled slowly, his shoulders relaxing as he leaned forward, his hand resting lightly on my shoulder. It was subtle, reassuring. "So," he said, his voice quieter now, like he was giving the moment space to settle. "You're really from the future?"

"Yeah," I whispered, the truth finally coming out. "I thought I was losing my mind when I first got here. I had nothing. Then I met you." My voice wavered, a broken laugh escaping as I looked at him. "And somehow things felt... less crazy. You—you helped, in more ways you'll ever know."

"Hey," Max said, his smirk crooked and unshakable. "You're not the first person I've pulled out of a downward spiral. Just the first one who makes me feel like I should be wearing a tinfoil hat while I do it."

He leaned back slightly, his eyes glinting. "Do you remember the cafeteria? The day we met? I roasted you about that jacket. Basically looked like you blew in from a blizzard."

I laughed, shaking my head. "Yeah, I remember. You called me out on being a time traveler in front of everyone. Felt *awesome*."

"Guess I wasn't wrong, huh?" Max said, his smile widening. "So, is all this why you're always sneaking glances at that... black mirror or whatever you have?"

The words hit me like a jolt, half-surprising and half-relieving. "You... you knew?"

Max shrugged. "I didn't *know*. But I saw. You'd pull it out when you thought no one was looking, like the night you went out on the porch. I figured if it was important, you'd tell me eventually." He tilted his head, his gaze steady. "And... now you have."

My chest tightened, relief mixing with disbelief. "You actually believe me?"

"Carter," Max said, leaning in with a smirk that softened into something more sincere. "Even if you're completely insane—and let's be real, the odds are solid—you're still you. That doesn't change."

For a second, the heaviness on my shoulders eased just a little. But then Max's brow furrowed, his grin fading as his expression sharpened. "So... Dr. Mercer," he prompted, his voice quieter now, tinged with something darker. "How does he fit into all this?"

I took a shaky breath. "He... found out I wasn't from here. And instead of helping me, he just... he wanted my phone. The tech. That's all he cared about."

Max's jaw tightened, his hand dropping from my shoulder as he straightened. "So he was using you," he said, his voice edged with frustration. "Stringing you along for his own ego. Always knew that asshole was bad news."

"Yeah," I muttered, bitterness rising to the surface. "He kept promising he could help me get back, but all he cared about was proving he was some kind of genius. Like, all I was to him was a ticket to... I don't know. Fame? Validation? He didn't care what happened to me."

Max shook his head, his expression darkening. "That motherfucker..." Max muttered, his jaw tightening. For a moment, his eyes flickered—anger, maybe, or something deeper. "And you've been dealing with this all on your own."

I nodded. "Pretty much. I wanted to believe he could help, you know? Like, maybe he was the one guy in this whole mess who actually knew what was happening to me. That he'd understand the science or... whatever." I exhaled, shaking my head. "But in the end, he didn't care about me. He only cared about what he could get out of it. And when he took the phone..." My voice cracked, dropping to a whisper. "He'd taken the last piece of home I had. The last link to my mom."

Max's hand tightened on my shoulder, firm but not heavy. It was anchoring, like he was telling me without words that he was here. His eyes softened, but there was a fierceness in his expression too—like he was already planning how to knock out Dr. Mercer if it came to that. "But you got it back," he said, his voice steady, solid, like a handhold on a cliff. "You didn't let him keep it."

I let out a small, shaky laugh, barely a sound but real. "I wasn't about to let him walk away with it. I mean, if the universe is gonna keep fucking with me, it can at *least* let me keep my damn phone."

Max's grip softened, his thumb brushing a small circle on my shoulder—a simple gesture, but it melted something inside me. "Look," he said, still carrying that undercurrent of confidence that felt like sunlight cutting through fog. "I know this whole thing feels impossible, like the kind of mess nobody gets out of. But you don't have to do this alone, Carter," Max said, his voice low but steady. "I'm not going anywhere. And as for Dr. Mercer?" He shrugged, his grin tugging at the corner of his lips. "We'll deal with him," Max said, his expression not quite matching his eyes. "Guys like him always have cracks. You just have to know where to push. And I'll make sure he doesn't push back."

The weight of everything lifted just a little, and before I knew what I was doing, my arms wrapped around him. For half a second, I panicked—*what if this was too much, too weird?* But Max didn't hesitate. His arms closed around me, steady and unshaking, like he wasn't afraid of the burdens I carried. For the first time in forever, it didn't feel like the world would shatter if I let myself lean on someone else.

We stayed like that for a moment that felt like forever and no time at all, the silence around us thicker than words. When Max pulled back slightly, his hands stayed on my shoulders, his gaze steady and warm. "Carter," he said, his voice quieter now, but still certain, "if your parents are here, in the 80s... maybe we should find them. You said your mom's sick in your time, right? But here? She'd be... healthy. Young. The way you'd want to remember her."

The thought surged through me like a tidal wave—hope sharp enough to hurt, crashing into the quiet ache of knowing it might never be enough. But it was something. And I couldn't let it slip away. "You think... this could be my last chance to see her like that?"

Max nodded. "It might be your last chance to see her at all if we can't figure that thing out," he said pointing to the phone. "After everything with Dr. Mercer, this might be your best shot. And if... if you're stuck here, then at least you'll have that. Her, happy and healthy. A memory that *doesn't* hurt. And who knows? Maybe it's part of this whole messed-up journey. Maybe it's what you were meant to do."

Tears pricked at my eyes, but they didn't feel like the kind that would drown me. I nodded, my voice quiet. "I'd like that. A lot."

Max's lips curved into a smile—not one of his usual quick, flashy grins, but something quieter, softer, like he meant it more than he was letting on. "And for the record," he said, his tone lightening like the first breeze after a storm, "I don't care if you're from the future, the past, or some weird alternate dimension where everything smells like soup. All I know is you're here now, and I'm not going anywhere."

Something cracked open inside me—something warm, something I'd almost forgotten I could feel. The kind of thing that feels more real than words. A smile crept onto my face, shaky and hesitant but completely, genuinely mine. "Thanks, Max. For... sticking around. Even with all this."

"Hey," Max said, leaning back slightly, "someone's gotta make sure you don't accidentally time-travel yourself into another train wreck. I could be saving the world for all I know."

His hand tapped lightly against my shoulder, a subtle rhythm that matched the buzz of energy always just beneath his surface. Max was usually all easy confidence and quick comebacks, but right now, I could feel something quieter—like he was holding back his own questions, his own worries about me.

He tilted his head, his smile taking on that familiar teasing edge. "So…" he started, his tone casual but laced with just enough mischief to make me wary. "Does this whole 'time traveler' gig mean you're too busy to do regular stuff here?"

I raised an eyebrow, smirking despite myself. "Regular stuff like what? Filing taxes? Getting a library card?"

Max's grin widened, his voice dripping with faux seriousness. "Oh, absolutely. And, you know, dances."

My smirk faltered as I blinked, caught off guard by the sudden shift. I totally forgot. Before I could process it, he continued, his voice taking on that teasing lilt that made my stomach flip. "You still planning on going with Tiff tonight, or is she getting cut loose by the man of the future?"

I laughed—half surprise, half relief that Max could take something so overwhelming and boil it down to something simple. "You're seriously bringing that up right now?"

"What?" he said, feigning innocence as his smile grew. "I'm just trying to help you keep your commitments. Time travelers are supposed to be dependable, aren't they?" His hand gave my shoulder a quick, playful squeeze, and I felt the warmth of it settle in my chest.

I rolled my eyes, my smile breaking through anyway. "Guess we'll see, won't we?"

The room around us seemed to brighten, like Max had flipped some invisible switch that chased all the shadows into the corners. It was actually like the future—whatever that even meant for me now—didn't seem so terrifying.

Then, like a sudden jolt of electricity, Max jumped to his feet, his voice brimming with energy. "Alright, enough of this broody time traveler vibe. Get up—we've got places to be."

I tilted my head, watching him with suspicion. "Places? You realize

I'm not dressed for school, right?" I gestured to my rumpled pajama pants, which were definitely not part of any acceptable '80s wardrobe.

Max bent down and grabbed my shoes, tossing them at me with a grin. "Well, if you're going to this dance, you're not showing up like that. Tiffany deserves better. And *you're* gonna need something with a little more... flair."

"Flair?" I said, pulling on my Chucks. "What, like sequins? A top hat? Maybe a pocket watch to complete the whole 'out-of-time' vibe?"

Max snapped his fingers, his smile widening. "Now you're getting it. But seriously, we're hitting the shops. No way you're skipping this thing, and no way you're showing up looking like you just rolled out of bed. Which... you actually did."

I chuckled, shaking my head. "Alright, let's say I'm playing along with this. Where exactly are you planning to take me?"

Max shrugged, his smirk turning slightly mischievous. "I know a place up in Burbank. Retro as hell, but they've got good suits. Plus," he added, his tone softening, "it's close to where your parents lived, right? Figured it might be nice. You know, just... seeing the neighborhood."

That hit harder than I expected. My chest tightened, a mix of nostalgia and something heavier. "You really thought this through, huh?"

Max shrugged again, his nonchalance carefully performed but no less genuine. "What can I say? I'm full of surprises. Throw on a shirt and grab your coat. I'll be damned if we're just skipping school to mope around."

I quickly dressed, slipped into my jacket and grabbed my phone, the overwhelming thoughts momentarily replaced by the strange, warm energy Max always seemed to bring with him. He grinned, holding the door open like he was inviting me into some new quest I hadn't signed up for.

"C'mon, time traveler," he beamed. "We've got an adventure to go on."

CHAPTER 29

Max slid into the driver's seat and the Corvette growled to life, a low, guttural sound that rattled through my chest. His movements were sharp and sure, like he belonged here in a way I never could. The radio crackled with static before bursting into a synth-heavy beat—Separate Ways. The music felt too loud, too clean against the jagged mess in my head. I sank into the passenger seat, letting the engine's hum bleed into my ribs, hoping it would drown out the static inside me. The bass rattled the windows, and Max grinned, shooting me a sideways look, his fingers drumming along to the rhythm like we were about to score a montage.

"Alright, Carter," he said, his smile widening. "Let's blow this joint."

I rolled my eyes but couldn't help the small smirk tugging at my lips. "Sure, cause nothing screams 'stealthy time traveler' like getting pulled over in a red Corvette."

Max laughed, tapping the gas and sending us peeling out onto the street. "Exactly. If we're gonna leave a mark, might as well leave tire tracks too."

The city unfolded in a haze of gold, light spilling over the cracks in its facade—faded signs, chipped paint, the jagged silhouettes of palm trees too stubborn to fall. It felt like a place caught between holding on and letting go. Like me.

The polished hood of the Corvette caught the light, blinding in flashes, as Max wove us through streets that smelled of gasoline and dried-out dreams. I leaned back, letting the rhythm of the car and the city sink into me. It felt... free. Like for once, time wasn't chasing me— it was just out there, waiting for us to catch up.

Max weaved through traffic with a kind of reckless precision, every turn and curve like he was carving out a private escape route. He leaned into it, completely at ease, like the road was his stage and every other driver was just a forgettable extra.

"You're gonna burn through your gas tank," I said, raising my voice over the music. "What's the plan then? Push this thing uphill?"

Max smirked, glancing my way without missing a beat. "C'mon, Carter. Have a little faith. This car and me? We've got history. She'd never let me down."

"Cool. Let me know how that works out when we're hitchhiking."

By the time the Hollywood Hills swallowed us whole, the engine's roar softened to a low rumble as Max eased us into winding streets. Boutiques gleamed under gold-trimmed awnings, their windows showcasing lives that didn't feel real—too curated, too far away from anything I knew. The air here clung to my skin, thin but suffocating, heavy with the promise of things I'd never have. Money, ambition—it wasn't just in the storefronts or the architecture. It was in the way people walked, like they'd already won.

Finally, Max pulled into a spot outside what looked to me like an upscale men's store, cutting the engine with a flourish like he'd just finished a grand performance. He hopped out and stretched, gesturing toward the shop's sleek black awning like he was unveiling a secret lair. "Alright, my man. Time to suit up. Prepare to be transformed."

I climbed out, raising an eyebrow as I looked at the store. "Transformed into what? A guy who can't afford to eat because he blew it all on a tux? I thought you said this place was 'retro'"

"It is to you!" Max said, nudging me with his elbow as we headed toward the door. "But hey, at least you'll be broke *and* stylish."

The air pressed down, thick with cedar and leather, the kind of place where even the quiet felt polished. It wasn't just the suits on display; everything here was untouchable. Perfect. Everything I wasn't. The lighting painted everything in long shadows, making even the simplest tux look like an heirloom. Max moved through the racks like he owned the place, his fingers brushing lapels with the ease of someone who knew they belonged. I followed, careful not to disturb anything, feeling like I was trespassing in a life I didn't want.

Suits and tuxedos hung in neat, perfect rows, their fabrics catching the light, seducing you into buying them. A salesperson glanced up from behind the counter, gave us a polite nod, and then disappeared into the back like they'd decided we weren't worth the hassle.

Max made a beeline for the racks, his fingers skimming the ties like he was auditioning for some kind of high-fashion heist movie. I followed at a slower pace, feeling like I'd wandered into a museum. I stopped at a rack of glossy black tuxedos, running my fingers over the crisp fabric. Fancy. Intimidating. Definitely not me.

"Hey, Carter!" Max's voice carried from the other side of the store. "Get over here. I found it."

I turned to see him holding up a sleek black tux, the fabric gleaming under the spotlights like it had been forged in some magical tailoring realm. He grinned, holding it out toward me. "This. This is you."

I snorted, taking the hanger from him. "How would you know what 'me' is? You haven't seen me in, like, a single shirt that wasn't yours."

"Yeah," he said, crossing his arms and pursing his lips to emphasize the point. "Tragic. Trust me, this? This'll fix everything."

"Right, because a tuxedo's totally gonna solve my life's problems."

Max shrugged, feigning nonchalance. "Maybe not all of them. But it'll solve at least one. Which is step one of my foolproof method."

"I'm gonna start punching you every time you bring up your methods," I said, smirking. "What is this… the 'look sharp' step?"

"Exactly," Max said, snapping his fingers. "See? You're catching on. And if you follow through on that offer, I'll punch you every time you say 'complicated.'"

I sighed, shaking my head as I headed for the dressing rooms. "Alright, fine. But if this thing doesn't fit, I'm blaming you."

Max scoffed, leaning casually against a nearby rack. "Relax. I know you better than you might think. It'll fit."

The tux slid on like it had been waiting for me—made to order, smooth and tailored in a way that felt completely foreign, like stepping into a superhero suit pulled from a different reality. The fabric hugged my frame with this sharp, effortless precision that screamed, *look at you, pretending to have your life together.* I adjusted the jacket in front of the mirror, tilting my head. For a second, I barely recognized myself.

The reflection staring back wasn't the awkward kid stuck on a runaway timeline. It was someone else—someone confident, someone cool. Someone who belonged. I let out a low breath, the moment settling on my chest. *Yeah, okay. You're totally pulling this off.*

I stepped out of the dressing room, the light catching on the fabric in a way that made me look sharper than I had any right to. Max was leaning against the wall, his arms crossed, looking like he'd just been dropped into the scene for dramatic effect. He straightened when he saw me, his grin widening as his eyes swept over me with a look that made my stomach do something weird. Something new.

"Well?" I asked, clearing my throat to break the silence. My voice cracked just a little, because of course it did.

Max tilted his head, his smile spreading like he'd just solved the world's most charming problem. "You look incredible, dude," he said, his voice softer than usual, but still carrying that effortless swagger. "Like, anyone would hire you to walk them down a red carpet. No questions asked."

I laughed nervously, brushing a hand down the front of the jacket. "Yeah? You think the paparazzi will survive?"

"They'll faint on sight." He stepped closer, his gaze lingering just long enough to make my face burn. "But uh..." His eyes narrowed slightly, flicking to the sides of my head. "Hold up. Was that always there?"

"What?" I asked, frowning. "What are you talking about?"

He motioned for me to turn my head, nodding toward the mirror. I did, squinting. Then I saw it. A streak of silver cut through my hair, a quiet crack in the mirror's reflection. My fingers hovered over it, afraid to touch, like it might unravel something delicate. It wasn't just a color—it was a warning, a mark I didn't remember earning.

"No…" I murmured, my voice barely audible. "I—I don't think so."

Max leaned in slightly, his expression softening. "I like it," he said, and there was something so genuine in his voice it threw me off. "It's got this whole 'I've seen things' vibe. It's very you—very cool." He smirked, and the glint in his eyes turned playful. "Everyone at the dance is gonna think it's hot."

"Hot, huh?" I laughed, but it came out shaky. My fingers brushed over the streak. I was touching a warning sign I didn't fully understand.

"Hot," Max repeated, his grin widening. "Trust me. If you don't get at least three numbers by the end of the night, I'll personally stage a re-do."

I shook my head, a small smile tugging at my lips despite the knot in my chest. "You're ridiculous."

"Ridiculous works." He gave me a quick wink, stepping back toward the racks of tuxes. "Alright, don't go stealing all the thunder. My turn."

He grabbed a tux, disappearing into the dressing room with the kind of nonchalant flair that only Max could pull off. I stood there, rooted to the spot, staring at the streak of silver in the mirror. Questions buzzed in my head. *How long had it been there? Why hadn't I noticed? Was this... was this a side effect of everything I'd been through, like stress induced? Or did it mean something much worse... something that time travel created in its sinister workshop.* The thought made my chest tighten.

Then Max stepped out of the dressing room, straightening his jacket. The tux hugged him perfectly, the dark fabric emphasizing the sharp lines of his jaw and the curve of his shoulders. He glanced up, catching me staring, and for a second, neither of us said anything.

"Well?" he asked, mimicking my earlier tone with a playful lilt, but there was something else underneath—something softer, quieter.

"You look…" My mouth went dry, the words stumbling over themselves in my head. "You look good, man," I said finally, my voice barely above a whisper.

A smile spread across his face, his cheeks flushing just slightly as he glanced away. "Guess that's one thing we've got in common," he said, his tone light but carrying an edge of something deeper.

I chuckled, shaking my head. "Shut up."

Max pulled out his wallet, flipping it open to reveal a shiny credit card that looked like it had never been touched. The light caught it, making it gleam like a prop from some old spy movie.

"New card?" I asked, raising an eyebrow as Max casually flipped the card in his hand like it was a poker chip.

"Dad's," he said, smirking like he'd just pulled off the heist of the century. "He's got a whole collection of these lying around. Trust me —he won't notice. Or, if he does, he'll just assume it was something important. Like textbooks. Or life-saving medical supplies."

"Right," I said, giving him a skeptical look. "Because a new tux totally screams *medical emergency*."

Max flashed a grin, tossing the card into the air and catching it with a little flourish. "Relax, Carter. What he doesn't know won't hurt him. Besides, we're performing a public service here. This store has been *tragically* uncool for years. We're just... elevating it."

I snorted, shaking my head as I followed him to the counter. Max strolled up like he owned the place, his easy confidence practically radiating out of him. The woman behind the register barely glanced at him as he pulled the tag off my jacket.

"Would you like a bag for your garments," she asked in the most deadpan voice I'd ever heard, "or are you just going to wear them out?"

Max tilted his head, glancing back at me like he was letting me in on some elaborate scheme. Then, with a smile that could probably charm the pants off a mannequin, he answered, "I think we'll wear them out. But still, give us the bags. Makes the whole thing feel more... *official*."

She didn't even blink, just rang up the clothes like she was counting down the seconds until we left. Max handed over the card with a practiced ease that made it clear this wasn't his first time pulling this stunt. Meanwhile, I stood there feeling like I was an accomplice in some minor act of rebellion, the kind of thing that feels huge when you're doing it but will barely register in your memory later.

When the transaction was done, Max turned to me, holding out one of the glossy shopping bags, which now held our old clothes, like he was bestowing a trophy. "Ready to make our getaway?"

"What, are we fugitives now?" I rolled my eyes.

"Fugitives in style," he said, nudging me toward the door. "Come on. Let's bolt before they realize how much cooler we made them."

We stepped outside, the cool evening air hitting my skin like a wake-up call. The sound of our shoes on the pavement felt strangely sharp, like the world was paying extra attention. Max glanced over at me, his grin softer now, the usual teasing edge replaced with something easier, something that felt safe.

"So," he said, holding the bag over his shoulder. "Ready to see your parents?"

I took a deep breath, catching my reflection in the car window. The streak of silver caught the light, a quiet reminder of everything I didn't understand yet. But when I looked at Max, his smile steady and unwavering, something inside me settled.

"Yeah," I said, a small smile tugging at my lips. "I think I am."

CHAPTER 30

THE STREETS of Burbank stretched out like a dream I'd only half-remembered. The kind where everything felt familiar but not quite real. Max drove with that easy confidence he always carried, one hand loose on the wheel while the other rested on the gearshift. He hummed along to the radio—something soft and distant that barely registered over the buzz in my head. I gave him directions, my voice quieter than usual, and he didn't push. He just nodded, taking the turns like he'd been here before, even though this wasn't his world.

"Left here, then a couple of houses down," I murmured, the words coming out like someone else was saying them. When we turned onto the street, my stomach churned. I knew where we were, even before I could see it. The houses lined the street like plastic models, each one too perfect to be real. Ivy crawled over porches in forced embraces, the kind that looked warm but always cut off your air. I hadn't grown up here, but I'd seen it before. My dad had shown me this house when we first moved to LA. He'd parked the car at the curb and told me, *This was where your mom and I first lived when we got here. Before everything.*

Max killed the engine and turned to me, one arm resting over the back of his seat. His expression softened, the usual easy grin replaced with something quieter, more careful. "You good?" he asked, his voice low but not intrusive, like he was leaving me space to answer however I needed to.

I swallowed, my throat tight, and nodded. "Yeah," I said, though my voice cracked just enough to betray me. I forced myself to smile, small and fleeting. "Let's... let's do this."

Max climbed out first, his movements easy and casual, like we were just here to pick up a pizza and not, you know, revisit my entire emotional baggage claim. I followed, my legs feeling like lead as we walked toward the house. The warm scent of freshly cut grass mixed with something floral—my mom's doing, obviously. She'd always loved planting flowers, even when she didn't have time for it.

The house hadn't changed. Red brick, white trim, the low-sloped roof. It stood there, unassuming, like it had no idea how much of my life was tied to it. The yard looked the same too, maybe a little neater than what I remembered.

And then, like the universe had been waiting for this exact moment, the front door opened.

I froze mid-step, my breath catching in my throat. There they were.

My mom stepped out first, laughing—really laughing—the kind of laugh that lit up her whole face, her hand pressing lightly against her stomach as if to hold it all in. Her dark, wavy hair spilled over her shoulders, catching the sunlight, and she wore a simple dress that somehow looked effortlessly elegant. My dad—James—followed close behind, his arm draped around her shoulders like he belonged there, his other hand spinning the keys to the station wagon parked in the driveway. His hair was all thick, messy waves, a little too perfect to be accidental, and his leather boots made this easy, casual click on the steps as he walked. His grin was all charm, the kind of grin that probably got him out of trouble more than once.

They looked like a snapshot from one of those perfect holiday cards people send when they want the world to think they have it all figured out. But they weren't just posing. They were *alive*. Young, glowing, the weight of everything that would come later still a distant mystery.

"You okay?" Max's voice was low, careful, but steady. He stood just close enough for me to feel him there without pushing, his presence grounding in a way I hadn't realized I needed.

I nodded slowly, the movement shaky and uncertain. My voice barely found its way out. "They look… happy."

And they did. My mom's face was bright, untouched by the shadows of her illness. James leaned in, saying something I couldn't hear, and whatever it was made her laugh again—soft, light, the kind of laugh that felt like a memory and a wish all at once. He pulled her closer, his hand brushing over hers like it was second nature. They fit together in a way that felt so seamless, so right, that it made my chest ache.

Max shoved his hands into his jacket pockets, his gaze following mine. "They seem like they were good together," he said, his voice softer than usual, almost reverent. There was no teasing, no one-liner to cut through the heaviness of the moment. Just Max, solid and present.

"They were," I said, the words scraping out of me like they didn't belong there. "I… don't even know what happened."

The urge to step forward clawed at me, raw and desperate. I could tell them who I was—warn them. Change everything. But the air felt thin, fragile, like one wrong word would shatter it. My feet stayed rooted, the moment holding me still.

Max must've noticed the way my hands were shaking, because he shifted closer, just enough for his shoulder to brush mine. "You don't have to do anything," he murmured, his voice steady, almost too steady. "We can leave whenever. Just say the word."

My fingers brushed the edge of my pocket, the familiar shape of my phone grounding me for a moment. I pulled it out, careful, like it might shatter just from being exposed to the air. The screen flickered to life, the glow catching against the cracks like veins of light. I swiped it open, the camera app loading sluggishly, and raised it just enough to frame them—my parents, caught mid-laugh in a way that felt rare, almost impossible.

It wasn't much. Just a second. A snapshot.

But before I could tap the button, the screen dimmed, and that damned icon popped up. *Low Battery.* The message hung there like a taunt, the light of the screen barely enough to illuminate the cracks running through it. I froze, my thumb hovering uselessly over the screen as the moment slipped past me.

Max glanced down at the phone, then back at me. "It's like that thing has a mind of its own," he said, his voice casual but curious. "You sure it's not haunted? Like, on top of being from the future."

"Definitely haunted," I muttered, trying to focus on breathing. "Because I clearly needed more complications in my life." I turned to him. "Nah, it's just programmed that way. It tells you when it's dying."

Max chuckled, a soft, reassuring sound that somehow cut through the static in my head. "I'm still gonna go with haunted. And, hey, if you're gonna be haunted, at least it's by something cool. Better than, like, a cursed stapler or something."

I couldn't help it—I laughed, the sound shaky but real. "Yeah, because nothing says *cool* like emotional breakdowns and dying batteries."

Max grinned, his hand brushing my arm lightly, just enough to ground me. "Hey, emotional breakdowns build character. Just think— next time you deal with something like this, you'll be a pro."

I rolled my eyes, but it felt easier this time. "Right. Because this happens so often."

He shrugged, his face softening again. "You'd be surprised."

I turned back toward the house. My parents were climbing into the station wagon now, my mom leaning her head against my dad's shoulder as he started the car. The memory felt like something solid I could carry with me, something I didn't need to change or fix. It was enough just to see it. To know it existed.

I took a deep breath, letting the moment settle. "I think—," I said finally, turning back to Max. "I think I'm ready to go."

We climbed back into the Corvette in silence, the seriousness of the moment trailing behind us. As Max pulled onto the street, I glanced back at the house one last time, watching as it faded into the distance. It didn't feel like closure, not exactly. But it was something— like a piece of the puzzle finally falling into place.

. . .

MAX PULLED the Corvette into his driveway, its low growl fading into the quiet suburban night. His house was the kind of place that looked solid, with a porch light that flickered faintly and a front door that always seemed slightly ajar. Without missing a beat, Max turned off the engine and leaned back, stretching like he'd just conquered the world.

"Alright," he said, popping the door open. "Stay here. Gotta grab something."

"What, your winning personality?" I asked, smirking.

Max smiled, opening the door. "Nope. That's all packed and ready to go. Be right back."

I watched as he bounded up the porch steps, his movements loose and easy, like he wasn't about to walk into one of the most photographed events of our teenage lives. He disappeared inside, leaving me alone with the steady hum of crickets and the faint creak of a porch swing being nudged by the wind.

A minute later, the door slammed open, and Max emerged with two small boxes in one hand and his dad, Dave, trailing behind him. Dave was wiping his hands on a grease-stained rag, a polaroid camera hanging from his neck like it belonged there. He was still in his work jacket, but his expression was warm and easy, the kind of look that said he'd already forgiven us for whatever trouble we'd get into tonight.

"Carter!" Max yelled, waving the boxes at me like they were trophies. "Get up here! We've got business."

I groaned, dragging myself out of the car. "Is this gonna be one of those things I regret later?"

"Absolutely not," Max said, grinning as I climbed the steps. "You're in for a real treat."

Dave chuckled softly, stepping aside to let me pass. "Don't let him talk you into anything too crazy, alright?"

"No promises," I muttered, side-eyeing Max as he popped open one of the boxes.

Inside was a boutonnière, the petals soft and white with a thin black ribbon wrapped delicately around the base. It looked like something out of a wedding catalog—way too fancy for a high school dance, which immediately made me suspicious.

"What is that?" I asked, pointing at it like it might explode.

"This," Max said, lifting the boutonnière with a dramatic flourish, "is how we announce to the world that we've got style."

"Style," I repeated, raising an eyebrow. "You mean *you* have style, and I'm just here for moral support."

Max laughed, already pinning the boutonnière to my lapel. "Exactly. You're my plus-one to the cool club. Hold still, would you?"

I smirked, not moving. "You're acting like I'm your date."

He chuckled, stepping back to admire his work. "What, you're not honored?"

Dave leaned against the porch railing, his camera in hand. "Alright, boys. Hold still. Let me get a picture." His voice carried something quiet, something that settled in the spaces between us—like he knew these moments were rare, fleeting.

"Dad," Max groaned, turning toward him. "We're gonna be late."

"You'll survive," Dave said, lifting the camera. "Now quit whining and act like you like each other."

Max sighed dramatically, throwing his arm around my shoulders with the flair of someone who knew exactly how to milk a moment. "There. Happy?"

"Ecstatic," Dave said, snapping a photo. He lowered the camera slightly as it spit the picture out, his gaze softening as he looked at us. "You two clean up pretty well, you know."

"Yeah, yeah," Max muttered, reaching for the second box. He pinned the other boutonnière to his jacket with practiced ease, then gestured toward me. "Alright, Carter. Ready to make some memories?"

"Memories, huh?" I said, smirking. "Is that what we're calling this?"

Dave chuckled, shaking his head as he adjusted the camera strap around his neck. "You boys have fun tonight. And Max—look out for Carter, alright?"

Max gave a mock salute, his grin softening into something quieter. "Always."

We headed back to the car, the boutonnières pinned in place, and as we climbed in, I glanced back at the house. Dave was still on the porch, watching us with that steady, thoughtful look that seemed to hold more weight than his words. His camera hung by his stomach, forgotten for now, but the moment stayed with me.

Max started the car, the engine roaring to life. "Sorry about that. My dad's pretty sentimental about photos. Sometimes it's all you have left, you know? Probably gonna frame it right next to my kindergarten graduation picture. Anyways," he said, throwing me a quick smile. "Ready to blow some minds?"

"Sure," I said, settling into the seat. "As long as you're ready to clean up the mess."

He laughed, and as the house faded into the night behind us, I felt that familiar, strange warmth settle in my chest. Max always had this way of turning things into a show, but somehow, it didn't feel like he was performing for anyone else. Just me. And for once, that didn't seem so complicated.

CHAPTER 31

THE HALL STOOD out against the December night like it had been ripped straight from a dream. Strings of lights draped along its façade shimmered in the crisp air, bouncing off balloons tied to the railings. Warm laughter and bursts of conversation spilled out through the open doors, carried on the pulse of bass-heavy music that thudded like a heartbeat through the sidewalk. It was magnetic, like the whole thing had its own gravity, pulling us in.

Max parked his Corvette just shy of the entrance, its glossy red paint catching the glow of the lights. He cut the engine, and for a moment, the only sound was the fading rumble of the car and the distant thrum of the music. We sat there, both of us lingering in the silence, like stepping out would break some unspoken spell.

"Ready?" Max asked, throwing me one of his trademark grins—the kind that said he didn't take anything too seriously but secretly cared more than he'd admit. His fingers drummed on the steering wheel, the rhythm betraying his excitement.

I exhaled, fiddling with the cuff of my jacket. "Ready's a strong word," I muttered, stealing a glance at the hall. The flickering lights felt almost too bright, too alive. "Let's just say I'm prepared to endure whatever this is."

Max laughed, a bright, effortless sound that cut through the tension like sunlight through fog. "Endure? Come on, Carter. This is Formal. You're supposed to *live a little*. Trust me, it's gonna be fun."

"Famous last words," I said, but my lips twitched into a reluctant smile. I didn't want to admit it, but his excitement was infectious.

"Alright, no more stalling." Max clapped his hands and swung the door open. "Time to show off our new looks."

I rolled my eyes but followed his lead, stepping into the cold night air. We adjusted our jackets as we walked toward the entrance, the sound of our shoes clicking against the pavement swallowed up by the growing hum of the crowd inside. At the door, Max held it open with an exaggerated flourish, his hand brushing mine as I passed. It was small, barely a thing, but it sent a spark up my arm, grounding me in the moment.

Inside, the hall hit us like a tidal wave. Music boomed from unseen speakers, spilling across the room in bursts of electric sound. Beams of light swept over the dance floor, catching on glittering decorations and casting kaleidoscopic patterns on the walls. Streamers hung from the ceiling like vines, swaying gently in the current of movement below. Laughter rippled through the air, mingling with the music to create a buzzing, electrified energy that felt like it might burst at any second. Hanging above it all was a hand-painted banner that read, *"How Will I Snow,"* clearly nodding to Whitney Houston.

Max let out a low whistle, his smile widening as he took it all in. "Now this is what I'm talking about! Look at this place—it's like the set of a music video. Or a cheesy prom movie. Either way, we're about to own it."

I couldn't help but laugh. "Yeah, we'll be legends. You know, as long as we don't trip over someone's feet or get tangled in the streamers."

"Don't underestimate us," Max said, nudging me with his elbow. "We're trendsetters. Visionaries. By tomorrow, everyone'll be talking about how we *redefined* the Formal experience."

"Wow, bold claim," I said, my voice heavy with mock awe. "Can't wait to see how we pull that off."

As we moved through the crowd, heads turned, and a few whistles and shouts rang out. "Matching tuxes? Bold choice!" someone called. Another chimed in, "Lookin' sharp, Max!"

Max flashed a confident grin, leaning close enough for me to hear him over the music. "What'd I tell you? Trendsetters."

At the refreshment table, Max grabbed two glasses, handing one to me with a wink. "To the best-dressed pair in the room," he said, raising his cup. "Cheers to our inevitable domination."

"Cheers," I said, laughing as I clinked my cup against his. The cold fizz hit my throat like a spark, cutting through the surreal buzz of the night. I could actually let myself sink into the moment, like I didn't have to hold the world up on my shoulders.

But then I saw him.

Dr. Mercer leaned against the far wall, his silhouette cutting through the chaos like a knife. The sharp lines of his suit, the curl of his smirk—they belonged to someone who had already decided how the night would end. His glasses glinted, catching the light like the flash of a predator's eyes.

The room tilted, the music fading into the background as my chest tightened. He wasn't doing anything—just standing there, a calm, amused observer. Too calm. His expression held that same detached confidence he always carried, like he was counting the seconds and just waiting for me to catch up.

Max noticed before I even said a word. He followed my gaze, and his jaw tensed as his shoulders stiffened. "Oh, fantastic," he muttered, shifting closer until his shoulder brushed mine, steady and grounding. "Looks like Mr. Chaos Theory himself decided to crash the party."

"What the hell is he doing here?" I whispered, my voice tight as I forced my grip to loosen on the cup in my hand.

Max shrugged, his tone light but edged with irritation. "Probably here to ruin your night." He bumped his arm against mine, his voice dipping into something quieter. "But hey, don't sweat it. He's not gonna pull anything in a crowd this big. He likes an audience, but he's not stupid. Just ignore him."

Easy to say, harder to do. My eyes kept flicking back to Dr. Mercer. He wasn't moving, wasn't even blinking, just watching me with that unnerving, too-knowing stare. His fingers tapped idly against his arm, like he was preparing himself for something only he knew about.

Max leaned in, his voice softer now, like he was letting me in on a secret. "Hey. Look at me, not him."

I forced myself to turn, meeting Max's eyes. He beamed, lopsided and confident, his expression so effortlessly sure of itself that it almost made me believe I could be too. "We came here to have fun, remember? Don't let him rent space in your head. Focus on me. I'm *way* more interesting."

I let out a shaky laugh, grateful for the distraction. "Wow. Humble too."

"Always," Max said, raising his cup and clinking it against mine again. "Now come on. Let's make some memories. Something worth boring our kids with someday."

I nodded, but Dr. Mercer's gaze stuck with me. Even as we moved deeper into the crowd, his presence hung in the back of my mind like a shadow, reminding me that no matter how bright this night felt, the darkness was always just a step behind.

As we wandered toward the dance floor, Max spotted Jessica, Josh, and Tyler in the middle of what could only be described as a hilariously chaotic dance-off. Jessica twirled like a goth ballerina on a sugar rush, her black velvet dress flaring out as she spun. A silver spiderweb necklace caught the light, and her black fingerless gloves made her movements look dramatic and deliberate, even when her balance wasn't perfect. Her hair, styled in thick, glossy waves, framed her face, the deep plum lipstick and smoky eyeliner making her smile look mischievous and sharp.

Josh, towering over everyone else, was locked in a stiff attempt at the robot. His light-gray suit didn't quite fit—it was clearly borrowed, the shoulders slightly too wide, and the sleeves a little too short, showing his wrists as he jerked his arms with exaggerated precision. His floppy dark hair kept falling into his eyes, and every few seconds, he'd blow it out of his face, determined not to break character.

Then there was Tyler, bouncing up and down like a hyperactive jackrabbit. His green-and-red plaid blazer, paired with a skinny black tie, gave him a distinctly Christmas ornament vibe, but somehow, he pulled it off with the dorky charm only Tyler could manage. His freckles were barely visible under the flush of exertion as he waved his arms like he was fending off invisible bats.

Jessica spotted us first and threw her arms up, her silver bracelets jangling as she waved us over. "Get over here, you cowards!" she called, her voice cutting through the music. "You can't just stand there —this is a dance!"

Max laughed, already stepping forward. He grabbed my wrist before I could protest, his grip warm and steady. "You heard her, Carter," he said, flashing me a grin that dared me to try and keep up. "Time for step two: *don't trip on your feet.* No sitting this one out. C'mon."

"I—" Whatever excuse I was about to come up with didn't stand a chance. He was already pulling me into their circle, his energy as unstoppable as it was contagious.

Jessica immediately spun toward me, grabbing both my hands with a smile that could've lit up the room. "Finally! About time!"

Josh broke character for a second to throw me a thumbs-up. "Welcome to the weirdest circle of the night," he said, his voice a little breathless as he adjusted his too-short sleeves.

Tyler jumped closer, almost colliding with me. "Just watch out for Jess's spinning! She's gonna take us all down!"

"Shut up, Tyler!" Jessica shouted, laughing as she twirled dangerously close to him. "This is art!"

Max let out a bark of laughter, already swaying to the beat. "Alright, Carter. Let's see what you've got." He threw me a wink, his confidence making it impossible not to at least try.

And just like that, I found myself pulled into their orbit—a chaotic, colorful mess of spinning, jumping, and laughter. The music pounded, each beat vibrating in my chest like it was trying to force me into the present. Max spun beside me, his laughter breaking through the noise. For a moment, I let the rhythm drown out the hollow ache clawing at my ribs.

I threw myself into the chaos with all the coordination of a baby giraffe on roller skates. All I could do was dougie. Jessica cheered me on with exaggerated enthusiasm, Josh doubled over laughing at some move I didn't realize I was doing, and Max—Max just laughed, his gaze flicking to mine every so often with a glint that said, *See? Told you this would be fun.*

And he wasn't wrong. For the first time in what felt like forever, I let myself just be. Everything I'd been carrying—the anxiety, the questions, the gnawing unease—faded into the beat of the music and the rhythm of everyone moving around me. Max stayed close, his presence grounding me in a way I didn't want to overthink. Whenever our eyes met, the world would shrink to just us, like the chaos around us didn't matter.

This is our night, his expression seemed to say. And for once, I believed it.

When a voice called my name, sharp and clear over the noise, I turned to see Tiffany approaching, her smile as dazzling as ever, her hair teased, and her sequined dress catching the light in a way that made her look like a goddess dipped in starlight. Her eyes flicked over my suit, and she giggled, a little too satisfied for my comfort.

"Carter! Wow, you clean up nice," she said, her gaze lingering. "And your hair—different. I like it! Really suits you."

"Uh, thanks, Tiffany," I said, my voice coming out uneven, like my words were tripping over themselves. "Same to you." A strange buzz started under my skin, faint at first but growing stronger, pulsing in time with the music. It wasn't nerves—it was something deeper, something wrong. My vision blurred for a second, the edges of the room smearing into a watercolor painting that dripped and muddied over the edges of the canvas.

Tiffany didn't seem to notice. "You've got to tell me where you got your suit. You look amazing."

I tried to respond, but the buzzing grew louder, thrumming through my chest like an invisible thread pulling tighter and tighter. My stomach churned, the floor tilting under my feet, but I forced myself to stay upright, my smile frozen in place.

Before I could excuse myself, the music cut out with a jarring screech, replaced by the crackle of a microphone. I turned toward the podium at the far end of the room, where a figure stepped into the spotlight.

"Ladies and gentlemen," Dr. Mercer's voice echoed through the speakers, smooth and deliberate, every word landing with unnerving precision. He stood under the stage lights, his face half-shadowed, but his gaze scanned the crowd like he was searching for something—or someone. My chest tightened when his eyes found mine, glinting with a look that could only be described as triumphant.

"It's time for the announcement of this year's Winter Formal King and Queen," he said, pausing just long enough to let the tension simmer.

Applause rippled through the room, the crowd turning toward the stage. For a brief second, I felt relief. At least Dr. Mercer was busy up there. But then his gaze shifted, his smirk widening as he locked eyes with me again.

"Tonight's King," Mercer announced, his voice sharp enough to cut through the room's buzz, "is Carter Sullivan." The spotlight seared into my skin, its heat crawling under my suit like a live wire. The cheers around me warped, stretched thin, until they weren't cheers at all—just static, a mocking echo that threatened to split me open. Everything seemed to be moving in slow motion.

Tiffany squealed beside me, grabbing my arm and bouncing with excitement, but the tug in my chest tightened, sharp and insistent, like the universe itself was pulling me apart.

I glanced toward Max, desperate for an anchor. He was watching me, his easy grin slipping into something more serious, concern flickering in his eyes. I wanted to go to him, to escape this suffocating moment, but Tiffany's grip on my arm held firm.

"And the Winter Dance Queen," Dr. Mercer continued, his smile stretching wider, "is none other than Tiffany Hart!"

A second spotlight illuminated Tiffany, who gasped and clapped her hands over her mouth like she couldn't believe it. The crowd roared, voices chanting our names, and Tiffany turned to me, beaming as she grabbed my hand.

"C'mon, Carter! We have to get up there!" she said, pulling me toward the stage.

My feet moved automatically, the pressure in my chest building with every step. I glanced back at Max, my gaze catching his for one desperate second. His mouth moved—words I couldn't hear over the noise—but the look in his eyes was clear: *You don't have to do this.*

But Tiffany's grip tightened, and the crowd surged around us, carrying me forward. The lights grew brighter, the noise louder, and the pull in my chest twisted into something unbearable. I stepped into the spotlight, unsure if I could hold myself together.

The dizziness hit like ripples from a stone dropped into dark water, each one pulling me deeper. My chest burned, hollow and frantic, my heartbeat stuttering like it was struggling to remember its rhythm. My legs wobbled as I tried to keep up with Tiffany, but the floor felt less like solid ground and more like a cheap carnival ride on its last legs.

"Carter!" Tiffany's voice rang out from the stage, bright and sugary, but warped, distorted—like it was traveling through water. She twirled under the spotlight, her dress glittering obnoxiously. "Come on! Don't be shy!"

I blinked hard, my vision swimming. Her words didn't feel real. Nothing did. My hand slipped from hers, and I stumbled back, my balance teetering dangerously. The pull in my chest—it wasn't just a feeling anymore. It was a force, something invisible and relentless, yanking me toward a place I couldn't see but could feel deep in my bones.

The crowd's laughter and chatter swirled around me, voices overlapping and twisting together like someone had hit fast-forward on reality. Faces melted into each other, features twisting and dissolving like smoke caught in a broken mirror, leaving behind only fragments of what they'd been. Somewhere near the edge of the dance floor, I caught sight of Max, his eyes locked on me. Concern flashed across his face, and for a moment, it was like a thread yanking me back— something solid in a world that was coming undone.

My legs gave a warning wobble, and I shoved past the dancers, ignoring their half-curious, half-annoyed murmurs. Every step felt like dragging myself through wet cement, but I aimed for the one thing that felt steady in the chaos.

"Carter, dude!" Jessica's voice pierced through the noise, sharp and teasing. She jabbed Josh in the ribs, laughing. "What, are you drunk or something? You're supposed to be up there, getting your big moment —what are you doing?!"

The words bounced off me, distant and meaningless.

"Max," I croaked, reaching him and grabbing his arm like it was the only thing keeping me from floating away. "Something's... wrong. I don't... I don't know what's happening."

Max didn't waste a second. His face shifted, the concern melting into something sharper, more focused. His arm wrapped around my shoulders, steady and warm, holding me up when my knees felt ready to give out. "Whoa, hey—Carter, it's cool. Breathe, okay? Just breathe." His voice was calm but firm, like he was anchoring me with the sound of it. "We're getting out of here. Come on."

He started guiding me toward the door, his grip solid, steady. Around us, people shot curious glances, a few whispers floating through the crowd, but Max didn't seem to notice—or care. His focus was laser-tight on me, like the rest of the room had just faded into the background.

Jessica's voice floated up again, a mix of teasing and genuine confusion. "Seriously? What's your guys's deal? You're bailing on formal already?"

Josh muttered something about me "needing a minute," but I couldn't even turn my head to respond. My world had narrowed to Max's arm around me and the relentless pull in my chest, growing stronger with every step.

CHAPTER 32

The doors finally swung open, and the cool night air hit me like a slap to the face. It wasn't relief, though. If anything, the pull grew worse, like something deep inside me was unraveling, drawing me closer to a cliff I could only sense but couldn't see. My breaths came shallow and sharp, and I clung to Max, the only thing keeping me grounded.

Max steered me toward a bench just outside the dance hall, easing me down onto it. "Alright, talk to me," he said, crouching in front of me, his hands on my shoulders. His voice was softer now, coaxing but steady. "What's going on? Someone spike the punch? Bad shrimp? Did Tiffany make you listen to her ten-year plan?"

I let out a shaky laugh, the kind that didn't even sound like me. "It's not… it's not the punch," I mumbled, my head sinking into my hands. "Something's wrong, Max. I don't know what it is, but it's—" My words cut off, a lump lodging itself in my throat. "It's like something's pulling me. Like… like I'm coming apart."

Max's brow furrowed, and for a second, he looked like he wanted to crack another joke but thought better of it. "Coming apart?" he repeated, his voice low. "Alright. That's… worrying. But hey, we'll deal with it. Whatever it is, we'll figure it out."

I glanced at him, my vision still swimming, threatening nausea, but his face came into sharp focus—his green eyes steady, his grin gone but replaced by something better: *reassurance*. Max wasn't panicking. He wasn't even flinching. Like no matter how messed up this was, he was sticking to the plan. And the plan, apparently, was me.

"You're freaking out, and I get it," Max said, his voice steady but stretched thin, like he was holding his breath for both of us. "I've got you. Whatever's pulling you apart, I'm not letting it take you. Worst-case scenario, you're having a meltdown, and we'll laugh about it later. Best-case, we skip out on the lame part of the dance and find a diner or something."

Another shaky laugh slipped out of me, and I finally met his eyes. "You make it sound like a win-win."

He smirked, his hands still firm on my shoulders. "It's what I do."

The pull surged again, a sharp, invisible tug deep in my chest. I gasped, my body stiffening, and Max's grip tightened. "Okay, Carter, you're scaring me here," he said, his voice dropping. "Is this, like… a medical thing? Do I need to call someone?"

"No," I said quickly, shaking my head. "It's not… it's not that. It's something else. Something I can't—" My breath hitched, and I doubled over slightly, clutching my chest. "I can't explain it."

Max stayed steady, his hands moving to my back, rubbing in slow, grounding circles. "Alright. So we don't explain it. Let's get you to my car. You, me, fresh air. Whatever's pulling at you, we're gonna beat it, okay?"

I nodded, clinging to his voice like it was the only thing keeping me anchored to the ground. For a moment, the warmth of his hand on my back, the calm in his voice, made the pull feel almost manageable. Almost. But it didn't stop. It dragged at me, harder and deeper, like some invisible thread was yanking at my insides.

We stumbled off the sidewalk, my steps heavy and uneven, Max practically holding me up. Rows of cars stretched ahead, the harsh glow of the security lights casting long, sharp shadows that made everything feel colder. We reached the edge, and I braced myself against a parked car, gripping the metal like it might stop the world from spinning.

Max crouched beside me, his hand still firm on my shoulder.

"Carter," he said, his voice softer now, careful but urgent. "Talk to me. What's going on? You're—you're about to collapse."

I opened my mouth to answer, but before I could say anything, the shadows shifted. A chill ran up my spine, and I didn't need to look to know who was standing behind us.

"Going somewhere?" Dr. Mercer's voice sliced through the quiet like a blade, smooth and sharp, with that complacency that made my stomach twist.

Max shot to his feet, putting himself between me and Dr. Mercer. His stance was rigid, protective, and his tone dropped an octave. "What do you want?" he snapped, his usual playfulness gone, replaced by something fierce.

Dr. Mercer stepped closer, his silhouette looming against the security lights. He tilted his head, his gaze flicking from Max to me with a calculated calm. "Carter doesn't look so good, does he?" His tone dripped with mock concern, like he was savoring the moment. "I warned you, Carter. This time isn't yours. And now, well... you're feeling it, aren't you? You're an anomaly. Time is recalibrating, erasing the error thread by thread. It's clinical. Precise. Unforgiving. I'd say it's poetic, but that might be giving you too much credit."

I clutched my chest as the pull grew sharper, deeper, like a hook lodged inside me was tearing me apart. "Fuck off," I croaked, my voice barely audible.

"Still defiant," Dr. Mercer said, his smirk curling wider. "Admirable, but pointless. Your body is rotting from the inside out— time scraping away at you, piece by piece."

Is this what he meant back in '95? Is this what takes me? What happens to me?

Max didn't back down. He stepped closer to Dr. Mercer, his jaw tight, his hands clenched into fists. "Whatever you're trying to prove," he said, his voice low and biting, "leave him alone. He's not your science experiment."

"Oh, but he is," Dr. Mercer countered, his smirk fading into something colder. "He's proof of everything I've worked toward. A living, breathing paradox, falling apart before my eyes. It's beautiful, really. Soon he'll simply be cast into the void."

The words hit like a punch to the gut, and my vision blurred. My grip on the parked car tightened as the pull became unbearable, a deep, wrenching force that felt like it was dragging me toward oblivion. My pocket buzzed violently, and I fumbled for my phone, my trembling hands barely holding it steady as her name flashed on the screen—Mom.

Mom, please... I need you. I— I'm scared.

Tears plucked at my eyes, my heart skipping. I hit play, and her voice crackled through the static, soft but urgent, like it was being carried across a vast, impossible distance. "You're almost there... don't forget... the red door, it's your way home..."

The message cut out, leaving only the faint hum of the dying battery and the silence around us. Her words echoed in my head, but they didn't make sense. *The red door? What red door? And how did she even know where I was?*

Max glanced down at the phone, his eyes narrowing. "Carter, what—"

Dr. Mercer cut him off, his voice darker now, almost a growl. "It doesn't matter. The battery's draining. And when it's gone, so is he. Dust in the wind. A ripple erased."

Max stepped closer to him, his shoulders squaring. "You're done here," he said, his voice steady, calm, and brimming with defiance. "You don't get to decide what happens to him."

Dr. Mercer stared at Max, his eyes narrowing as if sizing him up. "This isn't a debate, Max. It's inevitability. And soon, Carter will be nothing. Lost. No time, no place. Just... empty."

Max didn't flinch. He turned, pulling me close, his arm steadying me. "We're leaving," he said firmly. "And you're not stopping us."

Dr. Mercer's smirk flickered, his gaze cold as he stayed rooted to the spot. Max's hand was a steady weight on my shoulder, guiding me toward his Corvette like I was a drunk friend he had to haul out of a party.

"Come on," Max said, his voice easy but firm. "We're getting out of here. No debates, no drama."

The car loomed under the harsh glare of the security light, its red paint gleaming like fresh blood. The sight of it stopped me cold. My breath hitched, my chest tightening like something was clawing its way up my ribs.

It wasn't just a car. It was *the* car.

The red door, it's your way home.

Her voice echoed in my head, faint and distorted, but clear enough to set every nerve on edge. Mom. The voicemail. The warning. It all slammed into me like a brick wall.

"No," I croaked, my voice cracking as I grabbed Max's arm. My fingers curled around his jacket sleeve like it was the only thing keeping me from falling. "I... I can't. I can't go in."

Max frowned, his grip on my shoulder tightening as he turned to face me. "Carter, what are you talking about? It's just my car. It's not going to bite." He leaned down a little, searching my face, his expression softening when he saw how freaked out I was. "Hey, you're fine. You're safe. Okay? Fuck that guy and whatever he says. He's wrong. You're okay."

But I wasn't. The door wasn't just a door anymore. It was something alive, something humming with possibility, or danger, or both. The pull was sharp now, yanking at me, and no matter how hard I tried to hold my ground, I could feel myself slipping closer.

"I'm terrified, Max." I whispered, the words barely making it out. "I got this voicemail. From my mom." I swallowed, trying to steady my breath. "She said... a red door would get me home."

Max blinked, his frown shifting into something halfway between confusion and concern. "A red door?" His gaze flicked to the Corvette, then back to me. "Wait, you think my car—?"

I nodded, the air squeezing out of my chest. My voice cracked as I choked out, "If I get in... it might be the last time I see you, Max," my throat constricted. "I—I've spent so much time letting go. Letting go of my mom, my dad, my life. I don't have anything left to give up. I can't do it again—not to you."

Max went still, his hand resting on my shoulder like he was trying to steady me. For a moment, he didn't say anything. Then his expression softened, and he gave me one of those rare, serious looks that always threw me off. No teasing, no grin. Just Max, looking right at me.

"Carter," he said quietly, his voice thick with something I couldn't name. "If this is your way home… you're taking it. If this is it—really it —, if I have to let you go, I'll do it. I'd rather let you go before I sit here and watch you fade away. Because…" He hesitated, his jaw tightening. "Because if this is goodbye, I want it to be ours—not stolen piece by piece while I watch you disappear." His voice wavered, strained with everything he wasn't saying. "If this is it, Carter… then let it matter."

His words cut through the haze, grounding me, but they didn't make the ache in my chest any easier to bear. I swallowed hard, my fingers gripping his sleeve like it was the only thing keeping me together. "What if I never see you again?" I whispered, my voice trembling.

He let out a slow breath, his eyes soft but sad as he pulled me into a hug. His arms wrapped around me, warm and steady, his hand pressing gently against my back like he was trying to keep me from falling apart.

"Maybe this is how it ends. I hate it—I hate that it has to. But all the time we've had? It's been everything, Carter. *You've* been everything. I don't know how to say goodbye to you. But if this is it… you need to know you've mattered. You've mattered more than you'll ever know."

My chest tightened, his words hitting like a freight train. "Ditto," I managed, the word breaking on my lips. "I guess… step three's checked off." My fingers curled into his jacket, holding on like I could imprint this moment into my brain. The faint scent of his cologne, the warmth of his arms, the steady rhythm of his heartbeat—it all felt so present, so real, even as everything else felt like it was slipping away.

"See? I told you it was foolproof." His warm breath whispered against my ear. Finally, he pulled back, his hand lingering on my shoulder as he gave me one last, soft smile. "Left just enough mystery to last a lifetime. Now, go on," he said, his voice quieter now. "Before I change my mind and lock you in my trunk."

I let out a shaky laugh, even as my throat tightened. "Yeah… Like that'd stop me."

"Hey," he said, his smirk returning, teasing and genuine all at once as tears shined in his eyes. "I'm just saying, it's an option."

I nodded, forcing myself to take a step back. Then another. My legs felt heavy, like they were stuck in concrete, but I kept moving. When I reached the passenger door, I hesitated, my hand hovering over the handle.

Max's face lingered in the frame of the door, his eyes catching the light just enough to shine. He wasn't smiling anymore. His expression was an anchor, a silent plea not to forget him, even as the pull dragged me away. He shut the door for me, his hand lingering for just a second longer than it needed to.

And then, without warning, the world fractured—light and sound collapsing into a singular, suffocating pull. I didn't fall through the door. It devoured me, erasing everything: Max, the car, even myself. Nothing remained but the cold expanse of oblivion.

The darkness consumed me whole—dense and endless, like sinking into a sea of ink. It surrounded me from all sides, erasing the edges of my body, my mind, until I wasn't sure where I ended and the void began. Max's face, his voice, the sound of the dance—all of it slipped away, fading into nothing.

For a moment—or maybe an eternity—there was nothing. No light, no sound. Just cold, empty silence stretching out forever. I was falling, but there was no ground to hit. No end. Just the endless in-between.

And then, at the edges of the darkness, a flicker. A faint thread of light, barely visible but there, like the faint memory of a star long gone. I reached out for it, clinging to the sound of Mom's voice echoing in my mind. Her laugh. Her warmth. Her words.

I wasn't sure if I was moving forward, backward, or sideways through time. All I knew was the thread was all I had left, and I wasn't letting go.

CHAPTER 33

Reality punched through like a splintered windshield. The Highlander roared beneath me, the wipers frantically slashing at the rain that pelted the glass in relentless sheets. Panic detonated inside me—wild and suffocating, like it had been lying in wait, coiled under my ribs. "Shit!" The word tore out of me as my hands jerked the wheel.

The tires screamed against the slick pavement, water spraying up in violent arcs as the car skidded, fighting for traction. My chest hit the seatbelt hard, the impact knocking the air from my lungs. The world spun sideways, rain blurring into streaks of light and shadow, before collapsing into stillness.

Everything froze, except the pounding rain and the rhythmic drumming of my heartbeat slamming against my chest. My breaths came in jagged gasps, each inhale tasting like damp leather and electric air. Outside, the storm continued its tirade, the wind screaming through the trees like it had been unleashed with me.

I stayed there, gripping the wheel, my fingers trembling against the cold leather. The rain ran in rivers down the windshield, distorting the muted orange hues of the setting sun fighting to cut through the storm clouds. It should've felt like a reprieve, the kind of rain that washes things clean—but instead, it felt like the world was drowning alongside me.

I collapsed forward, my forehead dropping onto the wheel. The sob hit before I could stop it—raw and guttural, scraping up from somewhere too deep to name. It tore through me like a fault line splitting open. Tears burned in my eyes, hot and bitter, spilling down my cheeks and onto my lap. I couldn't stop them, didn't even try. Everything I'd seen, everything I'd lost, crashed over me in one brutal wave. *I was back. Finally back. But was any of it real? Was I going crazy? Did I imagine it all?*

Max's laugh floated up, fragile and far away, like a memory I wasn't ready to let go of. Nat's crooked smile followed, sharp and vivid, her voice cutting through the haze: *"Don't forget me."* It was almost enough to trick me into believing she was still here. My chest ached at the thought of them—people I hadn't meant to care about but had ended up tying myself to anyway. And now they were gone. I'd left them behind, pulled away like some cruel trick the universe was playing on all of us.

I thought about Dr. Mercer, about the way his sharp words always hid something heavier underneath. Was he still here, somewhere? Or had he moved on, stuck in his own endless loop of cause and effect? And Max... Max's face lingered the longest, the way he'd looked at me just before I was ripped away. The quiet acceptance. The sadness he tried to hide but couldn't.

Could I have stayed? Could I have found a way to make it work, or was it always going to end like this—with me alone, back in a life I didn't know if I wanted anymore?

On the passenger seat, my phone lay like a discarded relic, its cracked screen catching a fractured bolt of lightning that ripped through the sky outside. Thunder rolled seconds later, deep and resonant, shaking the car to its core. The battery icon blinked weakly— 1%. One fragile thread, unraveling fast.

"Don't die on me," I whispered, my voice trembling as I gripped it tighter. "Not you, too."

But the screen flickered once, twice, and then it was gone. Just a lifeless black mirror reflecting my face, fractured and hollow. I stared at it, willing it to come back, but it stayed dark. The last tether I had to the people I'd left behind, severed in a way that felt final. Over.

For a long moment, I just sat there, staring at the phone as if it might spring back to life. My reflection in the cracked glass mocked me, the lines of my face softer, younger, less tired than they've been in what felt like a year. The gray hairs I'd started noticing were gone too, but the memories they'd left behind felt worse than the change.

Finally, with shaking hands, I plugged the phone into the car charger. The screen flickered, dim at first, and then the battery icon appeared, glowing faintly—1%. Relief flooded through me, a fragile, fleeting thing. But before I could exhale, a notification popped up.

Voicemail: James.

My chest tightened, the air leaving my lungs in a rush. My fingers hovered over the screen, trembling. *I could ignore it. Pretend I didn't see it.* Let it slip away like so many other things I couldn't face. But something inside me stirred—exhaustion, desperation, or maybe just the faintest flicker of courage.

I hit play.

The line crackled, static carving through the silence before his voice slipped through—a rough, hesitant thing, like he was afraid it might shatter. "Carter… I know I screwed everything up."

I froze, the words slamming into me like a punch to the gut.

"Moving out here... leaving... I thought it was the right thing. I thought space would make it easier to breathe, for both of us. But the truth is… I was a coward."

His voice cracked, the emotion tangible even through the phone. "I shouldn't have left—shouldn't have taken you with me. I should've been there for her. For your sake. But I couldn't handle her slipping away. I was scared. I know it's no excuse and… and maybe it's too late for me to make things right, but… I'm trying. Please, just call me when you get this."

The voicemail ended, leaving a hollow silence in its wake. I let the phone fall from my hand, dropping it onto the floor of the car. My shoulders slumped, his words choking me harder than the quiet ever could.

I stared out the windshield, the horizon blurring into a smear of colors I couldn't name. I finally did it. I let myself feel the void he'd made—the empty space where normalcy should've been. Maybe he'd been running, just like me. Running from the fear, from the things he couldn't fix. And maybe, in some cruel, twisted way, we'd been running from the same thing all along.

But now, sitting there in the fading light, I realized something: *I was tired of running.*

Maybe, it was time to stop.

THE STORM BEGAN to ease as I turned into Mom's neighborhood, the rain softening to a persistent drizzle. The streets glistened, mirrors of asphalt reflecting streetlights just beginning to flicker to life. It was like someone had hit pause on the chaos of the storm, leaving the aftermath slick and glimmering under the muted glow of the fading sun.

Everything in her neighborhood was the same but softer, like someone had taken sandpaper to the edges of the houses, the trees, the cracked sidewalks. Each turn of the wheel felt like I was peeling back layers of memory, but they didn't fit quite right anymore—too warped, too faded, like a painting left out in the rain.

I pulled into the driveway, the low rumble of the car engine cutting out as I turned the key. The rain continued to tap against the roof, steady but lighter now, a quiet rhythm to fill the silence and soothe the soul. The house stood in front of me, unchanged but also completely different. Beige siding, slanted porch steps, the windows I used to sneak out of when I was twelve—all still there. But now it felt less like home and more like some museum exhibit called *"Relics of Carter's Childhood."* Same stuff, different Carter.

I sat there gripping the steering wheel, the leather cool under my fingers, staring at the house like it was daring me to walk in. This place had been everything once—my whole universe, where every scraped knee, every laugh, every grounding happened. But now I was on the edge of some chasm, staring into a version of my life I wasn't sure I fit into anymore. My pulse thudded in my ears, loud enough to drown out the creak of the car's cooling engine.

"Alright," I muttered to myself, because apparently I'd started giving pep talks these days. "Just get out of the car, Carter. Let's pray it's the right time. At least the house is… *here.*"

My fingers uncurled reluctantly from the steering wheel, and I pushed the door open. The metal groaned in protest, the sound sharp in the stillness. The air outside was thick with the scent of grass and old pavement, and the faint whiff of someone's dryer vent puffing out warm, soapy air. The kind of smells that shouldn't mean anything but still managed to punch me in the gut with memories I wasn't ready to unpack.

I took a slow step up the driveway, then another. My eyes drifted to the window beside the front door—the one with the lace curtains Mom had always loved. She was there, sitting in her chair by the window, her favorite spot. The one she'd claimed years ago to watch the neighborhood kids ride their bikes and play tag in the street. Her face was turned slightly away, her expression soft but distant, like she wasn't quite there. Her hand rested on the arm of the chair, still and quiet, and something in the sight of her hit me square in the chest.

She looked the same, but she didn't. The same shape, the same presence, but dulled somehow, like she'd been fading while I was gone. And I'd missed it. Missed all of it.

I swallowed hard, forcing my legs to move toward the red wooden door. Each step felt heavier than the last, my breath hitching as I raised my hand to knock. My knuckles hit the wood—once, twice, the sound echoing like it didn't belong in this moment.

The door creaked open, and I wasn't ready. A woman stood there —not Mom—with tired eyes and a calm, practiced presence that made it clear she'd seen this kind of moment a hundred times. She was dressed in pastel scrubs, her hair tied back in a simple bun with loose strands framing her face. There was something steady about her, like she shouldered this job without letting it break her.

She studied me for half a second, her sharp gaze softening almost immediately into something warmer. "You must be Carter," she said, her voice kind but sure, the way you'd want someone to sound when everything else feels unsteady. "I'm Kathy, Kathy Nguyen. I've been staying with your mom."

I nodded, my throat too tight to speak at first. "Yeah. That's me."

Kathy's smile was careful, practiced—a lifeline she'd thrown out a hundred times before for people like me. The ones who show up too late, hoping it's not. "It's good to meet you. Your mom talks about you all the time."

I forced myself to swallow past the lump in my throat. "Good things, I hope."

"Always," she said, her smile widening just a bit. There was warmth in her voice, steady and grounding, like she was holding up this conversation for both of us. "She's really proud of you."

The words hit me harder than I expected, a bittersweet ache settling in my chest. I glanced past her into the house, where the glow of the living room lights spilled onto the floor. It was so familiar, yet it felt like a whole lifetime had passed since I'd last been here.

"How is she?" I asked, my voice barely more than a whisper.

Kathy's expression shifted, the edges of her smile softening as she leaned just slightly against the doorframe. "She has good days and harder ones," she said carefully, like she was choosing her words with precision. "But she's hanging in there. I think seeing you is going to mean a lot to her."

I nodded, my breath catching as I tried to hold myself together. "I… I was scared I might be too late."

Her eyes softened further, her tone gentle but certain. "You're right on time," she said, stepping aside and gesturing for me to come in. "She's been waiting for you."

I hesitated on the threshold, the familiar scent of the house hitting me all at once—lavender air freshener, old wood, and the faint, lingering smell of coffee that seemed permanently soaked into the walls. It was like stepping into a time capsule, every sensory detail rushing back to remind me of everything I'd left behind. It held me rooted in place for a moment, my feet unwilling to move forward.

Kathy noticed. Of course she noticed. "It's hard," she said softly, her voice gentle but firm, like she wasn't going to let me drown in this moment. "Take a breath. You don't have to rush it."

I looked at her, and the steadiness in her expression gave me just enough strength to step inside. The floor creaked under my feet, and for a moment, it was like shaking hands with an old friend—one I was worried wouldn't remember my name.

The memories hit fast and hard. Mom and Dad laughing in the kitchen, his arm around her shoulders while she leaned into him, their smiles lighting up the room. Summers in the backyard, with Dad at the grill and Mom chasing me with a popsicle she swore I'd like if I just gave it a chance. The sound of their laughter filling every corner of the house like it belonged there.

And then it was gone. The warmth, the noise—all of it faded, leaving behind only the quiet hum of the present and the hollow reminder of what I'd been missing.

"Carter?" Kathy's voice cut through the haze, soft but steady. She didn't sound impatient, just there, like she was anchoring me to the moment. "You okay?"

I blinked, shaking the memories loose as best I could. "Yeah," I said, my voice cracking just a little. "I'm… ready."

I wasn't. Not even close. But Kathy just gave a small, knowing nod, her presence calm and unshakable. "It's okay if you're not," she said, her tone quiet but certain. "You don't have to have it all together right now."

Her words were simple, but they landed like a hand on my shoulder, grounding me. I forced a shaky breath, nodding back at her before stepping further into the house.

The living room felt like a memory someone had left out in the rain —soft, faded, and a little warped around the edges. The lamp on the side table cast a yellow glow that pooled weakly over the worn carpet, and the walls seemed too close, leaning inward under the strain of things unsaid. The air smelled faintly of lavender and mothballs, like it couldn't decide if it wanted to be comforting or just old.

Mom sat by the window, her gaze turned outward, toward the quiet darkness beyond. Her hair, once a deep chestnut that glinted red in the sunlight, was streaked with silver now, pulled into a loose braid that trailed over her shoulder. She looked smaller than I remembered, like she'd shrunk into herself, the faded sweater she wore hanging too loosely over her frame. Her hands rested on her lap, delicate and still, the skin paper-thin and pale enough to show the faint blue of veins beneath. She looked… fragile. Like if the light hit her wrong, she'd just disappear.

Her eyes narrowed slightly, unfocused, like she was searching for something in the night. "Is that man still out there?" she asked, her voice soft but tinged with unease.

Kathy's eyes flicked toward me for a split second, her expression unreadable but sharp. Then she uncrossed her arms and stepped closer to Mom, crouching slightly to meet her at eye level. "Hmm," she murmured, her voice dropping into something softer, gentler. "I'll check. But you know what? I've been keeping an eye out, and I haven't seen anyone. I think we're good."

She said it firmly, like it was a decision she'd already made and was now handing over, wrapped in a neat bow. Not dismissive, but final.

The ache hit me low and sharp, spreading out like a bruise. *That voicemail. Be careful of reflections. The man in the window isn't James.*

Kathy straightened, brushing her hands down the sides of her scrubs as she turned toward me. "She's been asking about him for a little while now," she said quietly, her tone clipped but not unkind. "You might want to sit with her. It'll help."

I nodded, throat tight, and stepped further into the room with a small, careful smile. "Hey, Mom."

She turned slowly, her gaze wavering between the window and me as if her eyes weren't sure where to land. For a moment, she just looked at me, her face unreadable. Then something shifted, the lines around her mouth softening, a flicker of recognition surfacing. "James?" she asked, her voice fragile and full of quiet hope. "Is that… you?"

The room went impossibly still, the air caught somewhere between then and now. My mouth opened, but the words didn't come right away. Like stepping out onto a frozen lake, one crack away from sinking.

All this time, she was never talking about Dad. She was talking about me. Standing in her driveway and looking up at her. That voicemail was about whatever fragmented version of me her mind was trying to piece together in the shadows.

"No, Mom," I whispered, finally finding my voice. "It's me. Carter."

Her eyes lingered on me, moving over my face slowly, piece by piece, like she was assembling a puzzle she'd lost the box for. "Carter…" she murmured, testing the name. Her expression softened further, and for a second, I saw her—the mom I remembered, the one who used to stay up late helping me build a poster board project last minute, the one who had a laugh like sunlight through curtains. "You —you came back."

Those words cracked something deep inside me, and I could feel the pieces shifting, breaking apart. "Of course I did," I said, my voice thick as I moved closer. "I wouldn't want to be anywhere else."

Her hand trembled as it lifted, slow and uncertain, before resting against my cheek. The touch was feather-light, as if she feared I might vanish if she pressed too hard. Her fingers brushed over my skin, as if trying to connect the boy she remembered to the person standing in front of her now.

"You've changed," she said softly, her voice tinged with wonder. "There's something in your eyes now. Wisdom, I think. But… you still look like my Carter."

I smiled faintly, swallowing against the ache rising in my throat. "Guess time has a way of doing that."

Her lips twitched into a small, wistful smile, but it didn't quite reach her eyes. She turned back to the window, her gaze distant again. "I–I thought I saw someone earlier," she said, her brow furrowing. "Standing where your dad used to stand. He'd lean right there, just like that."

I swallowed hard, my hands curling into fists at my sides. "It was me, Mom. I'm here. And I'm not going anywhere."

Her gaze drifted back to me, her eyes searching mine. For a moment, there was clarity there, a rare light breaking through the haze. "I'm glad," she said, her voice steady but soft. "I'm so glad you're here, Carter."

"Me too," I murmured, taking her frail hand in mine. "For as long as you need me."

She squeezed my hand lightly, her strength barely there but still enough to anchor us both. And for a fleeting second, the room felt whole again, filled with the warmth and steadiness of her presence. Her hand lingered against my cheek, her touch grounding me in a way that felt painfully fragile and beautifully real.

But then the light in her eyes dimmed, flickering out like a candle struggling against the wind. Her hand slackened in mine, her gaze slipping past me, searching the room as though I wasn't there.

"Carter?" she whispered, the name hesitant, like it wasn't hers to hold anymore.

"Yeah, Mom," I said softly, my voice steady even as my heart cracked wide open. "It's me."

Her lips parted, her brow furrowing as though she wanted to say more, but the words didn't come. Instead, her gaze drifted back to the window, lost somewhere I couldn't follow.

She looked back at me, her face softening, her eyes searching mine with a quiet intensity, as if somewhere, deep down, she knew I was important, even if she couldn't place me.

"You're kind," she said after a moment, her voice distant but warm. "Visiting an old lady like me. Not many people stop by anymore."

I forced a small smile, nodding. "It's my honor, really," I said, the words sticking in my throat.

Her smile grew, faint but genuine. "You remind me of someone," she murmured, her eyes softening. "My son. He used to look at me like that. Like he saw more than just the surface. He was a curious boy. Always asking questions, always looking for answers. He was a good boy."

My chest tightened, the ache blooming into something deep and relentless. "He was lucky to have you," I whispered.

She tilted her head, her gaze lingering on me for a moment longer before slipping away again, her thoughts retreating to some far-off place I couldn't reach. I sat there, holding her hand, letting the silence stretch between us like a fragile bridge. The moment was fleeting, the clarity fading, but I held onto it anyway, letting it anchor me even as it slipped through my fingers.

Love wasn't about clutching the fragments, forcing them back into place. It was about staying—quiet, steady—even as the cracks spread and the pieces slipped through your fingers.

And so I stayed, grounding her, grounding myself, as the night closed in around us.

CHAPTER 34

AFTER A WHILE, I couldn't take it anymore—the soft murmurs of Kathy's voice, the faint hum of the old TV in the corner, the oppressive stillness of the house. I excused myself and headed upstairs. My room hadn't changed—same stale air, same faint scent of mildew clinging to old fabric. It wasn't nostalgia that greeted me but something sharper, heavier, like stepping into a tomb I'd unknowingly built for a version of myself I'd abandoned long ago.

I closed the door behind me, leaning against it as I took in the room. Posters lined the walls, their colors faded and edges curling like they were trying to retreat from the present. Trophies sat on a dusty shelf above my desk, mocking me with reminders of glory days that didn't feel like mine anymore. My bed was covered with the same quilt Mom had given me when I was seven, a patchwork of dinosaurs and stars that now looked embarrassingly small for the person I'd become.

The air felt heavier here, like all the memories I'd ever had were resurfacing all at once, waiting for me to deal with them. My eyes wandered to the closet, its door half-open, revealing a row of clothes I hadn't touched in years. These were my emergency clothes—the ones I used to grab whenever I'd crash here after my parents split up. I moved closer, trailing my fingers along the fabric. They still smelled faintly of detergent and something undefinable. Home, maybe. Or what home used to mean.

That's when I noticed them, tucked away in the corner of the shelf above a forgotten sweatshirt.

Fuzzy dice.

The dice were so ordinary they almost didn't register at first—faded red, the fabric frayed at the edges. My fingers brushed the dice, and the air shifted. It wasn't just still—it was waiting, charged with something unseen. Max's voice echoed faintly, not in my ears but somewhere deeper: *"One day, when you're really up against it, they're yours."*

A chill ran down my spine. *How were they here?* Sitting in my closet, like they'd been waiting for me all along? My mind reeled, trying to piece it together, trying to understand if this was a coincidence or... something else. Something bigger. Had Max found a way to leave them here, to leave a part of himself in this time? Or had I just been carrying these threads all along, never knowing how they connected?

Before I could stop myself, I was halfway out the door, the dice clenched tightly in my hand. I needed answers. Needed to connect the dots that refused to form a picture. Maybe Mom would know. Maybe she'd have the missing piece.

Downstairs, Kathy was adjusting the blanket on Mom's lap. Mom sat quietly in her armchair, gazing out the window with a faint, dreamy smile, like she was somewhere far away. As I approached, her eyes flicked to me, and that faint smile grew, her expression softening.

"You see him, don't you?" Her voice floated, fragile as tissue paper, barely audible in the room. Her gaze drifted over me, unfocused, like she was staring through glass. "You're not... are you?" she murmured, her voice splintering on the last word. Something inside me crumbled, and I knelt, holding up the dice like they were proof that I was real.

"Mom, do you remember these?" My voice was thick with hope, though I was bracing for disappointment.

She blinked slowly, her cloudy gaze focusing on the fuzzy dice. For a moment, something flickered there—recognition, maybe—but it was fleeting. "Those… they were his, weren't they?" she said, her tone soft, almost wistful.

"Who, Mom?" I pushed, my heart sinking as I watched her drift. "Whose were they?"

She looked past me, her face calm, her eyes somewhere far away. "I told him," she murmured, her voice barely above a whisper. "I told him you'd come back."

I froze, her words settling over me like a heavy blanket. Kathy stepped closer, her movements deliberate, her expression calm but laced with understanding. She glanced at Mom, then back at me, her voice low and steady, the kind of voice meant to anchor you when the world felt too big.

"Sometimes she mixes things up," Kathy said gently, her eyes soft but clear. "It's like she's speaking to the past." She paused, watching me carefully, giving the words a moment to settle. "It's normal, Carter. Alzheimer's doesn't play by the rules we expect. It's like she's living in a kaleidoscope," Kathy said softly, her gaze steady on mine. "Pieces of the past, the present—they all blur together. It might not make sense to us, but for her, it's real. It's all real."

I nodded slowly, my throat tightening as I tried to process her words. "Yeah. I get it." My voice cracked, but I didn't look away from Mom. She was still staring out the window, her faraway smile unchanged, like she was locked in a moment I could never step into.

A sudden thought hit me, sharp and urgent. "She still has her phone, right?" I asked, turning to Kathy, my voice rising just a bit. The question felt ridiculous, but I couldn't shake it.

Kathy's brows furrowed for a split second before smoothing out, her professional composure steady as ever. "She usually keeps it in her chair," she said, her tone thoughtful. "Let me check." She moved toward the armchair, her steps quick but unhurried, like she understood this was important without needing to know why.

As she sifted through the cushions, she spoke again, her voice softer now. "Your mom… she holds onto things like they're anchors. Things that feel familiar. It's her way of staying connected, even if it doesn't always come across that way to us."

She pulled out an old, worn phone, the kind that had seen better days. The edges were scuffed, the screen faintly cracked, and when it lit up, the glow felt almost surreal. Kathy glanced at it, her lips pressing into a small, sympathetic smile. "Looks like there've been a few missed calls to you," she said, holding it out to me. "Probably accidental. I'm sorry, Carter."

Her voice carried no judgment, only care, and her cheeks flushed slightly, as if she felt responsible somehow. "I should've noticed sooner," she added softly. "She must've been trying to reach you in her own way."

I stared at the screen, my name staring back at me in neat, persistent text. Missed call. Missed call. Missed call. A lump rose in my throat, my heart sinking. "It's okay," I said quietly, my fingers brushing against hers as I handed it back to her. "Thanks."

Kathy didn't move right away. She stayed there, watching me with an expression I couldn't quite pin down. Empathy, maybe, but also a quiet strength, like she was holding space for me to process everything without forcing me to.

"You doing okay?" she asked after a moment, her voice kind but not invasive.

I nodded. "Yeah. I'm good," I lied, the words brittle in my mouth.

Kathy didn't call me on it, but the look in her eyes said she didn't believe me. Instead, she rested a light hand on my arm, her touch grounding. "Let me know if you need anything," she said softly, her words careful but genuine. "I mean it."

She straightened, her professionalism sliding back into place, though the warmth in her expression didn't waver. "Take your time."

The cold hit me like a sharp reminder the second I stepped outside. The air was heavy with that quiet, late-night stillness, the kind that made the world feel paused. I rolled the fuzzy dice between my fingers, their worn fabric rough against my skin. They felt heavier now, like they weren't just dice but some strange, small gravity well, dragging memories into their orbit. I let them dangle, swaying slightly in the breeze, as I pulled out my phone with my free hand. The screen glowed faintly, fractured into a mosaic of cracks, but it still worked. Barely.

My fingers hovered over Dad's number, hesitating. For a second, I thought about shoving the phone back in my pocket and pretending none of this mattered. But the dice swung in my hand like a reminder, their weight too much to ignore. I hit the call button before I could talk myself out of it.

The line clicked, and his voice came through, warm and a little surprised. "Carter, hey! Did you make it to your mom's place okay?"

"Yeah," I said, my voice quieter than I meant it to be. "She's… hanging in there." I leaned against the side of the house, the cold brick biting through my white t-shirt.

There was a pause, the kind that stretched just long enough to remind me how much we didn't say to each other. Then he sighed, his tone softening. "She's a fighter, you know. Always has been."

I swallowed, the words caught somewhere between my throat and my brain. "I, uh… I got your voicemails," I said, finally letting the words slip out. "I heard what you said."

Another pause, heavier this time. When he spoke again, his voice carried an edge I didn't hear often—raw and unguarded, like he was peeling back something he usually kept hidden. "Carter, listen. I'm sorry. For everything. I know I haven't always been… there, the way you needed me to be."

The weight of his words hit me like a gut punch. I didn't expect him to say it—didn't expect *any* of this. He cleared his throat, the silence stretching just long enough to make me wonder if he'd stopped himself. But then he kept going, his voice softer now, almost fragile. "Your mom, Carter…" He paused, and for a moment, the static on the line was the only sound. Then his voice broke through, low and unsteady, as if the words had been locked away for years. "I've always loved her. Still do. Always will."

The quiet that followed felt huge, stretching between us like a canyon I hadn't realized was there. "I didn't know you still felt that way," I said, more to myself than to him. My voice came out small, like I wasn't sure it belonged to me.

He let out a soft laugh, but it was shaky, full of something bittersweet. "Yeah, well... it's not exactly the kind of thing I go shouting from the rooftops." There was a pause, and when he spoke again, his voice was quieter, like he was talking to himself as much as to me. "You know, I never went on any dates after... everything. Not because I couldn't—I just didn't want to. She's always been... my person. And she always will be."

The finality of it hit me, sharp and unexpected. I'd spent so long seeing their love as something fractured, something broken beyond repair. But here he was, laying it out like it was still alive, still there even after everything fell apart.

"We knew things would get tough after she was diagnosed," he continued, his voice quieter now, the words slower. "When she found out she had early-onset Alzheimer's, it was... it was like this shadow hanging over us. We tried to be ready for it, to make all the right decisions, but..." He trailed off, and I could hear the weight of it in the silence that followed.

"But you left," I said, the words falling out like broken glass. On the other end, silence stretched thin, static crackling faintly.

When he spoke again, his voice was barely more than a whisper. "I know." he said, his voice breaking just slightly. "Your mom and I... we thought... we thought we were protecting you," he said, his voice breaking like he wasn't sure the words would hold. "We didn't want you to be stuck, Carter. To lose your childhood to her illness. We wanted you to have a chance at something better. Even if it meant losing us."

His voice cracked, and I could feel the regret in it, heavy and real. "I thought... maybe moving us back to L.A., to where it all started, could fix things. Like it'd be some kind of reset button. But I was wrong."

The honesty in his voice hit like a punch, cutting through all the years of silence. "It wasn't your fault, Dad," I said, my voice soft but steady. "None of this was."

He let out a shaky breath, the sound full of relief. "I just wanted you to have the best chance, Carter. Even if it meant... even if it meant being away from her. From us."

The ache in his voice settled deep in my chest, a knot I couldn't untangle. "I get it now," I said, the words surprising even me. "I didn't before, but… I get it."

He went quiet again, and when he spoke, there was something like pride in his tone, bittersweet and fragile. "You're a good kid, Carter. Your mom always said you would be. I guess I should've trusted her instinct more."

I glanced down at the dice in my hand, their fuzzy surface worn smooth in places. "Hey, Dad," I said, the question rising before I could stop it, "do you remember the fuzzy dice I had in my closet?"

He laughed, the sound softer now, as if the conversation had lightened just a little. "Oh, yeah. Those dice. A parent from your preschool gave them to you. You loved those things."

My stomach twisted, the pieces starting to click together in ways I wasn't sure I liked. "Do you remember the parent's name?"

"Uh…" He paused, thinking. "Bruce? Or Max, maybe? Yeah, Max sounds right. Your mom wanted me to throw them out, but you really latched onto them."

Max. His name hit like a shock, cold and electric, sending a shiver down my spine. I gripped the dice tighter, their weight suddenly heavier than before. "Thanks, Dad," I said, my voice trembling just enough to betray me.

"No problem, Carter," he said, his tone gentle now. "I just wanted to see you happy." He hesitated, and when he spoke again, his voice was softer, more fragile. "And Carter… I love you. I don't say it enough, but I do."

The words wrapped around me, sharp and warm all at once. "I love you too, Dad," I said, my throat tight and my chest heavy with everything we'd left unsaid.

And for a moment, the cold didn't feel so bitter. But the name—Max—hung in the air like smoke, curling through the cracks of my thoughts. It didn't just linger; it wrapped around me, impossible to shake. The past and present weren't just blending—they were bleeding into each other, pooling into something I wasn't sure I was ready to face but knew that I would. I had to. I didn't have a choice.

CHAPTER 35

THE DOOR CLICKED SHUT behind me, a sound so soft it might have been a sigh, yet it felt unmistakably final. The air inside was still warm with the scent of detergent and faint traces of coffee, a fragile kind of comfort that hovered just out of reach, as if mocking the idea of safety.

Kathy glanced up from the sofa, her smile flickering like a dying bulb when her eyes met mine. She set her book down carefully, tilting her head with the quiet precision of someone bracing for bad news.

"Everything alright?" she asked, her voice soft but edged with concern.

"Yeah," I managed, my voice too quick, too tight. "Just... a lot. To think about. A lot of, uh, thinking happening right now."

She didn't press, just nodded like she was letting me win this round. "You know where to find me, okay? Anytime."

I glanced at my phone, its battery teetering on the edge of doom. A bright 4% stared back at me, mocking. "Actually, do you have a charger? Mine's still in the car and my phone's about to flatline."

Kathy stood, her smile returning in that motherly *I'll take care of it* kind of way. "Of course. One second." She disappeared into the kitchen, the soft clatter of drawers and cabinets following her. A moment later, she returned with a frayed charging cable that looked like it had survived three wars and a power surge.

"This should work," she said, kneeling to plug it into the outlet by Mom's armchair. "I'll set it here for whenever you need it."

"Thanks," I said. I plugged in my phone and it sat there, inert, as though mocking the fragility of the thread that tied me to the present. "I owe you one."

She waved me off with a smile, already returning to her book. "You don't owe me a thing, Carter."

I climbed the stairs slowly, each step groaning underfoot as if protesting my return. The bed sagged beneath me with a creak that felt like an accusation, the past sinking into every fiber of the worn mattress. The glow of the hallway light didn't quite reach inside, leaving the edges of the room soft and hazy, like a memory just out of reach.

My fingers traced the edges of the desk drawer before pulling it open. My old laptop stared back at me beside a collection of shells, relics of simpler times. I dragged it out and flipped it open, waiting as it groaned to life with a sluggish whir. The glow of the screen flickered, throwing faint shadows across the walls.

Google stared back at me like an accusation, its blank search bar waiting for something I wasn't sure I was ready to give it. My fingers hovered over the keyboard, hesitating. The first name I typed in felt like crossing a line I couldn't uncross, a door I'd sworn to leave shut.

Dr. Harry Mercer.

The name appeared on the screen, harsh and unrelenting. My chest tightened as I hit *Enter*, and the search results rushed in, a flood of sterile headlines and lifeless academic profiles that blurred together like static. But then a headline caught my eye:

"Physics Professor Dismissed Amidst Fraud Allegations."

The words struck me like a slap, and my stomach twisted as I clicked the link. A grainy photo of Dr. Mercer appeared, his face younger, his eyes still sharp but dulled with something I couldn't name. He looked like the man I remembered, back in the 80s, before life had chiseled away at him for years.

The article laid it all out in brutal detail. Promises of groundbreaking research. Ambitious theories that couldn't hold water. The cracks began to show, and when the tension mounted, it all fell apart.

False data. Claiming findings that didn't exist. When the truth came out, the physics community turned on him like vultures on a carcass.

"Stripped of his credentials," the article said. "His work discredited, his reputation irreparably damaged."

I scrolled further, my fingers trembling as another headline appeared:

"Ex-Professor Banned from Future Research Grants After Allegations of Data Manipulation."

It was all there—the quiet, crushing downfall of a man who'd wanted so badly to matter. To prove himself. The irony was a cold blade, twisting with every word. The man who'd nearly unraveled my existence had dismantled his own piece by piece, his ambition devouring him from the inside out. He'd traded credibility for ambition, and in the end, it had cost him everything.

There was no swift, dramatic justice here. No grand finale. Just the slow, inevitable collapse of someone who'd built his house on sand. It should've felt like victory. Like closure. But instead, it felt hollow, a weight, like sadness, burrowing deeper on my chest.

I scrolled further, desperate for answers, for something more. But the trail ran cold. No photos. No interviews. Just one haunting line:

"Harold R. Mercer has been unreachable for comment since his dismissal in 1986. Last known address: Los Angeles, CA."

He could be anywhere. The words clung to me, heavy and unresolved. Even after all this, he was still a ghost. A reminder that some things don't tie up neatly, no matter how much you want them to. *Had he followed me all the way to DC, back in 1995, just to try and get the phone back? Who's to say he'd stop there?*

I leaned back, the dim glow of the screen painting my face in cold light. Dr. Mercer had become a cautionary tale, a name whispered with disdain in academic circles. But he was still just a man. Flawed. Broken. And maybe that was the real tragedy—not what he'd done to me, but what he'd done to himself.

As I stared at the screen, my mind began to drift. Another name surfaced, uninvited but insistent, tugging at the edges of my thoughts. A name that carried something softer, warmer. Something that didn't feel like a weight, but like a flicker of light in the dark.

Max.

The thought hit me harder than I expected, and I sank further into the mattress, the faint sound of the laptop's fan filling the silence. Max—his laugh, his endless patience, his way of holding space for me when I couldn't even stand myself—gone. Just like that. Like the universe had decided, once again, to take the best and leave me with the wreckage. *I had to know where he was.*

I hesitated, fingers hovering over the keyboard like they might combust if I actually typed the name. The soft hum of the laptop filled the silence, an unnervingly cheerful backdrop to the unsettling feeling in my chest. My fingers twitched, and then—*tap, tap, tap*—I typed it: **Max Carleton, Los Angeles, CA.**

For a second, I stared at the screen, half expecting nothing to happen. Like the internet might just shrug its shoulders and say, *Sorry, can't help you.* But then, like clockwork, a list of profiles appeared, scattered with faces I didn't recognize. My stomach twisted, the tiny cursor blinking like it was taunting me. I scrolled, slower than I needed to, until near the bottom, something caught my eye.

It was an old, faded MySpace profile, its photo grainy and sunlit. A young man stood on a beach, a surfboard propped casually beside him. That grin hit me first—wide, unbothered, the kind of grin that made the world look a little less heavy. *Max.*

I clicked, and the photo enlarged, filling the screen. For a second, I couldn't breathe. *It was him.*

Something cracked open in my chest—a weird, messy mix of relief and sadness, like finding something you didn't know you'd lost. My eyes traced every detail of the photo, my pulse pounding as I clicked through the profile. Scattered snapshots filled the page, a kaleidoscope of moments I hadn't been there for. Max smiling with friends, perched on the hood of a classic red Corvette. Max on sunlit beaches, holding that same surfboard like it was his signature prop. Him beside a grown-up Justin, who still looked every bit too eager to take on the world. Max looked… happy—alive in a way that felt almost unfair.

Then, I saw it. A picture of him in a tuxedo, standing with his arm around some dork with a gray streak in his hair. *It was us.* It was *me.*

My chest shook, the caption stating "Throwback to Formal with this crazy kid. Miss you Carter! Whenever you are!"

I paused, slamming the laptop down. My head spun as I dug my fingers through my hair. *It was real. It was all real.* To everyone else, they probably thought it was a typo. But to me, it was something else entirely.

Within a moment, I kept scrolling. I had to reach out. I had to let him know I was here. But as I continued down, the photos thinned out, scattering like leaves in the wind. By early 2005, they stopped altogether. No updates, no spouse, no kids, no cryptic captions—just silence. The last status update read: **"Be back soon."**

I leaned back, the glow of the screen painting the room in cold, pale light. My mind churned, desperate for answers that weren't there. Had he moved on? Left MySpace behind like everyone else? I wanted to believe that. God, I needed to believe that.

But the knot in my stomach wouldn't budge. I scrolled back up, my eyes landing on the "About" section. It was almost painfully empty —no location, no job history. Just those scattered memories, like bread crumbs leading to nowhere. I clicked through them again, searching for something—anything—that might tell me where he'd gone. Who he'd become.

Nothing.

The stillness of the room crept in, heavy and unrelenting. My thoughts buzzed louder, tangled with the fragments of Max's profile. This wasn't enough. I needed more. Something solid. Something real. I opened a new tab, fingers flying over the keyboard, chasing the thread before it slipped through my fingers.

Max Carleton obituary.

I hit *Enter*.

And there it was.

My stomach plummeted as the words hit me like a gut punch. **Max Carleton, 1967-2005.** The obituary was brief, almost cruelly so, reducing a life to a '*tragic, unexplainable accident.*' The words clung to me like smoke, suffocating and impossible to shake. I repeated them silently, trying to force them into meaning, but they dissolved into the void instead.

I blinked hard, the screen blurring for a moment. I wanted to scream, but the sound stuck in my throat, heavy and useless. Grief wasn't loud; it was quiet, insidious, curling around my ribs like smoke and stealing the air before I could take a breath. Max—*Max*. The guy who made space for me when I didn't know how to take it. Who let me crash at his place without asking for anything in return. Gone. Just like that. Like the universe decided to yank the rug out from under everything good.

Beneath his name was a hyperlink to his sister, Rebecca, the name a distant echo in my mind. Max had never told me what happened. Against my better judgment, I clicked it, and there it was in black and white. **Local woman claimed by town legend.** *"The Vanishing Eight."* I knew there had to be a link, some type of connection, though I couldn't understand what. How were we all tied in this?

I sat there, the laptop humming softly, the glow of the screen burning into my retinas. My hand hovered over the trackpad, shaking. I couldn't stop now. I couldn't.

I typed the next name: **Nat Thompson, Fairfax High School.**

My heart twisted as the search results loaded. One article stood out, its headline small and clinical: **"Natalie Thompson Missing Since 1995."** I clicked, and her photo filled the screen—a face I knew better than my own, caught in a moment of youthful energy. My breath hitched, a chill running through me as I skimmed the article. *Last seen near Fairfax High. No clues. No leads.*

My vision tunneled, my thoughts a hurricane of dread and disbelief. Nat had vanished. The same year I left. She was gone.

I shook my head, my hands trembling as I typed the next name. **Ethan.** Then **Jessica. Josh. Tyler. Tiffany**.

One by one, the names unraveled into tragedies I couldn't have imagined. Ethan—gone in a car crash on a rainy night in 1996. Jessica —her bright future cut short by an apartment fire. Josh and Tyler— friends until the end, both killed in a freak hiking accident. Tiffany— disappeared without a trace.

Each story hit like a stone through a window, piling on until I couldn't breathe. My hands clenched into fists, my thoughts spiraling. *What the hell happened after I left?* Was this all some horrible coincidence? Or had I done this—set something in motion without realizing it?

The questions clawed at me, relentless. And for the first time since this whole mess started, I felt something darker creep in. A deep, sinking dread.

I stared at the mirror above my desk, my reflection faint in the dusty glass. The person looking back at me felt like a stranger, lost and breaking beneath what they couldn't understand. I clenched my jaw, my chest tightening as I forced myself to look away.

The glow of the screen faded into the shadows of the room, but the questions stayed. Circling. Gnawing. And all I could do was sit there, drowning in the silence. Then Dr. Mercer's words returned to me, haunting and distant. *"You've always been here, in each of these times, even if you never knew it."*

Almost without thinking, I typed my own name into the search bar. My fingers moved automatically, like they had a mind of their own, while my brain stayed back, trying not to spiral. Part of me was ready for nothing to come up. Instagram, maybe. Tumblr. Vine. But overall, a digital blank slate where Carter Sullivan didn't exist.

But that's not what happened.

The first headline hit like a gut punch, the words sinking in before I could process their weight: **Local Teen Disappears After Alleged Time Travel Claim.** It felt like stepping off solid ground into nothingness, the air too thin to breathe. The date matched the Winter Formal. *My* Winter Formal. My chest tightened. *This was here all along?* Just sitting out in the open while I was flailing around, trying to make sense of everything in the 90s?

My hands trembled on the trackpad as I scrolled. Something else caught my eye: a set of old, grainy photographs. Black-and-white, faded at the edges, each labeled with my name. Not just Carter Sullivan. It was *me*.

I clicked the first image. It opened slowly, like even the computer knew I wasn't ready. It was a diner, all vinyl booths and chrome counters, and leaning against that counter was a guy who looked... like me. Laughing with a group of friends, one hand casually resting on the counter. No, not the counter. My breath hitched. A black mirror. The phone. *My. Phone.*

My heart started racing, my pulse loud and uneven in my ears. The face in the photo—it was me, but it wasn't. A little older maybe, or younger. The same eyes, the same shape to the jaw, but the context was all wrong. The photo was dated 1963.

I opened the next image before I could stop myself, the cursor moving like it had a will of its own. This one was from the 1910s, the photo scratched and worn with time. A man stood in the background in a stiff military uniform, his face unmistakably familiar. My face. Or something close to it. The uniform hung awkwardly on his frame, and his posture looked... uncertain. Like he didn't quite belong there, either.

"How?" I whispered, my voice breaking in the empty room. My throat felt tight, like I couldn't swallow the enormity of what I was seeing. *How was this possible? How could I have been there—been anywhere—after all this?*

The air in the room felt different, heavier, like it was pressing in on me from all sides. My vision blurred at the edges, my thoughts spinning so fast they stopped making sense. What if this wasn't the end of my journey but the start? What if those photos weren't just echoes from some forgotten timeline but places I hadn't even been yet, waiting for me to arrive?

I scrolled further, my hand moving almost without my permission, and then I saw it.

Carter Sullivan Obituary.

I froze, my breath catching in my throat. My hand hovered over the link, the screen glowing faintly in the dim light. There it was—my name etched alongside my death, a sterile line of text that felt more like a tombstone. It stared back at me, unblinking, as if daring me to click. My hand trembled, the unbearable heaviness of the mouse anchoring me as I hesitated on the brink of knowing.

"No! No, no, no!"

My mom's voice floated up from downstairs, soft but insistent, snapping me out of the spiral. There was something in her tone, something off—like a thread stretched too tight. It wasn't her usual distracted hum. It was sharper, tinged with something urgent.

I slammed the laptop shut, the screen going dark as I pushed back from the desk. The room still felt heavy, the words and images lingering like smoke in the air. My heart was pounding as I made my way downstairs, each step feeling slower than the last.

The living room was bathed in warm, soft light, the kind that should've felt safe. But it didn't. My mom stood beside her usual armchair, but something about the way she was standing stopped me in my tracks. My phone, cracked and faintly glowing, was unplugged and resting in her grasp. Her fingers hovered over it, her expression distant, like she was halfway here and halfway somewhere else entirely.

"Mom?" I said softly, my voice cracking in the quiet. She didn't respond. Her fingers moved slowly, tracing over the screen as if she could feel the numbers she was dialing.

"I'm late!" she murmured, her voice frantic and unsteady. "They must be worried sick. Mom and Dad are gonna kill me..." She trailed off, her gaze lifting slightly, as if she were looking at someone just out of sight. A faint, frown crossed her face. "Oh, God, please still be up..."

The air shifted. I didn't know how to describe it—something subtle, a static buzz crawling just beneath my skin. My chest tightened as I took a step closer. "Mom, what are you doing?"

Her hand hovered over the phone like it wasn't entirely her own, her eyes clouded, unfocused, like she was staring past me, or through me. The air around her seemed charged, electric, as if time itself was holding its breath. And then it hit me. *She was making a call.*

"Mom, stop—don't—!" I darted toward her, my voice shaking. But before I could reach her, she tapped the call button.

The room erupted in a violent burst of orange light, blinding and suffocating, the hum rising like a scream buried deep in my chest. It tore through the air, through my skin, unraveling the world around me until nothing was left but the void. My mom's face softened, peaceful and far away, as if she'd drifted somewhere I couldn't follow.

"Mom!" I shouted, reaching out, grabbing the phone, but the light swallowed me whole.

The world around me warped and blurred, the edges slipping away until there was nothing left but the glow. In the flash of orange, I caught a glimpse in the window—my face, stretched and distorted, a shadow on the edge of something infinite.

And then, there was nothing at all.

AFTERWORD

Thank you for joining Carter on his journey through time, love, and loss. Writing *All the Time* was an exploration of the moments that shape us, the connections that define us, and the fleeting nature of time itself. At its heart, this story is about the deep ache of holding onto the past while searching for a way forward—a feeling I believe we've all experienced in one way or another.

This book wouldn't exist without the support of so many people. To my readers: thank you for trusting me to take you on this mind-bending adventure. Your time is precious, and it means everything that you chose to spend some of it with this story. To my editor, beta readers, and everyone who provided feedback along the way, your guidance helped me craft this world and make Carter's journey resonate.

A Note on Themes

All the Time explores challenging themes, including grief, loss, and family estrangement. While these are central to Carter's story, I recognize that they may evoke strong emotions for some readers. If you found certain aspects of this book difficult, please know that it's okay to seek help or talk to someone about it.

Disclaimer

This book is a work of fiction. Any similarities to actual people, events, or locations are purely coincidental. The characters, events, and settings are products of the author's imagination, created to bring this story to life.

A Reminder

Time has a way of stealing moments from us, but it also offers endless opportunities. If this story left you reflecting on your own journey, know that you're not alone. There's strength in letting go and courage in holding on. You matter, your story matters, and there's always someone ready to listen.

Lastly, to anyone who feels stuck, lost, or out of place: this is your reminder that time, while fleeting, is also full of opportunities. Don't be afraid to hold on to what matters or let go of what no longer serves you.

Thank you again for sharing in this story. Here's to all the time we have left.

—Lincoln James

ACKNOWLEDGMENTS

A special thanks to these fantastic people who helped make this book possible:

Adri
Alex
Alice
Ana
Bree
Bobby
Cossy
Elena
Elise
Gogi
Jack
Jessie
Joanna
Kamran
Keaton
Lee
Mason
Maureen
Mike
Mila
Nadia
Rob
Ross
Sarah

Sean
Vlad

ABOUT THE AUTHOR

Author | College Professor | Thriller Enthusiast

Lincoln James, your favorite author's favorite author, is known for his haunting love stories, vintage thrillers, and slow-burn suspense. His characters feel, ache, and bleed, often trapped between the past and the people who won't let them forget it. When he's not writing, James is a Communication and English professor in New York City and cherishes moments with friends and family, proving that the most thrilling tales lie in the love and laughter shared with those closest to us.

www.ingramcontent.com/pod-product-compliance
Lightning Source LLC
Chambersburg PA
CBHW020056310726
48970CB00002B/353